AMAZON REV
FIRST DO N(
BY A. TU

This was one of my top picks. I was spellbound and couldn't put it down. First Do No Harm was Grishamesque. Loved it.

Kept me up reading 'til four in the morning. It speeds along and the suspense keeps building. This book totally helped me understand on emotional and technical levels the realities of being a lawyer. The characters are complex and intriguing, the story more so. As a plus, I got a small thrill every time I recognized a Middle Tennessee locale that was mentioned.

I am not an attorney but Mr. Turk was able to make the law and the procedures of the law understandable and very interesting. The characters in the novel were well represented. Mr. Turk was able to define the relative differences among the adversarial attorneys, who was professionally upright and others being dishonest and indifferent. I felt the emotional distraught of the plaintiff attorneys and those they represented. I look forward to the next book in the Davis series by Mr. Turk.

I was with Davis every step of the way! And I was in that courtroom with bated breath waiting for the verdicts. What an excellent *read.*

I can't wait for the next books in this series. I have dealt with some lawyers like the ones in this story.

This was one of those books that tend to be hard to put down. It centers on a young lawyer that takes on a malpractice case in a small town. I would like to read more by this author. I highly recommend this book to anyone.

First Do No Harm was a great read. I love a book with numerous plots and this one delivers. The story and characters were very believable. I look forward to reading more in the Benjamin Davis Book Series.

This book grabbed hold and didn't let go until the very end. I was driven to see how it ended and then disappointed that it was over. I can't wait for this author's next book. Hard to believe it was a first book. Seemed to be written by a seasoned author. Move over, John Grisham!

Couldn't put this down. I felt as if I was reading a true life documentary. The writing just flowed. Everything felt so real. Anyone who likes legal fiction has to read this. Can't wait for the next book to come out.

As cliché as it sounds I couldn't put it down. All those courtroom dramas on TV wrap things up nicely in an hour or two and the average Joe has no idea how much time and research go into a lawsuit. This should convince everyone to settle quickly out of court.

What an enjoyable book! I found myself making comparisons to parts of "The Lincoln lawyer." Held my complete attention for the entire book.

A superb book from beginning to end! It was one you couldn't wait to see how it ends, but you don't want it to end!

Great first book; couldn't put it down for long. Can't wait to read his second book and hope he is working on a third!

Second Degree

A Benjamin Davis Novel

A. Turk

Sue, like the by
This story, is inspired
first is inspired
true events
A. Turk

Second Degree is the second novel in the Benjamin Davis Series by author A. Turk. The story is a work of fiction, based upon and inspired by actual cases prepared and tried by Alan Turk, a prominent Nashville attorney. For the purposes of dramatic effect and to protect those involved in the underlying cases, the names of the parties have been changed, as have certain incidents, characters, and timelines. Certain characters may be composites, while others are entirely fictitious.

Printed in the United States of America

ISBN: 978-0-9892663-3-8 (paperback)
          978-0-9892663-4-5 (ebook)

Cover design by Dan Swanson • van-garde.com
Book design by Darlene Swanson * van-garde.com

CAST OF MAIN CHARACTERS

Davis Family and Team

Benjamin "Ben" Abraham Davis—protagonist

Sammie Annabelle Davis—niece of Davis, paralegal/attorney

Liza Davis—wife of Davis

Caroline Davis—daughter of Davis

Jacob "Jake" Davis—son of Davis

Morty Steine—legal and ethical mentor of Davis

Bella Rosario—longtime secretary of Steine and Davis

Dr. John Caldwell—Davis's father-in-law and Steine's cardiologist

Nichols Family and Team

Dr. Peter Nichols—cosmetic dentist, employer of Charlie Garcia

Lillian Nichols, deceased—mother of Peter Nichols

Peter Nichols Sr., deceased—father of Peter Nichols

Helen Nichols—wife of Peter Nichols

Albert Nichols—demented brother of Peter Nichols

Donna Burns—office manager of Nichols & Garcia, PC

Dr. Anita Dowdle—replacement physician for Dr. Charlie Garcia

Rocky McCormick—head hunter who found Dr. Charlie Garcia

Eden Family

Robyn Eden—victim, girlfriend of Charlie Garcia

Senator Valerie Daniels—sister of Robyn Eden

Garcia Family
Charles "Charlie" Juan Batista Garcia—antagonist, defendant
Señor Eduardo "Eddie" Miguel Garcia—father of Charlie Garcia
Maria "Kiki" Christina Batista Garcia—mother of Charlie Garcia

Attorneys and Judge in Civil Cases
Amy Pierce—attorney for Charlie Garcia in criminal case and before Medical Licensing Board
David Barton Harrelson—Garcia family attorney
Larry Pinsly—representative of Tennessee Mutual Insurance Co.
Lester Paul—attorney for Charlie Garcia in the Perkins and Howard cases
Robert "Bob" Sullivan—attorney for Nichols & Garcia in the Perkins and Howard cases
Jackson "Jack" Willis—attorney for plaintiffs in the Perkins and Howard cases
Karl Maddox—attorney for McCormick & Associates in the Perkins and Howard cases
Assistant District Attorney Jill Hoskins—Hewes County DA
Judge William "Billy" White—judge in the Circuit Court of Davidson County in the Perkins and Howard cases

Hewes City Police, Sheriff's Office, and Paramedics
EMT Louis Mackey—older paramedic who responds to 911 call
EMT Willie Whatley—younger paramedic
Officer Bobby Pew—senior officer responding to 911 call
Officer Donald Dawson—officer who remained at apartment
Chief Detective Kristin Haber—in charge of Garcia criminal investigation
Sheriff Buford Dudley—Sheriff of Hewes County

Patients of Dr. Garcia
Denise Alder—ex-wife of Dr. Frank Alder
Anna Perkins—sex partner of Charlie Garcia, plaintiff
Christy Howard—sex partner of Charlie Garcia, plaintiff

Jefferson County, Kentucky

Judge Corey Olsen—Jefferson County Criminal Court

District Attorney Peter Taylor—prosecuted Charlie Garcia

Alan Baxter—Charlie Garcia's probation officer

Medical Licensing Board

Judge Thomas Booth—administrative law judge

Randi Hecht—administrative prosecutor

Dr. Frank Alder—Medical Licensing Board panel member

Judge and Witnesses in Garcia Criminal Trial

Judge Joseph "Joe" Tanner—judge of the Criminal Court of Hewes County

Dr. Randolph Mann—emergency room physician

Dr. Robert Townsend—treating psychiatrist of Charlie Garcia

Dr. Thomas Barnard—treating physician of Robyn Eden

Dr. John Davenport—medical examiner of Hewes County

Dr. Lawrence Porter—addiction expert for defense

Dr. Brian Limbaugh—state's psychiatric expert

Dr. Gene Albertson—defense DNA expert, impeachment witness

Danny Nix—drug dealer, impeachment witness

**A Legal Glossary has been included in the
back of the book to assist the reader with legal terms.**

To Lisa, thank you for a lifetime of love.
The last year's been the best yet.

CHAPTER ONE
OVERDOSE
July 4, 2000

The lovers finished at the same time; neither disappointing the other. Their bodies, wet with perspiration, momentarily stuck together as each deeply sighed with satisfaction. Robyn rolled off him, kissed him on his cheek, and quickly jumped from the bed. She picked up her cell phone and took four provocative pictures of herself.

She walked naked past him, forgetting to turn off the video camera, and then disappeared into the master bathroom. Charlie noted in the last few hours she'd disappeared in there several times.

Charlie, exhausted, tried to gather his thoughts to resume the argument. He refused to give up on her. He loved her and hoped she could straighten out and change her destructive ways.

He'd arrived Friday from New York and went straight from the Nashville airport to Hewes City, twenty-five miles away. He'd come at the request of Robyn's sister, Valerie, to convince her she needed to go into rehab. He'd investigated the alternatives and settled on Cumberland Heights, a world-renowned treatment facility.

They argued for hours without any resolution, so he changed tactics and drank tequila straight up with a saltshaker and limes.

He felt ashamed; however, he thoroughly enjoyed the sex marathon. He now knew it was a huge mistake to buy into her addiction.

She needed to slow down. It was like she was spinning out of control, and as that thought crossed his mind, she flew out of the bathroom. Charlie looked into her intense green eyes dilated like two large black olives surrounded by a green rim. She was high on something. Her shoulder-length auburn hair was up, revealing her exquisite neck and shoulders. He loved to kiss her neck; she responded favorably every time. She danced around showing off her sculptured body and taking photos of herself.

Charlie watched as she grabbed a pill bottle from her nightstand and downed the pill without water. He noticed for the first time a small amount of white powder and a syringe on the nightstand. He blinked and tried to make them go away. They didn't.

She grabbed a large vibrating sex toy, posed, and took several more pictures. Charlie hoped the toy would satisfy her. His respite was broken when she spoke in rapid sentences: "Let's go again! Let's go again!"

In a weak protest Charlie reminded her, "I thought you had a splitting headache. Don't you think we should take it easy? We just finished ten minutes ago. I really don't want to take another Viagra. I've already taken the maximum dose."

"I'm better," she said. "My headache just disappeared. Let's go again. Take the damn pill."

Once in the bed she handed him the cell phone and demanded that he take photos of her clean-shaven pubic area. As he snapped, Charlie saw that she was bleeding in the femoral region. He yelled in an authoritative tone, "You're bleeding like a stuck pig. Get some gauze and put pressure on it."

He couldn't believe she was self-injecting in her groin. She jumped out of frame, went into the master bathroom, and then returned to the bed and started dabbing between her legs with a gauze pad.

Charlie yelled, "No, put pressure on it!"

She did, and the bleeding stopped

Charlie got out of bed and looked out the window at the courthouse square. The town had constructed a makeshift bandstand. Facing the audience was the mayor at a podium with an American flag draped across it. There was a Norman Rockwellian feel to the scene.

Just then fireworks exploded in the sky, lighting the courthouse dome with the various colors pressed against the blackened sky. Charlie forgot his troubles and relished the beauty of the moment.

Robyn grabbed him around the waist and brought him back to reality. She pulled him down onto the bed and planted a wet kiss a few inches below his belly button. She moved her lips the length of his body until they were nose to nose. She straddled him and began to rock back and forth. She was quick, less than ten minutes. At the moment she climaxed she stiffened and fell backward off the bed.

Charlie rushed to her side.

"Are you all right?"

She struggled to speak, "My chest feels real tight, like a hippo is sitting on it."

He checked her pulse, which was racing. The color had drained from her face, and she was short of breath. He knew she was in distress. He started to call 911, over her protests.

"I need an ambulance at 512 4th Avenue immediately. I've got a twenty-seven-year-old female in cardiac arrest."

She strained to crawl toward her nightstand, mumbling something about hiding her drugs. The effort was too much for her, and she collapsed facedown on the carpet.

He dropped the phone when her body hit the floor. He rolled her over, but she had little reaction. He checked her airway; it was clear. He put his second and third fingers on her carotid artery, looked at his watch, and counted to himself. Her pulse was racing, and her breathing was shallow, but evident.

She whispered, "Keep them out of my bathroom."

He looked around the room. Dirty dishes were everywhere; they'd been eating takeout and having sex since he'd arrived on Friday. He thought about the bathroom. The master bathroom was Robyn's drug haven. He'd intentionally used the spare bathroom, content to be blissfully ignorant. He knew he wouldn't have time to sanitize the entire scene before the ambulance arrived.

He glanced over at Robyn's nightstand; there were a pill bottle, syringe, mortar, and white powder strewn across it. Quickly using his cupped hand, he pushed the white powder into the nightstand drawer, and using a Kleenex, he wiped down the nightstand. He picked up the bottle, mortar, and syringe with the tissue and deposited them in the drawer carefully without leaving his fingerprints.

Charlie had more immediate problems, though. He needed to put on some clothes. He went to the other side of the bed and picked up his pants and shirt that were draped over a chair. He continued to watch Robyn as he moved around the room. Not bothering with underwear, he pulled on his pants.

He glanced at his watch; it was ten fifteen. He started unevenly buttoning his shirt, looked over, and saw that Robyn had stopped breathing. He rushed to her side, and he performed CPR. He got her breathing again and sighed with relief.

Another two minutes passed. Then loud knocks jarred Charlie away from his focus on Robyn.

He leaped from the bedroom floor toward the front door and opened it. Two paramedics burst in: one very old, and the other very young. The younger one carried a collapsible gurney, and the other held a duffle bag of equipment marked *Hewes City Fire Dept.*

The older EMT took charge and barked at Charlie, "You gave us the wrong damn address. This is 521, not 512."

Charlie defensively responded, "Your dispatcher transposed the numbers. I know where we are."

The experienced paramedic knew better than to engage a distraught person and dropped the argument. He turned his attention to his patient. He ripped open the Velcro bag, and the two professionals went to work.

Still focusing on Robyn, the senior one began peppering Charlie with questions: "What's she on, sir? I can smell alcohol. What else? How long has she been in distress?"

Charlie knew the EMT needed answers fast. He paused, gathered his thoughts, and in a commanding tone began answering the questions: "It's Doctor, not sir! Since Friday night the patient has consumed at least two liters of vodka, smoked several joints in front of me, over my strong objection, and disappeared several times into the bathroom. Robyn's an addict. I don't know what else she may have taken. She's also taking three prescription medications."

Charlie went to the nightstand on his side of the bed, and before he retrieved three bottles, without notice, he grabbed a Kleenex, so he could hand them over without leaving his prints. He left one bottle on the nightstand. "I don't know which of these she's taken, but she regularly takes hydrocodone, Xanax, and Prozac. I don't know from whom she got these prescriptions. It wasn't through me."

He strongly suspected that the drugs and the needles were in the bathroom somewhere. He absolutely knew what was in the nightstand drawer but remained silent. His silence was a lie. Charlie weighed the option of coming clean with the truth but forced himself to remain silent, justifying his silence by Robyn's plea.

The senior paramedic with gloved hands put the three vials into a plastic bag.

"What's that bottle?" He pointed to Charlie's nightstand.

"It's mine." Charlie picked up the bottle and handed it to the EMT.

He examined the label and asked, "Viagra, isn't that the new drug that's supposed to enhance sexual performance?"

"Yep, and it works." Charlie glanced over at Robyn.

He handed the bottle back to Charlie and returned to his patient. Charlie stuffed it in his front pants pocket.

The younger EMT established a line, and they lifted the naked Robyn onto the gurney. The white-haired paramedic resumed his questioning. Charlie thought the man did not quite believe everything he said. He didn't look in either nightstand; if he had, he would have hit pay dirt.

"Can I look in the bathroom so I can inventory what other drugs she may have taken?" asked the EMT.

Charlie got scared for himself and for Robyn. He looked hard at the paramedic and again in an authoritative tone told him, "There are dozens of pill bottles in the bathroom. She could have taken anything. You need to focus on your patient. She's in real distress."

"Doctor, what is your relationship to the patient?"

Charlie pondered the question a few moments. "She's my fiancée. I came down from New York for the long holiday weekend to convince her that she needed to go into rehab. We broke up because of her drug use."

"What was the patient doing immediately before cardiac arrest?"

Charlie knew the senior paramedic already had the answer to his question. There was no point in lying. She was stark naked. What else could they have been doing?

"Sex! She climaxed and then went into cardiac arrest! Rather than ask me a bunch of irrelevant questions, let's get her to the hospital. I'm riding in the ambulance. Move it!"

Charlie grabbed his shoes and followed the gurney out the door. He locked up with his key. At the elevator, the group was met by two Hewes City police officers. Officer Bobby Pew, a former University of Tennessee running back, in a deep southern drawl addressed the older paramedic whose nameplate read *Mackey*, "What've you got, Mac?"

"Drug overdose. He's the boyfriend, and he's a doctor."

Officer Pew turned to Charlie. "What's she on, Doctor? Is it prescription or street drugs?"

Charlie wished he were somewhere else, anywhere else. He tried to muster the courage to respond. He could tell that the black officer was listening carefully and about to weigh the truthfulness of his answer.

"She's an addict. I know she's been drinking and smoked some weed, but I don't know what else. She has done a lot of drugs the last few years. I can't say for sure what she's on right now."

"Do we have your permission to search the apartment? Maybe we can find a pill bottle or evidence of what drug she's taken," Officer Pew asked.

Frightened now, Charlie strained to understand the last question in part because he was nervous but also because of Pew's heavy accent. Charlie slowly repeated the question before he responded. The last thing he needed was legal problems. He'd had his fair share of them over the last few years, and he wanted no part of this.

He replied, "Absolutely not! The apartment's already locked up. We've got to get to the hospital. I'm riding in the ambulance. Let's go!"

Charlie surprised himself. He was proud of his commanding tone.

The officer backed down and stated he'd follow the ambulance to the hospital. What he didn't say and Charlie didn't know was that he directed Officer Dawson to call the station and report the overdose. Dawson was to stay behind to meet backup to secure the premises as a possible crime scene.

After the patient was loaded, Mackey jumped behind the wheel, looked at his watch, and called dispatch, "This is unit 12. It's ten twenty-nine, and we're leaving 4th for the hospital."

Charlie reflected, *I failed to get her into rehab, but I saved her life just now. Robyn's sister won't see it that way, though. She'll unfairly blame me. The last thing I want to do is face her, but damnit, I will.*

CHAPTER TWO

A HARD GOOD-BYE

Wednesday, August 23, 1995
(About Five Years Earlier)

D r. Peter Nichols held his mother's hand and looked into her blank face. She returned his loving look with a vacant stare. A single tear rolled down his right cheek because he knew that Lillian Nichols was dying. She didn't have much time.

Peter Nichols Sr., his father, died when Peter was eighteen; he'd been gone thirty-two years. Senior approved of Peter's decision not to go into the family business. Right before his death the elder Nichols joked, "Son, being a dentist is an honorable profession, not quite as glamorous as a retail butcher and grocer, but it's an honest living."

Peter Sr. died after being shot in a robbery. He knew as he bled out that the family business, Nichols's Market, in downtown Nashville at 4th and Church, would survive in the capable hands of his older son, Albert. At the time of Peter Sr.'s death the German-style deli market had been serving lunch and offering take-home dinners and household necessities to downtown Nashville workers and busy single businessmen for two generations.

"Mom, it's Peter. Blink if you hear me. Let me know if you understand that I'm here."

It might have been his imagination, but Peter thought his mother's face reacted to his voice. It seemed to strain, and her right eye closed ever so slightly. Peter desperately wanted to believe that his mother knew she wasn't dying alone.

He grabbed her hands. They were freezing, but he held them tightly and reminded himself that she always had a warm and kind heart. Peter looked down at the mangled digits, deformed by age and late-stage arthritis, and cried. He pulled his white linen hand-kerchief from his inside jacket pocket and wiped his eyes. His mother embroidered his initials PEN in gold lettering.

He could feel her pain, despite the lack of expression on her face. She was definitely conscious; she was just incapable of crying out.

According to the doctors, she was suffering from a rare form of dementia. She'd suffered from the horrid disease the last six and a half years. During that time she deteriorated both physically and mentally.

He'd been a good son. For the last six years his mother had lived in his home. His wife, Helen, and his two daughters were a solid support team, each pitching in.

Last night, against medical advice, he'd brought her home to die after a brief hospitalization. Dr. Morgan, her internist, kept in-sisting that with proper care and a little bit of luck, Lillian could survive her latest problems. That wasn't what Peter wanted, and more important, that wasn't what his mother wanted.

He recalled her once telling him, "If I can't play bridge badly, just shoot me."

At the time they both laughed. Peter accepted that she was way past that point now. She didn't know how to play any longer, and she wouldn't have even recognized her partner.

Dr. Peter Nichols was not a medical doctor. He'd been a cosmetic dentist for more than twenty years, yet Dr. Morgan, his mother's physician, questioned Peter's ability to provide her final care. Peter refused hospice, opting to personally care for his mother till the bitter end. Dr. Morgan argued that Peter was out of his field, but Peter rationalized, *What harm can I do?* Although he believed that Dr. Morgan and the hospital staff were well intentioned, Peter surmised they offered no better alternative than bringing his mother home to die.

He closed his eyes, bent over, and kissed her. She was not only cold to the touch but also cold to the lips. He felt a shiver go down his spine, as if he felt the life drain from her through him. By the time he straightened up and opened his eyes, she was gone. He checked her pulse. There wasn't one. He made no effort to revive her. She was in a better place.

He just sat there for a few minutes, staring at her corpse. He wondered what she was doing in heaven. Peter knew that if there were a heaven, his mother would be there. She'd been a great human being and a great mother. He muttered a prayer she'd taught him as a child.

They were alone in the house. At Peter's insistence, Helen and the girls had gone to the movies. He'd wanted to be alone with his mom at the end.

Peter walked downstairs, picked up the kitchen phone, and dialed 911.

"Nine-one-one, what's the nature of your emergency?"

"My mother just died. She's upstairs . . ."

The dispatcher cut Peter off: "Did she die of natural causes, suicide, or at the hands of someone else?"

"Natural causes . . ."

The dispatcher, without an ounce of sympathy in her voice,

interrupted Peter again: "This isn't an emergency, sir. I suggest you call a mortuary of your choice."

Peter realized she was right but didn't like her tone. Rather than argue, he slammed down the receiver. He took a deep breath and dialed Woodlawn Cemetery on Thompson Lane in Nashville. They'd prepare his mother for her eternal trip to be with her beloved husband.

Lonny Benedict answered the phone. There was no warmth in his voice; he sounded all business.

"Woodlawn, Mr. Benedict, how may I be of service?"

"Mr. Benedict, I'm Dr. Peter Nichols. My mother, Lillian Nichols..."

Peter paused to collect himself and in a strained voice said, "Just passed. I need your help. She needs to be picked up and brought to Woodlawn."

Benedict's tone made a complete one eighty, and compassion oozed from his voice.

"Dr. Nichols, I'm sorry to hear of your loss. In which hospital did Mrs. Nichols pass?"

"She died at my home. The address is 4515 General Robert E. Lee Drive off Granny White Pike."

"Dr. Nichols, we'll need a death certificate. Who is her treating physician?"

There was silence on the line as Peter realized he'd have to call Dr. Terry Morgan and get his cooperation regarding the release of his mother's body to Woodlawn. Then he told Benedict the name of the treating physician.

"Dr. Morgan will have to examine your mother, pronounce her dead, and agree to complete the death certificate before we can accept her. Doctor, are you a medical doctor?"

"No, I'm a dentist."

"Well, even if you were a licensed physician, as a family member, you couldn't by law sign the death certificate. If Dr. Morgan won't make a house call, we'll have to take her to a hospital first, so the death certificate can be completed."

Peter advised Benedict he'd call him back. He dialed the office of Dr. Terry Morgan. The answering service told Peter that Dr. Morgan was making rounds at the hospital. Peter asked that the doctor call him back about a very important matter. Peter decided not to characterize the call as an emergency. Fifteen minutes later, the phone rang. It was Dr. Morgan.

"How's your mother? Has her condition worsened?"

"Terry, that's an understatement. She's dead," Peter mumbled. "She's gone. I need a favor. Come by my house and pronounce her dead, so you can complete the death certificate."

Morgan was a real professional. His patients came first, even the dead ones.

"Give me a half hour. I've got two more patients to see, and I'll be there as soon as I can."

"She isn't going anywhere. Treat your living patients and get here when you can."

Forty minutes later, Dr. Morgan rang the doorbell. Peter, who'd been sitting with his mother, walked to the front door with his third strong cup of coffee in his hand. The formalities took less than three minutes. Thirty minutes later Lillian Nichols was on her way to Woodlawn.

Peter's daughters, Nan and Jayne, and his wife, Helen, arrived twenty minutes after the body left. Peter was glad they'd been spared the last agonizing moments of the life of their grandmother and mother-in-law. It had been a hard six and a half years for the family.

That evening, Peter met with Mr. Benedict; he knew his mother's wishes. Before the disease had ravaged her, she'd made her desires clear.

It was a beautiful day in Middle Tennessee when Lillian Nichols was laid to rest. Peter picked up his brother, Albert, at the assisted living facility at eight thirty.

Last year, Albert was forced to retire and sell the family business, which had operated for three generations, more than seventy years. Albert suffered from the same rare form of dementia that plagued their mother. Albert was only fifty-three, but the signs of the disease had appeared much earlier than with their mother. Albert could no longer be trusted to drive a car or cook. He couldn't run the family business or live alone any longer. Pointer Place offered him a safe environment, yet some independence. It also offered a progressive health care system, which would provide more services, as Albert needed them.

As Peter drove up, he found Albert sitting on a bench under a vestibule in the front of the facility. He was properly dressed in a suit, but he held his tie. He'd forgotten how to tie it. The two brothers looked like brothers. Both were about six feet tall with salt-and-pepper short hair.

At first they drove in silence. Peter broke the ice, "Mom wanted a closed casket. Would you like to look at her and say good-bye?"

"We said good-bye several years ago when she still knew who I was. I don't need to see the body. She's already left that shell and is in a better place."

Peter thought his brother sounded good this morning, better than the last time they'd spoken on the phone. At the beginning the disease was like that. There were good days, bad days, and worse days.

"How are you doing, Al? Is the therapy helping?"

Pointer Place specialized in dealing with all forms of dementia and worked with its patients to slow the process with drugs and various types of therapy.

"It's hard to explain. I remember our childhood in Germantown and the store downtown in the greatest detail, but last Wednesday, for the life of me I couldn't tell my therapist who the president of the United States was, and I voted for him."

"I wouldn't worry about that lapse. One politician is the same as another. Trust me, I know politics. It doesn't matter which bastard's in office as long as it's a Democrat."

They both laughed. It felt good to laugh on such a somber day. Peter returned to his brother's memory problem.

"It's more important that you remember our childhood and all those years you worked in the store. Those are things that really matter in life."

They forced a second laugh, but Peter was worried. He changed the subject, "I asked Morty to give the eulogy. I couldn't do it, and I didn't think you were up to it."

Morty Steine was the perfect choice. He'd been a childhood friend of their father and, after his father's death, a good friend to their mother and family. He'd acted as a father figure for both boys. Peter couldn't remember a time when the cigar-smoking Morty wasn't a part of their lives. He'd helped his mother through his father's death, was appointed to prosecute their father's killer, handled the estate matters, advised Peter when he established his practice, and until last year helped Albert with various legal problems so he could continue to run the market. Morty and his partner, Ben Davis, helped Albert sell the business last year.

The chapel at Woodlawn filled up quickly, and courtesy of Morty, the chapel overflowed with white lilies, her favorite flower; they were everywhere, including Lilly's casket. Morty was not only a loyal friend; he was a thoughtful person. Peter made a mental note to thank the man.

Mr. Benedict brought in a few folding chairs, but demand was more than supply. The room was uncomfortably overcrowded. Peter saw Senator Burton Eden and his daughter Valerie Daniels standing in the rear of the chapel. The senator looked frail and was supported by a cane. His mother drew in all walks of life, and they were all here to pay their last respects. Peter hoped the fire marshal didn't show up.

At ten sharp, the minister opened with the Lord's Prayer and introduced a family friend and the family attorney, Morty Steine.

Dressed in a black pinstriped suit, a crisp white button-down shirt, and a maroon tie, Morty walked slowly to the podium. At seventy-four he projected a stately image, but it was an aura that he wasn't a man you wanted to get on the wrong side of. He became a powerful force in any room he entered. He was in control of the room.

He looked incomplete without his cigar. Peter was reassured that Morty knew his mother well and had a way with words. He'd do their mother proud.

Morty cleared his throat and, in a southern-educated voice, began, "Family and friends of Lillian Nichols, it is with great pride and honor that I stand before you and address you today in remembrance of Lilly. She was a remarkably strong woman, who was also gracious and generous. I have no prepared notes. I thought it better that I spoke from my heart. I figured the words would come to me as I reflected on Lilly's life."

Peter thought, *Despite age, the old man still knows how to address a crowd. I bet he could still give an effective opening or closing argument in court.* Peter's mind drifted to the murder trial of his father. He remembered how Morty had been an advocate for Al and him to attend, over the initial objection of their mother. He returned to the eulogy.

"As a young girl, she met Peter at Nichols's Market when she was hired by him. It was love at first sight. I know because I was there when my friend first laid eyes on her.

"I was Peter's boyhood friend, and we learned retail together. I worked for my family business, Steine's Department Store, right across the street from Nichols's Market. We lived on the same block in Germantown, and the families opened their businesses in downtown Nashville a year apart. Both businesses flourished and became part of the Nashville community and helped its people through the Great Depression and through the war."

Morty, like the son Peter Nichols, elected not to make his career in the family business. Morty chose to go to law school and practice law.

Morty continued, "After Lilly and Peter married, they worked side by side in the market, and then Uncle Sam wanted Peter, who served in the navy while Lilly held down the store. Her two sons, Albert and Peter Jr., are here mourning her.

"For more than twenty years Lilly and Peter worked together until one summer night when Peter was murdered in a senseless holdup. The family asked me, as the family's attorney, to prosecute the murderer, which I did. That person is still serving his life sentence at Brushy Mountain State Prison.

"After Peter's death I became extremely close to Lilly. I tried to be a father figure to the boys and helped when I could. They became good men because of Lilly's hard work and efforts."

Peter remembered the times that Morty spent with him and his brother, providing the male touch.

"After Peter's death, Lilly and Albert operated the market together for another fifteen years until she retired seven years ago. Albert ran it until last year when a piece of Nashville history closed.

"Lilly knew almost everybody who worked downtown. She always had a pleasant word and always shared her memorable smile.

She was a beautiful young woman, but till her dying day she kept her beautiful, memorable smile."

In closing Morty remarked, "We're all going to die. They say taxes and death are the only certainties. I'll tell you another certainty: Lilly is in heaven, looking down on us with her beautiful smile."

The old man walked down from the podium and first embraced Albert and then Peter. It was a bear hug, and he kissed Peter on his right cheek, the same spot where he shed that tear for his mother the other day.

Peter whispered in Morty's ear, "I need to come see you."

Morty replied, "At your convenience."

CHAPTER THREE

LIFE MARCHES ON

Wednesday, August 30, 1995

Benjamin Davis got off the elevator on the eighth floor, where he'd practiced law for almost twenty years in what had been the shoe department of the old Steine's Department Store. As he walked down the corridor, he glanced down in the oak-framed ankle-high mirrors and noticed his shoes needed a shine. The brass plaque to the right of the door read *Benjamin Davis, Attorney at Law*.

Despite his wife Liza's protests for his safety, he still arrived at work around 6:00 a.m. Although the physical scars from his 1993 beating were barely visible, the emotional scars remained. Liza still worried because T-rex was still out there. She wished he'd wait until the office building was bustling to begin his day, but Davis refused. He loved the quiet of those first three hours. He was also pretty stubborn.

Reception was empty so he went straight to the kitchen. He spied two chocolate cupcakes on the counter, and he wolfed the first one down without even removing it from the wrapper. He stared hard at the second. These were somebody's snack, but he was the boss, so what the hell! He decided to eat the second one a little slower to savor the taste. He struggled with his weight, but the reason why was no mystery: too much food and no exercise.

That was another subject that Liza focused on. She was a nurse and knew what the extra fifty pounds were doing to him. He'd deal with his weight tomorrow.

Yesterday Bella Rosario, his longtime secretary, had set the timer on the coffee maker for him. He grabbed a cup of black coffee and jumped right into one of the piles of papers on his desk.

By seven, almost all of the staff had arrived. Bella manned the reception room, while Sammie, Davis's niece and a first-year associate and a Vanderbilt Law School student, was hard at work writing an appellate brief for her uncle. Davis had great expectations for his brother's daughter.

She'd arrived in Nashville via Miami, three years earlier, a freshly minted paralegal and a party girl. She'd been initiated by fire into the firm as she spent her initial tenure working on the Plainview cases. That experience motivated her to go to Vanderbilt Law School. She'd finished her first year in May while continuing to work for her uncle's law firm.

She was having some difficulty in recent weeks balancing her commitment to school and to work. She missed a few classes, rationalizing that she was blessed with the best teacher of all, Morty. He gave her the practical application of the law. He also taught her to love the law despite all its shortcomings.

She selected classes in the afternoon and at night, so her mornings were free to work. She had a full and busy life, unfortunately with no time for romance.

She'd changed not only intellectually but physically as well. Her girlish ponytail was gone, replaced with a stylish short cut. With the help of her aunt Liza there'd been a total wardrobe metamorphosis. At the law firm, tight jeans and sweaters were replaced with expensive business attire courtesy of Davis's American Express Card.

He was a willing accomplice. Sammie was a beautiful and strong woman, and she projected that image. Clients couldn't ignore her even if they wanted to. Through hard work she'd become an intricate part of the Davis team.

This morning every member of the team had arrived except the most senior member, Morty Steine. Morty was fast asleep on the ninth floor, where he maintained a loft apartment right above the eighth-floor offices. For more than fifty years Morty had been a nationally recognized attorney practicing out of the old Steine's Department Store building, where Davis currently operated his law office. Davis had worked with Morty for twenty years, starting as his three-dollar-an-hour law clerk, then his associate, partner, and finally boss. The substitution of authority had been seamless. Davis totally respected the old man, and Morty was self-confident enough that he no longer needed the aura of authority and control. The men truly loved each other; there was no room for them to get closer.

Morty arrived about ten, visited with his co-workers, and then took an early lunch. He'd slowed down quite a bit, but when needed, he still had what it took. Davis often admitted to himself as well as others that Morty was why he was the lawyer he'd become.

Morty once ruled the office, smoking his illegal Cuban cigars wherever he damn well pleased. They were eight inches long, and he made one last most of the day, chewing on the stub. Doctor's orders and his heart condition dictated that he stop smoking. In defiance of his cardiologist, John Caldwell, Davis's father-in-law, he still chewed his Cubans but never lit them. He was now relegated to smoking small cigarillos and hiding in his loft bathroom, blowing the smoke into the exhaust vent. Davis and the rest of the staff hounded him to stop his one pleasure. Morty was constantly cranky for lack of nicotine.

Davis buzzed Bella. "My calendar indicates that my first appointment is Valerie Daniels. You must have made this appointment when I was in court late yesterday. Did she tell you why she needed to see me?"

"No, she didn't. Remember, her father died recently. You missed the funeral because you were in the Kane trial. I suspect she has some questions about his estate."

"Pull her father's Last Will and Testament, so I can answer her questions."

Davis went back to one of the files on his desk. Before he knew it, Valerie Daniels was walking into his office. They took a seat in the teal blue leather chairs at the mahogany conference table, which took up most of Davis's private office. Bella offered the client a coffee or a soft drink, which she declined.

Daniels was not only a client but also an old friend. She was slightly younger than Davis, but they shared many of the same friends. They also knew each other through Morty, who was politically connected to Daniels's father, the late senator. She was also in public service. She'd been the superintendent for the Nashville school system, its administrative head, for the last eight years. Before that she was a high school principal. The Daniels family was part of the Old South, and Valerie was a real lady with an eloquent voice.

She said, "Sorry I missed your 4th of July barbeque, Ben. We were in Washington, visiting Daddy. I can't believe he's gone. My life has been bedlam."

Davis, a transplanted New Yorker, was amused by her pronunciation of the words *bedlam and barbeque*. He responded in his own equally heavy accent, "My condolences, Valerie. I missed your daddy's funeral because I was in court. Liza represented our family. She told me it was a beautiful service. You'd be proud to know that Judge

Wise interrupted our trial with a moment of silence. He mentioned that your daddy nominated him for his appointment to the federal bench. I was impressed that the governor ordered that the flags be brought to half-mast in his honor. He was a great public servant."

"You knew Daddy. He didn't do anything in a small way."

Senator Burton Eden last year had been elected to a fourth term as the senior U.S. senator for Tennessee. Davis and Morty had campaigned for and financially contributed to his re-election. Burt and Morty had been friends about fifty years, both yellow dog Democrats.

Daniels came to the point, "I've been going over Daddy's accounts. He left Mom broke. The man was a charmer but not much of a businessperson."

Davis was aware that her father was in desperate financial shape. Several months earlier he'd met with the senator and referred him to a bankruptcy attorney to consider his options.

"Valerie, have you found your father's will? I have a photocopy here if you haven't."

"I've read it. He left everything to Mom, but it's still nothing. I've totaled his debts, more than $500,000."

Davis knew he needed to shoot straight with Daniels. There was no point in sugarcoating the truth. "Your daddy may have mismanaged his finances, but he wasn't a fool. Your mom isn't liable for any of those debts, and the house and the farm are in her name only. Despite the demands of your father's creditors, I wouldn't let your mother guarantee any of his debts. Then there's the insurance."

"What insurance?"

Davis smiled and, with one of his piercing blue eyes, gave his client a knowing wink. "Your daddy had three life insurance policies. One in the amount of $500,000 that named your mother as beneficiary, and two others, each in the amount of $200,000, that named you as beneficiary and you as trustee for your sister, Robyn. Your daddy knew that Robyn would need help managing her money and wanted you to manage it for her. I'm actually the substitute trustee if you're unable or unwilling to serve."

"Let me get this straight. Daddy's creditors get nothing. Mom gets the house and the three hundred and fifty acres free and clear and the life insurance proceeds of $500,000. I get $200,000 for myself and manage another $200,000 for Robyn."

"That sums it up."

Davis assured her that no paperwork was necessary regarding the house and farm. "We'll have to send a death certificate to the insurance companies. The money should be here in less than two weeks. I'll have to probate your daddy's estate to get rid of the creditors."

"Ben Davis, I love you."

"I have that effect on most women, but don't tell Liza."

Davis turned serious, which was his intent. He asked her, "Have you thought of who might finish out the five-year balance of your father's term? You know, by law, his replacement is appointed by the governor."

"Why would that be my concern?"

"Because, my dear, you should finish his term."

"You're out of your mind. I'm not qualified."

"Like hell you're not. You've watched your father first in the House of Representatives and then in the Senate for the last nineteen years. You're a capable administrator, and you've been managing hundreds of people and dealing with unions. Your daddy's staff will help you. You've got their loyalty. If the governor appoints someone else, then they're probably out of a job. Anyone else would bring in his or her own staff."

Davis could tell that despite her protest Daniels was interested. Why not?

She looked thoughtful and said, "How would I get Governor Clark's consideration? He was close with Daddy, but we haven't spoken in years."

Davis expected the question and was prepared. "The men for the job are Morty Steine and Dr. Peter Nichols. Morty still knows everyone in the party, and Peter went to Vanderbilt with Governor Clark. They were fraternity brothers. Peter knows where all the skeletons are buried and has been a financial supporter. Between the two of them, they can get you the job. They'll make a perfect team."

Davis gave Daniels a moment to digest the information. He jarred her with his next question: "Are there any skeletons in your closet? We might as well address them on the front end."

That was an important question, and Daniels needed to be candid and truthful for his idea to work.

After a long minute, she responded, speaking slowly and softly, "My marriage to Bill is solid. Both my kids have stayed out of trouble. There's just one big problem, my sister, Robyn. She's got serious addiction problems. Drugs, alcohol, promiscuity, you name it."

She explained that Robyn was currently touring as a backup singer with Hank Williams Jr. and that life on the road had taken a toll on her. Davis promised to try to help Daniels get Robyn off the road and into rehab.

They hugged, and Daniels left the office with a lighter step and a big smile. She hugged Sammie Davis as she passed her in the doorway.

Sammie walked into her uncle's office with a perplexed look on her face.

Davis recognized her confusion and with a straight face remarked, "Just another satisfied customer."

Davis and his niece spent the next hour discussing the appellate brief she was working on and other pending cases. Sammie brought new energy and enthusiasm to the Davis practice. As Davis pondered the growth of his niece, he knew she'd be his partner someday. But they needed to address the present.

He asked, "Has Morty showed up yet?"

"No, he's still upstairs. Should I go rouse him?"

"Leave the old man alone. If we need him, and we will, we'll know just where to find him. Just get that brief ready. Remember, it's due day after tomorrow."

Sammie walked out without another word, and Davis sat there considering how best to solicit Morty's help on the Daniels nomination. He knew his luncheon appointment would move the issue forward.

Davis walked four blocks to the Merchants restaurant on Broadway. Dr. Peter Nichols was waiting at their table with a glass of wine in front of him.

"Hi, Ben, can I order you a beer, a glass of wine, or an iced tea?"

A waiter in a white coat walked over.

"I'll just have a glass of water with a lemon wedge," Davis told him.

"Peter, I'm sorry about your mom, but Morty gave her a beautiful send-off."

Nichols became emotional at even the mention of his mother. He quickly regained his composure and said, "Morty was superb. She's in a much better place."

He paused and changed the subject. "Thanks for meeting me for lunch. I need to talk to you about Albert. My brother's dementia is getting worse. He's becoming more and more dependent."

"I'm sorry to hear that, Peter. Your mother's estate is in good shape, and Al's in good hands in the Alzheimer's unit at Pointer Place. He'll get the progressive care he needs. You can feel good about the decisions you've made."

"Then why do I feel so terrible?"

"Life isn't easy sometimes. You just have to march on. You've got Helen and the kids, and as far as Al's concerned, all you can do is try to do the right thing."

Davis figured that his good friend and client needed a diversion, so he launched into his idea of filling Senator Eden's Senate seat with his daughter. Peter listened, asked a few questions, and then threw his full support behind the goal.

As they were walking out the door of Merchants, Davis turned to Nichols and reminded him, "I'll see you Saturday."

CHAPTER FOUR

THE READING
OF THE WILL

Saturday, September 2, 1995

D r. Nichols accepted Davis's offer to come to the house to read his mother's will. Peter wanted his girls to be at the reading since they'd been named as beneficiaries. He knew that their home would be less intimidating for the family than Davis's law office. Peter's home was a Tudor, just like his office, which was located on historic Music Row. When he left the house to pick up Albert, Helen, Nan, and Jayne were sitting in the screened-in porch overlooking the swimming pool. Helen greeted Davis and Morty with a pitcher of fruit tea and a homemade pecan pie at the ready.

Peter and Albert entered the porch, and after exchanging a few pleasantries, Davis turned serious and professional and asked everybody to take a seat. Peter was Morty's lifelong friend and client. However, like most of Morty's clients, over the last few years, he had been transitioned to Davis. For this reason Morty told Davis to take the lead at the reading. Davis explained that Lillian Nichols had not been competent to change her will for at least the last six years. Peter knew that his mother hadn't tried, or he would have been aware of it. He'd kept her original will in his possession and held up the document so everyone in the room could see it.

Davis confirmed that his copy was identical to the original and continued, "On May 14th, 1988, this will was prepared by Morty, witnessed by me and Sherry Duncan, and notarized by my secretary, Bella Rosario. Mrs. Duncan, a dear friend of Lilly, died three years ago, but because her signature was notarized, her availability now isn't necessary."

Davis stopped and let that information sink in. Then he handed each member of the Nichols family a copy of the will. He indicated that he preferred to explain the document rather than read it verbatim. No one objected.

He began, "The will names her sons, Albert and Peter, as co-executors, which means it was her intent in 1988 that both of you act as co-administrators of her estate."

Peter looked over at his brother to determine whether he was following along and understood. Albert's face was noncommittal.

"The will does provide that if one of you predeceases her or is unable or unwilling to participate in the probate, the remaining son should proceed to probate alone."

Albert had the same blank stare. Peter came to Davis's rescue and asked, "Al, do you think you're up to going to court and paying the bills of the estate?"

"I'm too busy running the market," he answered.

Everybody in the room just looked at each other. Albert hadn't run the market in more than a year.

Again, Peter interceded and said, "Al, we sold the market last year. You remember that, don't you?"

Albert didn't answer at first, and there was an uncomfortable silence.

"We sold the market? I didn't agree to that. I ran that place for more than thirty years, and you sold it out from under me? What the hell's going on here?"

Albert was becoming very agitated. He started wringing his hands together so hard that he cut off his circulation, and they began to turn white.

Peter helplessly sat there as Davis tried to calm Albert down. "Al, don't you remember you and your mother sold the market last year, and half the sales proceeds were placed in trust for you? That's when you moved into Pointer Place. They've been taking good care of you, haven't they?"

Albert jumped to his feet, and as he turned toward Davis, Peter saw a wild look in the man's eyes. In a matter of moments his brother transformed from a mild-mannered man to a raving lunatic. He turned and aggressively accused Peter, "Where'd the other half of the sales proceeds go?"

Morty tried to help handle the question, "It's now part of your mother's estate."

"Who gets that half?" Albert shot back.

Peter had read the will and knew that Davis planned to talk about taxes and other matters before he explained the distribution of the estate, but Albert wasn't giving him much choice. It was evident that Albert was not capable to serve as co-executor, and Peter hoped Albert would voluntarily step down.

Davis broke his train of thought: "Al, your mother left all of her jewelry, silver, and china to Helen. She left $50,000 each to Nan and Jayne in trust, which each will receive on her twenty-fifth birthday. Peter is the trustee until they reach the appointed age. If either of them were to die before her twenty-fifth birthday, the other gets the deceased granddaughter's share. The two girls also get their grandmother's collections, by alternate selection, with Nan picking first because she's older. The remainder of her estate is divided between you and Peter. Your half will go in trust with your other money to help care for you as you get older. There's plenty of money to last you until your time comes."

"What if I want something?"

"Well, Peter's your trustee. I'm sure if it's a reasonable request, he'd get it for you."

"What if he thinks it's unreasonable?"

"Under the trust, he controls your funds, and if it's an unreasonable request, he has a fiduciary obligation to say no."

"I'd like a couple of new pipes and some tobacco."

Albert had smoked a pipe for more than thirty years. The market always smelled of vanilla. The customers didn't seem to mind or got used to the odor. Peter loved it. His father smoked the same tobacco, so Albert's pipe reminded him of his dad. Unfortunately, it had been a problem at Pointer Place, which was a smoke-free environment.

Peter broke in, "No problem. I'll take you to Uptown's tomorrow, and you can pick them out. How about a Dunhill or Peterson?" Those were two brands that his brother liked.

"I'd also like a red Corvette, a convertible."

Peter replied, "That's a problem, Al. You don't have a driver's license anymore."

Albert looked visibly disturbed; he'd obviously forgotten he no longer had a driver's license.

Peter offered a solution: "What if I bought a new red Corvette with my half of the money, we kept it here at my house, and you could drive with me whenever you wanted?"

Albert seemed satisfied and calmed down. Peter hoped his brother had been appeased.

Davis took a moment to eat a piece of his pecan pie and take a sip of his fruit tea. As he did he thought of the song lyrics "you say potato and I say patattah." Where Davis was from, pecan pie was pronounced pea-can pie. The southern pronunciation was much more soothing to the ear.

Davis finished explaining the will and asked if there were any questions.

Jayne, a Hillsboro High School junior, asked the first question: "My grandmother's collections are boxed in the basement. Can Nan and I open them up and keep some of them in our rooms but leave the rest boxed up until we get places of our own?"

Peter answered his daughter's question: "We'll just leave them in the basement for the time being until you girls are ready for them."

Nan, the college sophomore, asked the next question: "Can we use any of our $50,000 now, or do we have to wait till we're twenty-five?"

"That's up to your dad. He's the trustee."

Albert raised his hand.

Davis acknowledged him: "You don't have to raise your hand, Al. What's your question?"

"What happens to my money when I die?"

"Well, Al, Morty prepared your will about ten years ago." Davis turned to his old friend and let him respond.

"If I recall correctly, you left your estate in trust for Nan and Jayne, with Peter as the trustee. The girls get distributions at various ages. I think it was at twenty-five, thirty, and thirty-five, but I'd have to check."

"Can I change my will?"

Everyone knew that was a loaded and dangerous question. The question was directed to Morty, so he responded, "Do you want to change your will?"

"Maybe I do."

"Let me pull it and read it, and we can talk about it, okay?"

"I'll make an appointment."

There were no more questions so Peter showed Davis and Morty to the front door.

Davis spoke up, "You'd better make an appointment for yourself, so we can start probate. I'll prepare a document for Al to refuse to serve for health reasons. If he won't sign, we'll have to go to court and explain the situation. Call Bella on Monday, and she'll make you an appointment. We may have a problem."

CHAPTER FIVE

SEEKING A
NEW PARTNER

Thursday, September 7, 1995

Benjamin Davis was no stranger to hard work. His cases required absolute dedication. A trial could last two or three weeks while the rest of his practice came to a shrieking halt. In the past Bella went it alone. Morty was no longer interested in the day-to-day grind of the practice of law. He acted like Davis's consigliore, as in the *Godfather*. He answered Bella's questions but only wanted to be involved in the exciting stuff. That was the benefit of having senior status. Now with the addition of Sammie, Davis had another set of hands to help Bella, particularly when Davis was unavailable. But Sammie always wanted to come to court; there was a delicate balance to maintain.

What both Davises knew about trial work was that after a favorable jury verdict, an appeal could last three or four years. Davis's work demanded patience and attention to detail. Through both her uncle and Morty, Sammie knew this. What Sammie found so interesting was that each case varied as to the facts and the law. They all loved the challenge of a new case.

In contrast the hard work of Peter Nichols, DDS, had gotten routine over the last twenty years. He performed the same four procedures again and again. Occasionally for a friend he might provide general dental services, but his reputation was built on cosmetic dentistry. He worked six days a week, sometimes fourteen-hour days, and he was still not keeping up with demand. Nichols's specialty was a unique and profitable niche in the marketplace. His practice was almost exclusively adults, except the children of close friends. Many of Nichols's patients were celebrities. He was the "Dentist to the Stars."

Davis's two children, Caroline and Jake, and even Davis's wife, Liza, enjoyed going to Dr. Nichols's office because there was always someone famous in his waiting room. Caroline for years, over Davis's protests, pestered Dr. Nichols's patients for their autographs. The stars politely signed their names and wrote a special note to one or both of the children. The memorabilia hung on each child's bedroom wall.

Jake also loved Dr. Nichols's television commercials where he sang a duet with one of his famous patients. Nichols actually had a pretty good voice and made several appearances on the Grand Ole Opry and local television shows with or without one of his patients.

Nichols's distinct office building, a Tudor mansion, was always shown in those commercials. It had become a Nashville landmark over the years since so many people had seen it so often. It was located on Music Row, close to Nichols's patient base.

Davis knew most of Dr. Nichols's patients because they were also Morty's clients; many remained represented by Davis after Morty's semi-retirement. Others fled to representation in either LA or New York.

Davis preferred that his meeting with Dr. Nichols be at Davis's office for two reasons. First, Davis could charge Nichols for the meeting, rather than the other way around; and second, Davis would suffer no pain at this appointment. Davis's chronic problems with his teeth and gums tainted his professional relationship with Nichols; Davis simply associated the man and what he did with pain.

Bella Rosario, first employed by Morty and now by Davis, buzzed Davis on the intercom and announced Nichols's arrival. Davis told Bella to park Nichols in the conference room and to let Morty and Sammie know that their one o'clock appointment had arrived.

Despite his odd office hours, Morty indicated that he'd attend the meeting with his old friend.

Davis got to the conference room first and greeted Nichols. Sammie was also a patient. Unlike Davis, Sammie, at age twenty-seven, had perfect teeth and a perfect smile. Nichols liked to joke that it was hard to believe, based upon their dental records, they were related. But uncle and niece were cut from the same cloth.

When Morty arrived, the two old friends bear-hugged hello. In deference to Morty, Davis let him open the conversation.

"Peter, how are you, Helen, and the girls holding up?"

"It's hard to believe that Mom is gone. She lived with us more than six years. The house just doesn't feel the same."

"Lilly was a great lady. I'll miss her," Morty interjected.

"How's your brother doing? Al seemed a little agitated at the will reading. Did you get him his pipes and the red Corvette?" Davis asked.

"I got him the pipes the next day. It took some nagging, but I did finally get the red Vette. We argued over the interior. He wanted white, I wanted tan, and we compromised on black. Here's the executed document, where Al waives his right to serve as co-executor on the estate. I like the car. It was a small price to pay to avoid the embarrassment of going to court to declare him incompetent."

Davis had to agree. Proving Albert was incapable of serving as the co-executor wouldn't have been difficult, but it still required a public hearing, and the Nichols family, ever since the murder of Peter Sr., was a very private family.

Morty looked at Nichols as he said, "You called this meeting. What can we do for you?"

"I'm worried. I look at Al and wonder if I'm next. He was only fifty-one when the first symptoms of the dementia reared its ugly head."

"How old are you?"

"I'm fifty. I'll be fifty-one soon."

Davis wanted to ask a question, but Sammie beat him to the punch with a critical one: "How many more years do you intend to work?"

"I'd like to slow down in four years. I've got one daughter in college and another about to graduate from high school. When they've both finished school, Helen and I would like to spend winters at our place in Highland Beach, Florida."

Morty followed up: "Does either Nan or Jayne have any desire to go into the family business?"

"Nan wants to move to New York and has no further interest in school after she graduates. Jayne's never indicated any interest to follow in my footsteps, but she doesn't know what she wants. She's seventeen."

Davis interrupted and in a serious tone said, "The reason I ask is that a non-professional cannot own a professional corporation. Helen cannot inherit your practice and continue to own it. If you were to die, your estate would have to sell the practice pretty quickly at a fire sale."

"I spent my life building that practice. I couldn't let it go for next to nothing."

Davis could see and hear the disappointment in Nichols's voice. He said, "You'd be dead, and Helen and your executor, who's Morty, would have no choice. People aren't going to sit around and wait for your replacement. They'd find another established cosmetic dentist. Even more likely, with you gone the competition would simply move in. There are not that many cosmetic dentists in Nashville."

Davis paused to let that sink in. He wanted Peter to recognize that his estate planning was important and what happened to his practice when he retired or died was a big part of it.

"I pulled your Last Will and Testament. Morty drafted it in 1988, seven years ago. Helen is the sole beneficiary. If you and she died in a common disaster, your brother is the trustee for the girls. Morty's the backup trustee. In light of Al's current condition, at the very least we've got to change that provision of your will."

Nichols looked at Morty.

Morty stated honestly, "I'm too old. You need someone younger than you and Helen. You also need to replace me as executor and substitute trustee."

Davis could see that Nichols didn't like the idea of replacing Morty. His face pruned up like he'd just bitten a lemon.

Morty offered a solution: "How about Ben? He's younger and better looking than me, and both you and Helen trust him."

It was agreed that with Helen's permission, Davis would serve as executor and trustee if both Nichols and his wife died. Again with her approval, Helen's will would be reciprocal and identical. Davis directed Sammie to use the old wills to draft new ones. Davis explained to Nichols that the documents would contain a waiver of conflict provision since the wills were prepared by Davis's office and he would be serving as the executor and as a trustee.

Davis looked over at Morty and with a nod from the old man took charge. "Getting back to your practice, you've got two choices as I see it. The first is to sell out to a larger and well-established practice. As part of the deal you would either work for the new owners or join as a partner."

"I've got to be my own boss. At fifty, I'm not changing my ways, and I'm not taking orders from anyone, except Helen. What's your other alternative?"

Davis explained that Morty had also been a solo practitioner for most of his career, but in 1975, he'd reluctantly brought on Davis, an inexperienced law student, which Davis emphasized turned out to be one of the best decisions Morty ever made.

When Morty made a sarcastic face, Davis ignored the old man and continued, "Find a young DDS, pay him well, and give him incentives to buy into the practice. Require, as a condition of employment, that he set aside money over the next few years to buy your practice. After two or three years, you determine if he or she is the right candidate; if no, then you cut the person loose and move on to someone else. However, after a few years, we'll call them the honeymoon years, if it feels right and you get to know each other, you slowly let this person buy stock in your professional corporation using the agreed upon savings from his compensation. Help him build up his credit so when you're ready, your young partner can buy your remaining interest in the practice using the bank's money. You might even elect to keep a small percentage of the practice to supplement your retirement."

"Morty, is that what you did with Ben?"

"I'm not that smart. After seven years, I gave him twenty percent, and then in 1992 when Goldie got sick, I retired and gave him the remaining eighty percent. Listen to what I say, not what I do."

Davis could see the surprise on Nichols's face as he said, "But you're still working. If I remember correctly, you only stayed retired about two months."

"Yeah, but Ben overpays me as his associate, and he works me so hard, I don't even have time to spend the dollar he does pay me each month. That's after my raise. At first he only paid me a dollar a year."

Twelve dollars a year didn't go very far. It was their private joke.

Davis asked the next question: "Doctor, you trained in the sixties. Are there any procedures that a young dentist could offer your patients that you don't perform? That would be a good way to expand your practice. So a younger dentist would perform slightly different procedures and would use different techniques."

"Yes, but we'd get to the same place."

Davis saw the opportunity he'd been waiting for to broach his brainchild of an idea: "What if you looked at this issue differently? What if you hired a medical doctor, let's say an oral surgeon?"

Nichols replied, "I'd never thought about that possibility."

Davis spoke with authority: "The fields of cosmetic dentistry and oral surgery overlap and have great synergy. An MD degree opens up what the practice could offer your patients. The MD license has much more flexibility than a DDS. Another possibility is a plastic surgeon who specialized in the face."

Nichols warmed up to the idea: "I refer patients to oral surgeons all the time. I bet they earn fees in excess of a hundred grand a year off my referrals. With an MD associate I could keep those fees in house."

Davis had anticipated the direction of this discussion and had directed Sammie to research several legal issues, including whether a DDS and an MD could practice together.

Sammie took her cue from her uncle and started reading from the memo she'd prepared for the meeting: "The Tennessee legislature does permit DDSs and MDs to practice together, but Dr. Nichols would have to reincorporate. Dr. Nichols's current professional corporation only permitted the practice of dentistry. A new corporation would have to be formed, and its charter would provide that the corporation could provide both medical and dental services to the general public. The only snag is that the young doctor would have to own at least one share of stock in the new corporation because at least one of the owners would have to be licensed to practice medicine."

Davis interrupted his niece: "That's not a problem. The young doctor can own one share, and the bylaws can provide that all decisions are controlled by a majority vote. If you own ninety-nine percent, you'll have absolute control. We can make a condition of ownership, employment by the corporation. So if the MD resigns or gets fired, he'll have to sell his share for a predetermined price. We'll also include a non-solicitation of patients. We can't prevent the new associate from competing with you because he'll be an MD and you're a DDS, but we can prevent him from competing with the practice and that's the same thing."

"What's the difference?"

It was Morty's turn: "Don't worry, Peter. We'll take care of the legal side and protect your interests. You just find the right candidate, and we'll get the paperwork done. Just make sure you do a thorough background check. All potential candidates must be vetted before they are interviewed. This person will represent you in the community. Your reputation will be tied with his or hers. A partnership is like a marriage except there's no sex involved."

Everyone in the room laughed, and the meeting broke up.

CHAPTER SIX

THE SEARCH BEGINS

Wednesday, October 25, 1995

Dr. Nichols was tired of working a twelve-hour day, six days a week. The office opened at seven and closed at seven. Nichols believed that he owed the highest obligation of service to his patients, and that included availability. His patients were busy people, whose work schedules often dictated when they could be seen.

The staff worked the same hours, and even with overtime they were on the verge of rebellion. Nichols's office manager, Donna Burns, kept the chaos manageable. She'd been with him since the beginning, more than twenty years.

In life, as in business, timing is everything. As the new millennium got closer, there was an unprecedented public awareness of the importance of one's smile and a fascination by women, and even some men, with looking younger. This took many forms, but one of the rages was for women to enhance their lips, plump them up. Dr. Nichols, who already catered to the music industry, could cover the smile, but only an MD could perform surgery on the lips.

Nichols finished his last patient at five and let his staff go home early, except Donna. Tonight the search began for an exceptional MD candidate to expand Nichols's practice.

Through the American Medical Association (AMA), Nichols had found a recruiting firm in Washington, DC that specialized in the placement of medical professionals. Nichols and Donna reviewed the company literature sent by McCormick & Associates and were impressed. When Nichols discussed his decision to hire the recruiter, Davis reminded him of Morty's warning that each candidate had to be vetted. Nichols assured him that according to the literature McCormick did a complete investigation before any interview was conducted. That eased Davis's mind; it was one less thing for him to worry about. McCormick professed to be the expert.

As the last staff member walked out, a tall gentleman with immaculately groomed silver hair walked in. He was well tailored, in a dark blue suit, crisp white button-down shirt, and red bow tie. He was tall, at least six four. He was extremely tan. He must have just come back from a long vacation in the sun.

Donna approached him, and when she shook his hand, she got a good whiff of his cologne. He smelled of gardenias.

"Mr. McCormick, I'm Donna Burns. We spoke on the phone several times. Welcome to Nashville."

McCormick in a baritone voice responded, "Ms. Burns, a pleasure, your directions were perfect. I've checked into the Hermitage Hotel, and I'm looking forward to meeting Dr. Nichols. These site visits by my firm are important in the processes of finding the right candidate. What an unusual place for a dentist's office. How old is this Tudor?"

"It's turn of the century. There are a full kitchen upstairs and several offices. There are two third-floor turrets. That's where the lookouts watched."

"What do you mean?"

"This used to be a speakeasy during Prohibition. Before that it was a house of ill repute. Those turrets housed lookouts to watch for cops who might show up to raid the place. We still have chairs up there but no need to have anyone watching. Our dental practice operates within the bounds of the law."

McCormick laughed and pointed out, "That can be a selling point for the new physician. Everybody enjoys a colorful story. I've been busy. We've got lined up three promising telephone interviews for tonight."

As McCormick was finishing his sentence, Nichols walked up to him and extended his hand. "Dr. Peter Nichols. It's a pleasure to meet you. Donna has told me a great deal about you, your firm, and the service you provide. Your survey questions and our prior telephone conversations were certainly thorough. I look forward to these telephone interviews you've chosen."

McCormick smiled and, in a warm, friendly voice, said, "Call me Rocky. You're Donna and Peter, right?" He assured Peter that each physician had been properly vetted, and each had been interviewed by first one of his associates and then by him.

Nichols thought the man was professional. Why shouldn't he be? His fee of $10,000 applied toward twenty-five percent of the gross salary of the hired physician was pretty steep. Nichols was convinced if they found the right MD, McCormick's fee would be well worth it.

"Thank you for agreeing to come to Nashville to meet with me. Can I offer you a soft drink or something stronger?"

"It's all part of our service. We can't make the right match without a site visit. By my being here for these interviews, we get to discuss our impressions right away and in person. That has real value in the selection process."

"What will it be?"

"I'll take a Jack Daniel's on the rocks, since you're offering. I understand the distillery is just south of Nashville."

"Yes, it's about forty miles south of Nashville. Would you believe it's in a dry county? It's a national brand, but the locals can't even buy a bottle in their hometown of Lynchburg."

Nichols led McCormick and Donna into his office and fixed all three of them a drink. After a few pleasantries, he asked, "Have you placed a physician with a dental office?"

"Yes, but only three times, all in California. We've been highly successful. Each practice grew exponentially by offering new services. I think your idea of combining a dental practice with a related medical field is ingenious."

Nichols gave credit to his attorney and then moved on to describe the nature of his practice. The discussion included information that had already been provided by Donna when she completed the practice survey, but Nichols wanted to explain and McCormick was willing to listen and sip his drink.

Nichols indicated that either an oral surgeon or a plastic surgeon, who specialized in the maxillofacial area, would probably be the best fit. Nichols explained that he wasn't a snob, but he preferred someone from an Ivy League school or at least a first-tier medical school.

Donna, who was far more cost conscious than Nichols, asked McCormick one of the more important questions: "What type of salary range and benefits can we expect to pay?"

McCormick replied, "That's the million-dollar question, not literally a million. I would guesstimate that a good plastic candidate will cost at least $150,000 out of the box. An oral surgeon will be a little less, maybe $135,000. For benefits, you should expect moving expenses, malpractice insurance, continuing education costs, 401k, three weeks of vacation, and health, disability, and dental insurance. At least the dental insurance shouldn't be a problem."

The three laughed.

"Benefits usually run about twenty-five percent of salary," McCormick added.

Nichols winced. "Just like your fee?"

Donna put in her two cents: "Boy, with your fee, that's a total cost of almost $200,000. That's quite an investment."

Nichols was a bit nervous about the cost, but he wasn't going to get cold feet. He needed an MD associate and eventually a partner to buy his practice.

McCormick broke Nichols's chain of thought: "Well, one thing you've got working in your favor is Nashville. If your practice were in Detroit, I couldn't attract anybody from a top-notch school. But Nashville is a good-sized town, not too big, not too small. Its demographics are almost perfect."

Nichols, Donna, and McCormick spent the next thirty minutes discussing the three candidates: Dr. Mary Brennan, Dr. William Cattleman, and Dr. Charles Juan Batista Garcia. Each had impressive credentials.

Brennan was currently completing her fellowship in plastic surgery at Mass General Hospital in Boston. She went to Harvard Medical School and to Amherst as an undergraduate.

Cattleman, an oral surgeon, had been in private practice for two years in Chicago and went to Georgetown Medical School and William and Mary as an undergraduate. On the application, under his reasons for seeking a new position, he indicated he wanted to move to a smaller city, preferably in the South.

The last candidate, the youngest, was exotic. He was born in Majorca, a small island off the coast of Spain. He was schooled in Switzerland, graduated from Princeton at nineteen, then went to Columbia Medical School, and was about to complete his residency in oral surgery at New York Presbyterian Hospital.

Nichols asked about the credentialing process. McCormick assured him that even though none of the candidates were licensed in Tennessee, McCormick & Associates knew how to expedite the paperwork and get their candidates licensed in their states of employment.

It was agreed that Nichols would handle the telephone interviews and that Donna and McCormick would make notes and if necessary pass a note to Nichols for a follow-up question. He dialed the female candidate, Dr. Mary Brennan.

The conversation started off badly. She had disdain for insurance cases and preferred cash cosmetic procedures. She wasn't open to the delay of collections. Nichols's practice relied heavily on insurance payments. In what Nichols thought an inappropriate tone, the young female fellow insisted that she'd work only five days a week, no more than fifty hours.

McCormick had warned Nichols that most candidates would complain about the proposed six-day work schedule. In Nichols's mind, that point was non-negotiable. If they didn't want to work hard, like he did, then they were the wrong candidates. Brennan wasn't the right candidate. He'd wasted his time.

The next call was to Dr. William Cattleman, an oral surgeon. Cattleman, now in Chicago, missed Virginia. He'd grown up in Richmond.

"The farthest north I'd been before Chicago was DC. I just prefer the slower pace of the South and its people. Tell me a little bit more about your practice, sir."

Nichols described his cosmetic dental practice and how he wanted to retain an associate who could offer his patient base a wider degree of facial cosmetic procedures, including chins, lips, and noses.

Cattleman listened and then asked, "What are the partnership opportunities?"

Nichols explained that he was looking for a young associate who could work his way up to partner by buying into the practice over time, and Nichols could reduce his involvement as he relinquished control.

Cattleman questioned whether that would be possible because of his more than $100,000 of student loans. Nichols didn't like the sound of that. Every dollar Cattleman paid back on his student loans was a dollar he couldn't pay Nichols for his interest in the practice. Cattleman was just too far in a hole to be a reliable purchaser of the practice. Nichols told Cattleman he'd be back in touch.

Donna had been quiet during both conversations after the introductions. She broke her silence: "Brennan isn't the right doctor for our practice. This isn't a nine-to-six place."

McCormick, who'd also been quiet, spoke up, "What did you think of Cattleman? He's hungry. At least you'd know he'd work hard to get out of debt."

"I'm not sure what that means. He's in debt because he couldn't afford college and medical school. That's no crime. In fact, it's admirable. But it also means his extra cash will go to pay off loans, not to purchase my practice."

Donna shared her opinion: "Don't be in a hurry. All of these candidates look great on paper, but you've got to expect that they're all going to have some hidden and probably obvious blemish. Nobody's perfect. You need to find a good fit. They've got to have the right personality. They've got to be willing to listen and learn from you, and when the time's right, they've got to be able to lead. That will take a special individual. That kind of doctor isn't just sitting around. We're going to have to find him or her. Don't be impatient."

Nichols knew that Donna was right. *I need to be patient*, he thought as he dialed the last number.

"Dr. Garcia, may I help you?"

"Hello, this is Dr. Peter Nichols. My office manager, Donna Burns, and Rocky McCormick are also on the line with us. It's a pleasure to meet you by telephone."

Despite his exotic background, Dr. Garcia had no accent. "I've been looking forward to this call. Mr. McCormick has told me a great deal about both you and your practice. I think it's a brilliant idea to associate an oral surgeon with your established cosmetic dental practice."

"There seems to be a synergy in combining my practice with a related medical practice. I've gone as far as I can as a solo practitioner. I'm bringing patients in the door. An MD surgeon would offer a world of other options to my patients."

Nichols and Garcia spent the next twenty-five minutes talking about themselves and where they thought a combined dental-medical practice could go. Dr. Garcia was very articulate and personable. He obviously was well educated and well spoken. The young surgeon impressed Nichols.

"I'm looking for a place to start my career. I've been to Nashville, the city is growing, and I could see myself settling down there, finding the right woman, and starting a family. I'm willing to make an investment of my time and money in the right practice."

"You don't have student loans?"

"I'm debt free. I've been very lucky. I had the skills, but my parents could afford my education. My parents have also supplemented my income as a resident. They're behind me a hundred percent.

"Just so you know, I love country music. The thought of treating some of your celebrity clients is very exciting. When I operate, I listen to country, over the objections of some of the doctors and nurses. It's one of the perks of having been selected chief resident."

Garcia hoped his last remark didn't come off as bragging.

"I'd love to come down and visit your office and meet you in person. I'd be happy to pay my way down for the interview."

Nichols assured him that wouldn't be necessary and promised to be in touch.

After Garcia hung up, Nichols got really excited. He said, "He sounds perfect. He's smart and personable and is willing to work hard. He's not talking about working fifty hours a week; he's got a fire in his belly."

Donna waited for Nichols to take a breath. He'd really gotten himself worked up.

"He sounds a little arrogant to me, and it's been my experience, if something seems too good to be true, then it is too good to be true," she observed.

"Don't be so negative. Let's have him come down here, look him straight in the face, and make a decision."

McCormick felt compelled to comment, "He's exactly as advertised. He's highly educated and motivated. He's what you want and what he appears to be."

"What about Cattleman?" Donna asked.

"Not interested; too much debt. Just get Garcia down here. I think we've found our man."

Arrangements were made through McCormick for Dr. Garcia to visit the office two days later. Nichols picked up Garcia at the airport and drove straight back to the office. During the tour of the facility, Garcia explained that the existing treatment rooms were legally inadequate to accommodate the types of procedures that he anticipated would be performed. Garcia also made a list of all the equipment that would need to be purchased and installed.

Nichols hadn't realized that in order to perform cosmetic medical surgery at his office, there would have to be substantial structural changes, such as a new ventilation system. Fortunately, in the back of the Tudor were an oversized parking lot and a storage-garage building that could be reconfigured into a medical surgical suite.

During the five-hour visit, Garcia suggested that the most efficient way to meet the ventilation requirements was to build a new surgical suite onto the back of the building in the existing parking lot. Garcia reasoned that Nichols needed his existing three treatment rooms for his own patients. Garcia argued that the construction and equipment cost could be recouped in less than two years.

After Garcia left on the last flight back to New York, Donna and her boss were alone. Nichols asked her to speak freely. Without reservation, Donna did. She thought he was arrogant and overly confident.

"He hasn't spent a day in private practice, and he's telling you that we'd recoup hundreds of thousands of dollars in two years."

She was far less impressed than Nichols and told him so. He tried to defend Garcia's requests: "We knew we'd be buying new equipment. He couldn't use our existing dental equipment to perform medical surgery."

"I understand, but to demand we build a new surgical suite instead of ventilating an existing treatment room . . ."

"He didn't *demand* anything. He suggested that in the long run, it might be more economical to build the suite right rather than modify the existing room, which I needed for my patients anyway."

The heated conversation ended badly, with Nichols asking Donna to price the equipment list and get bids for the construction of the surgical suite.

Donna wasn't happy with the directions she was given.

CHAPTER SEVEN

TOUGH NEGOTIATIONS
Monday, November 13, 1995

David Barton Harrelson, based in New York City, was the Garcias' family attorney. At $800 an hour, he catered to the rich. He was a fixer and a deal maker. On the surface he appeared polite, but underneath he was calculating and ruthless. He was proud that he was cunning, and he was more than willing to cut corners to get the job done. He farmed out the heavy lifting, such as litigation, but always remained in the background pulling the strings.

Harrelson was short, only five feet seven, with short brown hair just a tad longer than a crew cut. He always wore a dark pinstriped suit with a matching vest. In the right-hand vest pocket he kept a gold pocket watch, a Waltham, with an eighteen-inch gold chain prominently displayed across his flat belly. The watch belonged to his maternal grandfather. Attached to the gold chain were his Phi Beta Kappa key from Princeton, an Army Distinguished Service Cross, and two Purple Hearts for service as a LRRP in Vietnam. The men of long-range reconnaissance patrols were no strangers to getting up close and personal with the enemy and being successful in tracking them down and killing them in personal combat or calling in artillery. The kill ratio of the enemy by LRRPS was extraordinary.

And Harrelson's group even made it in and out of Cambodia alive. Harrelson didn't mind killing; he rationalized his actions were for the good of his country.

Later in life, as an attorney, Harrelson continued to rationalize his often unethical and harsh conduct for the good of his clients. He did business around the world. This tainted his ethics since most of the world still relied upon bribery as an effective way to success. Harrelson truly believed that the end justified the means.

In his youth, Harrelson was a badass, and he still was. He was in excellent condition, working out every morning and running marathons in his spare time, which recently wasn't happening. He knew he needed to make time to stay in shape. He'd do better.

After his stint in the service, he went to law school at Oxford and Georgetown, where he gravitated toward wealthy foreign students who needed someone smart to manage their affairs. He befriended them, and they later became his clients.

He'd met Señor Eduardo Miguel Garcia across a conference table in Prague on the other side of a deal. He impressed Garcia as a tough negotiator and was retained the next day. For the last nineteen years he'd represented the Garcia family in dozens of real estate transactions, four company purchases, and one company sale and provided family members with general legal advice.

Unfortunately over the last three years, several Garcia ventures turned sour. A hotel in Milan was forced to close because of a food poisoning scandal, an explosion and cave-in killed eighteen miners in Peru, and certain junk bonds, purchased against Harrelson's advice, tanked. The Garcias were still rich by anyone's standards, but they continued to spend without regard to their financial reversals. Harrelson on multiple occasions advised controlling costs to rebuild the family balance sheet.

Señor Garcia agreed with Harrelson, but he was reluctant to

share with his wife, Kiki, and his son, Charlie, their need to stop spending indiscriminately. Señor Garcia and his family loved to play the aristocrats and flaunt their wealth, even as it diminished. Harrelson bit his tongue and kept the decaying secret, under the attorney-client privilege and as a friend. His loyalty only reinforced his relationship with Señor Garcia, and in private he was allowed to call him Eddie, despite Señor Garcia's aristocratic airs.

Señor Garcia was deeply proud of his Spanish bloodline. His wife, who brought the original fortune to the marriage, was the niece of Batista, the Cuban president-dictator. Her family fortune sailed to Miami before the Castro revolution.

Harrelson was sitting behind his mahogany desk on the sixty-fifth floor of his 4 Park Avenue office staring out the twelve-foot-high wall-to-ceiling windows when his secretary broke his train of thought because of a call from Charles Garcia.

"Hello, Charlie, I've been waiting for your call. I guess you've read the deal memo I sent your father about your employment contract and the other documents."

Harrelson liked Eddie, but his son, Charlie, was a major pain in the neck. Charlie learned his self-importance from his father, but at least Eddie was a successful businessman. He'd known Charlie most of his life, and the kid had been trouble since he was fifteen. Harrelson was forced to resolve one scrape after another. The kid was a revenue source for Harrelson but also a headache. He could be counted on to screw up at least every six months.

With Harrelson's help, Charlie was admitted to Princeton, his alma mater and, with the Garcias' money, to Columbia Medical School. The kid was smart enough, but he was also a spoiled brat who used bad judgment and cared only about himself. Harrelson warned Eddie that he needed to be less indulgent, but wealth has its privilege. Charlie proved his point.

"It's only $400,000. It's no big deal. Nashville would be a perfect place for me to grow my practice. I need you to get on a plane with my parents and get it closed."

Who the hell does this kid think he's talking to? thought Harrelson. *I don't even let my clients who pay me disrespect me like that.*

Charlie may have been right about Nashville, but Harrelson didn't like the new terms and contingencies that this country lawyer, Benjamin Davis, insisted upon. He'd turned the tables on Harrelson. It started off fine with a handwritten term sheet drafted by Charlie and the dentist, but Davis complicated the transaction.

The term sheet read:

1. Base salary without board certification—$150,000. An increase in base salary with board certification—$200,000.

2. No bonus until equipment and renovation costs have been repaid to practice from profits.

3. Bonus after repayment of costs, one-third of revenue above $600,000 per year generated by Garcia.

4. Nichols will give Garcia one percent of the practice as part of employment.

5. Three-year honeymoon period. If Nichols agrees that Garcia is a good partner, Nichols will give Garcia nine percent of the practice, increasing Garcia's ownership to ten percent.

6. Nichols over the next four years will sell the remaining ninety percent of the practice to Garcia for an agreed-upon price based on market value, to be agreed upon after honeymoon period.

That handwritten term sheet was given to Davis to draft an employment document. The proposed contract included conditions never addressed in the term sheet, which imposed cross obligations on Charlie and his parents if the honeymoon period went badly. Davis's documents required that if Charlie failed to complete the three-year employment term, Charlie was restricted from practicing medicine within a fifty-mile radius of Nichols's Nashville office for two years. Such a non-compete clause was not uncommon but was never discussed between the parties.

In three telephone calls, Harrelson first tried to get Davis to eliminate the provision, then shorten the time period to six months, and finally to reduce the radius to ten miles. At first Davis was adamant that the provision remain as written, but he eventually agreed to a radius of ten miles.

Harrelson's other major concern was that Charlie's parents were required to guarantee Charlie's performance and put up collateral equal to Dr. Nichols's cost to construct the surgical suite and purchase the new equipment to perform medical surgeries. That guarantee was more than $400,000. Harrelson argued that Davis's insistence on the parents' guarantee was unreasonable and that Davis was taking advantage of the fact that Charlie Garcia was a member of the golden sperm club. To his credit Davis didn't deny Harrelson's claim, but he wouldn't budge.

Harrelson decided it would be best to try to improve the deal when he got to Nashville. Harrelson knew that Charlie was personable and good looking. He hoped that Charlie could capitalize on his rapport with Nichols, who might override his attorney.

Harrelson outlined his proposed strategy with Eddie Garcia on the plane. The limo ride to downtown Nashville took less than fifteen minutes. The group checked into the historic Hermitage Hotel, where Minnesota Fats, the legendary pool player, once hustled nine ball.

From the Hermitage it was a short walk to Davis's office in Printer's Alley. A tall, stunning blonde in her mid-twenties met Harrelson and the Garcias in reception. She was dressed professionally in a black pantsuit and white top. Despite her conservative dress, Harrelson could tell she had an impressive figure, and he observed that his young client also took notice. Like Charlie Garcia, she had deep blue eyes; her hair was short but businesslike. Harrelson thought she looked a lot like the actress Sharon Stone. Harrelson's radar went up. If this beauty was Davis's attempt at distraction, it was working.

"I'm Sammie Davis. I'm currently in law school at Vanderbilt. My uncle Ben will be handling these negotiations. Welcome to Nashville," Sammie said with her beautiful smile as she shook hands with each of them.

Harrelson watched the younger Garcia make his move. "You're much too beautiful to become a lawyer. Are you a junior, and can you dance and sing?" asked Charlie.

"I'm Jewish, but so was Sammy Davis Jr.; he converted. I'm not black, and I can kinda sing and dance. My mother just had a twisted sense of humor."

They all laughed, and the tension eased. They followed Ms. Davis into the conference room.

Harrelson watched Charlie watch the young law student. He didn't like what he saw.

Davis and Nichols were already in the conference room, and introductions were made. Charlie and Nichols had already met when Charlie visited the practice after his telephone interview.

Harrelson thought Davis turned all business rather quickly, but they were there to make a deal and sign the papers.

"Mr. Harrelson, have you reviewed the last redlined version of the documents that I faxed you?" asked Davis.

Harrelson confirmed that he'd received and reviewed the employment agreement, promissory note, guarantee, and security agreement. Harrelson then asked, "Aren't you making this transaction more complicated than it needs to be? Why should Charlie's parents guarantee the cost of equipment and construction of a surgical suite? Dr. Nichols owns the building. It's his property that's being improved, and if Charlie fails to perform, Dr. Nichols keeps the equipment."

Harrelson knew Davis's reasons why, but he thought it worth forcing Davis to explain.

"It's simple. Those costs are incurred only because Dr. Nichols is hiring Dr. Garcia. If he quits or is terminated for cause within the three-year honeymoon period, Dr. Nichols must recoup his $400,000 investment. Dr. Garcia has no assets to secure the cost of these expenses. He's an empty shell. The Garcias are another story. All we're asking them to do is stand behind their son and guarantee his performance. Bottom line, if Dr. Garcia does what he promises, there is no risk or cost to his parents. However, if Dr. Garcia breaches the contract by quitting or is terminated for cause, the Garcias pay up."

Davis's explanation of the transaction and challenge to stand behind Charlie's performance worked, and Señor Garcia nodded his agreement. Harrelson backed off on that issue.

Davis and Harrelson discussed the specifics of the documents. They argued over the definition of *termination for cause.* Harrelson kept arguing that the definition was vague. Davis refused to concede the point although Harrelson knew that Davis wanted it as broad and vague as possible. After much debate, it was defined as "acts and omissions including gross neglect of duties, suspension or revocation of medical license, bankruptcy, conviction of a crime, including a misdemeanor of moral turpitude, alcohol or drug abuse, or any misconduct that would damage the reputation of the professional corporation."

Harrelson questioned what Davis meant by damage to "the reputation of the professional corporation." Davis explained that Dr. Nichols spent more than twenty years building an unsullied reputation. He argued that if Dr. Garcia were to sexually harass an employee or do something in a similar manner, he could damage Nichols.

Harrelson asked, "So that wouldn't include professional negligence then?"

"We've got malpractice insurance for that. This provision is to protect the practice's reputation. It's pretty standard language."

The employment agreement included the compensation package in the handwritten memorandum. The corporation agreed to pay Dr. Garcia's malpractice insurance, health insurance, dental care, and continuing education and provided for three weeks of paid vacation. The agreement also gave Dr. Garcia one share of stock, or one percent in the new professional corporation named Nichols & Garcia PC.

It was agreed that the Garcias would deposit in a new account $400,000 of bonds to secure the transaction. The promissory note and guarantee provided that the bonds could not be sold or transferred from the account without Dr. Nichols's release.

Davis then asked, "The Garcias speak, read, and understand

English, right?"

"Mr. Garcia has command of English, but Mrs. Garcia's understanding is limited."

"That's a problem. We'll need to get these documents translated into Spanish."

"I can get that done," Harrelson offered.

"No offense, I'd rather hire my own translator."

Harrelson accepted Davis's position, and it was agreed that Davis would redraft the documents in English, which then would be translated. The revised documents would be messengered to the Hermitage Hotel the next day.

The Garcias shared that they planned to sightsee, and they had dinner reservations at Jimmy Kelly's, a well-known steakhouse. Charlie planned to go out after dinner to the Bluebird Café and hear some good country music. It was writers' night, and every so often an established country star would show up to perform and test new material.

Charlie addressed the younger Davis, "Will you join us for dinner, Sammie?"

Harrelson observed that the young woman blushed slightly but quickly responded, "Why don't we wait till we have an executed transaction before you make those dinner plans?"

Harrelson couldn't have agreed more. He thought, *She's a sensible young woman, business first.*

Not to be discouraged and confident that the transaction would close, Charlie ended the meeting by saying, "I'll see you tomorrow night then for dinner after our little deal closes."

CHAPTER EIGHT

HOUSEWARMING

Thursday, November 23, 1995

P eter Nichols was a happy man. The paperwork was executed, and Dr. Charles Juan Batista Garcia would soon be making him a lot of money. He'd also be able to breathe again. After Garcia got rolling, he and Helen were going to take a long cruise. He needed a vacation.

The Garcias didn't waste time. Within days of the closing, they bought their son a beautiful home in Hillwood, the same neighborhood where the Davis family lived. Nichols was excited about Garcia's decision to throw a housewarming party so he could introduce him to the community and Nichols's patient base. They'd sent out more than three hundred gold-embossed invitations. Nichols helped Garcia make out the guest list—a who's who of Nashville that included several country music celebrities, Morty, and the Davises.

The staff liked Dr. Garcia, all except Donna Burns. Nichols noticed that Garcia made it a point to ingratiate himself to his co-workers, all of whom were female. He was suave, and he knew it. He brought new life to the office when morale was low because of their long hours.

Nichols was impressed with Garcia's effort to fit in. It was working; almost everybody seemed happier and accepted him.

Garcia continued to pursue Sammie. He'd confided to Nichols that she was the most beautiful woman he'd ever seen, which she was. He'd also shown Nichols a personalized note he'd written to Sammie on her invitation: "We've signed our deal. Your conflict has evaporated in thin air. You must give me a chance. You're studying the law. That means you appreciate giving me a chance. Isn't that what justice dictates?"

Nichols figured, *They are both over twenty-one, consenting adults. Why the hell not? She's pretty enough, smart, hardworking, and from a good family. Garcia could do a lot worse. Marriage would be a stabilizing influence, closer to buying my practice.*

The event at Garcia's new home was important. Nichols was confident that Garcia would make an incredible impression on his female patients and even his male counterpart. At six feet one, with jet-black hair and deep blue eyes, Garcia would have a line forming outside the office for consults. He knew how to talk to people. He discussed with authority varied subjects, such as sports, world politics, or family. He knew how to carry on a conversation, and Nichols recognized that not everyone possessed that skill.

The plan was to have Garcia focus on surgical consults while the surgical suite was being built out, and then once it was completed, Garcia would tackle the backlog of insurance-approved surgeries. Those not covered by insurance would be cash or credit card.

Parking attendants greeted the guests and gave each one a stub to retrieve his or her car at the end of the evening. As Nichols and his wife reached the front door, the Davises and Morty came up behind them. Seeing the couple, Nichols grabbed Liza by the waist and kissed her on the cheek. He asked, "What's a beautiful woman like you doing with such an overweight, homely guy like him?"

Liza quickly responded, "Peter, that's a question I've asked myself every day for almost the last twenty years. The simple answer is pity."

They all laughed at Davis's expense. Davis, with his tall and broad frame, carried his two hundred and forty pounds better than most, but there was no question he needed to lose weight. Davis coped with the stress of his job by eating, and the stress never seemed to let up; neither did the meals. Nichols knew it was a sensitive subject with Liza.

Before anyone could continue the abuse, Davis changed the subject: "This is quite a house. Are you sure you're not overpaying this kid?"

"He didn't buy this on his salary. It was a gift from his parents, although he mentioned it's still in his father's name. These people have almost an air of nobility about them. Try not to embarrass me, Ben."

Nichols was only half kidding. Davis, who'd lived in Nashville more than twenty years, still wasn't a southerner. He was plain spoken, grounded in his New York roots, not to mention trained and taught by Morty Steine.

Morty, a man of strong character and conviction, had been a stable influence in Nichols's life after his father was murdered. The two men had the same teacher and shared the same values. Morty didn't put on airs for anybody. Morty had to be dragged to the party by Nichols's special invitation. Nichols knew when the old man was not at the office, he preferred to remain at his beloved Squeeze Bottom, a 288-acre farm outside Nashville. He'd spend the night at the Davises' home tonight. Nobody wanted Morty to drive at night, not even Morty; he recognized his limitation.

As the group moved from the marble foyer to the formal living room and dining room, Nichols was astonished at how well appointed each room was. He admired several pieces of colorful and intense blown glass. He also noticed several paintings by his favorite local artist, Ron York. Nichols wondered out loud, "How did this kid acquire all these beautiful things?"

Liza knew the one-word answer, "Money!"

The Nicholses and Davises walked through the rooms. A white baby grand piano and a fifteen-foot-high bookcase with leatherbound volumes and expensive-looking knickknacks were in the great room.

Nichols wondered, *Okay, he has money, but how does a young doctor furnish his new house so quickly? He must have used a decorator, more likely a team of decorators. It also involved someone with good and very expensive taste and, as Liza says, a lot of money.*

Garcia couldn't have looked better. His suit was a light gray Armani, with a charcoal-colored Yves St. Laurent shirt and a canary yellow tie. He looked educated and rich. He had a Bond-like aura about him. Nichols wondered if Garcia would order a vodka martini, shaken not stirred.

While Nichols was deep in thought, he heard Charlie Garcia address his wife, whom he'd previously met.

"Mrs. Nichols, so nice to see you again."

Then Helen introduced Davis's wife, Liza.

"Mrs. Davis, it's a pleasure to meet you. Your niece has nothing but the most wonderful things to say about you. Even though you're not related by blood, I can see where Sammie gets her good looks. It must be by osmosis."

"Dr. Garcia, please call me Liza. My husband and niece have told me quite a bit about you and your interesting background. Your homeland sounds beautiful. Welcome to Nashville, and congratulations on your new home."

"You must call me Charlie. May I introduce you to my parents?"

Nichols, Helen, Morty, and Davis silently followed Liza and Dr. Garcia across the crowded room, where Sammie was talking with a well-dressed couple in their late fifties.

Charlie interrupted their conversation. "Excuse me, Father. You've met Mr. Davis. This is his wife, Liza."

Señor Garcia turned to Liza, and in a smooth gesture actually practiced, he bent and kissed her hand. Nichols noticed that both Liza and Señor Garcia had French nails.

As he raised his head, Señor Garcia's mane of gray hair fell miraculously back into place. His trimmed goatee was the same color. He said in a heavily accented voice, "Eduardo Miguel Garcia at your service. It is a pleasure to make your acquaintance. What a beautiful dress, Mrs. Davis. That color green is my favorite. May I present my wife, Maria Christina Batista Garcia. We all call her Kiki."

The two women politely nodded to each other. Nichols had difficulty understanding Señor Garcia's very accented English. He had a deep voice, and he spoke slowly, Nichols suspected, to be understood.

Nichols reintroduced his wife to the Garcias. They'd all eaten dinner together at Jimmy Kelly's when their son decided to begin his medical career in Nashville.

"Mr. Davis, it's nice to see you again. So good of you to come to my son's little housewarming party. Thanks to you and Dr. Nichols, Charles has found a home here in Nashville."

"You've got Dr. Nichols to thank for that. All I did was a little paperwork."

"Nashville has opened its heart to my son. Charles has confided that your niece is one of the unquestioned attractions of Nashville. Aren't you from New York originally?"

"Brooklyn."

Nichols knew that Davis was born in Brooklyn, but he grew up in

Woodbury, Long Island. Davis once told Nichols that he thought it made him sound more colorful telling people he was from Brooklyn.

"Your niece, is she also from Brooklyn? Do we have Brooklyn to thank for this great beauty?"

"She grew up in Miami."

"Most of my wife's family members live in Miami. They left Cuba, right before the revolution."

Nichols was having problems following the conversation; both Davis and Señor Garcia had strong accents. Davis seemed to understand Garcia much better than Nichols did.

Charlie broke in, saying, "Father, the Davises don't want to hear about our family history or about the revolution. Let's not talk politics. I'd rather talk about my new life in Nashville. I couldn't be more excited about starting in private practice and getting to hear some incredible music."

Charlie's family and by now, even Nichols, had come to accept Charlie's love of country music. He revered the pioneers, Hank Williams Sr., Patsy Cline, and several others. He'd spent his nights going from one honky-tonk to another listening to great music. Every waitress, salesgirl, and temp was a singer/songwriter. He didn't have to go far to hear incredible music.

Charlie gave the group the twenty-five-cent tour of the house. After the tour, Sammie and Charlie disappeared into the garden.

Nichols saw newly appointed Senator Valerie Daniels standing by the white baby grand piano and talking to a fellow Democrat.

"Congratulations, Senator. How's DC treating you?"

The senator gave Nichols a hug and went into a tirade about the inefficiencies of the U.S. Senate. She explained that she'd been directed by party leadership not to discuss certain sensitive issues when approached by Republican colleagues. "At first I thought they were kidding, but another freshman senator confirmed the lunacy."

Nichols was intrigued by Daniels's story. He knew the federal government wasn't bipartisan, but he thought they'd at least talk through the issues. She explained that she ignored her party's directive and had several productive conversations with the other side of the aisle.

Then she changed the subject: "Your new protégé is quite a charmer. I've heard you're expanding by adding a surgical suite to your building."

"We'll be offering a whole new set of services. Charlie's an MD, and he's qualified to perform facial cosmetic surgery. I've got not only the cost of construction but also all new equipment. It's an investment in the future."

"Will you be hiring more clerical staff?"

"Yes, clerical and nursing staff."

The senator's face dramatically changed. She became somber, and her voice softened. The transformation in demeanor was immediate. In a single moment she went from being one of the most powerful women in the room to almost a subservient posture.

"I need a big favor."

"Ask away, we go way back. Besides you're now a mover and shaker in the party. That's what we do, give and receive favors."

Daniels lowered her voice even more, "It's not that type of favor. I need to get Robyn off the road. She's been touring, drinking, doing drugs and God knows what else. I want her to move in with my family in Nashville at least till she gets on her feet. My husband and kids can keep an eye on her at night, but I need someplace safe for her to be during the day. She needs to be kept busy. You've known her all her life. Can you give her a job? I need someone I trust to keep an eye on her. With your help we can straighten her out."

She was obviously beaten down by her problem. Like so many

in a similar situation, she loved her addict but didn't know how to deal with her or change her.

"It sounds like you need to have an intervention. She needs to be confronted and thrown back into reality. If you'd like, I could participate. I've known Robyn her entire life. You need to gather a group of people whom she respects and those who have influence over her. I wouldn't waste any time. Intervene, and then get her in a good twelve-step program, off the touring road and on the road to recovery. We get her in the program, and she could start the first of next month as a file clerk/substitute receptionist. Robyn is an exceptionally beautiful young woman. She'd make a good receptionist with some training."

Relieved, Daniels gave him a hug and acknowledged that she owed him one.

Nichols was in his element, and he decided to enjoy himself. Most of the guests were his patients as well as clients of Morty, then Davis. After several Jacks, Nichols joined Dolly Parton at the piano and sang a duet. They had sung together before in a commercial promoting his practice. Ms. Dolly then sang a solo, "I Will Always Love You." It was directed to her longtime attorney.

At midnight Helen dragged her husband out the door; she drove because he couldn't. Davis, Liza, Sammie, and Morty left at the same time. Even in his condition, Nichols noticed that Sammie was different. When he first saw her at the event, she looked striking in a strapless evening gown. Upon leaving, she had the entire top half of her body covered by a shawl, and she looked hunched over. It struck Nichols as odd.

He took a deep breath as Helen drove them home. He thought the evening was a resounding success for the newly employed Robyn Eden, the practice, himself, and the irresistible Dr. Charles Garcia.

CHAPTER NINE
A REAL CHARMER
Thursday, December 14, 1995

D r. Charles Garcia began offering consults to Nichols's patients and the general public on December 7th, a date that had lived in infamy.

Almost overnight Garcia was the talk of Nashville. Nichols carefully reviewed his patient list and photos to determine which ones would be good candidates for Garcia's services. He'd been treating many of these women for years; he'd performed various cosmetic dental procedures on them and knew which ones would be susceptible to Garcia's good looks, charm, and skills to make them appear younger.

Nichols and Garcia wanted high-profile women in the community as patients. These women were fashion and social leaders and could act as walking billboards for Garcia kissable lips. Garcia surgically figured out how to create plump lips that could be marketed to women as attractive to men. Nichols coined the phrase "Garcia kissable lips." He thought it had a nice ring to it.

They'd spent time and money marketing the practice. Garcia, who was artistic, designed a new logo that was mounted proudly behind the receptionist's desk. It also appeared on their stationery. Garcia's name was proudly set below Nichols, where it reported that he was licensed to practice medicine in both Tennessee and New York.

Robyn had a successful intervention on November 26th, and after two weeks in rehab, she sat at the helm of the ship. She'd been hot boxed at her sister's home. Nichols and Morty, who'd known her since birth, participated. They brought poor Sammie along because she was about the same age and maybe Robyn would identify with her. Davis had refused, arguing that he added nothing to the equation. Two high school friends of Robyn, both of whom had husbands and families and had achieved traditional success, filled out the group. After the five-hour process, Robyn agreed to enter Cumberland Heights for a tune-up and then enter a twelve-step outpatient program. She also accepted the position of receptionist/file clerk at Nichols & Garcia, under the watchful eye of Peter Nichols. It was Robyn's second day, and she was scheduled to leave early enough from her job to make her meetings.

After her first day, Nichols and Garcia, while brainstorming, realized that Robyn was the perfect first candidate for Garcia kissable lips. She was beautiful, and since she already sat in reception where the patients contemplating the surgery would sit, she was an effective advertisement.

Nichols raised the issue of her recovery and that she'd be given anesthesia during surgery and would probably need some form of painkiller after surgery. In response Garcia, who was unaware of her addiction, argued that she'd have no recollection of the administered Versed and that they could carefully monitor her use of narcotics after the surgery. Nichols insisted that before the offer was made, he'd discuss the proposed surgery with Senator Daniels.

Valerie Daniels had some reservations about her sister undergoing surgery. She was already beautiful and already preoccupied with her looks. In the end, though, she was an adult, and Daniels admitted that the decision was her sister's to make.

Robyn didn't need convincing to have the surgery. It was free, and Robyn was already self-conscious about her looks. Although a competent receptionist, she still saw herself on stage performing, and she knew that the more beautiful she was, the greater that possibility. She signed the appropriate waiver, a surgical suite was rented, and Robyn was transformed. She healed quickly, and in about a week some promotional and marketing material handouts with Robyn's improved lips were sent to Nichols's patient base. On the back of Robyn's photo there was basic information about the surgery, but the focus was the promotion of Dr. Charles Garcia as a surgeon and a caring professional and person.

Life was good. As anticipated by Nichols, Garcia's practice broke out of the gate like a racehorse. Garcia kissable lips were appearing throughout the Nashville elite at a rapid pace. His schedule began to fill up, and Robyn had to tell patients it would be a month before they could get a consult. It was almost contagious; one housewife told another, and before long, the entire book club scheduled consults.

A shrewd businessman, Nichols knew he needed to figure out how to effectively market his new employee and this groundbreaking procedure. Smartly, under Garcia's employment contract, the professional corporation owned the trademarks. Nichols made an appointment with Jean Stokes, a publicist, to map out an advertising campaign for Garcia kissable lips.

Garcia was working sixty-five hours a week. The first consult was a sales job, the second was a planning session to set goals and determine how best to achieve those goals, and the third appointment was the surgery itself.

Nichols kept a close eye on Robyn. He required that she provide him an attendance slip from each meeting she went to. By his count, she was averaging between three and four meetings per week. Robyn's recovery and the practice were both going well.

Nichols and his wife planned to vacation at their place in Highland Beach, the town adjacent to Delray Beach, Florida, after the surgical suite was completed.

Nichols and Davis kept the pressure on the contractor, Tim Tisdale, to complete construction of the surgical suite by the agreed-upon January 18th deadline. The rear of the office and the parking lot looked like a war zone. Thick plastic sheeting separated the working office from the dust and debris.

Mrs. Denise Alder, age fifty, had been waiting thirty minutes. She was a first consult.

"Mrs. Alder, I'm Dr. Charles Garcia. So sorry to keep you waiting; it's a pleasure to meet you."

"Hello, Doctor, I'm a friend of Randi Franks. You're going to do her lips and chin in February. She told me that you showed her computer-generated photos of before and what she'd look like after the surgery; she's absolutely thrilled. She was very impressed by you, and she insisted that I schedule a consult."

Garcia gave Mrs. Alder a big smile and thanked her for the compliment. Their eyes met, and he looked deep into her soul. Garcia had more than charisma; he had a Svengali effect on women. He mesmerized them, and Mrs. Alder was not able to resist his focused attention on her.

Mrs. Franks, a longtime Nichols patient, was well connected. She was a member of an old southern family, and she had three sisters. Before the end of next year, Nichols suspected that there'd be four sets of Garcia kissable lips in the Franks family.

Garcia began his examination of Mrs. Alder by taking measurements and using a black marker on her face.

He assured her, "Don't worry. This isn't a permanent marker. It will wash right off. By the way, you have beautiful skin. It's hard to believe that you're fifty."

His compliment hit the mark. Mrs. Alder blushed slightly.

He continued to turn on his charm. "It would be my professional advice that not only should you enhance your lips and reconstruct your chin like Mrs. Franks plans to do, but you should also have Dr. Nichols whiten your teeth. It would be a shame for us to improve the appearance of your lips and chin and not improve your smile. Your smile is beautiful, but your teeth are a bit yellow. Why hide that pretty smile?"

Garcia was a good salesman. Mrs. Alder was sold on the idea of having her lips and chin done like Mrs. Franks, and she'd go one better by improving her smile. Garcia figured she'd smile right in Mrs. Franks's face.

"What's all this going to cost?" she asked.

"My fee for the chin and lips is $9,000 if done together. I'd charge $5,000 for each procedure separately. It just makes sense to do them together. You'd also save with only one anesthesia."

"And the teeth whitening, how much will that cost?"

"That procedure will be done by Dr. Nichols. He's been doing that for more than fifteen years. He's your man for that procedure. The usual fee is $2,500, but as part of a package deal, I'm sure he'd reduce his fee below $2,000. We want our patients to be satisfied and feel that they get good value."

"I'm divorced, and it's close to Christmas. I'll have a lot of additional expenses this time of year. Eleven thousand dollars is a lot of money."

He was deep in thought and then looked like he was conceding a point. "Let's say we make it an even $10,000 for all three procedures. Call it a Christmas present from Nichols & Garcia to you. You deserve it. If you don't do this for yourself, who will? You're a beautiful woman. You deserve this. Treat yourself."

"You're absolutely right, Dr. Garcia. Who's going to do this for me? Certainly not my ex-husband, that's for sure."

"Who knows, Mrs. Alder? Mr. Right may be waiting for you around the next corner. I promise he'll melt under your new smile. I can do your lips and chin on January 20th as long as my surgical suite is ready as promised on the 18th. You'll have to heal two weeks before Dr. Nichols can do the whitening. I'm sure we can schedule Dr. Nichols's work sometime the beginning of February. By Valentine's Day, you'll be ready for Mr. Right. What do you say?"

He knew her response before she even opened her crooked little mouth and showed her yellowish teeth. Garcia walked Mrs. Alder out to Donna's office, where he explained his financial agreement with Mrs. Alder and they booked all of the surgeries. As he was leaving Donna's office, Mrs. Alder was handing Donna her MasterCard.

After Mrs. Alder left, Donna walked briskly into Dr. Garcia's office. "Did you clear that package deal with Dr. Nichols?"

"No, there was no time. The patient was concerned about money, and I didn't want to lose her. I had to make a snap fee adjustment to close the deal."

"Look, Doctor, you're not selling electronics. You're providing medical services. It's my job as the office manager and bookkeeper to apportion the $10,000 fee among the surgeries performed by both you and Dr. Nichols. He charges $2,500 for a teeth whitening. Does that mean you're doing Mrs. Alder's chin and lips for $7,500?"

"I'll work it out with Dr. Nichols. You're getting your skirt in a wad over nothing. The key is that I closed the deal, and she gave us her MasterCard today for services we're not providing until next year."

"Let's go talk to Dr. Nichols about this," Donna insisted. "He's got the final say."

Fifteen minutes later Donna and Garcia were standing in front of Dr. Nichols. Garcia could tell Nichols was annoyed that Garcia and his office manager were not getting along and complicating his life. Garcia decided to play it cool and let Donna talk herself into trouble.

She began very aggressively: "We've got a problem. Dr. Garcia negotiated a fee off our fee schedule, and he's offering not only his fees at a discount but yours as well. I think he should get your permission before he reduces your fees. I think he's got a lot of nerve."

"Hold on, Donna. Let's hear what Charlie's got to say."

Garcia knew Nichols gave him an opportunity to cut Donna's throat. He needed to appear sincere and calm. He began, "Dr. Nichols, I meant no disrespect to either you or the practice. I told Ms. Burns if she wanted to allocate your full $2,500 fee to the payment for your teeth whitening, it was okay with me. I'm not the experienced businessman you are, but it's my understanding that after Christmas, most of our patients have spent their disposable income and are not in a position to think about cosmetic surgery until Valentine's Day. I've studied the practice's financials, which you provided me, and January is historically the slowest month of the year. I cut the deal with Mrs. Alder, which she put on a credit card, so we'd get $10,000 when we probably needed it most. I told Donna that you and I would talk about how to apportion the fee. It was more important to tie down the business."

Nichols looked at Donna and, for the first time in their relationship, questioned her motives. For some reason, she didn't like Dr. Garcia, and she was challenging him at every turn.

"Donna, I would have approved the package deal. Charlie's right. In January, we need to give a little on price in order to keep a steady flow of business. He was in the room. It was his judgment call as to what it would take to get the business and whether the offer was necessary not to have lost the fee. Charlie, you have my authority to negotiate package deals without my prior approval. Be smart, and don't get too ambitious. We have product that people want, and generally our patients can afford to pay for what they want."

Donna could not conceal that she was furious. Garcia knew that she wasn't used to being overruled by Nichols. Round two in Garcia v. Burns, like round one, went to Garcia.

CHAPTER TEN

INTEROFFICE POLITICS
Wednesday, December 20, 1995

D avis drove with the tan top of his black Eldorado down even though it was late December and a bit colder than usual for Nashville. To compensate, he had the heater on full blast. It was only six fifteen, and it was still pitch black outside.

Tim Tisdale was parked in front of the building in his sky blue pickup. Davis, wind blown, his longish sandy hair in disarray, ran his hands through his hair trying to return some degree of control. He knew it was a waste of time.

He surveyed the construction site. It was a mess, equipment everywhere, but a shell of a structure where the parking lot once had been was sticking up in the air.

"Hey, Tim, how's our progress?" he asked the lanky contractor.

"The tricky part's done," Tim replied. "We've got county approval of the ventilation system. That cost an extra $3,500 to expedite."

"What the hell are you talking about?"

"It cost us $3,500 to get to the top of the inspection list. Otherwise it would have taken more than a month to get approval. Your client was in a rush, so I did what it took to get those bureaucrats out here. It will be a line item on the bill. Do you have a suggestion, Counselor, as to what I should call it?"

Tisdale deserved an answer. "Call it an expediting fee."

Davis was glad that he was only an accessory after the fact to Tisdale's bribery. Unfortunately, backroom politics and friendly green gestures were still how things were done in Nashville. Morty was a master at it; he didn't invent it, but he certainly perfected it. People all over Nashville owed Morty a favor. He collected them and, when necessary, cashed them in. Whenever possible, Davis deferred to Morty, so he could keep his hands clean.

"Do you think you'll be finished by the 18th deadline?"

Davis knew what Tisdale was going to say before he even opened his mouth. He'd never met a contractor yet who wouldn't promise a job on time, but this time there was a $10,000 bonus if he did. It was Davis's idea, but he didn't think Tisdale would earn it. There was also a penalty clause in the contract if Tisdale didn't finish by February 1st. Every day the punch list wasn't completed cost Tisdale $500. Tisdale was motivated to finish on time.

Davis said good-bye and entered the construction zone through the double plastic curtains and went into the office.

Donna met him in reception. She said, "He's waiting in his office. He can only give you a few moments. He's got a crazy day."

"He wanted me to show my face as a motivator for Tisdale. I think it worked. He's at least promising to get done by the 18th. It would probably be best if he got done around the 20th, but I won't begrudge him his bonus if he gets done on time."

Davis went on back, knocked on Nichols's door, and entered after he was acknowledged.

"Hello, Peter, I'm here as requested. What can I do for you?"

"Donna and Charlie aren't getting along, both personally and professionally." Nichols described several of their encounters. "I know he's young, but he's motivated and knows how to close a deal. The patients love him."

Davis said, "I know this kid's going to make you money, but he doesn't know anything about running a practice. Donna's done an incredible job for more than twenty years. She knows what she's talking about, and her instincts are good."

Davis knew what he was talking about. He'd worked closely with Donna the last ten years, and he recognized what an important part she'd played in Nichols's success.

He advised, "Make sure Donna doesn't think you're taking Garcia's side against her. Remind her that he's young and inexperienced, and ask her to be tolerant while the two of you teach him the ropes."

Davis felt that good advice might minimize the tension in the office. Bottom line, Donna didn't like anyone challenging her authority. She'd operated without any interference for more than twenty years. Davis knew she wasn't going to take a lot of guff from anyone. He made a mental note to follow up. He left Nichols, got back in his car still with the top down, drove off with the exhaust spewing white smoke, and sped down Music Row.

An interesting Nashville landmark, it began with the Spence Manor Hotel and its guitar-shaped swimming pool where Elvis skinny-dipped, and at the other end was Belmont University. The residential neighborhood converted to recording studios and small music companies, with a few modern high-rises that housed the larger record labels.

He parked in the Commerce Street Garage, walked down Printer's Alley to the back door of his office building, and got off at the eighth floor.

As soon as he walked into the office, Bella and Sammie bombarded him with questions.

"Let me get my coat off, and please pour me a cup of coffee."

The two women gave Davis his requested breathing room. They knew what he was like until he had his third cup of coffee.

Sammie sat down at the table in Davis's private office and waited for him to return from the kitchen. He sat down, and with her yellow pad in hand, she started rattling items off her list. The list changed daily as tasks were completed and new tasks arose.

"I'm ready to close the Lillian Nichols estate. I have the final accounting for Dr. Nichols's signature and the final order for the judge. If I'd known you were going there this morning, I would have given it to you last night. Why'd you go to his office?"

"Office politics. Donna and Dr. Garcia aren't getting along."

"That doesn't surprise me."

"Why's that?"

"Let's just say that Dr. Charles Juan Batista Garcia is used to getting his own way and that he doesn't understand the meaning of no."

Davis decided to drop the subject. His niece was a grown woman, who was also used to getting her own way and also didn't like to hear no. Despite her stubborn streak, which she probably inherited from him, he was so proud of her. She was smart, dedicated, and had not one, but two great teachers. Davis actually envied Sammie. Morty had the time to really mentor her, which he didn't have when Davis showed up in 1975.

Law school made demands on her time, but the Benjamin Davis Law Firm was her passion. She tried to make all of her classes but missed some. There were no periodic tests or midterms—just a final exam. Sammie wasn't shooting for top ten of her class, Order of the Coif, or Vanderbilt Law Review. Her goal was to graduate in the middle of her class and log in three years of hard work at the office and learn ten times more from her uncle and Morty. Just watching and listening to the two of them were the best possible education. What was going on between Donna and Garcia was just another learning opportunity.

"Call Donna and find out a good time for me to stop by, meet with Dr. Nichols to review the accounting, and get his signature."

Sammie was told that Davis should come by the office at seven the next morning.

Davis was right on time, and Nichols browsed through the document and signed it.

As Davis was leaving, Donna ambushed him and asked if they could talk. "There's something wrong with Dr. Garcia, but I can't put my finger on it yet."

"Dr. Nichols told me the two of you weren't getting along. You need to create and maintain boundaries. The operating room is his bailiwick, and the office is yours. You should both stay out of each other's way."

"I'd be willing to do that, but he insists on invading my sphere of influence." She was very upset.

Davis asked, "What's going on?"

"I don't trust him. He's so charming. Everybody is completely snowed by him, except me. Dr. Nichols looks at him and sees dollar signs. I see trouble."

Davis thought that Donna was a good judge of character. He told her, "Just keep an eye on him. If you have any concerns, call me and I'll help protect the practice and Dr. Nichols from himself."

"You know I think the world of Dr. Nichols. He's very excited about the addition of Dr. Garcia. It's blinded him. It's not all about the money. Dr. Nichols believes that by adding young blood he can keep the practice going and despite his retirement continue to serve his patients."

Davis was sure that Donna had only the practice and Dr. Nichols's best interest at heart.

CHAPTER ELEVEN
MERRY CHRISTMAS
Thursday, December 21, 1995

It was a few days before Christmas, and based on office scuttle-butt, Garcia learned that it was tradition at the office to close at three and celebrate the holiday together with a lavish party.

Garcia was impressed. Nichols spared no expense. There were carving stations of turkey, ham, and roast beef. As he watched Nichols in a white chef's hat and apron skillfully carve the turkey, Nichols announced, "Remember my family was in the deli business for fifty years. I learned as a boy."

There was also a full bar with bartender. Garcia asked for a Jack on the rocks. Earlier in the day Nichols volunteered that histori-cally the same staff drank too much. Based upon experience, Nich-ols arranged for several cabs to be on call to take staff home. Garcia thought that was a good idea; it avoided DUIs and liability of the practice. Several years ago Davis insisted on the cabs because of the dram shop law, which imposed liability on a party host if drunken guests injured someone or even themselves. The decision allowed the party to continue, and this one was shaping up pretty well.

Garcia couldn't have been happier with Nashville or Nichols's efforts to introduce him to the town. The start of their business relationship exceeded Garcia's every expectation. In fact, Nichols invited Garcia to his house for the holiday, but Garcia had already booked a flight to New York to be with his parents.

Someone turned up the music, and several people started dancing in place. Nichols walked over to Garcia and said, "Merry Christmas. So what do you think of our little luncheon?"

Nichols turned around and, looking at his staff rather than Garcia, commented, "They're a great group of people."

Just then Robyn burst out laughing and spilled her drink on herself and the floor. Garcia watched as Nichols's face got stern and Donna used a paper towel to clean up the spill.

Garcia remarked, "Robyn may be having too good a time. I don't think she drinks too often."

He wasn't aware she had a real problem. Nichols hadn't discussed with Garcia Robyn's addiction problem. He wanted Robyn to have a clean slate with the other employees. Donna knew, but that was it.

Garcia's contact with the beautiful young woman had been only in passing by her in reception. He'd admired her. It was impossible to ignore her, but he was so busy that he'd not had the time to use his charm on her.

Nichols made a mental note to sit Robyn down and read her the riot act. He thought she'd not only stopped drugs but alcohol as well. The fact she was drinking angered and surprised him. He had the number of her sponsor, and he decided he'd use it. He wondered if this was a one-time momentary lapse because of the holiday party or an indication of something else. He felt responsible for the young woman. After all, he made a promise to Valerie Daniels to keep an eye on her sister. Deep in thought, Nichols didn't respond immediately.

Garcia remained silent, which made the moment more uncomfortable.

Finally, Nichols spoke, "That's what the cabs are for, I guess. Say, before you leave I wanted to give you this Christmas present. Buy something nice for yourself." He reached into his inside coat pocket and pulled out and handed Garcia a beige envelope with the new Nichols & Garcia logo. It was the same logo that hung behind the reception desk and was newly embossed on their stationery. It also had appeared in several of the latest newspaper ads. Nichols kept his promises. He promised Garcia he'd develop a recognizable brand that they'd both be proud of.

"Should I open it now?" asked Garcia.

"Go ahead. I want to see your face when you open it."

Garcia ripped open the envelope, and inside was a check payable to Dr. Charles Garcia in the amount of $5,000. In the memo line it read "Merry Christmas, Peter and Helen."

Garcia felt a little strange. He hadn't gotten his partner anything. He ran back to his office, retrieved the gold cuff links he'd bought for his father, and walked up to Nichols.

"This is a small token of my appreciation. After the holiday, I'll have them inscribed with your initials."

Oh, well, Garcia thought, *I'll just get Father something else.*

As Nichols started mingling with his employees, distributing the Christmas bonus checks, Garcia went over to see if he could help the drunken Robyn. Before he knew what happened he was alone with her in the copier room. The room contained two large copiers and an imitation wood-grained folding table, which the staff used to collate documents.

She made the first move with lightning speed. Her right hand cupped his privates. He winced but didn't mind the twinge of momentary pain. He sighed as his brain translated and replaced the intense sensation with one of pleasure.

He was a sophisticated man, who didn't need to be hit over the head. Garcia didn't have to read any signals. This drunken, beautiful woman wanted him badly; she'd given him a green light. He was a healthy twenty-nine-year-old man.

But he knew this wasn't the right time or the right place. Despite his desires, he needed to get control over this situation. While he was thinking of how to do that, she began rubbing him hard on the outside of his pants. He could feel her body react, first getting rigid and then shivering. She undid his belt and pants, lowered his zipper, and grabbed him. She eased up, removed her hand, reached up to a shelf, and retrieved hand sanitizer. She squirted some into her palm and returned her hand to his member. Now lubricated, Robyn vigorously resumed working on Garcia, and he quickly finished.

"That was great," he managed to choke out.

When she spoke, Garcia appreciated for the first time just how drunk Robyn was. "That was so much fun. Should we go again?"

Garcia realized how compromised the situation had become. He zipped up his pants and said, "We'd better get back to the party."

Robyn left first. Garcia made the mistake of walking out of the copier room only moments after her. Donna was waiting five feet away and gave Garcia a very knowing stare.

Garcia decided not to try to explain what happened. He prayed Donna might forget over the long weekend what she'd just seen. He was very much mistaken because his problems with Donna were just beginning.

CHAPTER TWELVE

A WELL-CONCEIVED PLAN
Friday, December 22, 1995

Charlie and Robyn left the party together in a cab. They'd been busy all night. Charlie thought he'd only slept an hour or two. Robyn wouldn't leave him alone. They'd gone four times and finally spent from exhaustion fell asleep in Charlie's king-sized bed.

He glanced over and admired the sleeping young woman. Her long auburn hair was unkempt but shined against his periwinkle blue silk sheets. He thought about waking her and going a fifth time, but Nichols & Garcia was closed to give employees another day off for the holiday, so they had no reason to be in a hurry. There'd be plenty of time later in the day. Charlie wasn't scheduled to fly to New York until six.

Charlie took a deep breath and just stared at her. Not as a satisfied lover but as a surgeon examining a patient who'd undergone surgery and was being inspected by her surgeon for the first time. His professional opinion was that Robyn, without a doubt, was a beautiful creature, but her beauty was raw. He studied every inch of her naked body. The improvements were subtle but apparent to his trained eye. He knew her new Garcia kissable lips worked perfectly. She'd kissed and pleasured him all night. Her teeth had to be straightened and whitened. That was a job for Nichols. And she needed a softer chin. Her breasts were firm and ample, but he liked a full C cup.

After he completed surveying her body, he began kissing her neck. He tried to wake her, and it worked. Her green eyes opened wide, and she squirmed.

"Don't you dare leave a mark, or I'll kill you," she warned him.

"I may slightly mar your neck this morning, but I've got big plans for you. I'm going to make you a walking advertisement for what Dr. Nichols and I are capable of accomplishing."

"What do you mean?" she asked as she snuggled up against him. Her closeness aroused him. He decided to ignore his urges and try to get said what he needed to say.

"You sit in reception every day, and our patients who are contemplating surgery can't help noticing how beautiful you are."

Robyn smiled and batted her green eyes.

"What if both Dr. Nichols and I could make you even more beautiful? Dr. Nichols could straighten and whiten your teeth, and I could give you a new chin. I will find someone to enhance your breasts. You're much too talented to remain a receptionist. I've heard you sing. These procedures will help you go from a 9 to a 12. With your talent and new looks you'll have the formula to succeed in the music business."

Charlie actually meant what he said. These subtle improvements cumulatively would make a huge difference. She had the talent, she was pure country, and she could write about the Old South that hit hard times. With a break or two, Robyn could make it.

Robyn was obviously pleased. She planted a wet one and rolled her tongue along the roof of his mouth.

They held each other for a good ten minutes, and then she broke into song. It was an old Allman Brothers' song, more rock and roll than Charlie's taste preferred. He made her sing a Patsy Cline song next. *She's truly talented*, Charlie thought. *These procedures will give her just the edge she needs.*

Fifteen minutes later Charlie, very excited, had Nichols on the phone and shared his plan, saying that he had Robyn's seal of approval, but failing to mention he'd spent the night with her. He argued that if the results of Robyn's surgeries just convinced two or three patients, bearing the cost of the surgeries was a good business decision. When Nichols raised several potential problems, Charlie had the answers. He could tell that his partner was swaying when he remarked that the senator had no serious objection to Robyn's new lips and even commented that they enhanced her beauty.

Nichols came around. "Let's do it. The works. She'll be our combined masterpiece."

Charlie had no doubt that Donna, probably because it was his idea, would object strongly. He couldn't wait to see her face. He wanted to implement the decision quickly, despite Donna's anticipated opposition. He suggested, "Let's call Ben Davis and get his opinion."

"Can't this wait? It's the Friday before Christmas."

"Davis is Jewish. He's probably working anyway."

Calling Davis was a smart strategy on Charlie's part. Nichols trusted Davis implicitly, and his support was crucial. Charlie knew it was a good business decision. Nichols also insisted that Donna be included on the phone call. She was connected to the call, without any real explanation.

Despite his religion, Davis was at home with his family. He worked so hard he took both Christian and Jewish holidays off. He joked it was one of the benefits of being one of the chosen people living in a Gentile world. He called Bella at home, and she arranged the four-way call between him, Donna, Nichols, and Charlie.

Nichols presented the proposed surgeries as a legitimate practice expense with marketing benefits. Charlie thought Nichols made a convincing argument. Davis listened a full five minutes before he interrupted.

"Malpractice will cover the procedures because the surgeries are within the scope of the practice. Whether you charge or not isn't relevant. She's over eighteen, and she'll sign all the necessary waivers. What about your promise to Valerie Daniels?"

The question was directed at Nichols. Charlie didn't understand the question.

After a moment Nichols answered, "These surgeries will dramatically enhance her looks. She's a musician, not a receptionist. In the long run these surgeries will help her career. If it will make you feel better, Ben, I'll give Valerie a call and see whether she has any objection. It is Robyn's life and body. Ultimately it's her call."

Donna spoke for the first time, and her question was directed at Davis. "Well, are these surgeries a good idea or a bad one?"

Davis didn't like being put on the spot, but he was paid for his advice and they were asking for it.

"Donna, you've been quiet, but I take it from the tone of your voice you're against proceeding with the surgeries?"

Donna didn't respond, so Davis continued, "It's my professional opinion that you should run the office and leave marketing and what goes on in the operating room to the doctors. Robyn's surgeries fall outside your area of control and fall within Dr. Nichols's and Dr. Garcia's sphere of influence. I admit there's some overlap because this issue involves an employee, but Dr. Nichols and Dr. Garcia are the owners and it's their call. They have legitimate business reasons for their decision."

Charlie couldn't have been happier. The great Ben Davis sided with him over Donna; that was a major office politics victory for him.

Good-byes were said, but Nichols, Charlie, and Donna remained on the line. Nichols said to Charlie, "Since your surgical suite isn't finished yet, I'll go first and whiten her teeth. Donna, I think we have an hour and a half next Saturday."

Charlie couldn't wait to tell Robyn. He also decided he'd call his friend Dr. Melvin and schedule Robyn's breast enlargement. He'd have to pay the discounted fee himself. It was a small price to pay to get Robyn sculpted into his vision of beauty.

CHAPTER THIRTEEN

OVERSLEPT

Wednesday, February 14, 1996

The construction wasn't completed on January 18th as planned and hoped. Tisdale didn't get his $10,000 bonus. Nichols was disappointed; Tisdale was very disappointed; in fact, Nichols learned that because Tisdale was four days late, his fee was reduced by $2,000.

Although the delay pushed Dr. Garcia's entire surgery schedule back, Mrs. Alder would have her new look by Valentine's Day. In January Nichols whitened and straightened her teeth. It was reported to Nichols that Mrs. Alder's second consult with Dr. Garcia went perfectly. He mapped out how he would alter her chin and deliver Garcia kissable lips. Mrs. Alder was still smitten by Dr. Garcia.

From the schedule, Nichols knew that the Alder surgery was at seven thirty. Mrs. Alder arrived at seven fifteen; she was nervous but ready. Nichols watched as Tracy, Garcia's surgical nurse, walked the patient back to prep her for surgery. Dr. Garcia had not yet arrived.

Seven thirty came and went, but there was no Dr. Garcia. Nichols picked up the phone and called Garcia's cell phone. Donna was standing right next to him with a knowing smile.

When Garcia answered his phone, Nichols blasted him, "Where the hell are you? Mrs. Alder is waiting!"

Garcia sounded as if he'd just been awakened, "You're out of your mind. Mrs. Alder isn't scheduled until tomorrow. Check the schedule!"

"I did. If it's tomorrow, why would the patient and Tracy be here ready to go?"

"I'll be there in half an hour. Make some excuse to the patient."

"I'm not going to lie. I'll simply tell the patient you were delayed, and you can explain your reason when you arrive."

Thirty minutes later, in front of Nichols and Donna, Garcia was very apologetic. He made up an excuse about a medical emergency. Before she went under, Mrs. Alder bought it, but Nichols thought Garcia acted very unprofessionally by oversleeping. It was his responsibility to be on time. His entire day would be backed up due to his carelessness. Not only was Mrs. Alder inconvenienced, but all of his other patients today would be also.

When Nichols came up for air to take a break, Donna was waiting for him in his office. She shook her head and said, "He's dishonest and unreliable. Honesty and reliability are two important traits to have in a partner."

Nichols immediately became defensive: "He made a mistake. Everybody makes mistakes, even you! Why don't you like him?"

"There's something sleazy about him. I think he's messing around with Robyn. They're always whispering about something. What if he's having sex with her?"

"What business is it of mine?"

"They're your employees, and you promised to keep an eye on her for her sister."

That was a low blow, Nichols thought. *I am not her babysitter. Robyn is an adult.*

She'd religiously produced attendance slips from meetings and met her obligation of three a week. Her attendance and performance at work were excellent. And to Nichols's knowledge and limited supervision she was drug and alcohol free since the Christmas party. He saw that as a momentary slip.

Donna pressed further and suggested, "Let's call Ben and see what he has to say." She got Bella on the line and then was connected with Davis. She put him on speaker and explained the situation.

Nichols waited uncertainly for Davis's response. He was afraid about what the lawyer's advice might be.

Davis began, "Well, the company doesn't have an employee fraternization policy. There's never been a need since Peter's been the only male employee. It's critical that they keep their personal relationship out of the office. She reports to Donna, not him. Both of them are over eighteen and can make their own choices, good and bad ones. Peter, you did promise to keep an eye on her . . ."

Nichols cut him off, "Wait a goddamned minute. I meant I'd help keep an eye on her sobriety, not her love life. She's a beautiful young woman. She's supposed to be having sex with somebody. Why not Charlie? He's smart and good looking and has a bright future. He'd be a good boyfriend and even greater husband. Let nature take its course."

Davis didn't argue. Donna was unhappy with how the phone conversation ended.

By Nichols's watch, the Alder surgery started about an hour and a half late. Donna reminded him that the office lived and died by its schedule. She described the Alder incident as a fiasco. Nichols regarded it as a small hiccup and didn't share Donna's concerns. He knew that Donna wasn't going to let it go, though.

CHAPTER FOURTEEN

INAPPROPRIATE BEHAVIOR

Thursday, February 15, 1996

Anna Perkins walked into Garcia's office for a consult; she was the first of many patients of the day. Garcia came around from behind his desk and sandwiched both of her hands between his. He rubbed her bottom wrist gently and looked deeply into her eyes. Not a casual glance but intensely, as if he was trying to read her soul. Like most women, she reacted positively and smiled back at him.

As she started to pull back, Garcia increased his hold. He could feel her quiver under his touch. Her palms began to sweat. Her reaction was not uncommon; almost all women found him irresistible. Garcia could tell he'd made another conquest.

He closed the door. Nichols & Garcia had no policy that required a treatment room door to remain open or a nurse to be present in the room during a consult. Of course during surgery at least one other professional was in the surgical suite. Garcia preferred that all consults be private so he could focus on the patient without any interference from the staff.

With great interest in his voice, he said, "Those are exquisite jeans. Who makes them?"

"I don't rightly know," responded Ms. Perkins in a heavy southern accent.

"They fit you perfectly. They accentuate your shapely behind."

Perkins blushed, and Garcia, who'd been facing her, came around behind her and pulled down the top of the jeans so he could see the label. He playfully ran his finger along the small of her back, all the way down to the top of the cleft between her buttocks.

Ms. Perkins was taken aback by the doctor's presumptiveness but didn't protest. It was obvious to him that she loved the attention, as he thought she should. He was young, four years her junior, handsome, and an eligible professional. Her neck was a blotchy red, a dead giveaway that he'd struck a nerve.

In almost a whisper, he reassured her, "Don't worry. I'm a doctor. If we proceed with your contemplated surgery, I'll see a lot more of you than your lower back. You need to relax and let me examine you so I can evaluate which procedures to recommend.

"You're tense. Please relax. With these hands I'll make you desirable. I'm here to help. Please trust me."

Garcia began to rub her shoulders. He knew exactly what he was doing.

"You need to follow my lead. I'll take you to a place where you'll no longer feel lonely. Men will pursue you, and you'll meet the man of your dreams."

Garcia knew that for most of his patients finding or pleasing the right man was their ultimate goal. Generally, surgery wasn't considered for vanity's sake only.

"Let's begin with a thorough examination!"

He knew his words would be accepted as gospel. From behind, he grabbed each side of her jeans and quickly pulled them and her panties down to her knees. She gasped but didn't protest. He took her silence as a green light and placed the palm of each hand on each buttock and squeezed.

"You've got a very firm butt. No need for a Brazilian butt lift there. You have beautiful skin, soft and pale, like a baby's bottom."

"I came in considering new lips. . . . I read your ad about Garcia kissable lips," she said. She was so startled by Garcia's actions that she was uncertain about how to explain the reason for her visit.

"My consults consider all aspects. I recommend where there can be improvements made, and then we determine how to improve your appearance and your life. I'm trying to help you find happiness. That's our goal."

Perkins pulled up her panties and jeans and tucked in her shirt.

He took out his black felt-tip pen and assured the patient that the marks would come off. He was with her for more than two hours, an unusually long first consult.

Garcia was turning on his charm; he wanted to close the sale. Using his eyes and body language, he overwhelmed poor Ms. Perkins. They talked about surgical options and a timetable. He convinced her to alter her lips and her chin.

Then he addressed her breasts. He carefully and slowly unbuttoned her blouse. He reached behind and with the skills of a surgeon unhooked her bra in a single motion. He laughed to himself. He could make $1 million teaching high school boys that trick.

After consideration, he determined that she needed a lift. His colleague Dr. Melvin would give her a discount with his referral. He gently cupped each of her breasts and raised them to where he thought they were appropriately positioned. He squeezed them slightly.

"See the difference? Now they're perky."

Perkins giggled under his touch. With the sale made and Perkins hot and bothered, Garcia changed subjects. They talked about

Nashville and the fact he was new to town. At a break in the conversation, he asked her to dinner that evening. She jumped at the invitation.

He figured he'd try to expand the sale. "You know, Anna, you've got a beautiful smile. It's a shame your teeth are so yellow. My partner, Dr. Nichols, can change that and give you the smile you deserve."

She just couldn't resist him. When she left his office, she'd signed up for a new pair of Garcia kissable lips, a new chin, and a teeth whitening by Dr. Nichols. The package deal price was $12,500. No need for a discount with this patient. They said good-bye and agreed they'd meet at Houston's on West End at eight.

The rest of the day went like clockwork. Garcia had a procedure at three and another at five. By the end of the day, two more female patients were more beautiful and had been transformed by Garcia kissable lips.

Passing Nichols in the hallway, Garcia told him about his sale to Ms. Perkins. She was signed up for three procedures without a discount.

"That's wonderful, Charlie. You're learning the business side of the practice. We have a valuable service that women want, and most of our patients can afford to pay full price. If certain women can't afford our services, then we'll discount them slightly. I want to help as many women as possible. Even at the discounted price we're making a healthy profit."

At the end of the conversation Nichols reminded Garcia that they were scheduled to appear on *Talk of the Town*, a local morning TV talk show, the next day to promote Garcia kissable lips.

Garcia was glad that Nichols mentioned it, or he'd have forgotten. The two partners exchanged good-byes. The next morning the interview went better than expected. Garcia was not only his charming self but also vivacious. He overcame his tiredness. At the end Charlie Chase, the show's host, thanked them and asked if they'd agree to come back on the show soon.

Over the next week, Garcia's business increased by fifty percent. He was booked six weeks in advance for first consults. One of those first consults was Christy Howard, age thirty-six. She was a beautiful woman, and Garcia convinced her that he could make her even more beautiful. Her application stated she was a non-smoker and identified what medications she was on.

Business was good because the patients perceived him as charming and someone who could make them beautiful. Garcia's ego grew with every ring of the phone.

CHAPTER FIFTEEN

TROUBLE IN PARADISE
Sunday, April 7, 1996

Charlie was tired of listening to the broken record. Robyn was complaining again that they never went out.

"I've gone through all of these surgeries, and the only place I go is from here to the office and then back here to screw. The only time I get off my back in this place is when you demand to do it doggy style. I want to go out and have some fun. I want to go back on stage. I've got talent; you've insisted I did. Thanks to you I'm even hotter than ever, and you've got me chained to the bed."

Charlie replied, "You know that I don't use chains, but I do admit that I sometimes use handcuffs.

"I've explained we can't be seen outside the office together, not yet anyway."

"Who cares? What difference does it make? We're both over twenty-one. Are you ashamed of me?"

This conversation was about to get out of control. Charlie needed to calm her down, so he turned on his magic: "That's ridiculous. You're my masterpiece. I'm proud of what you've become, but I can't have that bitch Donna complaining to Nichols that the only reason I convinced him to provide free surgery was because you were my girlfriend."

"I certainly don't feel like your girlfriend. All we ever do is take out food and screw. I think you're using me."

"I need you to be patient just a little longer. Eventually we'll reveal our love, and the office can know about us."

"Why don't I just quit, move in with you, and pursue my music? You've always insisted that I have talent." Robyn whined, "I don't want to be a receptionist. I'm a very talented singer-songwriter."

"I don't think that would be the best thing for your sobriety."

Charlie learned almost immediately about Robyn's twelve-step program; she attended three days a week religiously. She remained sober from all addictions, except one, sex. During intimate moments Robyn described her struggle with drugs and alcohol. They also discussed the temptations of the music business. Taking drugs and excessive drinking were just part of the culture. The same demons that inspired Robyn in her music haunted her as a person.

In advising Robyn about her career path Charlie was torn. He loved country music and in particular her voice, but he was scared of the risk of her falling off the wagon, which prompted him to say, "You're better off behind a reception desk."

Robyn was good at her job. As predicted, the patients liked her, and she was a successful sales tool. Several patients specifically asked for the same chin as Robyn, and Charlie had actually called her into several consults to argue the merits of the surgery. Even Donna begrudgingly admitted that Robyn had made the difference in several sales.

Robyn's hand cupped Charlie. When in doubt the couple turned to sex as the best way to solve a problem or end an argument. She slid down to the bottom of the bed. The chocolate brown silk sheets made it easy for her to get into position. Charlie winced with pleasure.

"Hum," he begged.

She began to hum "Yankee Doodle."

After she completed two bars, she raised her head from under the sheets.

Having provided her services, she thought she could resume her complaining: "When's the next time you're going to New York? I'd love to meet your parents."

"You, of all people, know I'm too busy at work right now to get away. The only day off I have is Sunday, and I need that day to spend with you and to recover from the rest of the week."

Robyn didn't like that answer and jumped up from the bed and dashed into the bathroom. After a few minutes Charlie knocked on the door. He hoped to kiss and make up. No such luck. She wouldn't open the door. He was worried about what was going on behind that door.

He stood there a few more minutes, thinking about his next move. He was so fed up that he got dressed and left the house. If she was going to lock herself in the bathroom, what good was she to him? She'd been doing that a lot lately. He didn't really care what the hell she was doing. He knew other women, and they could satisfy his needs with no strings attached. He decided to call Christy Howard, a fiery redhead he knew for certain didn't dye her hair.

He changed his mind about calling and decided to just show up at her apartment. It was Sunday about ten. He'd knock and see if she wanted to go to brunch or something. He preferred something, but he was also hungry.

He knocked five times before she came to the peephole. From the other side of the door he heard, "Charlie, what the hell are you doing here? I'm not dressed."

"That sounds absolutely perfect. Can I come in?"

After a few seconds of hesitation, the door swung open. Standing in front of Charlie was a naked woman with dark red hair on top and below. Her bright blue eyes met his, and he stepped in the foyer and put his arms around her. She had alabaster white skin, which was only accented by her red hair. They disappeared into the bedroom, and for the next two hours Charlie forgot about Robyn Eden. Christy was not only Charlie's lover; she'd soon be a patient.

CHAPTER SIXTEEN
THE DISAPPEARANCE
Monday, April 29, 1996

As usual, Davis was the first to arrive at the office. By seven, Bella and Sammie were hard at work. Morty slept in; he was entitled to a late start. He'd worked hard for more than fifty years, retired for two months to care for his ailing wife, Goldie, and returned after her death as Davis's associate on the cheap. Despite his age, the old man was still brilliant and a great asset for Davis to have in his corner. At times he could get ornery. He missed his unchallenged right to smoke his cigars anytime, anywhere in the office. He was now on a very short leash with his doctor's daughter, Liza, leading the way. He vigorously objected, but everyone tolerated his outbursts. Morty was admired and loved by everyone in the office.

Morty's stated purpose in life was to train Sammie. He wanted her to be a better lawyer than either Davis or himself. The two worked closely together, meeting as often as school would allow to review the day's events and to ponder the next day's. He knew from hard work and diligence that she would be his legacy.

There was a sense of excitement and anxiety in the air as the team prepared for a trial, a wrongful death case. The first day of trial was only two weeks away, and there was still a lot to do. Davis represented Thomas Jackson, the surviving husband of Karen and father of Jimmy Jackson, age six. The proof would show that Karen died upon impact when the tractor-trailer struck their Volkswagen Beetle, but poor Jimmy lived three days before expiring.

Davis and Sammie were on their second day drafting jury instructions. Davis had eaten almost an entire family pack of peanut M&M's. When Bella interrupted, Davis had a Tootsie Pop in his mouth. He always sucked them till the end, never chewed them.

"It's Dr. Nichols and Donna. I told them you were tied up, but they insisted that it was important and can't wait."

Davis told her, "I'll take the call but no more interruptions. We need to get this draft done, so we can move on to preparing my opening argument."

Davis pushed the blinking button. "Peter, what can I do for you?"

"Ben, we've got a big problem. Our med count is off, and there's a tank of nitrous oxide that should be full but is only three quarters."

"Has this ever happened before?"

Donna answered, "In all the time that I've been here and in charge of the medication closet, it's happened twice, and we determined both times it was a clerical mistake. This is different. The seal on the tank was broken, and that's no clerical mistake. Also, since January and the addition of Dr. Garcia, we're using different narcotics and other drugs that weren't used in our cosmetic dental practice."

Davis asked the obvious question: "Who had access to the medication closet?"

Nichols started to answer, "Well, four of us have keys . . ."

Donna interrupted, "That's not true. Both Dr. Nichols and Dr. Garcia leave their keys on their desks all day, with their offices unlocked. Any employee could use them or even have duplicated them without either of them knowing."

Davis knew Nichols could be lax, but he had a legal obligation to guard the contents of his drug cabinet and canisters of nitrous oxide. These missing drugs were a serious problem; a crime had been committed.

Nichols was one step behind Davis. "Do we have to call the police? These are controlled substances."

Davis weighed his next words carefully. "Technically you've discovered a crime, and your DEA license is at risk. The problem is that your entire office would be suspect based on the information that you would report. The police would interrogate every employee, and it would affect not only operations but also morale."

Donna suggested, "We'll change the locks, and I'll keep the only key."

Davis didn't like that idea. He offered another one: "That won't catch your thief. I suggest we install a hidden camera and catch the culprit on video in the act."

"Can we do that?" Nichols asked.

Sammie entered the conversation for the first time. "There's no expectation of privacy in a medication closet. You couldn't place a camera in a bathroom or even a locker room, but as the owner of the building and the employer who's been the victim of a serious crime, you'd be within your rights."

Davis added, "Then, when you go to the police, you'd have a solid suspect on videotape."

Davis didn't want to be the bad guy, but someone had to point out the obvious: "I've got to ask. Does anyone suspect Robyn in light of her history?"

An uncomfortable silence followed. Then Sammie asked, "How's her performance and attendance? Any red flags that implicate her?"

Donna immediately responded, "Her performance is excellent. She's busy ten hours a day. Hasn't missed a day and has been late only once. My only concern is her private relationship with Dr. Garcia."

Immediately Nichols defended the romance: "We've addressed your concern. They are adults, and as long as their relationship doesn't affect their work, it's none of our business, right?"

The question was directed to Davis, but Sammie answered, "Doctor, you're legally correct, but that may not be the only consideration. You promised her sister, the senator, that you'd keep an eye on her. You've assumed a moral obligation for this vulnerable and impressionable young woman."

Davis looked at his niece sternly. He thought she'd just overstepped her bounds even if it was a legitimate point. In so many ways she was just like him, and he liked that. She was straightforward and no nonsense. A discussion was warranted but not a scolding.

In a louder than intended voice Nichols challenged her: "What are you saying? Spit it out!"

"Let's just say that Charles Juan Batista Garcia is no gentleman. He's trouble, and Robyn Eden with all of her other problems doesn't need him."

Davis didn't like his niece's last comment. It was unprofessional. He wondered whether Sammie was jealous of their relationship and it was clouding her judgment. He moved the conversation back on track. Davis gave Donna the name of a surveillance company that Davis's firm had used in the past. He suggested that they purchase a camera that had a motion sensor so the camera ran only when someone entered the closet. Davis reminded Donna that she would have to replace the tape every day or two depending on how long the loop lasted. He also suggested that they regularly check their med count so that if the count were off, it would narrow the scope of their review of the surveillance tapes. Donna agreed to assume responsibility for the surveillance. She felt that the missing drugs reflected badly upon her, and she wanted this problem resolved.

The company installed the camera in the medication closet the next evening. Two days later Donna discovered that the three-quarters full tank was now half empty. Someone had had a party.

Donna spent the next morning in her office, fixed to the monitor, expecting to discover their drug-stealing employee. She saw that at 5:10 a.m., the medication closet door opened, and Robyn Eden entered, attached a mask to the half-empty tank, and spent the next eight minutes breathing in the laughing gas. She had no idea that her actions were being recorded.

Donna reported her findings to Dr. Nichols, who called Davis and arranged to have him confront Robyn at the end of the next business day.

CHAPTER SEVENTEEN

THE JIG'S UP

Monday, May 6, 1996

Upon Davis's advice, Donna asked Robyn to stay late to inventory the office supplies. They actually began the process waiting for Davis and Sammie to arrive. The staff left at their usual seven, but Nichols hung back so he could be present for the confrontation.

Just as soon as Davis and Sammie arrived, Donna took them upstairs to Dr. Nichols's private office where he was sitting behind his desk. Davis assured everyone that he'd handle the meeting, and Donna left to get Robyn.

Davis brought with him a small combination TV/VCR, which he and Liza used on family vacations. Caroline and Jake sat in the backseat, and the TV/VCR was wedged in the middle front seat armrest and plugged into the cigarette lighter. *Jurassic Park* and Indiana Jones films made the long family car rides seem much quicker with the kids preoccupied. The TV/VCR now had another use.

When Robyn entered the room, she couldn't hide her surprise to find a room full of people. There was no need for introductions. Davis had known Robyn almost her entire life.

Davis's tone was anything but familiar when he addressed Robyn: "Ms. Eden, please sit down. I've been asked to meet with you because it has been discovered that you've taken company property and breached the trust that Dr. Nichols placed in you. Do you want to admit what you've done?"

The young woman looked frazzled. She tried to speak, but the words just wouldn't come out.

Davis encouraged her to tell the truth: "I bet you'll feel much better if you come clean."

Robyn hesitated, then said, "I didn't realize it was such a big deal. I bet I'm not the only one who took stuff."

Now it was Davis's turn to be surprised. The videos showed only Robyn's theft. "Who else do you know is taking things?"

"I've seen Tracy take stamps and yellow pads. I didn't think it was a serious problem. I'm so sorry."

"What the hell are you talking about?" Davis shouted and hit the play button to show Robyn the irrefutable evidence of her drug theft.

Robyn sat there several minutes without saying anything.

Finally, Donna asked, "You've got nothing to say? You should be ashamed of yourself. How did you get the key?"

"I took it off Charlie's key chain while he was operating. The keys were just sitting on his desk. I put it back the next day without him ever missing it. Do you have to tell him?"

Davis realized that she didn't understand the seriousness of her predicament. "Ms. Eden, I don't think you understand. You're gone. Either you resign and agree not to apply for unemployment, or you get terminated for cause for stealing drugs and Dr. Nichols reports the theft to the police. It's not much of a choice. I suggest you go quietly."

"Does Charlie know about your ultimatum?" Robyn's eyes flashed with defiance.

Donna snapped, "What difference does that make? He's not going to save your job. You're a thief and have a drug problem."

"I wouldn't be so sure. I work for him . . ."

Donna stopped her midsentence. "That's nonsense. You work for Nichols & Garcia, and I'm your immediate supervisor. You're fired. Now get the hell out of here and never come back!"

Robyn stood and, with a smirk on her face, said, "You haven't heard the last of me. You'll be hearing from my lawyer. Dr. Garcia has sexually harassed me, and I can prove it."

Losing her patience, Donna responded, "You're out of your mind, girl. No one harassed you. Whatever you did, it was voluntary . . ."

Davis turned litigator and ordered, "Donna, quiet! Let me handle this."

His tone was unmistakable; he was in charge, and everyone in the room appreciated the need to be quiet. Ben Davis was no one to cross. Now that he had the floor, the advice he gave needed to be extraordinary. He turned on the accused.

"You're using bad judgment. A federal sexual harassment suit will take at least two years till trial, and an appeal will take another two years. How are you going to pay your lawyer during those four years?"

Robyn stated evenly, "I've spoken to an attorney who has agreed to take the case on a contingency basis and will advance all of the expenses."

"Robyn, your lawsuit will focus on each party's credibility. You're a known drug addict with at least three unsuccessful rehabs and video of you stealing drugs from your employer. Dr. Garcia is a professional member of this community. Who do you think a jury will believe? Do you really think a jury will penalize Dr. Nichols for terminating you?"

"You have no idea who the hell Charlie is and what he's capable of. You've got your video, and I've got mine. I'm willing to bet that the jury finds my video more interesting than yours. Peter Nichols is liable for the wrongful actions of Charlie. Dr. Nichols allowed harassment right under his nose. Without his blessing I never could have been the prey of Charlie Garcia."

Davis decided to change tactics and asked, "Have you discussed your lawsuit with your sister?"

"Why the hell would I?"

"Because she got you this job, and she controls your trust, which you'll need to live day to day during the four years of litigation."

Suddenly Robyn was nervous. She was an actress who'd lost her script.

Davis watched her crumble to a confused drug addict faced by a powerful presence who was challenging her. The argument turned on her.

"I'm calling your sister. Let's confirm that she's not going to fund this fiasco.

"Here's what's going to happen. You'll resign your position with Nichols & Garcia effective immediately. The company will not oppose your application for unemployment in consideration for your execution of an airtight release and confidentiality agreement that I will prepare. You'll give us your video, all of your videos, and we hold ours, which we turn over to the police if you breach the confidentiality agreement. Take it, or leave it."

Davis looked around the room. Sammie knew to keep her mouth shut. Nichols wanted to say something, but Davis could tell he was afraid. Donna was fuming.

"Do we have a deal, Ms. Eden? I can have the documents ready in two hours, and you can begin collecting unemployment next week."

The scared drug addict answered, "I'll deliver my tape in the morning."

"How many do you have in your possession?"

"I stole just one. I knew he wouldn't miss it."

"You're claiming that Dr. Garcia has other tapes? How many?"

"He's got dozens of them, and they're not for the pure of heart. Prepare your damn documents, and I'll sign them."

Robyn practically ran from the room, and Donna locked the door behind her. Using the same authoritative voice he used with Robyn, Davis said, "Do you realize how pivotal that last confrontation was? I hope what happened wasn't lost on you. Think of what would happen to the practice if it were engaged in a four-year sex scandal. How many patients would you lose? If she gets a good lawyer before she signs my release, he'd argue that not only did Peter negligently supervise Charlie, but he allowed him to alter her looks while he exerted undue influence on a young woman whom Peter knew had a drug problem. Finally there's Peter's moral obligation to Valerie Daniels. I bet I could get that into evidence. I closed a good deal. My fees would have exceeded $25,000. It was a bargain."

Nichols rubbed his eyes. He looked tired and angry. He managed to ask, "When should we talk to Charlie?"

Davis answered immediately, "There's no time like the present. Let me handle him." Davis got Charlie on the phone and explained in a very businesslike tone in detail what just transpired. "Before you open your mouth, you'd better think and get your story straight."

Charlie admitted his bad judgment about his relationship with Robyn, but he swore he didn't know anything about the theft. He admitted it was careless to leave his keys on his desk, but he knew for a fact that Nichols did the same thing. "I've got other tapes. I'll destroy them."

Davis remained silent. The Eden case would be settled by the end of the day. The releases and confidentiality agreement would be signed. The tapes could be destroyed; they weren't evidence anymore.

CHAPTER EIGHTEEN
EGOMANIAC
Wednesday, May 15, 1996

Nichols arrived at the office before seven. As always, Donna was waiting for him.

"Morning, Donna, busy day?"

"Dr. Garcia has four lip enhancements. Two of them involve a new chin, starting at seven thirty. He and Tracy will be moving at a pretty good clip all day."

Nichols quickly calculated the fees in his head, $28,000. Not a bad day's work for Dr. Garcia. The kid was a money-making machine.

Donna interrupted his thoughts, "Doctor, have you noticed that Dr. Garcia has changed since Robyn's departure?"

"How so?"

"I'd say both professionally and physically. Last week we had to cancel two morning surgeries at the last minute. Haven't you noticed that he's come into the office disheveled? He has always taken such pride in his personal appearance."

Nichols was aware of the cancellations and how badly Garcia looked the last few mornings. He figured the kid was burning the candle at both ends. He debated sitting the young doctor down and having a man to man, but he'd put it off. Donna was forcing the issue.

"It's a terrible reflection on the practice and not only his reputation, but yours as well."

Donna always pushed hard but never too far. She'd run Nichols's practice for all these years, and she'd help make it what it was today. Nichols knew she was right. He had to address the problem.

The phone rang, and Donna picked it up. The temporary receptionist supplied by a service hadn't arrived yet.

Nichols was still standing next to Donna, who was listening intently to the caller. When she responded, Nichols could hear her end of the conversation.

"You've got to be kidding. You're scheduled to be in surgery in less than an hour. It's right on the schedule, in black and white. Don't try to push your problems on me. Well, I suggest you get yourself out of bed and get over here and perform surgery. I won't be talked to like that, Dr. Garcia."

Nichols motioned for Donna to give the phone to him.

"Charlie, Peter. What's up? Why aren't you here?"

"You tell that bitch to reschedule my seven and my ten. I'll be in around noon for my one o'clock. If you don't like that, then you perform the surgeries."

Nichols thought Garcia sounded hung over or still drunk.

"I'll reschedule your seven, but I want you here for your ten o'clock. Sober up, and get your ass in here. This is a place of business, not your private amusement park. You can't just show up when it pleases you."

"I'll try to make it in by ten."

"Don't try. You be here, ready to perform surgery. If you're not here, you can just pick up your stuff and get the hell out."

Donna canceled Janice Bender's appointment. Dr. Nichols apologized and assured her that she'd hear from Dr. Garcia as well.

Garcia arrived at the office at nine fifteen. He performed the three scheduled surgeries at ten, one, and three thirty. By six o'clock he was finished for the day and sitting in his office writing up his surgical notes.

Nichols walked in and sat down in the leather chair across from Garcia's desk. They hadn't spoken since their heated telephone conversation of the morning. Nichols decided he'd take a softer approach. "Charlie, listen, I'm not only your boss. I'm your friend. What's going on? I'm concerned about you."

"I've been drinking and carousing until all hours. I'm just acting my age. I've been serious my entire life, and I'm blowing off a little steam now. I've overindulged. I'll get it under control."

"You admit to drinking. What about drugs?" He could see hesitation in Garcia's body language. Nichols suspected the answer.

"Absolutely not. You can drug test me if you want. My drug of choice is Jack Daniel's. I can stop. You know what kind of disciplined person I am. I'll get it together. I promise this will never happen again. My drinking will never again interfere with our business."

Nichols wanted to believe him, but he couldn't. Something in the young doctor's eyes made him challenge his words. He decided he'd better call Ben Davis for advice.

"Bella, I've got to talk to Ben."

"He's in a meeting, but he can call you back between appointments."

Thirty minutes later Davis called back. Nichols explained that he had a strong suspicion that Dr. Garcia was using drugs and that he was in no condition to perform surgery. Davis was familiar with Garcia's employment contract since he wrote it.

After a brief mental review of the contract, Davis replied firmly, "I want you to cancel all of Dr. Garcia's surgeries for the rest of the week."

"Are you out of your mind? That will cost me tens of thousands of dollars."

"Would you rather have a suspected drug addict employee perform surgery at your office? That could get ugly real fast. I want you to have Donna type up a letter to Dr. Garcia demanding that he submit to a drug test at Abbott Labs on 28 White Bridge Road. The letter on the top should reflect the date and time it was hand delivered. According to his contract, he'll have only forty-eight hours to undergo the drug test."

"What if he refuses?"

"Then you'll have no choice but to terminate him for cause and demand that he repay his note and demand that his parents honor their guarantee. The money's sitting in an account at Goldman Sachs and shouldn't be too difficult to secure to repay your investment. Cancel the appointments, and deliver the letter."

Nichols wasn't happy. His golden goose was probably on drugs and would have to be terminated. No more golden eggs.

After talking to Davis, Dr. Nichols delegated the delivery of the hand-delivered letter to poor Donna. Garcia read the demand that he submit to a drug test, jumped up from his desk, and barged into Nichols's office.

"What the hell is this?" Garcia demanded.

"I suggest you read it and get your ass over to Abbott Labs as soon as possible. I've canceled all of your surgeries scheduled this week. You're not performing surgery until we get confirmation that you're drug-free."

"Just mind your damn business. I'm seeing my patients, and I'm making you money. That's all you need to worry about."

"I have no choice. I've consulted Davis, and you've got to get a drug test in the next forty-eight hours. If you're telling me the truth, you'll be back at work as soon as you're cleared."

"I'm not getting any damn test. And since you've mentioned it, I don't like my share of the split. You're making a fortune off me, and

I'm not getting my fair share. I deserve more. I'm also working in a hostile work environment. Either she goes, or I go."

Nichols was about to lose his temper. *Donna is right. This kid is really out of control. What an egomaniac!*

"We've got a deal, and you're committed for three years. If you're thinking of walking, it will cost your parents $400,000."

"Bullshit. You'll never enforce that contract. I can walk away anytime. If you don't believe me, then just watch me."

With that Garcia stormed out of Nichols's office and right out the front door.

Nichols called Davis and gave him the blow-by-blow details.

Davis organized his thoughts before responding, "If he takes the test and is on drugs, that's a big problem. I'll have to send a letter to his parents with a copy to Harrelson informing them that his drug use is a breach of contract."

"Can't we get him help? Put him in a twenty-eight-day program?"

"Yes, but after receipt of the results, you're on notice that your employee and agent is on drugs. It creates a real liability for the company with his patients. We'd better think this thing through. If he tests positive or refuses to take the test, we will have to contact your malpractice carrier. Who has the coverage?"

"Tennessee Mutual. That's my carrier, his carrier, and the company's carrier."

"Great. I hate those guys, and they hate me. Perfect."

"Why do they hate you?"

"It's too long a story. Hopefully he'll pass the test."

CHAPTER NINETEEN

THE GUARANTEE
Friday, May 17, 1996

Charles Juan Batista Garcia's response to the demand to be drug tested came in the form of a written response from David Harrelson Esquire, New York, New York. Harrelson explained that Dr. Garcia refused to take an arbitrary drug test at the behest of Dr. Nichols and suggested that Dr. Nichols might seek psychiatric help for his delusions. The letter also informed Dr. Nichols that Dr. Garcia resigned from Nichols & Garcia PC and that the guarantee of Señor and Mrs. Garcia was unenforceable. A copy of the letter was sent to Benjamin A. Davis Esquire, and another copy was sent to the contact person at Goldman Sachs where the $400,000 was held in escrow.

Davis heard from Nichols within minutes of his finishing the letter.

"What does he mean that the guarantee is unenforceable?"

Nichols sounded nervous. Davis realized he needed to calm down his client.

"He doesn't say why. We've got the Goldman Sachs money tied up. Goldman, by contract, is obligated if there's a dispute to deposit the funds into the Circuit Court here in Nashville. At least we've got home court advantage, we've got the parents' signed guarantee of $400,000 as security, and most important we've got the money."

"What's our next step?"

Davis thought a moment. "I'll call Harrelson and see if I can flush out his defense on the guarantee. You've got to find another MD to join your practice immediately. In order to enforce the non-solicitation of patients, your company needs to be able to offer the same services. You're a DDS, not an MD. You need either another oral and maxillofacial surgeon or a plastic surgeon on staff. That should be your first priority. Also his employment contract has a non-solicitation of employees. So let his nurse, what's her name?"

"Tracy Nelson."

"Let her know that she can't go to work for him. He's going to need a staff to compete."

The contract defined solicitation of employees as any employee who had worked for Nichols & Garcia within the *last two years.* Nelson was clearly barred from working for Garcia. They decided that the new doctor should pick his or her own staff. Donna also expressed concern about Nelson's loyalty. She was terminated, given two weeks of severance pay, and the search for a nurse began.

Davis explained that the definition as to what constituted solicitation of patients was less clear. Garcia wasn't permitted to target the company's patients, but the contract couldn't prevent him from treating former patients. It was the patient's choice as to his or her doctor. The contract between the doctors couldn't usurp the patient's right to choose.

"I guess I'd better have Donna start canceling his appointments."

"I'd go about two weeks out. Tell Donna to apologize and say he's become unavailable. I better fax a response to Harrelson ASAP."

Davis signed off with Nichols, put down the phone, and picked up his Dictaphone. He began,

Dear Mr. Harrelson, I am in receipt of your letter of May 17th and in response to it would state that Dr. Nichols, in accordance with paragraph 10 of Dr. Garcia's employment contract, has an absolute right to demand that Dr. Garcia undergo a drug test. First, narcotics have been taken from the practice's storage closet; second, several employees will testify that Dr. Garcia has recently been acting erratically and that his pupils have been dilated. Donna Burns, office manager, will testify that several morning surgeries have been rescheduled because Dr. Garcia failed to appear at the appointed time to perform those surgeries. Dr. Garcia's refusal to submit to the drug test constitutes a default.

Dr. Garcia has an absolute right to resign as an employee of Nichols & Garcia PC. It would be unlawful to require him to remain employed for the three-year term. However, Dr. Garcia by resignation triggers certain provisions of his employment agreement and the guarantee signed by his parents.

Please be advised that a copy of this letter has been sent to Mr. Wendell Smith of Goldman Sachs, which demanded that the $400,000 referenced in paragraph 15 of the employment contract and the guarantee be paid to Dr. Nichols to satisfy the default and breach of contract. If Dr. Garcia challenges this payment, the funds must be deposited in the Circuit Court of Davidson County, Tennessee, as provided for in the escrow agreement.

Please be advised that Dr. Garcia is prohibited as provided by paragraphs 18 and 19 from soliciting any patients or employees of the practice. I also remind you that Nichols & Garcia PC, of which Dr. Nichols owns ninety-nine percent, owns the phrase "Garcia kissable lips" and its related trademarks.

Finally, in your letter of May 17th, without explanation, you assert that the guarantee securing this transaction is unenforceable. Let me assure you that under Tennessee law, which controls this transaction, the document *is* enforceable. If you have additional information that you think I should consider, please provide it.

Yours very truly, Benjamin A. Davis.

A copy of the letter was also faxed to Dr. Nichols. At two o'clock Bella buzzed in and informed Davis that David Harrelson was on the phone. Davis asked Bella to request that Sammie sit in on the call. Within a minute Sammie was in Davis's office.

"David, I've got you on speaker. My associate will be sitting in. Based on the correspondence, it looks like we've got a mess on our hands."

"That's one way to look at it. We suggest we all go our separate ways, shake hands, and be friends."

"Why would my client do that? He has a perfectly good guarantee from the parents."

"It just seems like you have a good guarantee."

"What's on your mind? You might as well identify your position. You're not going to be able to keep it secret for long."

"I've got two arguments to set the guarantee aside. First, the employment agreement violates the Stark federal anti-kickback laws. A DDS can't earn a fee from services provided by a medical doctor. Second, you translated all of the documents into Spanish, right?"

"Okay."

"You knew the Garcias were from Majorca, right?"

"Okay."

"Well, Spanish is not the official language of Majorca. Catalan is. My clients don't understand Spanish, so they couldn't appreciate that they were guaranteeing the transaction."

Davis looked at Sammie in silence for a few moments but knew he had to say something.

"Horseshit. You represented the Garcias. You speak English, don't you? If you knew they didn't speak Spanish, you had the obligation to translate the documents into Catalan. If your clients didn't understand what they were signing, and I seriously question that, it was because of *your* negligence. Maybe I should recommend a good malpractice attorney."

"What about my Stark argument?"

"More horseshit. Tennessee allows a DDS and an MD to form a professional corporation together. Since both the DDS and the MD are employees of the same corporation, there are no cross referrals. Also, Stark only applies to Medicare, and I seriously doubt any of those Garcia kissable lips were paid for by Medicare. Nice try, David, but the parents are on the line for the full $400,000."

After the thirty-day notice period expired, Davis filed suit in the Circuit Court of Davidson County on behalf of Dr. Nichols against Dr. Charles Juan Batista Garcia and his parents. Three days later Goldman Sachs deposited the funds with the Circuit Court of Davidson County in Nashville.

CHAPTER TWENTY
RESPONDENT SUPERIOR
(Employer Liability for Its Employee)
Wednesday, July 3, 1996

It was the day before July 4th, a slow day for any cosmetic practice, with family commitments and the arrival of out-of-town guests. Despite these distractions, Nichols & Dowdle PC was open for business.

With the help of McCormick & Associates, Nichols replaced Dr. Garcia with a plastic surgeon, Anita Dowdle, MD within five days. Davis assured him it was a necessary hire to enforce Garcia's non-compete. She was competent, capable, and offered lip enhancement, but she couldn't duplicate Garcia kissable lips. They entered into a one-year contract; it would be a short honeymoon period. Dr. Anita Dowdle was hired as a quick replacement; if Dowdle worked out, so much the better.

Nichols sat at his desk fuming as he stared at the legal papers sent over by Sammie. The injunction secured by Davis stopped Garcia from specifically advertising Garcia kissable lips. However, it couldn't stop him from advertising or performing the surgery; he was just prohibited from using the name. More important, those papers couldn't stop the cancellation of appointments.

At nine a sheriff's deputy appeared out of nowhere in reception and asked to see Dr. Nichols. He was informed that the doctor was in surgery. The deputy took a seat and waited. Upon completion of the procedure, Nichols came to reception to speak with the deputy. The deputy rose, handed Nichols a legal document, and announced, "You've been served and so has your company, Nichols & Garcia PC. Good day, sir."

At first Nichols thought Garcia had brought a countersuit; Davis warned him of that possibility. As he skimmed the document, he realized it was something very different and literally ran to his office to call Ben.

"Hello, Dr. Nichols . . . ," Bella began.

"Bella, I need Ben. It's urgent!"

There was panic in his voice, and she said, "I'll get him immediately."

It took her what seemed like a half hour, but in reality it was only a few minutes.

"What can I do for you, Peter? Bella said it was urgent."

"I've been sued."

"Dr. Garcia filed a countersuit?"

"No, it's not a suit by Charlie. It's by a patient. I've only skimmed the document. A patient named Anna Perkins has sued Charlie, me personally, and the company. Somehow we're responsible for her having sex with Charlie. I don't understand. How can I be personally liable for Charlie having sex with a patient?" He was getting all worked up.

"Look, Peter, fax it over, and I'll read it. I can't give advice in the dark. Don't discuss it with anyone, not Donna, not even Helen, until we have a chance to review it. Can you come over here this afternoon? I don't want to discuss the lawsuit at your place until I know what we're going to tell your staff."

"I'll cancel my last three appointments. I can be at your place by three."

True to his word, Nichols arrived at Davis's office exactly at three. Davis explained that Morty was at his farm, resting. He'd join them later.

The complaint was twenty-eight pages long with eight exhibits. Anna Perkins, also known as the plaintiff, sued Dr. Charles Juan Batista Garcia, Dr. Peter Nichols, and Nichols & Garcia PC, defendants, alleging various wrongful conduct, and she sued for compensatory and punitive damages totaling $10 million. Ms. Perkins claimed that she chose Dr. Garcia as her surgeon based upon reading certain advertisements placed by Nichols & Garcia in the *Tennessean* and also after seeing Dr. Garcia and Dr. Nichols on a local television show. She attached to the complaint as exhibits a copy of the newspaper ad and the written promotional material provided by Nichols & Garcia PC about its employee Dr. Garcia and Garcia kissable lips.

Jackson "Jack" Willis, a prominent Nashville attorney, prepared the complaint.

Davis commented, "He's smart and juries like him."

"Is he as good as you?"

"I've butted heads with him twice and won both times, but they were close calls."

Sammie knocked and walked into Davis's office. Morty followed behind her and, with a copy of the complaint in his hand, parked himself at the end of Davis's conference table. He was chewing on a big black cigar. Davis gave him a stern look.

"Get off my back. I'm only chewing on it. See, it's never been lit."

Davis decided to drop it, and subdued hellos were exchanged.

The complaint alleged that during Anna Perkins's first consult with Dr. Garcia, he told her how much he liked her jeans and then proceeded to pull them and her panties down to her knees. Dr. Garcia then did a thorough examination, including an inspection of her breasts, which he commented were asymmetrical.

Sammie spoke first, "Why the hell is an oral surgeon examining a patient's breasts? And I don't understand this claim he pulled her pants to her knees. Any woman with any sense at all would have been out the door the moment he asked her to remove her shirt. Where was his nurse? Isn't it protocol to have a female staff member present when a male doctor performs an examination?"

Nichols answered, "Maybe for a gynecologist, but it's not the standard of care for an oral surgeon or a cosmetic dentist for that matter. I conduct consults without another staff member present, but I've never asked anybody to remove an article of clothing."

Sammie was getting angry. "This woman's an idiot. How does she explain her gullibility?"

Morty remained silent, reading the document.

Davis continued to recap the complaint. "She claims that during the first consult Dr. Garcia made physical advances and told her he was new to town, didn't know many people, and found her very attractive. She claims she was flattered by the attention of a young, handsome surgeon."

Davis's paraphrasing recounted that later that night Ms. Perkins and Dr. Garcia went to dinner together and, according to the pleading, had unprotected sex at his home. As they lay in bed, Dr. Garcia explained that there was a Porsche automobile in Miami that he was interested in purchasing, and he asked Ms. Perkins to accompany him on a test drive. Admittedly, the plaintiff jumped at the chance to spend more time with Dr. Garcia. The complaint alleged that he asked the plaintiff to make the flight arrangements Saturday morning with an overnight stay. He promised to repay the plaintiff for these expenses.

The complaint described the evening in too much detail. Quite frankly, Nichols thought Willis went overboard when he identified certain sexual aids used. The complaint asserted that Ms. Perkins agreed to these uncomfortable acts to pleasure Dr. Garcia in the hope that he would continue the relationship.

Ms. Perkins alleged that as soon as they returned to Nashville on Sunday, Dr. Garcia became distant and started talking about the fact they should just be friends. He even went so far as to tell her he was interested in other women and wouldn't be exclusive. The plaintiff became angry and demanded that day that Garcia reimburse the amount for the airfare and hotel accommodations she'd advanced. He claimed he didn't have enough cash and asked if she took American Express. He promised to get the money to her at a later date, but he never did.

In a very agitated voice Sammie commented, "I would have punched the schmuck out, right there in the airport. This woman has no self-esteem."

None of the men acknowledged her suggestion. Davis continued, "Two days later, Dr. Garcia called her and apologized. She accepted his apology. Three days after that, the plaintiff underwent surgery and paid the balance of her invoice, $9,000."

Davis began to read, "A week later she had a follow-up visit at the offices of Nichols & Garcia, and after the examination of her surgery sites, Dr. Garcia began fondling her breasts. Davis read, "... then without warning he pulled down her jeans, bent the plaintiff over the exam table, and entered her from behind. He was unable to maintain an erection and became angry, blaming the plaintiff. At this point, the plaintiff claimed she didn't know what to do because Dr. Garcia became louder and louder. He claimed he was distracted and asked the plaintiff to come to his home for a home-cooked meal. The plaintiff nervously agreed. That night she went to his home in Hillwood under the guise of sharing a home-cooked meal. Instead he lured her into the bedroom where he attacked her with a dildo. The sex toy was so big it caused tears to her anus and vagina, requiring her to seek medical treatment in an emergency room and from her gynecologist."

Davis paused, then he shared his concerns: "That's a big problem for Peter and the company. They had intercourse in the office. Up until that point, with the exception of the first exam, the inappropriate conduct took place outside the office. At the office he's clearly under Dr. Nichols's supervision and control. In Miami, Charlie's on his own."

Morty finally broke his silence. He'd been only half listening to Davis while he read intently. "I've seen a lot of lawsuits in my time, but this one has sex appeal. Willis has spun a good tale. His biggest problem will be his client. He can't let older women sit on the jury. They'll crucify his client."

Davis nodded in agreement and turned to Sammie. He asked, "What about the sex toy? What will women think about the fact that she allowed him to insert a dildo in both her anus and her vagina?"

"According to the complaint, he sodomized her, tearing the lining of her anus and her vagina. The girth of the device was so enormous it caused real damage, requiring medical attention. They'll have the testimony of not only the emergency room doctor but also a gynecologist. Physical evidence takes what happened out of the realm of he said, she said."

Morty broke in and took control of the conversation, "She's sued for both negligence and intentional wrongful conduct. She claims that a doctor having sex with his patient is malpractice, below the standard of care, and assault and battery. She blames the company and Peter individually for the negligent hiring of Garcia and failing to supervise him."

Nichols listened to the lawyers banter back and forth. He'd sweated through his shirt, and his head was spinning. He wanted to throw up. He'd always conducted himself at the highest ethical and moral standards, and now he was being sued for failing to supervise that asshole. How could Charlie have the nerve to have sex with patients in the office? Nichols was both angry and anxious.

Sammie kept flipping pages.

Davis continued, "She's even sued the company under the Tennessee Consumer Protection Act for false advertising as to the company's representations of Dr. Garcia's qualifications and ethics. What the hell is the Sexual Misconduct Victims Compensation Act?"

Sammie was the only one familiar with the act because she was in school and constantly learning about changes in the law and new statutes.

"It's a statute passed by the legislature concerning therapists taking sexual advantage of their patients. I would think oral and plastic surgery fall outside the definition of *therapy*."

Davis directed his next statement to Nichols: "We'll need to call your malpractice carrier and put it on notice of the suit. We can't take any real action without its knowledge and approval. Some of these allegations are covered by insurance while others are intentional torts, and I'm sure are excluded from coverage. We can't give his carrier an excuse to deny coverage."

Nichols tried to be optimistic, but Sammie's revelation shook him. "This isn't fair. I've done nothing wrong. It can't be my responsibility to make sure Charlie keeps his pants zipped up."

Sammie was listening sympathetically. She said, "Remember

the night of Charlie's open house? Well, he tried to introduce me to the dildo described in the complaint. When I told him I had no idea where that had been and that he could stick it up his own ass, he got angry. We haven't spoken since the closing, and I didn't say much to him that day. No person in her right mind would let somebody insert that in any orifice voluntarily. He's a sick man."

Nobody said anything. Everyone, including Sammie, was embarrassed.

Davis took a deep breath and said, "Look, Peter, there's no question the company can be held liable for Garcia's alleged wrongful conduct. Garcia was not only an employee of the company; he was a one percent owner. The company promoted him and made representations about his skills as a surgeon. He was an agent of the company. In response to the allegations, the company will assert that he was hired to provide medical services, not perform sex with his patients. When an agent acts outside the scope of his or her authority, it's called an ultra vires act, and the company is not liable. That's our best argument if these allegations are true, but there are no guarantees in the law."

Davis paused to let Nichols digest his concerns and then continued, "These claims by the patient that you are individually liable for Garcia's sex acts are a whole different story. You didn't personally employ him. Your company did. He wasn't your agent. You both worked for the same company. That's all. You have no personal liability. I should be able to get you personally dismissed from the lawsuit on summary judgment."

"What the hell is a summary judgment?"

"The judge, rather than a jury, decides whether under the law you can be held personally liable for Dr. Garcia's alleged sex acts. We need to file that motion early in the case, or we could lose that opportunity. Trust me, Peter, this is what I do. I'm a trial lawyer. My job is to out-strategize the other side. I'm looking out for you, but the law moves slowly. I can't do anything about that, except remain diligent and persistent."

While Davis was explaining the definition of *respondent superior* and their strategy, Sammie was half listening and looking over Nichols's malpractice insurance policy with Tennessee Mutual Insurance Company. After reading half the policy and skimming the other half, consisting of boilerplate language, Sammie informed the others, "The Company, Nichols & Garcia PC, has $5 million in coverage for the year 1996, with unlimited defense costs. Your company, Tennessee Mutual, is a mutual insurance company, owned by you and the other doctors. Usually, most members-owners maintain $3 million in coverage or less and an annual $1 million cap on legal fees and expenses. So this is an excellent policy, with better coverage than most."

"Morty helped me select the carrier and the amount of coverage. I'm glad he advised me," said Nichols. "How do I get Tennessee Mutual to hire your office to defend me in this mess?"

Davis looked at Morty, then Sammie, and then Nichols. "Tennessee Mutual isn't going to retain our firm."

"Why not?" asked Nichols.

Sammie answered the question: "The senior management hate our guts. They'd rather pay the plaintiff than pay us a fee. Tennessee Mutual hasn't forgotten or forgiven us for the Plainview cases."

"Is that when Ben got beat up? I contributed to the reward fund."

Davis didn't like to talk about Plainview, so Sammie answered, "We sued two doctors for performing unnecessary surgeries, and one of them was insured by Tennessee Mutual. It got pretty heated and lasted for years. We tried one and then settled the rest. It ended with bad feelings on both sides. They won't let us represent their insured and pay us."

"What are you talking about? I want you to be my lawyer!"

Nichols was near panic. He'd known Morty his whole life; he'd been by his side since his father was killed. Ben Davis was his lawyer. He needed his guidance and advice about this lawsuit. Damn the insurance company.

Davis could see the pain on Nichols's face and tried to calm him down by saying, "Don't worry, I will be. But you'll have to pay for me personally. You've been sued personally, you've been sued for $10 million, and your coverage is only half of that. I can't accept any money from Tennessee Mutual, or this firm would owe it certain obligations of disclosure and ethical commitment. If you hire and pay us, I'll be able to better maneuver and protect your interest. Tennessee Mutual will at first object to my involvement but will eventually agree because it's one less lawyer the company will have to hire. If you hire us, Tennessee Mutual will have to hire two lawyers: one for the company and another for Dr. Garcia. If the insurance company rejects our involvement, Tennessee Mutual ethically would be required to hire three lawyers: one for you, one for the company, and one for Dr. Garcia. There is a clear conflict among the three defendants. They select from its pool of defense firms to represent its shareholders/insureds. I'll work with whoever it selects. As much as I'd rather not, let's call Tennessee Mutual."

Davis gave Nichols the number, which was answered on the first ring. Davis told Nichols to ask for Larry Pinsly. He was connected almost immediately.

"Mr. Pinsly, my name is Dr. Peter Nichols. I'm one of your insureds."

"What can I do for you, Dr. Nichols?"

"I'm with my attorney, Ben Davis. I'll let him explain."

Davis took a deep breath. The last time he saw Pinsly they were in federal court, and Judge Wise had just chastised Pinsly's lawyer for unethical and possibly criminal conduct.

"Hello, Larry, I've got you on speakerphone, so my associates and Dr. Nichols can hear us. Dr. Nichols was served today with quite an unusual complaint, and he's giving you notice of the suit."

Davis spent the next twenty minutes telling Pinsly the nature of Dr. Nichols's relationship with Dr. Garcia, the pending breach of contract suit, and the substance of the lawsuit filed by Ms. Perkins.

Pinsly asked several questions and then said, "Thanks for looking out for our insured. We'll take over from here. I'll call Sean McCoy, and he'll get right on this."

Davis immediately responded, "Dr. Nichols has asked me to stay on as his personal attorney. He's been sued for $10 million, and there's only $5 million in coverage. He needs separate representation from that of his company and Dr. Garcia. My firm will be exclusively protecting Dr. Nichols's interest. As you know, the lawyers you hire will be protecting conflicting interests, those of the company and those of Dr. Garcia. I'd prefer not to work with Sean McCoy. You know our history together. I'm sure we can agree on another firm that's approved by your company."

The tone of Pinsly's voice was anything but friendly: "Look, Davis, you're not going to tell me who to hire to defend this action!"

"I'm not telling you *who* to hire. I'm simply asking you *not* to hire McCoy's firm. I don't like or trust him. Larry, you're stuck with me. We're on the same side of this one. Let's put our history and differences behind us, and then work together for the benefit of our common client. I'll fax over the complaint. Let me know which two lawyers you want to hire. I'll be reasonable. Try to do the same."

Pinsly didn't directly reply. He said good-bye to Dr. Nichols only.

As soon as Pinsly hung up, Nichols, who was obviously surprised by the tone of the conversation, questioned Davis, "Pinsly really doesn't like you, does he?"

"Let me assure you, the feeling is mutual."

"What's the story?"

"It's too long to tell. Someday, I'll write a book about it."

CHAPTER TWENTY-ONE

TELLING THE STAFF
Friday, July 5, 1996

It would be a busy day. Dr. Nichols had a full schedule, and the day began with Sammie showing up at the office on Davis's orders to pick up the Perkins chart and to attend a staff meeting. Nichols knew she was there to observe and report the staff's reaction to the news of the lawsuit. Nichols understood he needed the support of his staff through these difficult times. They'd figured that the presence of the beautiful young Sammie would be less of an intimidating effect than that of Davis or Morty. She was there to answer any questions that Nichols found either uncomfortable or too difficult to answer.

As agreed, Sammie stood in the back of the conference room, trying to blend into the walls. Nichols stood at the front with Donna faithfully at his side. Sammie told Nichols to remain calm and to speak in an even tone.

It wasn't easy, but he began the explanation: "I'm sure most of you have heard about the sensational lawsuit that has been filed concerning the alleged conduct of Dr. Garcia. Let's face it. This is a small office, and news, both good and bad, travels fast. But rumors are dangerous, so I want to set the record straight. The practice and

I are named in that lawsuit because Dr. Garcia was an employee of the company at the time. The lawsuit is a matter of public record, and therefore there will be publicity. I'm assured by our lawyers that not only will a summary of the lawsuit make the papers, but we can expect local TV news coverage as well."

Nichols paused to collect himself. It was harder than he thought to face his staff and discuss the lawsuit.

"These are allegations. Nothing has been proven, and I'm told that the burden is on the person making the claims to prove them. I was shocked by these accusations and have always expected employees to conduct themselves with the highest degree of ethics and professionalism. I have done nothing wrong, yet I am saddened that I will have to defend the company and myself.

"It is critical we work together to minimize the impact of this lawsuit on the practice we've built together. I need your help and cooperation. You may be asked about the lawsuit by patients. If so, your response must be, 'I'm not permitted to discuss the matter, but I assure you that it is this practice's policy to uphold the ethics of our profession.' If they persist, direct them to either Donna or me. If a member of the news media calls you at home or follows you from the office, your response must be, 'I have no comment.' Take the person's name and the news outlet and give the information to Donna or me. I hope you all know how much I appreciate your loyalty and support. I have done nothing wrong. We all need to take solace in that fact and stick together through this difficult situation."

Nichols was exhausted. His mouth was dry as could be. He desperately needed a drink of water or something stronger, but it wasn't even eight. He wasn't used to giving speeches, and he didn't like controversy since the murder of his father.

"How'd I do?" he asked Sammie.

"You were great, poised and confident. I just hope you don't have to give the speech again."

"What the hell does that mean?"

"Well, we don't know if Charlie Garcia kept his hands to himself. Anna Perkins may not be an isolated incident. The man's a pig."

Sammie's words really bothered Nichols. Maybe because he suspected she was right. He was so worried that right in front of her, he picked up the phone and called Davis. He explained his concerns about other possible victims.

After a slight pause Davis gave his opinion, "You'll see other lawsuits. Unfortunately you're going to have a target on your back. Peter, some of these suits will have merit while opportunists trying to take advantage of the situation will file others. They'll contact Jack Willis because he brought the Perkins lawsuit. The key is to get to Willis, settle fast, tie him down with a confidentiality agreement, and hope for no more press. If the case continues, drags out, and draws more coverage, the other cases are likely to surface. You need to communicate with Garcia's counsel quickly before the insurance companies get involved and screw it up. You also need to settle your breach of contract lawsuit against him. You're co-defendants in the Perkins lawsuit. It's not good form to be suing each other when you're being sued together."

Sammie had been listening on the speakerphone, and she volunteered, "Why don't I fax the Perkins complaint over to Harrelson, and we'll all give him a call?"

Courtesy of Bella, an hour later Sammie, Nichols, Davis, and Morty had Harrelson on the line.

Davis took the lead: "Good morning, Mr. Harrelson. I've got my team on the line. As you can see, we've got a problem."

"Who is Dr. Garcia's carrier? I assume it's the same carrier as your client. How much coverage do we have? Have they assigned my client a lawyer yet? Has the media got hold of this story?"

Nichols found Harrelson's shotgun blast of questions almost amusing. The lawyer was panicked.

"Boy, you've got a lot of questions," Davis observed. "It seems your client needs my help after all, doesn't he?"

"Don't try to get smart with me, Davis. Your client, Nichols, is in the same hot water as my client. Don't forget that they're co-defendants, and they'll need to put up a common defense."

"I don't think so. All they've alleged is that the company negligently advertised the skills and the ethics of your client and did a negligent background check when hiring him. All of the claims against my clients are based in negligence. On the other hand, your client has been charged with intentional torts, the most serious ethical violations a doctor can commit, and he's exposed to several possible criminal prosecutions. David, you're overplaying your hand. Nichols isn't in the same boat as Garcia, and he has no intention of getting in that sinking boat with him."

Despite the fact that their conversation was not face-to-face, Nichols could tell that Harrelson was hot. It was obvious to Nichols that Davis was provoking him and was getting to him. It was equally obvious that Davis was enjoying himself in the process.

Harrelson responded loudly, "Do I really have to teach you the law? Respondent superior, Nichols & Garcia, is liable for the acts of its agent and employee, Dr. Garcia."

Davis was prepared. "I've got *Black's Law Dictionary* open to the page that defines that term: 'Let the master answer for the acts of his servant.' It goes on to state that the master is liable only if the servant is acting within the scope of his duties and not on the side. We didn't hire Dr. Garcia to have sex with his patients. I think it's fair to say that using a ten-inch dildo is outside the scope of employment."

"We'll have to agree to disagree."

Nichols thought Davis got the best of Harrelson in that exchange.

Davis plowed forward. "If you really want to work together, we need to address our pending lawsuit."

"What about it?"

"It might be easier for us to work together if Dr. Garcia's parents met their obligation and paid Dr. Nichols back under the guarantee."

"That's not going to happen. We've got good defenses, and we can drag that case out for years."

Now it was Davis's turn to be annoyed. "You think so? Your answer is due tomorrow. I'll be filing a motion for default judgment the next day. So, unless you can get licensed in Tennessee in the next week or so, you'll have to hire a Tennessee attorney. I'll withdraw my motion once your answer is filed. I'll then move to take the depositions of Señor and Mrs. Garcia and their little boy, Charlie, as quickly as possible. You'll be able to delay a month or two, but I'll get my depositions. Within four months, not years, I'll file a motion for summary judgment. Since neither the facts nor the law supports your defenses, the court will throw them out and award me a judgment against all your clients for $400,000 and my attorney fees and costs. Let me assure you, Mr. Harrelson, I'm within a month or two of acquiring the money deposited by Goldman Sachs with the court."

Harrelson snarled, "You're dreaming, Davis. I'll let you know the name of my Tennessee co-counsel by close of business Monday."

Davis was obligated to provide Harrelson the contact information of Dr. Garcia's malpractice insurance carrier so that Harrelson could contact Larry Pinsly of Tennessee Mutual about the defense in the Perkins case. With the exchange of that information, the heated conversation ended.

Nichols was unnerved by how the call went. He said good-bye to Morty and Davis, and Sammie gave him a hug. The hug felt good.

Sammie rubbed his back and whispered, "This is going to be a long, hard fight. Morty, my uncle, and I are in your corner. You need to accept the fact this isn't going to remain quiet. The news will eat this story up. Morty can minimize coverage because he knows the editor of the newspaper and the news directors of all three local TV stations."

Sammie called it right. That evening all three local stations ran the lawsuit as the third story, and the *Tennessean* ran the lawsuit on the front page of the business section. In each account Nichols & Garcia was identified as a defendant and Garcia's employer. No coverage mentioned Dr. Peter Nichols as a defendant, courtesy of Morty. At least that was something, but not much.

CHAPTER TWENTY-TWO

THE MESS GETS WORSE

Monday, July 8, 1996

D avis decided it was time to call Jack Willis, Anna Perkins's attorney. Willis was a smooth-talking southern boy who could convince a jury the sky wasn't blue on a clear sunny day. Juries identified with him. He was short and maintained a long mane of gray hair. He constantly ran his hands through it to regain control when it was disheveled. Davis knew, despite grooming problems, Jack Willis was up to the job.

Before he made the call, he ate two chocolate-covered doughnuts. It calmed his nerves. He looked up the number in the attorneys' directory and dialed. Willis answered his own phone.

"Jack Willis here. Can I help you?"

Davis got right to the point. He represented Dr. Peter Nichols and had nothing but disdain for the alleged conduct of Dr. Garcia. Willis assured him that he could prove his client's accusations against Garcia.

Willis, a smart lawyer, knew about the dispute between Nichols and Garcia, and he decided to test Davis. "Ben, we're not as adverse as it appears on paper. Maybe we can help each other. I'll tell you something you don't know, and you tell me something I don't know."

Davis replied, "That might work. Seems fair as long as it doesn't violate a client confidence."

"I'd never ask you to do that, Ben."

"You go first."

"Your clients are about to be served with another lawsuit because of the sexual misconduct of Charlie Garcia and for medical malpractice. The Christy Howard lawsuit has one significant difference from that of the Perkins suit; this patient did drugs with Garcia, which may explain why she let him sexually abuse her."

Davis decided he'd better get as much information as possible while Willis was being so candid.

"What kind of drugs did they do?"

"They did Ecstasy. He's a sick guy. It's a shame your client hired and promoted him to Nashville. I did my research on your client. He has a good reputation and a clean record, but he's responsible for at least any acts of negligence, maybe more, depending on the facts."

"Come on, Jack, Nichols has no personal liability. If Garcia's wrongful conduct falls on anyone, it's the company, not Nichols individually. Tell me about the malpractice aspect of the lawsuit."

Willis in a very organized and articulate way explained the Howard lawsuit. He described in detail how Howard's lower Garcia kissable lip turned necrotic. He'd already retained a plastic surgeon to testify that Garcia breached the standard of care.

"What do you want?" Davis asked.

"A little cooperation and quick settlements. Let's start by your telling me the dollar amount of malpractice insurance your clients and Dr. Garcia have and with whom."

"You know that the dollar amount of coverage is confidential and not discoverable, but I can't help it if you guess." Davis smiled, knowing that Willis couldn't see him on the other end of the line.

After two guesses, he coughed when Willis said $5 million, and Davis volunteered that Tennessee Mutual provided coverage. It was agreed that Davis's loyalty and fiduciary duties were to Dr. Nichols, not Garcia and definitely not Tennessee Mutual. Davis hoped that a quick and quiet settlement could be negotiated with Willis.

The allegations of the Howard complaint included many of the same ethical and tortious claims asserted in the Perkins case, but it also included a traditional malpractice element. Willis included a picture of Ms. Howard's necrotic Garcia kissable lips. The lower one had turned black and a deep purple, and there was dried pus in the corners of her mouth.

Davis knew that the Perkins case would be defended differently than the Howard case because it was a straight sexual misconduct case. In Howard, Willis would have to prove that there was a breach of the standard of care, that Dr. Garcia provided negligent medical care, and that such care proximately caused damage. There was no question that Ms. Howard's lower lip became necrotic, but Willis had to prove the problem was caused by Garcia. He'd need expert testimony to prove negligence. That surgeon would have to agree to testify against Dr. Garcia, and that might be difficult since Tennessee Mutual insured about eighty percent of the doctors licensed to practice in the state. On the other hand, Tennessee Mutual would have no problem finding and retaining medical expert witnesses. These physicians would be insured and shareholders of Tennessee Mutual. They'd have no problem protecting their company and testifying that Dr. Garcia didn't breach the standard of care. Willis would hire his own out-of-state medical experts, who would testify that Dr. Garcia did breach the standard of care. The Howard lawsuit would become the war of experts, while the Perkins case would focus only on Dr. Garcia's sexual misconduct.

In the Howard complaint the sexual allegations were even more graphic than in the Perkins lawsuit. Willis described the ten-inch sexual device in particular detail: black in color with deep purple bulging veins, divided into three ribbed sections. The Howard complaint alleged that Ms. Howard required vaginal reconstructive surgery as a direct and proximate result of its use.

The Howard complaint alleged that at first, like in the Perkins case, the plaintiff was impressed and flattered by Dr. Garcia's sexual overtures. There were dinners, dancing, and consensual sex, including at Howard's condo. According to the Howard complaint, Dr. Garcia changed once he introduced the dildo into their relationship. He became physically and verbally abusive. The complaint claimed that at first the plaintiff thought that they were engaged in some type of role-playing game, but as that evening went forward, Dr. Garcia forced the plaintiff to do things that would psychologically mar her for the rest of her life. It alleged that Dr. Garcia, because of the relationship of doctor-patient, had some sort of power over Ms. Howard, like Svengali. The plaintiff alleged that she was currently under psychiatric care twice a week.

There were now two women claiming they had sex with Dr. Garcia in Dr. Nichols's office. Davis wondered, *How was that possible? Where was the staff? Why would these women subject themselves to be treated in such a humiliating fashion? How could voluntary lovemaking change so quickly? Why would these women allow themselves to be abused by Dr. Garcia?* These were all good questions, and Davis intended to get to the bottom of them. He decided he'd let Sammie interview the staff—all women. They were more likely to open up to Sammie than to Morty or him.

Davis thanked Willis for the information, promised him they'd talk in the next few days, and agreed that a quick settlement might be in everyone's best interest. In return Willis agreed to hold off filing and, more important, agreed not to give any interviews or make any comments about the Perkins case. Davis hoped that without any further information from Willis the news coverage of the lawsuit would end.

Davis was only partially right. There was no TV coverage, and only a brief follow-up article appeared in the newspaper. Morty swore he'd get even at his next poker game with its editor.

CHAPTER TWENTY-THREE

SPANISH INQUISITION
Wednesday, July 10, 1996

Davis changed his mind; he wasn't willing to simply rely on Sammie's notes or recount of the meetings. He needed to hear the tone of each woman's voice and observe her body language. He'd let Sammie handle the interviews, but he decided to be present.

She started with the new receptionist and asked about her duties. They were the same as those of Robyn Eden. She'd never met either Perkins or Howard so her interview was short and sweet. Sammie worked her way up to Donna, the office manager.

All of the staff, except Donna, found Dr. Garcia charming and were shocked when he left. They were even more shocked by the allegations of the lawsuits. Even though Dr. Nichols had warned his staff not to discuss the lawsuits, they talked about nothing else. That was human nature. None of the staff ever saw Dr. Garcia act inappropriately with any patient. According to the staff, he always acted professionally. A few commented that it was obvious that Dr. Garcia and Donna didn't get along, but they all felt that Donna, who was used to running the office, was threatened by Dr. Garcia.

By the time Sammie got to Donna, it had been a long day, and most of the answers from the Nichols staff had been identical and unhelpful. Davis, who knew Donna pretty well, could tell immediately that she had more information than the others. That was not surprising since Donna had been involved in the storage closet videotaping and ran the office. Her body language showed him that there was a serious problem; her arms were crossed, and her brow was furrowed. Davis, an exceptional trial attorney, knew how to read people.

Davis took over the questioning of Donna and told her, "Relax, we're on the same side. Just tell me what you know about any sexual misconduct by Dr. Garcia. You'll feel better getting it off your chest."

"At the Christmas party, Dr. Garcia and Robyn Eden came out of the copier room together, and I don't think they were making copies. He looked real suspicious, and I stared them down . . ."

Davis cut her off. "Donna, before every deposition, I tell the witness to tell the truth but not to guess. I also explain that a guess is as bad as a lie because that uncertain answer can be used against you. The door to the copier room was closed. You don't know what went on in there. The only two people who know what happened in the copier room are Robyn and Dr. Garcia. There's no reason for you to speculate."

Donna nodded, and Davis hoped that there would be no further discussion about speculated misconduct. He certainly hoped that Donna wasn't asked a direct question under oath about the Christmas party or about Dr. Garcia and Robyn. Sammie's notes of their meeting with Donna, although protected by the attorney work product privilege, did not contain any reference to the copier room.

Davis then asked the million-dollar question: "What about patients? Did you ever see any evidence that he fooled around with patients in the office?"

"Never, but the treatment room doors were always closed, and they are well insulated for privacy."

Davis liked the first part of that answer but not the second part.

"Do you remember anything unusual about either Ms. Perkins or Ms. Howard?"

"No, both women were in their mid-thirties, attractive but aging. They each purchased multiple procedures. No indication outside the treatment room of hanky-panky."

"We need to change the office policy," Davis said. "I don't want any treatment of patients without another staff member in the room. Consults can remain private."

"What about Dr. Dowdle? Does she need another female in the room?"

"For consistency we'd better maintain the same policy for both doctors."

Davis figured he learned what he could from Donna, but he ended the interview with a common question he asked of witnesses: "Donna, is there any question I haven't covered that you think I should have asked?"

"I didn't like Charlie Garcia. I knew there was something wrong about him, but I couldn't put my finger on it. Obviously I was right, but he had everyone else snowed."

Sammie, who had been quiet, chimed in, "Not everybody!"

Glancing at his niece, Davis ignored her comment. There was nothing to be gained by exploring it. She wasn't going to be a witness in the case.

Davis called both Harrelson and Pinsly about the Howard lawsuit. They claimed to be shocked, but Davis suspected that Harrelson knew better. Based upon the allegations of the Perkins lawsuit, no one should have been surprised by Dr. Garcia's conduct. Pinsly was now in a real fix. Tennessee Mutual, under Dr. Nichols's malpractice insurance policy, would be required, now that there were two lawsuits, to pay out more legal fees, and Tennessee Mutual was exposed to two potential judgments.

Pinsly was concerned about how many more lawsuits were out there. He'd begrudgingly accepted that Davis would represent Dr. Nichols, at Nichols's expense, and that his company would hire separate counsel for the corporation and Dr. Garcia. He suggested Bob Sullivan for the corporation and Lester Paul for Garcia. Davis liked Sullivan and respected him. They could work together. That was important since Nichols owned ninety-nine percent of the corporation, and Sullivan would be representing the company. Lester Paul was another story; he was a typical arrogant member of the defense Bar. They were both qualified, with substantial trial experience, so Davis decided it wasn't worth fighting with Pinsly over his choices.

Davis faxed the Howard complaint to Harrelson, Pinsly, Sullivan, and Paul. He waited two hours and then called Paul.

"Hello, Lester. It looks like you've pulled the tough defendant in these cases."

Paul, a short bald man about sixty-five, mistook Davis's comment as criticism and fired back: "Look, Ben, don't try to turn on my client. If my boy goes down, so does yours."

Paul was quick tempered, and he disliked Davis because Davis was 6 and 0 against him. Constantly losing had a way of affecting one's judgment. For that reason the conversation was off to a rocky start. Davis wasn't going to let Paul implicate his client. "All the complaints allege as to the company is that your client was falsely advertised and promoted. That's Sullivan's client, not mine. Dr. Nichols hasn't even been accused of doing anything wrong by these women."

"I spoke to Harrelson and the parents. Why don't you drop your contract lawsuit? That litigation is only going to hurt us and give Willis an advantage in his cases."

"I don't think so. Why don't you have Mom and Dad just pony up and release the funds held by the court?"

"You'll have to litigate to get those funds, and it may take you a while to get them. I've been retained to represent Dr. Garcia and his parents," Paul informed Davis.

"Don't hold your breath, Lester. FYI, Willis let me accept service in the Howard case for Dr. Nichols and the corporation. You might want to accept service for Dr. Garcia."

"Why would I do that? It just makes Willis's job easier. What are you doing talking to Willis anyway? He's the enemy."

Paul was just being himself. He couldn't help it. He was predictably uncooperative.

Davis decided he'd see just how far he could push him. "You know, Lester, both of these lawsuits raise serious ethical concerns. The Medical Licensing Board frowns on a doctor having sex with his patients. Someone has to report this to the board. It would be far better for your client if he did rather than someone else."

"I don't think that's necessary."

"It sure is. I'm sure you'd prefer not to, but someone has to. I'll give you forty-eight hours to self-report, or either I on behalf of Dr. Nichols or Sullivan on behalf of the corporation will report your client and provide the board with copies of the two complaints."

"That's not going to help either of our clients."

"You're probably right, but neither will the press if Willis files the Howard complaint. We've got to stop that from happening. The only way to prevent that is to settle. Tennessee Mutual has to do the responsible thing and settle these cases. Your client deserves all the bad press he gets. My client's only mistake was hiring your son-of-a-bitch client."

"I'll talk to Pinsly."

Davis wasn't going to hold his breath. Paul was greedy and arrogant. He didn't care that Nichols spent more than twenty years to build his practice and reputation, and because of Garcia's libido, all that hard work was about to come crashing down.

After they hung up, Davis faxed Paul a confirming letter giving him the forty-eight hours and copied Sullivan. At the close of the business day he called Sullivan. They were on the same page. Sullivan represented the company, which was owned ninety-nine percent by Nichols. Sullivan and Davis would work together to protect Dr. Nichols's interest.

Sullivan was a few years older than Davis. He had a red full beard with flakes of gray in his moustache and a full head of red hair. When he was nervous, he took out his black comb and groomed his beard. During their dealings, Davis found it an annoying habit, but Davis still liked and respected him. Lester Paul was a whole other story.

CHAPTER TWENTY-FOUR

STRANGE BEDFELLOWS
Monday, July 22, 1996

As Davis promised, he filed a motion for default judgment against the Garcias in the breach of contract case. The Garcias, under the Tennessee Rules of Civil Procedure, had to file an answer to the complaint within thirty days of receipt of the complaint. Davis mailed Dr. Garcia and his parents their copy of the complaint by certified mail, return receipt requested. The green cards evidenced delivery to Charlie on June 18th and to his parents on June 19th.

An answer is a responsive pleading that admits, denies, or claims there is insufficient information to either admit or deny a specific allegation of the complaint. Thirty days passed; none of the defendants filed an answer.

By suing not only Charlie Garcia but also Nichols and the practice, Jack Willis created quite a conflict for Tennessee Mutual. All of the liability derived from Garcia's wrongful conduct, sexual in the Perkins case, but professional and sexual in the Howard case. Davis wasn't worried about the professional negligence aspect of the Howard case. Her necrotic lip was a simple malpractice action, and insurance would cover it. Davis was worried about the sexual allegations of both cases. Garcia would argue it was voluntary, but

Nichols didn't want to join that argument or try to explain Garcia's conduct at all. This was a major conflict, and that was why each defendant retained separate counsel.

Davis was pleased to be working on the same side as Bob Sullivan. He could not say the same about Lester Paul, Garcia's counsel, who was a typical defense lawyer with very little imagination. He had poor eyesight and wore glasses with very thick lenses that exaggerated the expressions of his eyes, sometimes giving him a bizarre look. His physical shortcomings aside, Davis didn't trust him; they'd butted heads several times. Morty thought Paul was a weasel.

Davis's loyalty was clear in the sex cases. He represented Dr. Peter Nichols, who'd been sued individually. He'd be the easiest defendant to represent. He did nothing wrong, and Nichols wasn't Garcia's employer. Sullivan's client, the company, was.

Bella buzzed in. "I've got Lester Paul on line one."

"Good morning, Lester. What can I do for you?" Davis asked.

"In the contract dispute as local counsel with Mr. Harrelson, I need a thirty-day extension so I can familiarize myself with the case and the documents."

"That's bullshit, Lester. Harrelson's your co-counsel, and he's staying in the case. He already knows the facts and the documents. He created them. Second, Harrelson has already shared with me his absurd defenses. They'll be struck down on summary judgment. Sorry, no extension. My motion for default is scheduled to be heard in thirteen days. If you file your answers before the date of the hearing, I'll strike my motion."

"Steine taught you better than that. I'm asking for common courtesy."

Paul was actually right. Morty did teach Davis professional courtesy, but he also taught him not to be pushed around and delayed by the other lawyer's tactics. It was a thin line, and a good lawyer learned to walk it through experience and good judgment.

"I'd talk to Harrelson. I'm sure you boys can whip up an answer in thirteen days. It only took God six days to create the heaven and the earth. In light of your client's conduct and the fact my poor client has been named a defendant in two lawsuits and has been forced to file a third to collect his money owed, I think *you* should be extending the professional courtesy."

"I don't owe Peter Nichols anything. His insurance company hired me to represent Dr. Garcia in the Willis lawsuits. My obligations are to Dr. Garcia."

"You may be right, Lester, and like you, I owe nothing to the Garcias. It's not in Dr. Nichols's best interest to delay. His money is sitting with the court. I'd like to schedule the depositions of your clients as soon as possible."

"My clients live in New York."

"Those are your paying clients. Dr. Garcia lives right here in Nashville. To expedite these depositions, I'll travel to New York, even though I could compel your paying clients to come to Nashville."

Davis was trying to provoke Paul. He just didn't like him. Davis was determined to push the breach of contract case forward toward summary judgment.

"I'll let you know about our availability."

Within fifteen minutes, Davis had faxed Paul a letter offering to take Dr. Garcia's deposition at Paul's office on August 7th, 8th, or 9th. He also offered to take the parents' deposition at Harrelson's office in New York, New York, on August 16th or 17th.

About two o'clock Sammie walked into Davis's office. "We've got a problem."

"What else is new? We're practicing law. All we do is handle other people's problems. Look at the bright side. At least they're other people's problems, and we're well paid to worry about them and resolve them."

"Very funny. I'm not there yet. I still have a full year of classes and the Bar to take. But for now, Peter Nichols called. Garcia is advertising Garcia kissable lips."

"I can't believe the little putz has the nerve to advertise with these lawsuits pending. I'll write Paul and Harrelson a letter threatening to get an injunction if their client doesn't cease and desist from using the trademark, Garcia kissable lips."

Legally, Nichols & Garcia owned the name. Charlie Garcia didn't have the right to use it. As Davis was dictating the letter, Bella walked into his office and brought him a fax from Jack Willis. The letter suggested that Davis schedule a meeting between Willis and defense counsel to discuss the cases and see if a settlement could be reached before there was any undue publicity. Davis asked Bella to set up a conference call with Paul, Sullivan, and Pinsly.

At four, Bella had everyone on the line. Davis never could have accomplished a four-way call by himself. Bella was invaluable in so many ways. Davis knew this but should have told Bella more often. Like Morty, she helped professionally raise him, and he appreciated her effort. He still should have told her; it was the right thing to do.

"Gentlemen, I have you on speaker so that my associate can hear our conversation. I faxed to you Jack Willis's letter . . ."

"It's blackmail, plain and simple," Paul blurted out.

Davis didn't like the fact that Paul interrupted him.

Pinsly then spoke up, "Lester's right. Willis wants a big payday without doing any work. File lawsuits and get paid. That's a pretty good deal."

Davis thought he'd better take control. "Larry, this guy's capable of doing the work and destroying Dr. Nichols's practice, even though Nichols didn't do anything wrong. Why litigate for a year, spend a lot in lawyer fees and costs, and then settle? You can use the money Tennessee Mutual was going to pay Paul and Sullivan to settle the case. And let's not forget the bad press. If we don't settle now, Dr. Garcia will be crucified, and association will damage my client. Willis will make it a nightmare, and my client did nothing wrong."

Sullivan jumped in. "I'm all for making a fee, but Ben's right. My job is to protect the practice, and bad publicity won't help the practice. What do we have to lose by listening to Willis? I've dealt with him before. He's reasonable and capable. Do we really want to try a lawsuit and have Willis mark as an exhibit a ten-inch dildo?"

Davis thought Sullivan's last remark was funny. Paul and Pinsly didn't think so. They all agreed to think about it and let Willis stew a day or two.

After they hung up, Paul called Davis back. "I was thinking, Ben, I might be more inclined to agree to meet with Willis if you dropped your breach of contract lawsuit and release the funds to my clients."

"Go to hell, Lester. Now who's the blackmailer?" Davis slammed the phone down.

Davis had a temper and tried to control it. He didn't always succeed, though. If Morty knew what he had just done, he would have scolded Davis for losing it. *Talk about blackmail. Look who's calling the kettle black,* Davis thought and started dictating a letter in an unrelated matter.

CHAPTER TWENTY-FIVE

CHECKERED PAST

Wednesday, July 31, 1996

Paul convinced Pinsly to let Willis's deadline expire with no response. Two days later Davis wrote Tennessee Mutual a bad faith letter to protect Dr. Nichols:

> Dear Mr. Pinsly,
>
> I am writing on behalf of my client, Dr. Peter Nichols, your insured and shareholder, to whom your company owes a fiduciary duty. Your refusal to meet with Jack Willis to discuss the possibility of settlement is a breach of that duty and constitutes bad faith. As you will recall I strongly urged you to attend the proposed meeting. It is my understanding based upon our telephone conversation of July 22nd that your decision was based upon the advice of Mr. Lester Paul.
>
> Dr. Nichols has been sued for more than his policy limits. He has personal exposure. Tennessee Mutual has an obligation to determine whether these

cases can be settled within those policy limits. Your failure to open communications with Mr. Willis is clear breach of your company's duty and constitutes bad faith. As a result of this bad faith, please be advised that Tennessee Mutual shall be liable for any judgments awarded in those cases in excess of the $5 million policy limits. Further, please be advised that Dr. Nichols shall seek recovery of his attorney fees paid to my office and other costs incurred after your refusal to meet with Mr. Willis.

It is important to note that Mr. Paul, whom you selected to represent Dr. Garcia, does not have Dr. Nichols's best interest in mind. As you know, Dr. Nichols's alleged liability is based solely on the alleged wrongful conduct of Dr. Garcia. Further, Mr. Paul is representing Dr. Garcia and his parents in a breach of contract suit brought by Dr. Nichols. I would think that these factors would discount any advice provided by Mr. Paul. He is unconcerned as to the risk you might expose Dr. Nichols, and his practice will suffer as a result of no effort to settle these cases.

My client's position is clear. These cases should be settled promptly to avoid adverse publicity.

Benjamin A. Davis

A copy was faxed to Lester Paul, Bob Sullivan, and Dr. Nichols. Fifteen minutes later Sullivan called in part to support Davis but even more to rib him. Sullivan particularly liked the part about discounting any advice from Paul. He was stroking his red beard as he read the letter.

He also called to report important news. His private eye had completed the background checks, and the reports were incredible. He started with Garcia. As a freshman at Princeton, age sixteen, he was arrested and pled no contest to possession of a DUI, driving under the influence. Because he was a minor, the file was sealed and later expunged.

"If it was expunged, should McCormick have found it?"

"My guy did."

Sullivan then went on to tell Davis that another student at Princeton, Sarah Thomas, charged Garcia in his senior year with sexual battery.

"His weapon of choice was a large dildo. A report of the Princeton campus police is attached, but the charges were never pursued. I'd bet Mommy and Daddy bought Ms. Thomas off rather than have their brilliant son's life ruined by a scandal."

"A Princeton campus police report, should McCormick have found that?"

"My guy did."

Davis and Sullivan discussed whether to notify McCormick of his exposure. They agreed that disclosure, prior to filing the cross claim by Nichols & Garcia against McCormick, wouldn't be helpful. They also agreed that nothing would be gained; he would deny liability anyway. Sullivan said he would prepare the cross complaint to bring McCormick into both lawsuits.

Then Sullivan asked, "Should we tell Paul? I feel like I owe him a heads-up of his client's prior record before he reads about it in a legal document."

"Send us both copies of the full report with the attachment, just in case Paul convinces Pinsly to try to force you to sit on the evidence. If he does, then I already have a copy. In fact you should send it to Pinsly and just copy Paul and me on the letter."

"You're a devious son of a bitch, Ben."

"Yeah, but those boys deserve it."

Sullivan asked Davis if he could stand more good news. After Davis assured him that he could, Sullivan dropped the bombshell, "Christy Howard is no innocent."

Sullivan's PI discovered a website with very provocative pictures of Ms. Howard. "The title of the website is wwwplaychristyforme." The photos included Moore with other women, using large dildos.

Sullivan described the pictures in detail. He was giggling a little as he did. He choked out, "They're attached to the PI's report. I guess I should send those to Paul and Pinsly as well?"

"Send it all to them. Do you think Willis knows about the photos?"

"No way his client told him, and he isn't looking too hard for dirt on his client."

Davis thought about it for a second and then responded, "Willis is smart. Any good lawyer knows his plaintiff isn't perfect. Everybody's got a skeleton or two in the closet. He's looking, but he probably just didn't find it. Tell your man, good work."

"Howard's got more than a few. These pictures are pornographic. I had to look at them four times before I called you, and I bet you look at them at least four times."

"I'm a thorough attorney. If I need to look at them four times, then I will suffer through the task."

Both men laughed. The discovery of naked pictures of a plaintiff that were admissible into evidence was a defense lawyer's dream.

Sullivan suggested, "We might even get them blown up to poster size."

Sullivan was only half kidding, but Davis thought it was a great idea. The two men hung up after exchanging their good-byes.

It had been a good day. Both Garcia and Howard could be discredited. Based on the PI's report, McCormick was at least comparatively at fault for the hire of Garcia.

Davis turned his attention to the mail. He opened a letter from Paul's law firm. He read:

> Dear Ben,
>
> Our clients are co-defendants in two lawsuits and are about to spend the next two years fighting over the breach of contract lawsuit you filed. Your lawsuit will only provide ammunition to Willis in his suits. I propose we settle the breach of contract lawsuit by splitting fifty/fifty the funds held by Goldman Sachs, $200,000 for each side. This offer expires on August 2 at 5:00 p.m.
>
> Yours very truly,
>
> Lester Paul

Davis leaned back in his desk chair and put his hands behind his head. He liked the fact that Paul made an offer, but the dollar amount wasn't acceptable. He needed to call Nichols and advise him of the offer and make a recommendation. He knew the defenses raised by the parents were red herrings. The Garcias had adequate representation, and although there were no other MD/DDS practices in the state, it certainly didn't violate the Stark Act.

Donna got Nichols out of a treatment room to take Davis's call. Nichols told him, "I trust you. Use your best judgment. I agree we need to settle the case and focus on the two Willis cases. We need those settled too."

Davis agreed that getting rid of the breach of contract case increased the possibility of settling the Willis cases. He promised to maximize the settlement amount. He hung up and picked the phone right back up to call Lester Paul.

"Hi, Lester, got your letter. Thought it might be in our clients' best interest to talk settlement."

"You've got my offer. What's your response?"

"The contract calls for transfer of the $400,000 to my client. That's my offer. Dr. Nichols will eat my fees, which are recoverable under the contract."

Davis was trying to needle Paul, and it was working.

"You're out of your mind. That contract you drafted won't hold up. It's very unfair to the parents."

"Unfair? Who's out of his mind? A contract doesn't have to be fair to be enforceable. The parents were over eighteen; they were represented by counsel; and in light of their son's history, they were in a far better position to assume the risk of their son's performance than my client. The kid quit, Lester, rather than take a drug test he would have failed. In addition, I'm going to amend the suit and allege that his conduct with Perkins and Howard violated the moral clause of his employment contract not to discredit the practice. Willis will love that, won't he?"

Paul took an unfiltered Camel out of the pack and lit it.

Davis was making a hollow threat. Such a move would damage both Garcia and Nichols. The threat worked, though.

"Ben, you've got to give me something. I've got to have something to take back to the parents."

Davis remained silent for a moment, pretending to be deep in thought.

"Tell you what, Lester. I'll give you something. I'll deduct from the $400,000 your fees and Harrelson's fees, and the balance will then be paid to my client."

It was Paul's turn to be quiet. Davis took that as a good sign.

"Okay, I'll draw up the paperwork."

"Nah, since your fees are being paid by my client, I'd rather draft the documents. I'll have a draft to both you and Harrelson by tomorrow. Get me an itemized bill for the two of you. And, Lester, be reasonable or the deal's off."

The bill submitted by Harrelson was $14,000, and the bill from Paul was $6,000. Davis's fees were $5,000, but his office had to draft the complaint. The bills were padded, but Davis figured his client got $375,000 and ended the lawsuit. It was a good deal.

CHAPTER TWENTY-SIX

PROBLEMS NEVER STOP

Monday, December 2, 1996

C harlie, at his parents' insistence, tried to put his lawsuit with Dr. Nichols behind him and focus on his new practice. His new office was eleven miles from the office of Dr. Nichols. The contract required that he couldn't practice within a ten-mile radius of the office. The settlement agreement reinforced this point and also prevented him from soliciting patients or employees of Dr. Nichols. He was also prevented from advertising Garcia kissable lips, but the document didn't prevent him from performing the procedure.

Dr. Charles Garcia arrived at his new office at seven thirty; his first procedure wasn't scheduled till eight. Leslie, his nurse, arrived five minutes after him and checked the surgical supplies and the equipment. Dana, his receptionist/bookkeeper/office clerk, appeared five minutes to eight. The staff of Garcia Surgical Care PC was ready for action.

Joan D'Annunzio, age thirty-eight, was right on time. She sat nervously in the waiting room, ready to be called back for her surgery. Dr. Garcia strolled into the reception room and welcomed his patient with a big hello and a hug. Dr. Charles Garcia was many things, but stupid was not one of them. He knew how to schmooze his patients and how to close a sale.

As he was leading Ms. D'Annunzio to the surgery suite, a man in a dark suit appeared in the doorway.

"Dr. Charles Garcia?"

"Yes, may I help you?"

Garcia was annoyed that this person appeared at his office unannounced.

"I'm a private process server. I've been retained by the state of Tennessee to serve these legal documents on you. Consider yourself served." He handed the doctor an envelope and walked out.

Garcia didn't know what to do. Ms. D'Annunzio was staring at him. He had to say something. "Damn parking tickets. I thought I'd paid those."

He put the envelope on his desk and walked Ms. D'Annunzio back for her surgery.

"Joan, you're going to look ten years younger with your Garcia kissable lips." Garcia knew he wasn't supposed to use that term, but neither Nichols nor Davis was there.

Leslie, his new nurse, assisted Garcia during the surgery. Garcia's mind was somewhere else, the envelope. After the procedure, while the patient was still in recovery, he retrieved the package. He sat down at his desk, took a deep breath, and opened it.

It was a notice of charges by the state of Tennessee, brought by the Medical Licensing Board. He read the document slowly. The charges followed the allegations of the Perkins and Howard lawsuits filed by Willis. It was alleged that he acted unethically and unprofessionally when he had sex with both AP and CH. *Why the hell were they using those whores' initials? They'd filed lawsuits that graphically described the sex acts they'd performed.*

Garcia picked up the phone and called Harrelson. He was told Harrelson was in a meeting.

"I don't give a shit if he's in a meeting. Interrupt him. This is an emergency!"

He waited what seemed like an hour. In reality, it was ten minutes.

"Charlie, what do you want? The settlement's signed, and the lawsuit's behind you. I'm really busy right now." Harrelson played with the gold chain of his watch, almost twirling it in small circles.

"I just was served with notice of charges by the Medical Licensing Board. It's trying to fine me and take away my Tennessee medical license for having sex with those women. Can they do that? I never should have gotten involved with those bitches. All I did was have sex with them. They each wanted it. I didn't put a gun to their heads. Those bitches are ruining my life. They need to take responsibility for their own actions. It's not like they didn't get multiple orgasms from being with me. It was the best sex of their lives."

Harrelson didn't say much. He stopped playing with his watch chain and put the watch back in his vest. He was sick of the arrogant little brat. He'd been cleaning up Charlie Garcia's messes for years, ever since he was a teenager.

Charlie didn't think Harrelson felt much sympathy for him. As far as Charlie was concerned, Harrelson wasn't a friend, just his father's lawyer, a paid shark.

"I don't know. Let me finish up here, and we'll call Lester Paul together. Give me twenty minutes to wind up . . ."

Charlie cut Harrelson off. "Call me back in twenty minutes."

True to his word, Harrelson called back on time, and they conferenced Paul. Paul pulled a Camel out, took a deep drag, and waited for the bad news. Charlie described the document and then read several paragraphs. They were serious allegations, and more important, they were true. The civil lawsuits filed by Willis had a strong defense, at least in the defense's eyes; the sex was voluntary. Each of

166

the plaintiffs, on several occasions, had sex with Charlie freely, despite the claims of duress. According to the charges, the mere act of having sex with a patient, voluntary or not, violated Charlie's ethics and subjected him to fines and revocation of his license.

After ten minutes Paul broke in: "These are serious charges, and Charlie's malpractice insurance carrier, Tennessee Mutual, won't provide coverage for this."

Paul, a chain smoker, had a full ashtray in front of him. His fingers were yellow from his addiction. He lit another cigarette and waited for Charlie's response. There wasn't one. Charlie was surprised and quite frankly didn't know what to say. He finally squeaked out, "Why not?"

"Because these are charges brought by the state, not the patients you treated."

"You mean I've got to pay your fees to defend this matter?"

"Not my fees. I already represent you in the civil actions and Davis's breach of contract case. We need to get you somebody who really knows the law and regularly appears before administrative disciplinary panels, such as the Medical Licensing Board."

"Who'd you recommend?"

"Amy Pierce. She's had success before the Medical Licensing Board, and she knows her stuff. I'll call her and make the first available appointment."

Harrelson thought, *When did Charlie Garcia ever pay a legal fee? I pity his parents. They just lost almost $400,000 because he couldn't pass a drug test, and now they're going to expend tens of thousands of dollars because he couldn't keep his dick in his pants. What an arrogant, stupid fool! He's a waste of space.*

Two days later, Charlie and Señor Garcia were seated in Amy Pierce's waiting room. Pierce specialized in defending physicians brought up on charges before the Medical Licensing Board. Señor

Garcia had flown down to Nashville on a private jet to come to the aid of his son, yet again.

Pierce greeted Dr. Garcia and his father and led them back to her office. She sat at her desk, and the Garcias sat across from her in blue leather wingback chairs. Señor Garcia noticed a picture of a young man, who looked about ten or eleven. He asked, "Is that your son?"

"Yes, his name's Carter, my only child."

Pierce didn't get into the reasons that she was a single mother and that her disbarred husband, Dan Smith, a drug addict and alcoholic, had seen Carter only once in the last several years.

"Charles is my only child, so you must know how I feel and that I would do anything to help him."

Pierce knew about protecting children. She'd tried to protect Carter from Dan throughout Carter's life. When the son of a bitch was drunk, he was unpredictable and sometimes violent. Once when they were still married, Pierce was working late, and Dan was supposed to be watching Carter. But he started drinking and behaving wildly, and the child became agitated. Dan picked up the little boy but dropped him, headfirst, onto the edge of the coffee table. Carter was not seriously injured but required stitches, and he still had the scar. Pierce never left her son with Dan again, and she swore he would never have a chance to hurt Carter again or have a role in their lives.

"Of course. I've read the charges as well as the two lawsuits filed in the Circuit Court by Jackson Willis. Mr. Paul was kind enough to fax them over. I must be frank. These charges are very serious, and they could cost your son his Tennessee medical license."

Señor Garcia spoke again, "You'll make sure that doesn't happen."

"I understand from Mr. Paul that there was a third lawsuit that just settled, brought by Benjamin Davis. He represents Dr. Nichols in the other two lawsuits."

No one in the room liked Ben Davis, but they agreed that he was a force to be reckoned with.

"I've had my share of trouble with Ben Davis. You'll be happy to know that the last time my client was charged by him in front of the Medical Licensing Board, my client got off."

Pierce failed to mention that her license was suspended for three months at the end of that case because she breached confidentiality and reported a settlement to the IRS.

She directed her next question to Charlie: "Mr. Paul tells me that you're also licensed in New York. There haven't been any charges filed there yet, right?"

Charlie got very upset. "You mean I might get charged in New York too?"

"It's certainly a possibility. Tennessee would send its findings to New York if your Tennessee license were revoked."

Señor Garcia stated firmly, "Ms. Pierce, we can't let that happen. How much is your retainer?"

"I need $10,000, and I bill at $400 an hour."

She's a bargain. Harrelson charges $800. I guess that's Nashville's prices compared to New York's, thought Garcia.

Pierce had recently started her own firm, Pierce & Associates. She had been a partner at Dunn, Moore and Thomas, but when she was suspended, they dropped her like a hot potato. At first she was furious, but now she liked being on her own, her own boss, answering to no one. She'd actually pilfered two associates from DMT, and she supervised them with an iron hand.

Señor Garcia didn't blink an eye. He pulled out his wallet and counted $10,000 in hundreds. Pierce wrote a receipt, and she had a new client, Dr. Charles Juan Batista Garcia.

CHAPTER TWENTY-SEVEN

A LIAR IS DEPOSED

Monday, April 21, 1997

Jack Willis was persistent. He reminded Davis of himself. Willis was relentless in trying to get discovery. The purpose of discovery, interrogatories (questions answered on paper under oath), request for admissions (affirmative statements, which had to be either admitted or denied), request for production of documents (providing the other side with responsive documents), and depositions (questioning a witness in person, under oath) is either to find out information or to box witnesses into a corner and force them into taking a position. Dr. Garcia, through his attorney, Lester Paul, had done a masterful job of saying nothing in response to Willis's discovery.

Today, Dr. Charles Garcia had no place to run. Lester Paul would be at Garcia's side, but he could not prevent the inevitable. Dr. Garcia had to answer the questions. Willis wouldn't take "I don't remember" as an answer.

Paul insisted that the deposition take place at his office. Davis thought such posturing was childish. Where a deposition took place was irrelevant. Davis was mistaken. Paul wasn't posturing; he simply wanted access to his private office at breaks so he could smoke his cigarettes. It was his haven. It smelled like an ashtray, and several of his partners constantly complained.

The deposition was scheduled to begin at nine. Davis brought Sammie along for the experience. She could learn from Willis. The deposition promised to be exciting, the subject matter wasn't going to be boring, and the deposition of a bad liar was always the most fun.

Willis walked in with Christy Howard. She was a pretty woman, conservatively dressed in a black business pantsuit. Her long red hair was pulled back into a fiery bun, which was set off by her pale skin and blue eyes. She looked like a schoolteacher rather than the woman who posed so provocatively on her website.

Everybody sat at the conference table. Dr. Nichols elected not to attend; he'd read Dr. Garcia's deposition. He didn't want to be in such a confined space with Garcia. He'd confided to Davis, "The little slime ball makes my skin crawl." And he was concerned he'd become too emotional.

In Nichols's place, Donna attended as the company representative. Bob Sullivan was Nichols & Garcia's attorney.

Because it was his office, Lester Paul took charge of the room. "There's coffee, juice, soft drinks, and water over on that table. Please help yourself. It's nine thirteen. I thought we'd break at noon for a one-hour lunch. The deposition will end precisely at three thirty. Dr. Garcia has a five o'clock flight to New York."

Willis remained calm, but he was annoyed that Paul was trying to limit the time of his examination of Dr. Garcia. He said, "That's fine. We'll respect Dr. Garcia's travel arrangements, but I already know I cannot complete this deposition in less than five hours. I insist that we set a continuation of the deposition right now, or I'm getting the judge on the phone."

Willis wasn't bluffing. Davis used the threat all the time. Most lawyers were afraid to get a judge on the phone when they were being obstructive or difficult. Paul tried to convince Willis to begin without the agreed upon date to resume, but Willis wouldn't budge. Everybody but Davis had his calendar, so he had to call Bella to get his available dates over the phone. It was agreed that if Willis didn't complete Dr. Garcia's deposition by three thirty, the deposition would resume on May 19th, and they would not break until completed. The plaintiff Howard's deposition was scheduled for May 22nd. She'd have the benefit of hearing Dr. Garcia's testimony before she'd have to give hers.

By the time the logistics were worked out, it was ten fifteen, and the deposition had been scheduled for nine. They were already an hour and fifteen minutes late because of Paul's and Willis's maneuvering. Paul wanted to take a smoke break but was afraid to ask the others. He started cracking his knuckles, and Davis noticed his yellow fingers from the nicotine.

The court reporter administered the oath, and the deposition began. The video camera was turned on, and the image of Dr. Garcia appeared on the television screen. Willis had gotten permission from Judge William "Billy" White, the judge in the Howard and Perkins cases, to videotape the depositions of Dr. Garcia, Dr. Nichols, and Donna. Lester Paul, Dr. Garcia's attorney, got permission to videotape the depositions of Anna Perkins and Christy Howard. White, for economy reasons, had been assigned both cases. A jury demand was made by Willis in each case.

Willis spent the first forty-five minutes establishing Garcia's background and education. Willis asked a lot of questions about Majorca, where Garcia spent part of his childhood. He established that Dr. Garcia came from wealth and that his mother was the niece of the Cuban dictator, Batista. There was plenty of time to get to the juicy stuff.

Willis established that Garcia maintained a Tennessee medical license and a New York medical license and that the Tennessee Medical Licensing Board had brought charges against him based on the allegations of the Perkins and Howard cases.

When Willis started asking questions about the charges pending before the board, Paul objected, "I don't represent Dr. Garcia in the board proceeding. Ms. Amy Pierce represents him in that matter. This is a deposition in the Howard civil case, not in those proceedings. I had no notice that the board charges would be an issue. I insist that Ms. Pierce be present when you question Dr. Garcia about those charges. She needs to be afforded an opportunity to object and advise her client regarding those pending charges."

Davis knew that argument was without merit, but Willis took it in stride.

"Mr. Paul, please advise Ms. Pierce that on May 19th, when we resume this deposition, I will be inquiring into the board charges. She's invited to attend if she feels her presence is necessary. However, with or without her, I will question Dr. Garcia about the board charges on that date. I'm not changing that deposition date. If she can't attend, she can have one of her associates attend, or she'll need to get relief from Judge White or forever hold her peace."

Willis then pulled the patient chart of Christy Howard maintained by Nichols & Garcia. He established when Ms. Howard became a patient in February 1996.

"At the time were you employed by Nichols & Garcia?"

"I was an employee of the company, and I owned one percent."

"What was the purpose of the first meeting?"

"It was an initial consult to evaluate and discuss options available to the patient."

"You would agree that at the first consult, you established a doctor-patient relationship with Ms. Howard?"

"She was there for a consult. I wasn't treating her at that time."

"As her doctor, you owed Ms. Howard all of the professional and ethical obligations that a doctor would owe one of his patients?"

"I don't know. If I give someone an aspirin, is she my patient? If I answer a medical question asked, does that make her my patient?"

Paul objected, "I think that calls for a legal conclusion."

"He's a doctor. I'm entitled to know when in his opinion he believes a doctor-patient relationship begins."

"He's answered the question. He doesn't know. Move on."

"At that first visit you said you made an evaluation and then discussed her options, correct?"

"Yes."

"After you made your medical evaluation and then gave her, in your medical opinion, her options, did that establish the doctor-patient relationship?"

"I don't think so because I hadn't treated her yet."

"Isn't giving medical advice treating a patient?"

"Is it medical advice to discuss with someone whether to use Motrin or aspirin?"

"Look, Doctor, I'm the one asking the questions, not you. You need to start answering my questions, or I'm going to get Judge White on the phone."

Paul stood at the table and, louder than intended, said, "Don't threaten my client."

It was starting to get ugly. Davis just sat there. If Willis called the judge and was able to get him on the phone, it wouldn't be good for Dr. Garcia. Davis didn't care whether Garcia got in trouble with the judge or not, but Dr. Nichols was paying Davis $400 an hour to sit there, so something productive might as well happen.

"Jack, you've preserved your record. Why don't you ask him

whether he eventually established a doctor-patient relationship with Ms. Howard after he started treating her?"

"Mr. Davis, this is my examination of the witness, not yours. If you have an objection on behalf of Dr. Nichols, make it, or mind your own business."

Davis looked at Sullivan, and they silently agreed this wasn't their fight. They'd let Willis and Paul just go at it.

Willis was so angry with Davis he'd lost his train of thought and moved on to the next subject without establishing that a doctor-patient relationship ever existed.

"Who is Robyn Eden?"

"She was an employee at Nichols & Garcia. She was the receptionist."

"Is she a patient? Did you treat her?"

Paul actually came out of his chair. "Objection, you have no right to ask the doctor about other patients. I direct him not to answer that question."

"If you want to get the judge on the phone, let's go. This lawsuit is about this doctor dating and having sex with his patients. If Ms. Eden has been treated by Dr. Garcia and he had sex with her, that's relevant to this case."

Paul responded, "We agreed that we'd break at noon. It's noon." He desperately needed a smoke.

Willis didn't care. "No, *you* said that we'd break at noon. I never agreed to that. Check the record. I'm going to finish this line of questioning."

"That's fine. You'll do it without my client and me. We're going to get a sandwich and will be back at one."

With that Paul, Harrelson, and Dr. Garcia got up, left the table, and walked out the door. The others at the table sat there dumbfounded.

Rubbing his beard, Sullivan was the first to speak, "I guess we better get some lunch."

Davis and Donna stood to follow Sullivan.

Willis grabbed Davis's arm and said, "Ben, I'm sorry I lost my cool. Paul is such a horse's ass. I know you were only trying to help and move things along. I can't stand Garcia, and I don't like Paul any better. Sorry."

"It's okay. We all get frustrated at times. You've got his answers, and his demeanor is preserved on video. At some point you'll go to Judge White. Build your record, and give Dr. Garcia enough rope to hang himself."

"You're absolutely right. After today, I'll get to depose this asshole at least twice more: in the continuation of this deposition, on May 19th, and in the Perkins case. He'll be sick of me before I'm through with him."

Everyone left the conference room and had lunch. By one, all of the players were back in their seats.

Willis started right back in. "Who at Nichols & Garcia knew that you were dating Robyn Eden?"

"I don't know."

"Did you keep your relationship with Ms. Eden a secret?"

"It was my personal life. It wasn't anybody's business."

Willis artfully established that Ms. Eden was an employee and patient of Dr. Garcia. He established that their personal relationship began around the end of 1995. Davis laughed to himself. Lester Paul just missed Willis's sly way of proving Robyn Eden was a patient, and Dr. Garcia had a doctor-patient relationship with her. Paul must have been half asleep, dreaming about his unfiltered Camels.

"Did you date your other patients?"

"Yes."

"Did you date Ms. Howard after she became your patient?"

Garcia admitted having sex with Ms. Howard but claimed she instigated sex. Willis asked if there were other patients.

Paul objected, "He's not going to identify the names of his other patients."

"What about Anna Perkins?"

Paul yelled out, "That's not relevant to the Howard case."

Now it was time for Willis to get angry. "Like hell it's not. It shows a pattern of conduct. As counsel for Ms. Perkins, I waive any confidentiality she might have to Dr. Garcia disclosing that they dated and had sex."

"I don't think you can make that waiver."

"Ms. Perkins has sued the man for $10 million. I don't think she'd mind his admitting to having sex with her."

Paul was getting red in the face, and his glasses made his eyes look like they were bulging. "I don't care what you think, Mr. Willis. What the law says is relevant is what counts."

Willis turned to Garcia, "But you admit you had sex with Ms. Howard after the doctor-patient relationship was established?"

"Yes."

"How many times?"

Garcia couldn't remember how many times. Willis established that it was less than fifty and more than five.

"What about Ms. Perkins?"

Paul objected again, "This isn't a deposition in the Perkins case."

"We'll be talking to Judge White before May 19th, the next time we're together. I'm confident he'll rule that this line of questioning is relevant."

In his mind, Davis agreed with Willis.

"Let's try it a different way. How many female patients did you have sex with, with whom you had a doctor-patient relationship?"

Paul didn't object, and Garcia just sat there. Davis assumed he was mentally counting the number of patients.

"Six."

"Does that include Ms. Howard, Ms. Perkins, and Ms. Eden?"

"Seven."

"So, you had sex with seven female patients when you worked for Dr. Nichols?"

Davis, who was listening intently, objected. "Dr. Garcia never worked for Dr. Nichols. Nichols & Garcia, a professional corporation, employed him. Dr. Nichols was not his employer; he's just another employee. I don't even understand why he's a defendant in this case."

Willis, on edge, snapped at Davis, "Dr. Nichols is a defendant because I sued him. If you're so sure he shouldn't be here, file a motion for summary judgment, and see if Judge White will let Dr. Nichols out."

"That's why I'm glad you're conducting this deposition, so I can file parts of it with the court in support of my motion."

Davis forgot that the camera was running, or he wouldn't have made the last remark. After the taking of Dr. Garcia's deposition, he did in fact plan on filing a motion for summary judgment.

"Did you have sex with all seven while employed at Nichols & Garcia *PC*?" Willis emphasized the PC part of the question.

"No, some of them were when I worked in New York as a resident and fellow."

"How many at Nichols & Garcia?"

"Three: my girlfriend, Robyn Eden, the two plaintiffs."

Davis considered whether Garcia was lying. If what he said were true, then no other lawsuits against the company or Nichols personally were out there.

"Did you have sexual relations with other Nichols & Garcia employees in addition to Ms. Eden?"

With his answer he was about to give Willis a new client. Davis looked at Sullivan who, through his eyes, acknowledged the importance of the answer to the last question.

Sullivan raised his voice and objected, "We're here on the Howard case."

Sullivan hesitated, looked at Davis, decided they wanted to know the answer to the question, and then withdrew his objection. Davis agreed they should let him answer. It would come out anyway. They were better off knowing the name of the other employee.

"How do you define *sex*?"

It was Bill Clinton all over again. Davis knew Willis must have thought about the possibility of defining *sex*. Willis actually looked at his notepad for the first time. Despite their exchanges, Davis admired Willis's ability. He'd gotten Garcia to admit he'd had sex with Howard and Perkins.

From the next few questions Davis realized that Willis anticipated Garcia's playing games with semantics. He read from his notepad, "Let's divide the definition into parts. How many Nichols & Garcia PC employees did you have intercourse with?"

"Is that anal and vaginal, or just vaginal?"

"Let's stick to the vaginal, and we'll get to anal next."

Garcia was playing with Willis, but Willis didn't care because it was on video. Neither a judge nor a jury would appreciate a smart-ass. Willis planned on filing the video with the court in support of some yet undetermined motion. Assuming that human nature was what it was, Judge White would watch the video despite its more than four-hour length.

"I had vaginal intercourse with Robyn Eden and another Nichols & Garcia employee."

"Who?"

"Donna Burns."

Paul stood, and Garcia followed.

"It's three thirty-four. We've reached our deadline. Dr. Garcia has a plane to catch. He's got to go back to the hotel to pick up his bag first."

Willis protested, "I never agreed to any deadline. You made that statement, and none of the attorneys present agreed."

Davis and Sammie were momentarily stunned. Davis's mind was racing. What was the point of objecting at this point? What would the objection be? Charles Garcia had just slandered Donna Burns, but Davis couldn't just yell out "liar!"

The liar spoke, "I've got a plane to catch. We're leaving."

Harrelson walked out, followed by Lester Paul and Dr. Charles Juan Batista Garcia.

Over his shoulder, Paul looked at Donna Burns and said, "You're welcome to use my conference room. I'm sure you've got a lot to talk about."

The door closed. The court reporter and the videographer decided to leave their equipment set up.

Willis was right behind them. As he left, Willis, loud enough for everyone to hear, said his parting words to the videographer: "I'm sure we'll all want copies of the tape, even Paul. Can we have them by tomorrow?"

"No problem."

The door shut again. It was just Donna, Sammie, Sullivan, and Davis.

"It's not true! The little bastard's lying," Donna shouted in rage.

Davis certainly knew that was a possibility. Garcia was many things, and a liar was one of them. Pervert was another.

Sammie spoke up for the first time since the deposition began. "Are you willing to take a lie detector test to prove your innocence?"

Donna shot back, "I thought you were innocent until proven guilty?"

"Not in employment law. You've got no contract. Remember what happened to Dr. Garcia when he refused to take a test."

Confidently Donna said, "When and where?"

Davis responded, "Tomorrow at my office. I'll call you with the time. Don't talk to Dr. Nichols about what happened. Either Sammie or I must be present when you speak to him. We'll show him a small part of the video, including the end. He can form his own opinion."

Sullivan, as the company's attorney, informed Donna that she should take the morning off and that they would call her at home when they got the video and the lie detector test set up.

Donna practically ran from the room.

Sullivan looked at the Davises. "Holy shit! I didn't see that one coming. What do you think, Ben?"

"No way. She's solid, she's honest, and she cares about Nichols. She's been with him for more than twenty years. I know this woman. She didn't let Garcia near her. He's a damn liar, and he, Paul, or Harrelson thought of this. My guess is, it was Harrelson. He's disreputable, and Paul's not that creative."

Neither Sullivan nor Sammie agreed or disagreed. Davis suspected they wanted to see the results of the test. So did he.

CHAPTER TWENTY-EIGHT

THE POLYGRAPH

Tuesday, April 22, 1997

The videotape was delivered to Davis's office at ten fifteen. Davis had been informed that because of a backlog, it could take as long as a week to get the transcript. They needed the video; the transcript could wait. The tape was far more revealing. You could hear the intonation of the witness's voice and watch the body language.

A black cloud was hanging over the team. Did Donna have sex with Garcia? Dr. Garcia produced no proof of their relationship, yet the pressing question was, why did Lester Paul cut off Garcia's testimony? The day certainly ended dramatically. Everyone in the room but the Garcia team was shocked by the last answer. Willis didn't expect it, and Donna Burns almost had a coronary.

What if there was proof of his sexual relations with Donna? She knew there was a running video camera in the storage room, but then again she was the person responsible for collecting the tapes and reviewing them every morning. Davis delegated that assignment to her because he trusted her implicitly.

Davis believed in and had relied on polygraphs for years. A polygraph was only as good as the person who administered the test and analyzed its results. For the last ten years, Davis had used Robert Escher, a former FBI agent, who performed them for the bureau for more than twenty years. He lived in Bowling Green, Kentucky, and agreed to drive to Nashville to administer the test.

In the meantime, Davis sat Dr. Nichols, Morty, Sullivan, and Bella in the conference room to watch the last thirty minutes of the tape. He trusted their judgment and wanted their opinions as to Dr. Garcia's truthfulness. Sammie also sat in; she wanted to see and hear the testimony again.

Davis decided he'd better call Liza. Tonight was the first night of Passover, and the family and Morty would be gathering at Davis's home for their Seder. Davis was supposed to help with the preparation of the Passover meal, which began at sunset.

Passover was Davis's favorite holiday; it was Thanksgiving with more than five thousand years of tradition. Each year Davis told the story of the Jews' escape from Egypt. His was the Cecil B. DeMille version, starring Yul Brynner and Charlton Heston. For Davis it was an acceptable reason to overeat Jewish delicacies.

Liza answered on the third ring. "Hi, honey. When will you be home?"

"I've got quite an emergency. Bob Escher is coming in this morning to do a polygraph, and I'm not sure how long that will take. If the results go badly, it's going to be a long day. I promise to leave the office as soon as I can. I'll give you a status report at noon. I know you're busy cleaning and cooking for tonight. I love you."

Liza knew not to ask any questions. Davis wouldn't answer them. Liza didn't argue with her husband on the phone. She had a Passover meal to prepare. Unlike Sammie and Morty, she wasn't part of the firm and therefore wasn't privileged to confidential information. She was an outsider and had been his entire career.

Davis returned to the conference room to see Nichols looking stunned. He'd absolutely trusted Donna Burns to manage his office and his money. How could this be possible?

"What do you think, Ben?"

"No way. Garcia's a lying piece of shit. I'm a good judge of character, and Donna's not his type."

Nichols turned to Morty. The old man looked deep in thought.

"She certainly didn't like Garcia. Was that because she was smarter than the rest of us or because after they had sex, he shunned her for a younger woman? I've known Donna a long time. She genuinely cares about you. I vote no way also."

Nichols apparently wanted to get a consensus before he expressed his opinion.

Sullivan conceded that he didn't know Donna, but based on the tape, he thought that Garcia was lying. Nichols turned to Bella.

She didn't hesitate. "I'm ashamed of you, Peter Nichols. Donna is my contemporary at your office. Could you see me having sex with Dr. Garcia? In fact, I'm ashamed of all of you for even considering what this pervert has said about this fine woman. As far as I'm concerned, she's innocent until proven guilty."

Sammie looked down at the table and felt disgusted with herself. She'd said things yesterday to Donna that she shouldn't have.

When Donna walked into the conference room, she put on a brave face. Dr. Nichols jumped to his feet, ran over, and gave her the biggest bear hug he could.

Davis interjected, "This is a bunch of bullshit. Let's get this test done and let the Davises celebrate their holiday."

For some unexplained reason the mood changed on a dime. Donna started crying. Bella and Sammie started right afterward. The men held it together, but they also felt the emotion of the moment. No one felt good about questioning the integrity of this fine woman.

Just then Robert Escher walked in the conference room, unannounced. Reception had been left unattended. Introductions were made, and Escher suggested that they use Davis's private office. He'd performed polygraphs in there before. Only Escher, Davis, and Donna were present for the test.

He placed Donna behind Davis's desk and explained that Davis's office would intimidate her and her defenses would be lowered. Escher asked her dozens of questions, some easy, while others were very direct and accusatorial. Escher mixed them up.

"What is your favorite color?"

"Have you ever stolen money from Nichols & Garcia, or before Dr. Garcia arrived in 1995?"

It took forty-five minutes to complete the exam. As an experienced FBI agent, Escher had no problem asking the embarrassing questions, such as, "Did you have sex with Dr. Garcia?" Only Escher had access to the machine, so Davis had no idea how the test was progressing. It really didn't matter because he couldn't understand the results anyway.

Escher didn't keep them waiting long. He spent ten minutes analyzing the data. "In my professional opinion, with ninety-seven degrees of certainty, Donna didn't have sex with Dr. Garcia."

Escher joked, "She eats a box of chocolates, alone, every Christmas and doesn't share a piece. They're her chocolates, not stolen, so no harm, no foul. However, if a box goes missing, she's your best suspect."

Davis smiled. Escher knew how to break the tension. Davis and Sullivan were relieved the company representative didn't have intercourse with Garcia.

Nichols blurted out, "What can we do to this little bastard?"

The lawyers and Sammie, all four of them, sat silently around the table. After stroking his red beard and clearing his throat, Sullivan spoke first: "You could file a slander lawsuit against Dr. Garcia, but he's already got two civil lawsuits and the board charges pending against him. One more suit isn't going to make a significant difference. You have the added problem that he slandered you while testifying. There's a qualified privilege for testimony given in a civil case. Witness's testimony is afforded extra protection."

Morty went next, "We need to prove that Dr. Garcia's a liar, in Judge White's mind. Let him watch the video, and then file a motion for contempt against Garcia for perjury under seal. Provide him with Donna's affidavit and the results of the polygraph test. Even if White doesn't find perjury, he'll still figure Dr. Garcia's a liar. This must all be filed under seal or our court filing would be a republication to the world of Garcia's slander. You also need to write Willis and Paul and demand that they not file the video or the transcript open in the record but under seal."

Davis began dictating to Bella, who knew shorthand,

To Jackson Willis, Lester Paul, and David Harrelson,

At the end of Dr. Garcia's deposition he slandered the representative of Nichols & Garcia, Donna Burns, by falsely asserting that they engaged in sex. Please be advised that this office intends to file under seal the video and other supporting evidence that prove Dr. Garcia's perjury. Please be advised that if you intend to file either the video or the transcript with the court, you should do so under seal. An open filing would be republication of the slander, and this office would seek to hold you personally liable for such wrongful conduct. If you have any questions concerning this demand, please do not hesitate to contact me.

Benjamin Davis

The letter was faxed to all concerned. After the holiday, both Davis and Willis would file motions and the video under seal.

Judge White put his feet up, grabbed his bag of popcorn, and watched the four-hour video.

CHAPTER TWENTY-NINE

A CONTINUATION OF LIES

Monday, May 19, 1997

The resumed deposition of Dr. Garcia began as scheduled at nine o'clock. David Harrelson wanted to continue it, but short of Garcia being hospitalized, the deposition was going forward. Judge White entered an order, which provided the following:

> I reserve judgment on the defendant Nichols & Garcia's motion for contempt against Dr. Garcia. This motion will require a hearing to be scheduled at a later date.

> I grant the Plaintiff Howard's motion to set guidelines for the deposition of Dr. Garcia. The deposition will begin on May 19th, 1997, at nine o'clock and shall continue as deemed necessary by Mr. Willis, Mr. Sullivan, and Mr. Davis until completed. There shall be a luncheon break at noon and, if necessary, a dinner break at six. Comfort breaks shall occur after an attorney has completed a line of questioning. If necessary, the deposition shall resume on May 22nd, the date Ms. Howard's depo-

sition is scheduled to begin in this case since counsels for the parties are available.

All questions are relevant under Rule 26 of the Tennessee Rules of Civil Procedure, unless protected by the attorney-client privilege or the attorney work product doctrine. All names of patients and/ or employees of Nichols & Garcia PC, who the defendant Garcia had sex with, of any kind, will be identified, but remain confidential, and the video and transcript of the deposition may be filed only with the court under seal. No one in attendance of Dr. Garcia's deposition will discuss the substance of Dr. Garcia's testimony with any third party, particularly the press. I will hold any person who violates this confidentiality clause in contempt, subject to fine and incarceration.

I will be available to counsel on May 19th and 22nd to prevent any obstructive conduct by counsel or non-responsiveness by the witness.

Signed the Honorable William White, Judge of the Circuit Court of Davidson County, Tennessee

Harrelson resented that the court's order was made the first exhibit for the resumed deposition.

Willis began, "When we left off, we were talking about the employees of Nichols & Garcia with whom you had various types of sex, and you indicated that you had sex with Donna Burns, correct?"

"Yes."

"When did this occur?"

"The first month I was there, in December 1995."

"Who other than you knew about this act?"

"She does."

"So it's your word against hers?"

"I suppose. There are no pictures or videotape."

"Where did this allegedly happen?"

"The first time on the couch in Dr. Nichols's office. The second time was in the copier room."

"When was the second occasion?"

"It was in late January. I'd say one of the last days of the month."

Harrelson was surprised that Donna was still the company representative for Nichols & Garcia. He thought she might skip the deposition. He was dead wrong. She was there, and she was fuming. Sullivan and Davis kept looking at each other and then at Donna. Garcia stepped in it. The videotapes of the copier room were saved, and by omission they could prove Garcia a liar. Harrelson kept waiting for her to explode and lunge across the table at Garcia.

Willis continued, "You indicated the last time we were together that you had sex with four other patients when you were a resident and fellow in New York?"

"Correct."

"Who at New York Presbyterian Hospital knew you were having sex with patients?"

"I know at least several of the other residents and Professor Gaines. He questioned me about it."

Harrelson already knew about the incident. Garcia almost got thrown out of the residency program over it. Harrelson was watching Davis, trying to determine whether he appreciated the importance of the last answer. He was convinced that Davis did understand based upon his body language. Dr. Gaines's name was one of the references on Garcia's resume. The arrogant kid never changed his resume after the reference learned of his sexual exploits. Harrelson knew that Dr. Gaines was one of two of the references that McCormick & Associates were unable to reach because he was on sabbatical.

McCormick's attorney, Karl Maddox, objected; Davis suspected he probably didn't know what else to do. Dr. Garcia's testimony just created a good argument for the claim against McCormick & Associates. If McCormick had reached Dr. Gaines, Gaines might have warned Nichols of Dr. Garcia's tendency to have sex with patients.

"So McCormick & Associates or Dr. Nichols could have found out about your little escapades with patients if they asked Dr. Gaines or some of the residents you worked with?"

"I don't know. I don't think Dr. Nichols knew."

"That's not my question. He could have discovered it?"

Davis and Maddox at the same time objected, "Speculation."

"Was there ever anything about your sex with patients during your residency or fellowship written in your personnel file?"

"I don't think so."

Willis spent the next hour reviewing Ms. Howard's medical chart. He showed Dr. Garcia photographs of her necrotic lower lip and asked if that was an acceptable result. Garcia argued that a bad result didn't necessarily mean he was negligent. Garcia blamed the outcome on the fact that Ms. Howard was a smoker and that he was unaware of that fact.

"Is it your testimony, Doctor, that Ms. Howard's smoking . . ."

Garcia interrupted. "It contributed to it."

"So you did know she smoked?"

"At some point I did."

"You had sex before the surgery. So you knew before the surgery that Ms. Howard smoked?"

"I can't agree. I don't remember."

"When you were having sex with these female patients, were you aware that having sex with a patient was ethically wrong?"

"No."

"When did you become aware?"

Paul objected on the grounds of the attorney-client relationship. Harrelson thought that was a valid objection.

Willis must have too. He moved on. "Have you heard of the American Medical Association?"

"Yes."

"Are you a member?"

"Yes."

Willis spent the next half hour reviewing with Dr. Garcia the rules of the AMA, which prohibited doctors from having sex with patients. A physician wanting to get romantically involved with a patient had to terminate the doctor-patient relationship first.

"They didn't teach you about ethics in medical school?"

"There may have been one course. I don't remember."

"You didn't pay very close attention, did you?"

Garcia made no response, and Lester Paul objected. They broke for lunch. Paul rushed out of the conference room and went back to his office for a smoke. Willis skipped lunch and went for a brisk walk.

Davis, Sammie, Sullivan, Donna, and even Maddox ate lunch at Merchants on Broadway. Davis ordered a strip steak smothered in onions and a baked potato on the side. He drank two Frescas. He also ordered key lime pie for dessert. He figured he wasn't going to fall asleep during this deposition. As they walked back to the court-house, Davis topped off lunch with an orange Tootsie Pop.

When they got back, Willis started right back in. "Do you know what the standard of care is for an oral surgeon performing a lip enhancement in Nashville, Tennessee?"

"I went to medical school and did a residency and fellowship in oral surgery, and I've been in private practice since December 1995. Yes."

"Are you of the professional opinion that your care and treatment of Ms. Howard were within the standard of care?"

"Objection," Paul pronounced, "that calls for a legal conclusion."

Willis snapped back at Paul, "No, that calls for a medical conclusion, and he's an oral surgeon."

He switched his attention to Garcia: "Answer the damn question, or I'm calling the judge."

"I don't know. Bad results don't necessarily mean that the standard of care was broken."

Willis spent the next half hour discussing the breach of contract litigation. Bob Sullivan objected several times to correct the fact that the litigation was with Nichols & Garcia, not Dr. Nichols individually. Dr. Garcia got angry when Willis asked whether his parents had paid the entire $400,000 to settle the case. Sullivan, rather than Paul, objected on the grounds of confidentiality of their agreement.

"Did your relationship with Nichols & Garcia terminate because of the lawsuits filed by my clients?"

"No, but I'm sure the lawsuits didn't help our relationship."

"Did your relationship with Nichols & Garcia terminate because of your drug use?"

"No."

"Didn't you refuse to take a drug test?"

"Yes."

"Weren't you using drugs at that time and would have failed a drug test?"

Paul directed the witness not to answer that question. He indicated that Ms. Pierce was again not present and that drug use related to the charges brought by the Medical Licensing Board.

Willis would not be put off. "I offered for Ms. Pierce to be here today and told you that I would proceed to questioning the witness if she chose not to be here. She's not here, an associate is not here, and no motion was filed. I'm asking him these questions."

Paul was ready for this problem. "She didn't choose not to come. She had a prior commitment, which she was unable to break."

"What was it?"

"You'll have to ask Ms. Pierce. I'm not her social secretary."

Willis persisted, and eventually Dr. Garcia testified that while employed by Nichols & Garcia, he didn't use illegal drugs. Harrelson knew that was a lie.

"Why didn't you agree to take the drug test?"

"Out of principle."

Davis almost came out of his chair, but he used self-control. *What is this clown thinking? There's a video camera running. Who does he think he's kidding?*

Willis continued, "Those principles cost your parents the settlement dollar amount paid, right?"

"I guess so."

"Those principles didn't prevent you from having sex with your patients, did they?"

Paul objected, and Willis moved on. There was no jury to impress. He'd made his point.

Willis pulled out a copy of the complaint he filed on behalf of Ms. Howard and the answer filed by Dr. Garcia. Garcia admitted most of the sex acts described in the complaint but denied that any of the sex was forced. According to Dr. Garcia, Christy Howard was a willing participant and enjoyed every perverted turn. He denied offering her Ecstasy or ever taking Ecstasy.

It was almost five o'clock when Willis called it quits. Bob Sullivan asked thirty minutes of questions, which established that Dr. Garcia worked for the corporation and that Dr. Nichols never discussed sex with Dr. Garcia or his relationship with any of the patients or employees.

Garcia also admitted that he had sex with Donna Burns, which he described as "fucking her." According to his testimony, Donna Burns, to his knowledge, wasn't aware of his relationship with other employees or patients.

Karl Maddox went next. He got Dr. Garcia to admit that he never told Rocky McCormick about his relationship with patients when he worked in New York.

Davis announced that he had no questions for the witness. Sullivan had asked all the important questions for Davis's motion for summary judgment. The deposition adjourned right before six twenty-five. It had been a long day for everybody.

CHAPTER THIRTY

INNOCENT AS THE DRIVEN SNOW

Thursday, May 22, 1997

The deposition of Christy Howard was scheduled for May 22nd. There was quite an argument between Davis, Bob Sullivan, and Lester Paul as to who would get to question her first. Finally, Davis sided with Sullivan, and that made the vote two against one, so Sullivan took the lead.

Davis gave in to Sullivan for two reasons. First, he'd come to dislike Paul, who smelled of cigarette smoke. Davis smoked good cigars and also worked for more than twenty years with Steine. He was not sensitive, but Paul really did stink. Second, Sullivan's investigator found the Howard website. It was only fair he got to drop the bombshell. Besides, this deposition would make Sullivan look good with Tennessee Mutual, which was paying him for his legal services. Sullivan had been a good friend, and Morty taught Davis how to treat a friend.

After it was agreed that Sullivan would start the deposition, the next disagreement between defense counsel was whether to use the provocative photos at deposition or save them for trial. Paul wanted to save them for trial and surprise the witness on cross-examination and destroy her credibility in front of the jury. Trying to ambush the witness at trial carried certain risks, though. If an exhibit wasn't disclosed and exchanged before trial, Judge White could refuse to allow the defense to introduce the photos. A document used to contradict a witness's direct testimony at trial is an impeachment exhibit.

A compelling reason to use the photos at the deposition was that Davis and Sullivan didn't want to put their clients through a trial. They reasoned that Willis would be so shell-shocked by the photographs that a settlement could be negotiated with no further depositions, including Dr. Nichols and Donna Burns.

Sullivan started slowly. He questioned Ms. Howard about her background and education. He then went through her employment history, which included several modeling jobs. Sullivan asked her specifics about those jobs. She described several of the shoots. She'd done some ads for department stores and for a grocery chain.

"Do you always wear your hair in a bun, like today?"

"No. Sometimes I wear it down or in a ponytail."

"Are you wearing contact lenses?"

"Yes."

"Do you ever wear glasses?"

"When I'm alone at night in bed watching TV, but I wear the contacts when I'm in public."

"You wouldn't model in glasses, would you?"

"No."

Willis was getting impatient.

"Where is this questioning going, Mr. Sullivan?"

"Give me a minute, Jack. I'm about to get there."

"Well, let's get there already. You're wasting all our time."

Davis thought, *Jack, you just asked for it, and you're about to get it.*

Sullivan slid an eight-by-ten glossy in front of Willis and his client. He handed one to Maddox, who was the only other attorney in the room who hadn't studied the photographs for months.

The reaction on Jack Willis's face was priceless. His mouth opened, and his eyes went wide. It was as if somebody wearing golf shoes kicked him in a vulnerable place.

Howard's reaction was quite different. She started crying. All the time the camera was rolling.

"Is the redhead wearing glasses in that photograph you?"

Christy Howard couldn't answer. She was crying hysterically.

The photograph was of her and another woman. Christy had a black gag in her mouth and was sitting on a desk. She was wearing a very short schoolgirl's green plaid uniform skirt. Her white oxford shirt was wide open. She wasn't wearing a bra or panties. The other woman was sucking on her right nipple.

Sullivan pulled out another one, slid it to the witness and her attorney, and gave one to Maddox, whose face was bright red. This one had Howard's green plaid skirt hiked up to her waist, and the other woman was performing cunnilingus.

The second photo got another reaction from Willis, who was an experienced litigator. He put the palms of both hands to his face, then repeatedly ran his fingers through his hair and shook his head. Davis thought it was a shame that the camera was fixed on Howard only and that Willis's reaction was off camera.

At that moment, every attorney in the room understood that the value of the Howard case just plummeted. Howard continued to cry, but no one had sympathy for her. She knew she'd made these photos and intentionally put them on her website. She hadn't told Willis, who was obviously taken completely by surprise.

Davis wondered what he would have done if he represented Howard. In his interview of the client, would he have revealed that she'd made pornographic pictures? Davis thought about how he would word such a question on his intake form completed by his personal injury clients.

It had been fifteen minutes since the first photograph was shown, and Christy Howard still hadn't acknowledged that she was the redhead in the photographs. Sullivan wanted to move the deposition along. He didn't want to make all of the photos exhibits for her deposition. He intended to save some.

"I've got forty-eight of these. I can wait for you to stop crying, and we can go through them one by one. I need you to acknowledge that you're the redhead."

Willis finally shook off his daze. "Let's take a break. I need to talk to my client."

Sullivan could have insisted that the examination continue, but what the hell? The pictures wouldn't change during the break, and the witness would still have to face them when she got back.

When Willis and Howard left to go to another office, Paul smiled and congratulated Sullivan for his good work.

"I didn't take the photos, Lester. My investigator found them."

Maddox, who was as shocked as Willis, asked, "How did you get them?"

"She has a website. They were just sitting there on the Internet." Even though Davis had copies for months, he still found them shocking.

After a half-hour break, Paul left the conference room to find Willis and his client to discover when they could expect to resume the deposition.

Paul came back and reported, "Willis can't get her to come

back in the room. As you might imagine, he's shocked and upset. She lied to him and damaged his other lawsuit. He asked if we could continue the deposition to a later date. She's broken. If we press her, and she won't come back, Judge White might dismiss her case. That will leave just Perkins . . ."

Davis interrupted Paul, "Think about it. You said it yourself. Howard brings the value of the Perkins case dramatically down. I say we enter an agreed order right now and adjourn the deposition as long as Willis stipulates that the redhead in the two photographs is Christy Howard. Willis also has to agree to resume the deposition before the end of the month.

"Later today, I'll call Willis and suggest that we try to settle both cases, or we resume Christy Howard's deposition. We just might have these cases settled by the end of the month."

Paul was the designated representative to approach Willis. Paul returned to the conference room five minutes later and suggested May 27th to resume the deposition.

Sammie was designated to prepare the agreed order continuing the deposition, which also stipulated that Ms. Howard was the redhead in the two photographic exhibits. She came back in less than ten minutes.

During that time, Willis didn't say a word. He just sat there looking very defeated.

"How's this sound?" Sammie began to read, "On May 22nd, 1997, the deposition of the plaintiff Christy Howard was taken. During the course of her deposition, two photographs were shown to the witness, marked Exhibits 5 and 6, which are attached hereto. As evidenced by the signature of Jackson Willis to this agreed order, Christy Howard stipulates that she is the redheaded woman in the photographs and that said photographs are admissible at the trial of this cause. It is hereby stipulated that the deposition of Christy Howard shall resume at the law offices of Lester Paul on May 27th, 1997, at 9:00 a.m.

There was a place for each lawyer to sign.

"I never agreed that the photographs would be admissible," said Willis. "I can't do that. The judge will make that decision, not us."

Davis suggested that they delete the language concerning admissibility and sign the agreed order. Everybody agreed.

Willis walked out to retrieve his client, who was sitting by herself in a small conference room. Davis suspected that Jack might have a Jack Daniel's when he got back to the office. The videographer also left, leaving all of his equipment set up. He knew to make himself scarce. There wasn't going to be a record of what was said at this next meeting.

Davis suggested that Dr. Garcia and Ms. Burns leave the conference room separately and that only the attorneys remain. Paul agreed. Dr. Garcia left first and was placed in Paul's office. Davis hoped he choked on the smell in the smoke-inundated furniture. Donna Burns walked out with instructions to tell Dr. Nichols what happened and inform him that Davis and Sullivan would be calling him later.

When only the defense attorneys were present, Davis took charge. "We have an opportunity to end this. My client, Dr. Nichols, doesn't want to be deposed, and he certainly doesn't want to go to trial. I'm confident that Dr. Nichols individually will be dismissed from the case. He wasn't Dr. Garcia's employer. The company was. As part of any settlement Dr. Peter Nichols individually must be dismissed with prejudice, without any admission of liability."

No one voiced an objection, and they all remained silent, which encouraged Davis to go forward.

"As I see it we've got the remaining defendants insured by two different insurance companies. McCormick & Associates is insured by Equitable, and Tennessee Mutual insures both Dr. Garcia and Nichols & Garcia. I think it's our job to convince our respective companies to pay their fair share, so we can get these cases settled. Lester and Bob will take the lead with Tennessee Mutual, and, Karl, you've got Equitable. We'll need to agree how much of the comparative fault to apportion to each of the other defendants, and their carriers will pay for that percentage."

Karl Maddox spoke up, "Well, Dr. Garcia caused ninety-nine percent of the problem. He's an animal, a pervert. Ms. Howard may be a tramp, but Dr. Garcia's a filthy pig."

Lester Paul jumped up. "Don't talk about my client like that. This wasn't rape. These women voluntarily had sex with him."

Davis saw he was losing control of the meeting. There were a lot of egos in the room, and they were getting in the way of a constructive discussion.

Davis stopped him in his tracks. "Lester, the voluntary nature and the character of the plaintiffs go to the amount of the settlement, not how it should be divided up among the defendants. You've got to admit that the vast majority of any settlement payment should fall on Tennessee Mutual for the conduct of Dr. Garcia."

Sullivan made a contribution: "Let's examine what Nichols & Garcia, the company, is charged with, and what McCormick & Associates has been sued for. Nichols & Garcia is sued for negligent supervision of Dr. Garcia and his negligent hire. Let's put the supervision to the side for a moment. Nichols & Garcia asserts that it hired McCormick & Associates because of its expertise, to help in the hire decision. McCormick found Dr. Garcia and held him out as an excellent candidate. McCormick did a negligent background check on Garcia."

Maddox couldn't listen any longer. "How do you know McCormick did a negligent background check?"

"McCormick didn't speak to Dr. Gaines or the other residents at the hospital where Dr. Garcia did his residency and fellowship. Those conversations would have revealed that Dr. Garcia had a proclivity to have sex with patients. Also . . ."

Sullivan slid his investigator's report to Maddox. "This report cost me $5,000, one-sixth of what McCormick charged Nichols & Garcia to find Dr. Garcia. McCormick missed the drugs and the Princeton coed violent sex act. Dr. Nichols had a right to rely on McCormick & Associates, and McCormick screwed up."

Maddox responded, "Well, your client's also been sued for negligent supervision. He admitted having sex in your offices. He was screwing patients and maybe even your office manager."

Davis could hardly control himself, but he forced himself to calm down and speak in a low, measured tone: "Stop! I have two conditions for settlement. The first, as I mentioned, is that Dr. Nichols must be dismissed individually. The second is that Dr. Garcia must apologize and withdraw his testimony about Donna Burns. I will not let that lie stand."

Lester Paul was getting red in the face. He said, "You're asking my client to admit to perjury. He can't do that. He'd be lucky if all Judge White did would be to hold him in contempt and fine him. The court could turn him over to the DA for criminal prosecution of perjury."

Davis stood his ground. "There's no deal unless Donna Burns's name is cleared."

Maddox said, "Ben, let's not fixate on this point right now. Let's focus on apportioning liability. I could recommend to Equitable ten percent, not exceeding $100,000. That would give you $1 million to settle the cases." Maddox was from New York; he placed a higher value on the cases than the Nashville attorneys.

Davis saw an opportunity. "Karl, how much do you think your defense costs and expenses will be to try these cases in Nashville?"

"I'd guess we're a year away from the first trial, and the other may be tried in 1999 or 2000. I would suspect both Howard and Perkins would take at least a week to try. Rough guess, $150,000 in attorney fees and another $50,000 in expenses."

Davis liked Maddox's answer. "I think you're a little low since you'll be in a hotel for at least three weeks eating room service. I think your number is closer to $225,000."

"It would probably be somewhere in the middle. I'm listening."

"We had a great day today, but Dr. Garcia's deposition didn't go so well, did it? A jury verdict is an unknown, as McCormick will get hit for something, and it will be hit twice. How about if Bob can get Tennessee Mutual to agree that if Equitable contributes $150,000 toward settlement for both cases, then Equitable gets to walk away? That's less than your estimated cost of defense."

Lester Paul almost came out of his skin. "You don't have authority to make that deal."

"No, but Bob has the right to recommend that deal, and we've discussed . . ."

"Why wasn't I part of those discussions?"

"Because the company sued McCormick, not Dr. Garcia. This has nothing to do with you or your client."

"It has to do with Tennessee Mutual. It's their money you're spending . . ."

Maddox decided he better take the deal. "Bob, if you can get Tennessee Mutual to take full responsibility, I'll get Equitable to kick in $150,000. I'd rather recommend a known risk than an un-known risk."

The meeting broke up. It was agreed that Sullivan would call Pinsly of Tennessee Mutual to set up a meeting between Pinsly, Sullivan, Paul, and Davis. That promised to be quite a meeting.

CHAPTER THIRTY-ONE
BAD BLOOD
Friday, May 23, 1997

As promised, Davis called Willis the next day. Davis figured it had been a long night for him. Willis had brooded, cursed Christy Howard, and now in the light of day could realistically evaluate his position and his lawsuits. Despite his reflection, Willis was not in a good mood. "I figured they'd have Lester Paul, rather than you, call. I can't stand that guy or his client."

"I'm not a big fan of them, either. Right now, I'm your best friend in these cases. I want the same thing you do, settlement, but I have almost no control over the insurance companies. Sullivan has some, but I have little credibility with Tennessee Mutual. Pinsly and I have a long history together, and it's not good. He's listening to Paul. The reason's simple. Paul tells him what he wants to hear."

"What do you think I can get for the two cases?"

"Howard is practically worthless. She's a train wreck. You haven't studied those pictures. A jury will send her home in a box. Nobody will believe that she didn't participate in those sex acts with Garcia voluntarily. Her claim that he forced her to do any of those acts will not just be rejected; you'll be laughed out of court. Can you imagine what a middle-aged housewife is going to think about Ms. Howard?"

"You've got to get me something."

"Maybe I can get you $30,000 if you're lucky."

"Ben, because the Howard case included an element of malpractice, I selected that case as the lead one. That necrotic lip is pretty disgusting looking. I've got close to $20,000 in expenses. If you pay $50,000, the client will only get $20,000 after expenses and my fee. I can't sell that."

"Jack, the only reason I think I can get you *anything* for Howard is her necrotic lip. I can't get you a penny for the claimed sexual acts. Paul will play that video of her deposition for Pinsly, and his hand will stay in his pocket. What if I get Tennessee Mutual under Rule 54 to reimburse your expenses, and then it pays Howard $20,000 for her malpractice claim? You're reimbursed your expenses, and Howard gets two-thirds of $20,000 or just under $14,000."

"Now, for Perkins, I'd like $400,000. You're not going to find pictures of her on a website."

Willis was catching his breath and gaining confidence.

"Maybe not, but she got what she paid for. There's no medical malpractice in her case, just sex. There's no necrotic lip. The jury might question whether there was any forced sex. You've got those same middle-aged women on the jury."

"You've heard what I need. See what you can get."

They said good-bye, and Davis asked Sammie to come into his office.

"What did Willis have to say?"

"He wants a total of about $430,000 for settlement and expenses."

"If so, you made a pretty good deal with Maddox. McCormick would be picking up more than a third of the total payment. Maddox wanted to limit McCormick's contribution to ten percent."

"Let's call Sullivan together and find out when we're meeting with Pinsly."

Sullivan had been on the phone all morning with Pinsly. Paul had gotten to Pinsly first and poisoned the well. A meeting was set at Paul's office at four.

When Davis and Sammie arrived at Paul's office, Sullivan, Paul, and Pinsly were already there. Obviously their meeting had started earlier.

"Bob, what time did you get here?"

"Three."

"Well, what'd we miss?"

Paul interjected, "We were talking about how you exceeded your authority by promising Maddox that McCormick and Equitable could get out for $150,000."

Sullivan came to Davis's defense. "I've explained to you, Lester, that Davis and I had discussed that offer before the deposition began. We agreed that I'd take the deposition and that Davis would approach Maddox and then Willis."

Paul turned to Sullivan. "Why wasn't I included in that strategy session?"

Sullivan responded, but Davis was thinking the same thing. "Because neither one of us trusts you, Lester. You've been a prick so long. That's all you know how to be."

"I resent that, Sullivan."

"You can resent it all you want, but the facts are the facts. No amount of resentment is going to change those facts."

As much as Davis agreed with Sullivan, the bickering was slowing them down in handling business matters. Davis tried to be conciliatory. "Gentlemen, and I use that word loosely, if you'll let me, I can get these cases settled by Monday, and Tennessee Mutual can close the files and stop paying legal fees to both of you."

Davis hoped that a little levity would break the ice. He was right. The mention of settlement and cessation of legal fees got Pinsly's attention, and he got real interested. Davis asked Pinsly, "If we go to trial in both cases, how much will you pay Bob and Lester in legal fees to defend?"

Pinsly pretended to think about his response, but he'd already calculated the dollar amount. "I'd pay out $280,000 and another $43,000 in expenses. What will it take to make the cases go away?"

Davis described in detail his conversation with Willis. When he finished, Paul commented, "We should take more advantage of the Howard deposition in the Perkins case."

From Davis's point of view, Paul always seemed to say the wrong thing. "We need to help him make the right decision. Willis is a fighter; he'll recover from this disappointment. First, we need to agree to pay his expenses of $43,000."

Again, Paul tried to sidetrack the settlement. "That's outrageous."

"Wait a second, Lester. How much has Tennessee Mutual paid your firm for expenses in these cases?"

"That's none of your goddamn business, Davis."

"I'm sure your fees and expenses are more than Willis's, and as Pinsly points out, significantly more going forward."

Neither Paul nor Pinsly said anything. Both of them knew that Davis was right.

Davis tried to close the deal. "I think reimbursing his expenses of $43,000 and another $130,000 should fund the settlements."

Pinsly asked for clarification: "You're saying a total of $173,000 from us and $150,000 from Equitable?"

"That's right. Equitable is paying more than forty percent of the settlement and expenses. Equitable's insured, Rocky McCormick, didn't have sex with any of these women. And of course, Ms. Burns gets her written apology from Dr. Garcia."

Paul was quick to reply, "You're joking, right?"

Pinsly had prepped Lester Paul about Davis's demand that Dr. Garcia had to apologize to Ms. Burns.

"I'm as serious as a heart attack. If that lying little asshole doesn't apologize to that fine lady, I'll blow this settlement up and sue him for slander. You've all dealt with me before. I'm not bluffing, and I know at least two of you think I'm half crazy. Maybe I am."

The other men looked at one another. Sullivan was the first to speak. "You're a crazy son of a bitch. I believe you."

Davis smiled. "All three of you know I'm crazy then."

Pinsly directed Paul to draft a letter of apology for Dr. Garcia to sign. They agreed that it would be a private letter as long as Dr. Garcia's deposition remained sealed and that Dr. Garcia never slandered Ms. Burns again.

When they got back to the office, Sammie and Davis tried to call Willis, but he'd left for the day. It was after six. Davis decided the call was important enough to contact Willis at home. Susan Willis, the lawyer's wife, answered the phone. She knew Davis casually.

A minute later, Jack Willis was on the line. "What's up, Ben?"

"I think we can get this done. I got your $43,000 in expenses under Rule 54. Your clients will recover, without reimbursing you in any costs incurred in any of the cases. I've convinced the two insurance companies to pay another $280,000. I can't get a dime more, so don't ask. I'm offering $30,000 in Howard, and $250,000 in Perkins. What do you think?"

"I need a few days."

"You can have all the time in the world as long as the deals are done before we're scheduled to resume Howard's deposition on the 27th."

"I'll call you in the next day or so."

The next day, Willis called and informed Davis that they had a deal. The paperwork was executed three days later. It contained a strong confidentiality clause that prevented the parties from talking about the case or the settlement. That same day Davis delivered Garcia's apology letter to Donna for lying about their relationship, and he personally apologized for her having to take the polygraph.

CHAPTER THIRTY-TWO

MEDICAL
LICENSING BOARD

Wednesay, October 15, 1997

It had been five months since the settlement of the Willis lawsuits. The claims of malpractice and sex were behind Dr. Charles Garcia. Life moved on; Sammie graduated from Vanderbilt Law School and took the Bar. The results were published in the *Tennessean*. She passed.

It was a big day. Not only had Sammie become an attorney, but also it was the day of Dr. Charles Garcia's hearing before the Medical Licensing Board. The entire Davis team was attending the hearing, including Bella and Liza. Davis arranged a little breakfast party to honor Sammie's achievement.

Aunt Liza started things off. "We're so proud of you. We've watched you grow up and become a woman and a great attorney."

She gave her niece a hug. Davis, Bella, and Morty gave her a hug in turn. Davis produced a wrapped package from under the conference room table and handed it to Sammie.

She opened it immediately, ripping the paper that her aunt had chosen and so carefully wrapped. She pulled from the box a leather calfskin briefcase identical to the one her father had given her uncle. Inscribed below the buckle were her initials SAD, Sammie Annabelle Davis. She kissed her uncle on the cheek. Davis squeezed both her arms and said, "At least yours doesn't have any blood on it. Use it in good health."

Just a few buildings down, Amy Pierce was preparing to deal with Charlie Garcia's last serious problem. The charges brought by the Tennessee Medical Licensing Board were still pending. The *Tennessean* and two of the local TV news stations ran stories the day before the hearing. News cameras weren't allowed in the hearing room, but the reporters would attend and the cameras would be waiting outside the building when the hearing ended.

Pierce had done a masterful job of delaying the administrative hearing, but the day had come. At her insistence Señor Garcia and Mrs. Garcia were in attendance. Harrelson, the loyal family attorney, sat next to them. As he sat there, he twiddled with his watch chain and then finally put it in his vest pocket.

The absolute instructions to Pierce were to prevent the revocation of Dr. Garcia's Tennessee medical license at all costs. If it was taken away, his New York license was sure to follow. Charlie's professional future was riding on this hearing's outcome.

Charlie was sitting at the defense table next to Pierce and dreading the opening of the session. His father signaled him to come to the back of the room, where the Garcias and Harrelson were seated. Charlie sat down next to his father and whispered in his ear.

He looked over to his right, and in the third row were Davis, Steine, Sullivan, Sammie, and two other women. Four vultures were ready to pick his bones after the hearing. Paul didn't show; he wasn't getting paid to attend.

Charlie's father broke his chain of thought. "Mr. Harrelson and I met with Ms. Pierce this morning, and based upon her recommendation, we've changed our strategy."

Charlie had complained to Pierce that he didn't like his chances under the old strategy. Even though the settlements were confidential and the depositions were sealed, he could be called as a witness by the state. He would either have to perjure himself or take the Fifth. That would be difficult to explain.

"What's the new strategy? How has it changed? This is my life. I not only have a right to know, I'm the one who has to live with the outcome. What's up?"

"Don't worry, son. Mr. Harrelson, Ms. Pierce, and I have everything under control. I'd never let you down. Just trust us. We know what's best for you."

Pierce walked to the back of the courtroom to retrieve her client. Her real client was not the son, but the father. He paid the fee and controlled the strategy. She could tell by the look on Charlie's face he didn't like being in the dark, but it was better this way.

He was thinking about the years he'd spent studying to become a doctor and now because of some stupid mistakes and some horny women, all that hard work was at risk.

He turned and whispered to Pierce, "All I did was give these women what they wanted. Nobody held a gun to their heads."

"You'd better not share those thoughts with the board. You'd better not be arrogant."

Charlie Garcia was angry and felt no remorse for his actions. His attitude wasn't going to be sympathetic.

Pierce stretched to her full height of five nine and a half, and with authority she said to Charlie, "Trust me. I know what the hell I'm doing."

At ten, the Medical Licensing Board panel walked into the

room. It consisted of three licensed physicians: Robert Becker, internist; Lawrence Karl, urologist; and Frank Alder, cardiologist. Each doctor had been appointed by the governor to serve on the board. Each read the charges brought by the state against Dr. Garcia and his answers to the charges.

The next person who entered the courtroom was the administrative law judge, Thomas Booth. Judge Booth was a state employee and worked closely with the state prosecutor, Randi Hecht. Ms. Hecht was young and inexperienced; her boss had assigned her to the Garcia case because it was a slam-dunk.

Unlike the civil suits filed by Willis, consent to the sex was not a defense. Ethically, the act of sex with a patient, whether voluntary or not, was still a violation of the Code of Conduct. A doctor who wanted to date or, even worse, have sex with his patient was obligated to discharge the patient as a patient first before any romantic involvement.

Pierce had discussed with her client that he might have to take the Fifth Amendment, asserting he might be incriminating himself if he testified. Pierce anticipated that the state would argue that there were no criminal charges pending. In response Pierce would argue that no criminal charges were pending yet, but who knows where these matters might lead? That was the last strategy Charlie had been told about, and he didn't like it. He hoped the new undisclosed strategy was better and less incriminating.

Judge Thomas Booth called the hearing to order. He had the panel members identify themselves and their medical specialties. He had Ms. Pierce and Ms. Hecht identify themselves, and Ms. Pierce introduced Dr. Garcia to the panel.

Then Judge Booth took control. "Are there any preliminary matters that should be addressed?"

Pierce stood and addressed the judge. "Yes, Your Honor. Dr.

Garcia moves for the court to recuse and disband the panel because of a clear conflict of interest and potential bias."

That got everybody's attention in the courtroom, particularly the panel members.

"Explain yourself, Ms. Pierce. That's a bold statement."

"Your Honor, please be advised that Dr. Frank Alder's ex-wife is a patient of Dr. Garcia, and under the Code of Ethics, that would constitute a clear conflict of interest."

"I don't understand . . . ," Dr. Alder blurted out.

Pierce was ready for anything Hecht might have to say, and Hecht was on her feet prepared to argue. "This is not a medical malpractice issue. I could see the conflict argument if the board was seeking to revoke Dr. Garcia's medical license for negligent practice. Then Dr. Alder's ex-wife's patient relationship might be relevant. But this is about Dr. Garcia having sex with patients, not about the care he provided."

Grasping for straws, the judge addressed Pierce, "Ms. Hecht makes a good point, Ms. Pierce."

Pierce snapped back, "How do you know Dr. Garcia didn't have sex with Ms. Alder? That would disqualify Dr. Alder, wouldn't it?"

Dr. Alder jumped up. "Did he?"

The panel member was both angry and confused. Pierce knew she'd disqualified Dr. Alder. There was no way Judge Booth or anyone else in the courtroom would consider him unbiased at this point.

Judge Booth took a ten-minute recess to think about the pending motion and to read certain sections of the Code of Ethics.

Sullivan leaned over and whispered to Davis and Morty, "A brilliant delay tactic!"

Morty quickly responded, "It's brilliant, but it's not a delay tactic. Watch this."

When the judge returned, he ruled that Dr. Alder was conflicted from sitting and that the hearing would have to be continued to date uncertain until a full panel could be appointed.

"Any other preliminary motions since we're all together before I adjourn this hearing?"

Pierce stood again and handed a document to the clerk and to Ms. Hecht. Charlie had no idea what was on the piece of paper, but judging from Hecht's reaction, it was spectacular. The document was also handed up to Judge Booth, who also reacted strongly.

"Ms. Pierce, what is the meaning of this?"

"I think the document is clear and straightforward. Dr. Garcia has surrendered his Tennessee medical license. Therefore this administrative body has no jurisdiction over him. He is not subject to your authority. He is a non-licensed person as far as Tennessee is concerned. All charges must be dismissed for lack of jurisdiction."

Pierce handed the clerk and Hecht a ten-page brief with more than a dozen cases cited. The judge took a one-hour break to read the brief and do his own research.

During the break, Pierce, Dr. Garcia, his father, and Harrelson met in a private office near the courtroom. As soon as they got in the room, an agitated Charlie asked, "What the hell just happened in there?"

Harrelson responded, "Ms. Pierce just saved your New York medical license and saved you the embarrassment of losing your Tennessee medical license. You couldn't testify, and you couldn't successfully take the Fifth. It was a no-win situation. Ms. Pierce got Dr. Alder recused so that there wasn't a full panel and the charges couldn't proceed. Once the court ruled that the hearing was continued, it allowed Ms. Pierce to surrender your license, and the court no longer had any authority over you. It was absolutely brilliant."

Harrelson tipped an imaginary hat to Pierce.

Still confused, Charlie asked, "What do I do now?"

Señor Garcia answered Charlie's question, "You come home to New York and practice medicine there. Your mother and I will help you get started. You need to behave yourself, no more trampy women. I want you to find a nice girl and settle down."

Judge Booth dismissed the charges against Dr. Garcia, and two days later he returned home to New York. He just shut down his practice in Nashville. Damn his patients, even the ones who paid deposits. Harrelson would sort all that out.

CHAPTER THIRTY-THREE
ESCAPE TO NEW YORK
Saturday, March 14, 1998

It didn't take Dr. Charles Juan Batista Garcia long to settle into his new surroundings. Charlie knew New York City; he'd grown up in part there. He'd also gone to medical school and completed his residency and fellowship there.

His father set him up in a medical office on Park Avenue. Dr. Charles Garcia hung out his shingle and began practicing oral and maxillofacial surgery.

Charlie loved the city, and despite his promise to his father that he'd settle down, he was out almost every night. He vowed on a stack of Bibles and his sainted mother's life that he wouldn't sleep with his patients. In Charlie's mind, however, every other woman in New York was fair game.

He drank to excess and used various recreational drugs. He was convinced that he could stop at any time. His caseload was light, he didn't need the money, and he never scheduled a surgery before noon to allow for his recovery.

On this particular Saturday night, Charlie was in the company of a beautiful Brazilian woman, Monica. After dinner, they went to Charlie's favorite country bar on East 53rd Street. He'd found several country bars in the city and spent several nights a week at one or another. Charlie still missed Nashville and its music scene. When he lived there, he often went to music venues; his favorite in Nashville was the Bluebird Café.

He also missed Robyn. She was a head case, but she had her virtues. Those nights Charlie didn't go out, he stayed at home and watched videos of himself and Robyn.

As for his current date, Charlie couldn't decide whether he wanted to sleep with the woman or perform surgery. He knew that he had to make up his mind. He swore on his mother's life he couldn't do both.

He told her, "You're a very beautiful woman, but I could make you even more beautiful."

The young woman laughed and asked him how he would change her.

Charlie looked her up and down and, in a serious tone, said, "I'd first give you Garcia kissable lips. I wouldn't touch that smile. Your breasts are perky enough, but you could go up a cup size. I love the shape of your ass, but I'd recommend a lift. That's my professional opinion anyway."

Like so many women, the mocha-skinned beauty had fallen for Charlie's smooth talk and sexual appetite. She leaned in and planted her lips on his, and her tongue found its way into his mouth. Charlie felt a slight tingle. She ran the tip of her tongue along the roof of his mouth, and he achieved an erection. It didn't take much for that to happen.

Their table was located in a dark corner of the club. They were about forty feet from the stage. Under the table, she grabbed him.

Charlie thought, *There goes another potential patient.* She completed her task while a young man in a black cowboy hat sang the theme to the *Rawhide* TV show starring Clint Eastwood.

The next act was a group of six musicians with a female lead singer. Charlie could hardly believe his eyes: the woman was Robyn Eden. There was no mistaking her. She still had the most incredible green eyes of any woman Charlie ever seen.

The band played three songs and then left the stage. Charlie excused himself, "Darling, I've got to go to the little boy's room."

Instead he rushed backstage and knocked on the performers' dressing room. A member of her band, with shoulder-length hair and a scruffy beard, answered the door. He must have been at least six feet six inches tall. In a booming voice, he inquired, "Can I help you?"

"I'm a friend of Robyn. I'm Dr. Charles Garcia. Please tell her I'm here."

A moment later Robyn appeared at the door. She was just as he remembered her, with her white teeth, new chin, C cup breasts, and Garcia kissable lips. "Charlie, what the hell?"

"Just give me a few minutes. I know I did you wrong. Please have a drink with me, and let's reconnect."

"I don't think so. You hurt me, Charlie. You abandoned me. I went into rehab after I got fired. Thank God, my sister got me help. Where were you? You just left me high and dry." Robyn sounded more hurt than angry.

Charlie turned on the charm. He'd smooth talked her before. He could do it again.

"I'm a changed person. What happened to me in Nashville made me grow up. I'm back on track. Just give me a chance. I'm the man you fell in love with. I've put my demons behind me." Then he added, "You look great and sounded even better."

Robyn smiled, and he knew he had her. Her next words confirmed it. "I could go for a cup of coffee and maybe some breakfast. I'm not on the same clock as the rest of the world. I go to bed at noon and wake up at seven. Why don't you meet me at the front door in twenty minutes?"

"I'll count the minutes."

He left Robyn and went back to the table where his Brazilian date was waiting. He gave the explanation of a medical emergency as he put her in a cab. He wondered whether their brief encounter precluded her from being a patient. He'd ponder that thought and decided he wouldn't ask his father's opinion.

Charlie didn't have to wait long for Robyn. She'd changed into jeans and a black flannel shirt. Her hair was in a ponytail. Her intense green eyes sparkled, and Charlie felt his heart skip.

They ate breakfast around the corner at a Greek diner. Charlie listened as Robyn explained her struggle to remain clean. After he left town, her sister, Peter Nichols, and others ambushed her and held an intervention. They forced her into rehab, where she suffered through a difficult detox. After ninety days at Cumberland Heights, she was forced to live in a halfway house.

Despite the drugs and alcohol, music was her life, and she needed it even more than drugs. For her first year out of rehab she limited herself to studio work, but with time, she felt strong enough to go out on the road. She mostly stayed with club soda or near beer but occasionally slipped and fell off the wagon. When she did, she got right back up and started her sobriety from day one.

Charlie was a good listener. They drank coffee and talked for almost four hours. It was a great reunion.

The next evening after her show, they went back to his apartment. Charlie decided to take it slow, no sex toys, just pure lovemaking. But old habits are hard to break, and she was a willing participant. Charlie had forgotten just how kinky Robyn could be.

They started with a little bondage, at Robyn's suggestion. She got completely naked, and he admired her body. She lay flat on the bed, on her stomach. Charlie secured her arms and legs to the four-foot-tall bedposts with long gray silk scarves. He was careful not to tie them too tightly. Robyn squirmed in the bed, raised herself to her knees, and purred like a kitten. Charlie quickly undressed, and they did not stop until early morning.

They spent the next ten days together, with Charlie attending each of her shows. Robyn finished her two-week gig and was scheduled to go to Philadelphia for a week.

They both cried the morning she left town. Charlie told her that he loved her. They agreed to vacation together at the end of April. As he watched her drive off with the rest of the band, Charlie wanted her in the worst way.

CHAPTER THIRTY-FOUR

A TROUBLED ROMANCE

Sunday, July 12, 1998

After three months of a long-distance relationship, Charlie convinced Robyn to relocate to New York City. He promised her they'd be happy and she could find work in small local clubs. She found occasional work but not happiness. She wanted more from the relationship than Charlie was willing to give.

She moved into Charlie's Central Park West and 67th Street apartment. Its wrap-around balcony had a breathtaking view of the park.

It was Sunday. Robyn didn't have a gig, and Charlie had the day off. Their plan was to lie in bed all morning and read the Sunday *New York Times* from front to back. He propped himself up in bed and started with the front page on an article about Iran's efforts to build a nuclear bomb. It was a little depressing, so he put the paper down.

Charlie looked around his bedroom. It was professionally decorated to satisfy his masculine taste. His bed's headboard of dark rich chocolate leather allowed him to sit straight up in bed. His aqua sheets were made of Egyptian cotton, an expensive one-thousand-thread count.

In front of him was his six-foot-wide fireplace, which he used regularly in the winter months. On each side were twelve-foot-high walnut bookcases, which sported dozens of volumes of books and various knickknacks Charlie and his mother had collected over the years. The room was impressive, and so was the walnut and brass ladder that could slide from bookcase to bookcase in front of the fireplace.

He returned to his paper, starting with another depressing article about the Mideast crisis. When he looked up, Robyn appeared in the doorway. All she had on was the top portion of his midnight blue pajamas. He stared first at her incredible green eyes. It was where he and every other man started.

His eyes didn't stay there long. They worked down to her partially opened top. She'd only done the bottom two buttons, and her breasts were readily visible. The pajama top barely covered her shaved pubic area. As hard as he tried, he couldn't see it.

He gave up and focused on what she was carrying. She had a tray with a silver coffeepot, set for two. Charlie spied a basket of croissants, butter, and his favorite orange marmalade. She poured each of them a cup of coffee, and Charlie applied a glop of marmalade to his croissant. He took a big bite and, before he could swallow, said, "Thanks for the coffee, I needed a cup. I couldn't focus on the paper. Every story is so depressing."

"That's why I don't even bother to read the paper. Why get depressed?"

She put the tray on the nightstand, got in bed, and snuggled up against him. Her mere presence excited him. It didn't take that much. He threw the paper on the hardwood floor and started kissing her neck.

She protested, "You promised that we'd read in bed all morning. There's a legal thriller I wanted to start."

"What's it called?"

"First Do No Harm."

"Who's it by?"

"Somebody named Turk. It has a picture of Printer's Alley on the cover. You know I performed in several clubs in the Alley."

"Sorry, I didn't know you planned on reading it. I put it on the top right bookshelf."

She smiled and without a complaint moved toward the ladder and rolled it to the right. She began to ascend the ladder, and as she did her pajama top hiked up, revealing her perfect behind.

Charlie was immediately aroused, jumped from the bed, and followed her up the ladder. She'd made it to the fourth step, and he was on the second when she reached for the book. As she did, he placed a hand on each of her hips. She trembled under his touch.

She lowered herself to the third step, holding onto each rail of the ladder. As she did, he entered her from behind, pushing upward. She moaned with pleasure. This encouraged him, and he rhythmically moved inside her. Satisfied, she turned around on the ladder and was now facing him. Her bottom resting on the fourth step, he moved from the second to the third, and she met him the rest of the way. She used the sides of the ladder to move up and down.

After five minutes, Charlie finished, but he didn't even make an effort to pull out. He would have if he'd known she'd stopped taking her birth control pills.

They'd discussed children. He was against them, so she secretly plotted to get pregnant. She thought he'd have to marry her if she was carrying his bastard child. She was wrong. She misread Charlie Garcia. He'd never marry her because his parents would never approve. They had plans for their son, and Robyn Eden wasn't part of those plans.

They dismounted each other and then the ladder. She never got her book, and they lay there exhausted on top of the sheets. He was naked. She still had on the midnight blue pajama top, but it was now completely open.

"That was great, wasn't it?" She was looking for validation.

He'd give it to her. Why not? It was great. "Absolutely. Couldn't have been better."

"Do you love me?"

Charlie felt a little cornered, but why pick a fight?

"Of course." He figured he'd keep it short and simple.

But she continued to press. "I'm living with you. I'm screwing you. When am I going to meet your parents?"

He needed to think quickly. He wanted to avoid a fight, but if he promised, she'd hold him to it.

"The time's not right. My relationship with my parents is very complicated. The best I can promise is someday."

"Fuck you, Charlie. Someday isn't good enough. I've given up the road for you. You begged me to move in with you, so I did. What a fool I am. You said you'd changed. You're the same selfish son of a bitch you were in Nashville."

She jumped up from the bed. Within thirty minutes she was packed and walked out the door without another word. Charlie didn't try to stop her. He'd miss her, but what she wanted he just couldn't give.

CHAPTER THIRTY-FIVE

THE DERBY

Saturday, May 1, 1999
(Almost Ten Months Later)

Charlie couldn't live with Robyn, but he couldn't live without her either. They'd poke along a few months in silence, and one of them would break down and call the other. They were addicted to each other like a drug, certainly no damn good for each other. They'd hooked up twice since the day she walked out on him in New York, but each time the trip ended in a fight because of Charlie's unwillingness to commit to their relationship.

Despite their tumultuous existence, Charlie paid her each month $1,500 for an apartment and expenses in Hewes City, just south of Nashville. Those payments gave Charlie access to her. She'd just moved into a new apartment on the courthouse square. Her sister, Valerie, co-signed for her, and Charlie paid the deposits and the first month's rent.

This weekend would end differently, Charlie hoped. He flew down from New York to Louisville, Kentucky, and she drove up from Hewes City. He'd brought an entire pill bottle of Viagra; he received samples from the manufacturer.

It was Derby weekend, and despite the demand, Charlie secured a suite at a Marriott Hotel near the track. They arrived separately, Charlie first and Robyn an hour later. They decided on a quickie before going to the track. The Viagra made it easy.

Charlie bet on every race and lost $800. He figured he could afford it. Despite the fact it was only May, the sun was strong and beat down hard on the couple. Robyn got one of her cluster migraine headaches. She went to the racetrack store and took four Motrin but felt no relief. An hour later she complained, "Charlie, my head's splitting. Those Motrin didn't work. I need something stronger."

From conversations with Valerie, Charlie knew that Robyn's drug use was more pronounced than when they'd lived together in New York. They'd partied but within limits. It was somewhat under control. According to Valerie, Robyn was totally out of control now, and her drug of choice was hydrocodone. Robyn didn't name the drug, but Charlie knew that her request was for hydrocodone.

"We can stop at a pharmacy on the way back to the hotel. I'll write you a prescription," he told her.

"I'd like hydrocodone. It seems to work best."

"I bet it does," Charlie said sarcastically.

Robyn didn't catch the condescending remark. She was too busy dreaming about her hydrocodone.

He pulled into a Super AAA Pharmacy and got out while she stayed in the car. He walked up to the pharmacy counter.

"Hi, I'm Dr. Charles Garcia, and I'm going to write a prescription for my fiancée, Robyn Eden, for hydrocodone."

He handed Robert, whose nameplate identified him as a pharmacy tech, his DEA card that authorized Charlie by federal law to write prescriptions for narcotics.

"I'm sorry, Doctor, I can't fill this prescription. You're an out-of-state physician. I think it's my company's policy, but only a pharmacist can fill a Schedule III narcotic for an out-of-state physician. He'll be back in an hour. He just stepped out for a late lunch. You'll have to wait or come back."

After Charlie berated poor Robert for ten minutes, the young man relented and filled the prescription despite his understanding of company policy. Charlie paid and walked out the door with the pills.

Once in the car, he handed Robyn the pill bottle, and she downed two of them before they got back to the hotel. Charlie thought he'd lie down before they went out to dinner. He hoped to at least go to the hotel restaurant, assuming that Robyn's headache got better. Thirty minutes later, he inquired about how she was feeling. The answer was, "No better."

An hour later, he was getting really hungry, and he asked again. She grunted a negative response. He'd hoped for another go-round. He'd taken another Viagra.

By eight he was about to order room service when Robyn spoke for the first time in more than two hours.

"Where's our relationship going?"

"I think we're doing fine. Maybe we should see each other more. I'll fly down to Nashville."

"That's not what I want. First, I want to meet your parents. Next, I want to get engaged. Then, I want to get married and start a family. That's what *I* want. What do *you* want?"

"I want to see you five or six times a year and have a great time whenever that happens."

"Then we want different things out of life."

As her words came out, Charlie could tell Robyn was getting angrier and angrier.

"You're an asshole, Charlie, a fucking asshole." With that said, she ran into the bathroom.

Fuck her, Charlie thought. *I'm ordering room service.* She wouldn't answer, so he ordered only for himself. He ordered a double Jack on the rocks, shrimp and grits, and key lime pie for dessert. The food arrived in less than forty minutes, and he devoured it.

He turned on the TV and selected a *Seinfeld* episode. It was the one where Kramer befriends some Cubans so he can continue to smoke Cuban cigars. When the episode ended, it was nine thirty, and Charlie knew that room service ended at ten. He knocked on the bathroom door. She'd been in there without a sound for almost an hour and a half.

"Do you want anything from room service? I've eaten. Room service stops at ten, so I've got to order it now. Speak now or forever hold your peace."

No response, so he knocked again harder. Still nothing, so he banged on the door. Silence.

"Look, you stubborn bitch, answer me!"

She didn't, so he broke down the door. He found her lying on the floor unconscious but breathing, with an empty pill bottle in her left hand.

Initially stunned, he regained his doctor's responses and dialed 911. The paramedics arrived in five minutes, and he rode in the ambulance to the hospital.

Once at the hospital he reported to the emergency room attending physician that she overdosed from prescription hydrocodone. The physician confirmed that earlier in the day she'd filled the prescription of twenty pills and that Charlie was the prescribing doctor. After she was taken to the OR to have her stomach pumped, Charlie went to the waiting room.

At midnight a police detective found Charlie in the waiting room and, after a few minutes of conversation, read him his Miranda rights, arrested him, and took him into custody.

At two thirty after being booked, Charlie got his one phone call. He debated whether to call his father, Pierce, or Harrelson. Although Pierce was closer, three hours by car, she wasn't licensed in Kentucky. He was afraid to call his father, so by process of elimination, Harrelson was the lucky one. Harrelson got things done; he was the man to call.

Harrelson was sleeping. It was three thirty eastern time, and he didn't appreciate being awakened, especially by Charlie. He told his client that he'd fly down on a private jet, but it was Sunday and there'd be nothing he could do. Once down there he'd figure out what to do. Harrelson agreed to call Señor Garcia later in the morning. There was no point in waking him up at that hour. The way Charlie Garcia treated and disappointed his parents was enough to break Harrelson's heart—that is, if he had a heart.

CHAPTER THIRTY-SIX

A DEAL IS CUT

Monday, May 3, 1999

A man of his word, Harrelson was at the Louisville, Jefferson County jail by one o'clock, but because it was Sunday, there were no judge, no DA, and no police chief to influence or bribe. The fate of Dr. Charles Garcia would simply have to wait until Monday, and Charlie would have to remain in jail. Harrelson checked into a Holiday Inn near the jail.

On Monday at 10:00 a.m. when Harrelson managed to get in to see him under the attorney-client relationship, Charlie complained about the delay, rather than being thankful. He wanted out. That really angered Harrelson. Charlie Garcia was a pain in the butt and was unappreciative. If it wasn't for his father, he'd let the kid rot in jail.

Harrelson looked at his pocket watch, his Waltham, and advised the younger Garcia that the bail hearing wasn't till three. Harrelson approached the DA to discuss Charlie's case. He learned that Robyn survived and was thinking about prosecuting Charlie for reckless endangerment. The DA, whose name was Peter Taylor, informed Harrelson that Charlie was also charged with wrongfully prescribing a narcotic.

Harrelson asked, "I don't understand. Dr. Garcia has a federally issued DEA number. How could he wrongfully prescribe a narcotic?"

"He's an out-of-state physician. Only a pharmacist can fill a narcotic prescription, and he bullied the pharmacist tech to fill Ms. Eden's. He violated the law."

Harrelson, who was extremely bright and motivated to get his client off so he could go back home, tried to twist the law. "Isn't that the problem of the pharmacy? They knew the law. Dr. Garcia didn't. He had no intent to violate the law. Is that crime a felony, punishable by more than one year?"

"It carries one to three years. Intent is not an element. He's guilty the moment he hands the prescription to the pharmacist tech."

"This is a simple misunderstanding. Who's the judge?"

"Judge Corey Olsen."

Harrelson excused himself to find the office of Judge Corey Olsen. It was on the third floor of the courthouse, and Harrelson walked straight in and introduced himself. He told the judge what happened and noted Charlie's ignorance of the law. He explained that a conviction would destroy a promising and lucrative medical practice. He assured the judge that Robyn Eden, Charlie's girlfriend, ultimately wouldn't testify, so it would be much more difficult to secure a conviction.

Ethics didn't bother Harrelson. This ex parte communication, without the county attorney present, didn't matter to his sense of justice. For some reason it didn't bother Judge Olsen, either. Harrelson was a deal maker, and he knew just how hard to push.

Olsen was sympathetic, and he accepted Harrelson's explanation for Charlie's conduct. For the next fifteen minutes they talked about possible solutions.

Harrelson asked the judge, "When a defendant pays a fine, where do those funds go?"

"That's a very interesting question, Mr. Harrelson. Half goes into the general county coffers, and the other half goes into the judges' and DA's retirement fund. Donations are appreciated."

Harrelson felt good about his conversation with Judge Olsen. No dollar amount was agreed to, a pretrial diversion was mentioned, but Harrelson was confident he could buy Charlie's way out of this one.

The deputy brought Charlie into court. Harrelson was licensed in several states but not Kentucky. For $500, he hired a local co-counsel, so he would be permitted to speak in court. Charlie's was the third case called. This was supposed to be a bond hearing and, if the parties agreed, an arraignment.

DA Taylor addressed the court, "Your Honor, Dr. Charles Garcia recklessly endangered the life of Robyn Eden and illegally prescribed narcotics. I've interviewed the pharmacy tech, Robert Cummings, and Ms. Eden . . ."

Judge Olsen cut Taylor off. Harrelson figured the more said in open court, the harder to cut a deal. Judge Olsen was his kind of guy. Olsen announced a fifteen-minute break and asked Harrelson and Taylor to meet with him in chambers.

"General, this doctor made a mistake. The girl locked herself in a bathroom, and she took the drugs. He didn't administer them."

"He broke the law, Judge. If not for him, that girl wouldn't be in the hospital. He bullied that tech into breaking the law. We can't just tolerate such conduct."

Harrelson interrupted, "According to my client, he was told the restriction was company policy, not a violation of the law."

"Well, he was misinformed," replied Taylor, who turned to the judge and asked, "What do you suggest, sir?"

Taylor knew Olsen and his skewed form of justice. He sensed the hammer was about to come down and wanted to hear what the judge said before he committed too far.

Judge Olsen looked deep in thought before answering DA Taylor's question, "Let's start with a fine. I'd say $20,000 should do it. He'll do pretrial diversion, and if Dr. Garcia remains out of trouble, we'll expunge his record. The document will remain under seal so that the New York Medical Board won't have access and won't be notified."

Harrelson watched Taylor closely. The young DA almost blew a gasket. His face got red, and his voice quivered with anger, "Judge, I can't sign off on that deal. He can't just walk away without consequences. He can't just buy his way out of this problem. Ms. Eden almost died. This is serious, and with all due respect, I wouldn't characterize this as a mistake. The victim wants us to prosecute."

Harrelson saw his opportunity. "Excuse me, General Taylor, I'm willing to submit any deal we make to Ms. Eden for her approval. These people know each other intimately. They have a long-term relationship. She doesn't want Dr. Garcia prosecuted. Let's make her approval a contingency."

Harrelson knew that Charlie could influence Robyn to withdraw her cooperation. Charlie would simply sweet-talk her.

Judge Olsen spoke next, "That seems fair to me, General. If the victim wants this resolved quickly, why should we pursue it? Pretrial diversion is the right solution. I want your help on this one, General. We see each other every day. We've got to work together. After Mr. Harrelson leaves following this hearing, you and I will continue to negotiate deals. I can be your best friend or your worst enemy. Help me get this done."

Harrelson could tell that ultimately the judge would win, but Harrelson wanted this matter to end today. He thought he'd sweeten the pot.

"What about if Dr. Garcia agrees to increase the fine to $50,000?"

Now Taylor saw his opportunity. "I want this man to feel responsibility for his conduct into the future. I'd say three years' probation would impose that sense of responsibility."

Harrelson cringed at the thought of Charlie Garcia on probation. He wasn't confident that Charlie could stay out of trouble that long. Unfortunately, Taylor's suggestion made sense, and the judge did have to work with the DA's office after Charlie walked out the door.

The judge stated, "Here's what we're going to do. Dr. Garcia is going to pay a $50,000 fine. I'm going to enter a sealed order that provides for pretrial diversion, which will be expunged eighteen months from the date of entry of the order. During that eighteen-month period, Dr. Garcia will be on probation. I appoint Alan Baxter as Dr. Garcia's probation officer. Dr. Garcia is required to call Mr. Baxter every week and report his status and verify he's remained within the boundaries of his probation.

"In addition, every quarter Dr. Garcia will travel to Louisville and meet with Mr. Baxter to review the status of his probation. Dr. Garcia will surrender his passport, and his travel will be restricted to within the United States. This deal is contingent on the victim, Ms. Eden, agreeing that prosecution is not appropriate. That's the deal. I want the two of you to accept this deal and like it."

Harrelson extended his hand, and Taylor reluctantly took it. Harrelson needed to explain the deal to Charlie and turn him loose to charm Robyn Eden. Harrelson didn't have confidence that Charlie could stay out of trouble for eighteen months, but he was confident that Charlie could charm Robyn into approving the deal.

Charlie was more concerned about his confiscated Viagra prescription and how he could get more from the manufacturer. Despite his need to distance himself from Robyn Eden, he knew he wouldn't. He was addicted to her and knew eventually he'd be drawn to see her again.

CHAPTER THIRTY-SEVEN
THE HOSPITAL
Tuesday, July 4, 2000
(Almost Fourteen Months Later)

The ambulance with lights flashing and sirens blaring pulled into the emergency room entrance of the Hewes County Hospital. The staff came running out to meet the EMTs and their patient. Charlie jumped out the back of the ambulance; it was ten forty-six. They'd hit quite a bit of traffic leaving the town square because of the fireworks observers. It took probably twice as long, even with the sirens blasting.

Despite his medical training, Charlie was pale and nauseous. As a medical student and resident, he'd dealt with critically ill patients, but for the last five years he'd limited his practice to cosmetics. Besides, this was very personal. He loved this woman.

The paramedics carefully unloaded the gurney with its precious cargo. Charlie followed behind the gurney. Just inside the automatic doors of the emergency room there was an exchange of information between hospital staff and the paramedics. The patient was seemingly transferred. Although he was listening, Charlie didn't comprehend what was being said. He was going into shock.

He mindlessly tried to follow the gurney into a treatment room and was barred by a huge black woman in a nurse's uniform. "Where do you think you're going, sir?"

Charlie's mind was racing, but he dug down deep and with absolute control and authority in a loud enough voice for everyone in the treatment room to hear said, "Excuse me, I'm Dr. Charles Garcia, and she's my patient."

The nurse let him pass with no further comment. He needed information and walked straight up to the attending doctor. He was tall and black, wearing blue scrubs.

"How's she doing, Doctor?"

"You claim to be her doctor-fiancé. What's she on, and how much did she take? She's in real trouble."

Charlie hesitated for what seemed to him a very long time, but it was only a minute. He wanted to contemplate his words carefully. He knew what he said needed to be consistent with what he told the paramedics or there'd be trouble.

"She's been partying several days. She's an addict. I know she's drunk at least two liters of vodka, smoked a couple of joints, and disappeared into the bathroom almost a dozen times. What she did in there I just don't know. I've been trying to get her into rehab since I came to town."

He failed to mention the syringe, white powder, and her bleeding from the femoral region. Those were lies by omission.

Charlie fingered the bottle of Viagra in his front pocket.

The attending doctor, whose nameplate read *Mann*, looked doubtfully at Charlie and, with scorn in his voice, stated, "You've been with this patient all this time, and that's all you can tell me about her condition. As you know, Doctor, how I proceed in my treatment depends on what drugs she's on. What's her drug of choice? Without that information I'm flying blind."

"That's the best I can do, sorry. Over the years she's used more than a dozen different drugs. I didn't follow her into the bathroom. I would be guessing, and that would be worse than not knowing."

"What's your relationship with the patient?"

"She's my fiancée," he consistently lied.

With that, Dr. Mann turned and returned to his patient. Charlie remained in place a few minutes, then left for the waiting room. He sat down, and the bottle in his front pocket dug into his groin. He adjusted his pants.

A tall woman in a black pantsuit with a gold shield visible at her belt approached him. She extended her hand. Before Charlie shook it, he looked at his watch, ten fifty-nine.

"I'm Detective Haber, Hewes City police."

Chief Detective Kristin Haber arrived at the hospital, unbe-knownst to Charlie, a few minutes after the ambulance. She'd been at the station when the 911 came in. Haber instructed Officer Dawson to remain at the scene, seal the apartment with crime scene tape, and prevent anyone from entering the apartment.

When she got to the hospital, Haber didn't make her move right away. She wanted to observe him.

Charlie eyed Haber with suspicion. She looked tough, and she was. Haber was a sixteen-year veteran of the Hewes City police and was respected and regarded as a no-nonsense detective.

She was tall, almost six feet, but she clearly had a woman's body. She had short blonde hair, which gave her a tough dyke-like quality, but after being with her a few minutes, that stereotypical conclusion was rejected. She was a woman who had succeeded in a man's world.

"Is she alive? Her name's Robyn Eden, right?"

Charlie barely choked out, "She's still with us, but I don't know for how long."

Charlie was in a near state of hysteria. Tears were running down both cheeks. He was sobbing uncontrollably. In an effort to comfort him, the detective put her hand on his shoulder.

Haber put her arm around him and drew him close. She felt the pill bottle in his front pocket and wondered what it was. Charlie cried hard into her shoulder. Haber was not only providing emotional support to Charlie but also evaluating this potential witness/suspect.

Dr. Mann walked over and in a grim voice reported, "She's gone. I called it at eleven thirty-six. I'm very sorry, but there was nothing we could do."

Charlie fell to his knees, and his face went blank. Haber read the look as one of complete despair and grief. He wasn't acting. Haber could sense his deep loss. Haber lifted him up from under his arms. She was surprisingly strong for someone of only a hundred and fifty pounds. She worked out at least four days a week at the police gym, and on Sundays she took her two chocolate labs, Hershey and Nestle, for a six-mile run around Radnor Lake.

She led Charlie to the Meditation Room, a small room the hospital set aside for clergy to meet with grieving families. It was a room too often needed at a hospital. Detective Haber mustered up her most compassionate voice and asked, "Doctor, what happened?"

It was an open-ended question, non-threatening. Charlie burst into tears again and began sobbing.

She tried again, "What happened to Ms. Eden?"

"I don't know. We were making love, and her heart just gave out."

His whole body was trembling. He gripped the chair for support, and it started to chatter from his trembling.

The cause of death was drugs, not sex, thought Haber. *He needs to tell me what she was on and how she got them.* She was about to ask that very question when Charlie began to lose it again. *He couldn't be that good an actor, could he?*

Between his shakes and shivers, he squeaked out, "I've lost my baby."

Haber, trying to calm him, repeated the common assurance, "She's in a better place."

Charlie shook his head and blurted out, "*They're* in a better place."

"Who?"

"Robyn and our baby. She was pregnant; that's why I came to see her. I was trying to save both her and the baby. My baby, my child."

Haber was shocked. The news came out of left field, and she simply wasn't prepared. The pregnancy would have been revealed anyway via the autopsy report, but that would be provided down the road.

He calmed down a bit, and she put her hand on his shoulder before cautiously continuing to question him.

Charlie explained that he lived in New York and was in town for the long holiday as a good time to try to reason with Robyn.

"When did you come down?"

"Friday afternoon. Robyn's an addict. She was out of control. I was trying to convince her to get help. We were having intercourse, and she complained of severe chest pain so I called 911. I performed CPR until the paramedics arrived. I can't believe this happened again." The words just slipped out.

"When?"

Between sobs Charlie mumbled, "Derby weekend last year."

Haber decided to change the subject. She could call Louisville later and get the details. So she asked, "Did Ms. Eden have a history of heart disease or any other serious medical problem?"

He replied, "I wasn't her cardiologist, but she didn't have a history of heart disease." Then he changed the subject, "I need to call her family. Anything else?"

"Make those calls, and we'll resume my questioning. One last thing: whose name is the apartment under?"

"I don't know. I paid the rent for her. Robyn was a songwriter and performer. I paid most of her bills."

"Do I have your permission to search the apartment? If she was a drug addict, I suspect we'll find her stash, and that might shed light on the cause of her death."

The question changed Charlie's demeanor. It was like a light switch was turned on, a total transformation. He became all business.

"Absolutely not! No search warrant. I'm not going to turn Robyn's death into a three-ring circus. She was an addict, and her death was tragic. I've got to make those phone calls." He fled the Meditation Room and went into the hall.

Haber looked at her watch. It was eleven forty-eight.

Detective Haber didn't like being dismissed by him, but she had to admit that the conversation could wait while the family was informed. Better to let him be the bearer of bad news than her. Eventually she'd interview Robyn Eden's next of kin but not today.

CHAPTER THIRTY-EIGHT

SOME FRIENDS GET TOGETHER

Tuesday, July 4, 2000
(About An Hour Earlier)

It was just about eleven when the big finale of the Hillwood Country Club's fireworks lit up the sky with explosions of bright colors and deafening noise. Without fail, the club supplied twenty-five minutes of free fireworks. This year, the Davises' one hundred twenty guests gathered in their backyard around the swimming pool and oohed and ahed. The Davis home was so close to the source of the fireworks that the observers could smell the gunpowder in the air, and the smoke drifted into the backyard.

It is a clear night, not too many stars, the blacker the better, Davis thought.

As the fireworks ended, Davis checked his watch, eleven twenty-eight. It was pretty late, and the party would be breaking up quickly. Davis smiled as he looked around at the happy faces at the party. He mingled among his guests who seemed to be having a fun time. And why not? They'd been well fed and entertained. Sparing no expense, Davis arranged for the main courses: a roasted pig cooked over an open pit and fried chicken submerged in a wire basket in a vat of hot oil. The Davises also offered all the fixings: hush puppies, white beans, and fries. Davis joked with several others that his kosher grandfather would turn over in his grave if he knew that his grandson was serving pork on the 4th. It was funny because it was true.

Davis consumed three plates of food. Liza saw the first two plates. He ate the third out of her view. Davis knew he was already in trouble for going back for seconds.

The guest list included family members, clients, neighbors, politicians, and other members of the Bar. His in-laws, Dr. John and Patsy Caldwell, looked like they were really having a good time. Davis noticed Sammie and Morty sitting at an isolated table. He looked down and saw the smoke rising from Morty's cigar. Davis laughed. Morty was braver than he'd thought, smoking in front of his cardiologist, Davis's father-in-law. Morty fought the Nazis, so Davis guessed Dr. John Caldwell was manageable.

Davis took a deep breath and took a moment to ponder his success. He had a sense of accomplishment in what he'd done. Then he looked at his children, Caroline and Jake. They were standing around with neighborhood kids and kids of longtime friends, having a ball.

And then there was the lovely Liza. Davis was dedicated to her to a fault. She put up with all his quirks, which many wives wouldn't. She preferred to nag him instead of leave him. He was a very lucky man.

Davis walked over to Peter Nichols and Valerie Daniels, who were sitting on a wooden swing, pushing off with their feet under a one-hundred-year-old oak tree. Davis was very proud of that old tree.

Valerie was running for re-election. They'd been talking for hours. Davis thought they must have been talking strategy.

"Great party as always, Ben," Peter loudly announced.

They talked Democratic politics for a good thirty minutes; they were some of the last ones at the party. It was about midnight when Davis decided to change the subject.

In a concerned but hopeful voice he asked the senator, "How's your sister, Robyn, doing? Is she still with Charlie Garcia?"

Valerie's body language immediately changed and gave away her answer. Davis, a quick study of body language from reading witnesses and jurors, watched as this proud and powerful woman became humbled. He could also see the anguish on her face.

"She's out of control, and I admit, I'm desperate. I turned to Charlie Garcia for help; he's still a part of her life. She's pregnant with his child. He's with her now. I spoke to him on Thursday and told him about the pregnancy. He at least admitted to me that he'd been with her in Nassau recently, which makes him the father. We agreed that was the time of conception. He promised to try to convince her to go to rehab. She's a complete mess, a full-blown junkie."

Davis and Peter were aware of Robyn's problems. She'd worked for Peter, and they all knew that ended badly.

An emotional person, Peter said in an unsteady voice, "What a waste! She's such a beautiful and talented young woman. I'm sorry I ever gave her a job and introduced her to Charlie. He's nothing but trouble with a capital *T*. I was fooled by his aristocratic air and charm. I misjudged him. I made him my partner, and it was the biggest mistake of my life. Thank God for Ben, or I'd still be dealing with the problems he created. I can't believe, Valerie, that Robyn's pregnant and he is going to be a part of her life forever through their child. I pity Robyn, and I pity their child."

"Believe it or not, Charlie is my last hope to save Robyn. He still has influence over her, and I'm waiting to hear from him, whether he convinced her to face up to her addiction and enter rehab again."

Just then the senator's cell phone rang, and she excused herself. When she returned, she had a strange, blank look on her face. It was obvious that something was very wrong. Before either Davis or Peter could ask, in a weak and quivering voice, she squeezed out, "That was Charlie. Robyn's overdosed, and she's been admitted to Hewes County Hospital. Ben, could you drive me there? I don't think I'm up to driving, and I may need your legal talent."

Peter jumped to his feet. "I'm coming too. I know Charlie better than either of you. I'll get the truth out of him."

Davis excused himself, conferred with Liza, and he, Peter, and the senator jumped into Davis's black Eldorado convertible and sped off to the hospital. They were at the emergency room of Hewes County Hospital in less than twenty minutes; it was just before one.

The emergency room was crowded. There was an accident involving two cars of teenagers. There were also the predictable injuries of the 4th, including burns and mangled limbs from M80s and other incendiary devices.

Davis walked up to a physician with Peter and Valerie right behind him. "Good evening, sir. This is Senator Daniels. She's Robyn Eden's sister. What's Robyn's condition?"

A young resident in blue scrubs glanced up, cleared his throat, and looked Davis straight in the face. "I regret to inform you that Ms. Eden was pronounced dead more than an hour ago. My condolences, Senator Daniels. She was barely alive when the EMTs brought her in, and there was nothing we could do to save her."

Davis and Peter each grabbed one of Valerie's arms, preventing her collapse to the floor. The two men dragged her to a chair in the waiting room, and Peter left to get a glass of water. Davis put his arm around her, and she sobbed into his shoulder. Peter returned with the water, and she desperately gulped it down.

As the three sat there and tried to digest what they'd been told, another doctor approached and introduced himself, "I'm Dr. Randolph Mann. I'm the attending. Ms. Daniels, would you like to talk with me in private?"

Between sobs, she replied, "No, sir. This is my friend and attorney Benjamin Davis and my friend Dr. Peter Nichols. You can speak freely in front of them."

"Senator Daniels, you were aware that your sister was an IV drug user? She died of an overdose."

"She's had a substance abuse problem for almost the last ten years. Do you know what she died from?"

"I'm waiting on the blood work, and the police have already ordered an autopsy, but it was definitely an IV and her injection site was her groin area. That's not an easy self-injection site. It's used to try to hide one's drug use from others. Do you know a Dr. Charles Garcia? He came in with her by ambulance."

"He's Robyn's off-and-on boyfriend. Is he still here?"

"He's in the chapel. He was not able to give me a good medical history when your sister was admitted. I found some inconsistencies in what he told me. The police initially questioned him, but he asked to be left alone in the chapel before they resume their questioning."

"What was the exact time my sister died?"

"The code was called at eleven thirty-six."

"When did Dr. Garcia know she was dead?"

"The moment it happened he was standing outside the room."

Davis was overtaken by anger. He'd looked at his watch and tried to figure out when Daniels got the cell phone call. It was right about midnight. "That bastard knew Robyn was dead when he called you. Where's the chapel?"

Dr. Mann informed him it was the fourth door on the right. Davis ran down the hall and threw open the stained glass door. Charlie was sitting in the third wooden pew with his face in his hands, crying. Peter and Valerie weren't far behind Davis.

"Charlie, you good-for-nothing son of a bitch. You knew she was dead when you called Valerie!"

Valerie chimed in, "Ben's right, Charlie. You called me right at midnight, and the doctor just told us she was dead twenty-four minutes before you made your call. You should have told me she was dead."

Charlie looked up and, with tears in his eyes, responded, "I didn't know how to tell you that Robyn was gone. I tried and tried to convince her to go to rehab, but I was too late."

Peter spoke for the first time, "You didn't make her an addict, but you encouraged her. You knew better than any of us that she needed to be protected from herself and watched over. Instead you convinced me to turn her into a walking billboard. Shame on me!

"She underwent half a dozen surgeries, and each time she was given a narcotic for pain. Then you unethically made her fall in love with you, yet you were unwilling to make any commitment to her. Shame on you! The last thing that girl needed was unreturned love. When she walked out, she turned to the road and drugs. You're the one who pushed her out the door.

"And then there's last year's Derby. We don't know what happened because your henchman Harrelson covered it up, but we do know Robyn was hospitalized and you wrote the prescription. Shame on you!

"You knew your relationship was poisonous for both of you, yet you continued to see her, and then you reckless son of a bitch, you knocked her up. Shame on you!

"That brings us to this weekend. The cops aren't through with you, and you've got a lot of explaining to do. I'm going to enjoy watching you squirm."

Davis put in his two cents, "What a lousy excuse for a doctor you are, Charlie. You're also a lousy excuse for a human being."

"Don't jump on me, asshole. You've always had it in for me."

Charlie thought about the bottle in his front pocket. He wished he had another oxycodone, but he didn't.

"You've ruined so many people's lives. You're a real smart-ass, Charlie. I hope you've got the right answers when the cops resume questioning you about this poor woman's death. My advice is to get a good lawyer. I'm not available."

The three friends exited the hospital, leaving Charlie alone in the chapel.

CHAPTER THIRTY-NINE
A DEFENSE IS NEEDED
Wednesday, July 5, 2000

Haber was still in the lounge and needed to be dealt with. Charlie didn't care if Haber wanted to question him. He was going home. At least that's where he thought he was going.

Charlie was walking toward her, and without a word, he walked right past her. Haber wasn't used to being ignored. Who did he think he was?

With as much authority as she could muster, Haber asked loudly, "Where the hell do you think you're going?"

Charlie snapped back, "I'm out of here. I've got Robyn's mother and sister to contend with." Over his shoulder as he walked away, he said, "I've got to organize my thoughts. Those won't be easy phone calls."

"I thought you just left to make those phone calls. You're not going anywhere. I've got a lot more questions for you. I need to determine what happened. I'll ask you again. Do I have your permission to search the apartment?"

"Absolutely not! I know my rights. Arrest me, take me into custody for questioning, or let me out of here. I'm not saying anything without my lawyer."

As the words came out of Charlie's mouth, a severe migraine headache emerged over his right eye. He grimaced in pain. He was in no mood to answer questions.

"Back off! I've had a bad day. This conversation can wait."

She realized that it would be better to let him win this round and let him start feeling a little overconfident and arrogant. He'd be more likely to make a mistake under those circumstances.

Haber tried to soften her approach and asked, "Where would you like to go?"

"Back to the apartment to shower and get some fresh clothing."

"Can't go there. It's a potential crime scene. You've watched TV. We have to sweep for evidence."

"I've got nothing more to say."

Haber didn't have enough to hold Charlie for questioning. He'd play the distraught fiancé as long as he could. In her gut, she knew that his story wouldn't fly very long. She'd get her search warrant, and then she'd question the weasel.

"What's your cell phone number?"

Charlie reluctantly gave it.

"When you check in a hotel, make sure it's in Hewes County, and call the Hewes County Police Department with the name of the hotel and your room number. I'd like to see you at the station at one o'clock in the afternoon."

"I'll have to check my schedule."

"Bullshit. You'll be there at one, or I'll issue a warrant for your arrest for obstruction. You have a legal obligation to cooperate with the investigation."

Charlie didn't respond, but he was clearly infuriated. He walked into the chapel. As he was walking down the hall, he reached into his pocket and pulled out the bottle. On Friday there were twenty

Viagra pills in it. Now there were only eleven left. He'd consumed nine during the sex marathon. He opened the bottle and took his last oxycodone with a drink from a water fountain.

Haber left the hospital at 2:00 a.m. She stopped at home to take a shower and have breakfast. She got to the station at six, no sleep. She couldn't. She wanted to get a search warrant, and that required her to submit an affidavit to a friendly judge to get one. Based on what Charlie told her in a moment of weakness, she knew that he'd had a similar problem in Jefferson County, Kentucky.

By the time she drank three cups of coffee, it was seven o'clock Hewes County time, eight o'clock Louisville time. She reached the Jefferson County Criminal Court Clerk's office and spoke to a deputy clerk. She asked her to run a criminal record on Dr. Charles Garcia. Haber copied verbatim what the young clerk told her. She finished her affidavit, deposited it with the clerk of a friendly judge, and went home to get two or three hours of sleep. There was no doubt in her mind that any of the judges in Hewes County would issue a search warrant for Robyn Eden's apartment. At nine, Judge Tanner signed the search warrant, and the homicide investigation of Robyn Eden was in full swing.

After the confrontation, Charlie used his cell phone to call a taxi to get him the hell away from the hospital. *That bastard Nichols had no right to talk to me like that. They had a right to be upset but not at me. How could they vilify me? I was trying to save her and the baby.*

While he was waiting for his cab, he called his father again. Earlier, in the hospital, it was his father first and then Valerie Daniels. Those were the two calls he'd made while being watched by the detective in the hall.

"Father, the police are going to get a search warrant. They'll find drugs and other incriminating items at the apartment."

"What items?"

"Sex toys and tapes of Robyn and me having sex, videos of trios having sex. They're pretty graphic."

Señor Garcia was familiar with his son's proclivity to film himself with women. Harrelson had already solved one such problem during his residency.

Charlie spoke up, "I think the camera was running when she overdosed. I don't know, but I think it shows me performing CPR."

"You're telling me that her overdose and your participation are on video for the police and anyone else to see? That's pretty stupid, son. Does the tape show her using drugs?"

"No, she did those in the bathroom off camera."

"Did you prescribe the drugs to her?"

"My name isn't on the bottle."

"That's not what I asked, Charles. Never mind. Don't answer that question. I don't want to know. I'll be questioned about this conversation. I'm better off with plausible deniability."

Charlie's father was an international businessman, and not all of his deals were aboveboard. He often used bribes and other illegal methods to achieve his purposes. Señor Garcia was not naïve.

This wasn't the first time Robyn had been rushed to a hospital emergency room because of her use of drugs with Charlie, but this time Robyn was dead. The last time a good lawyer and money were enough to get Charlie pretrial diversion. A dead girl would take much better lawyering and a lot more money. They'd figure it out. Señor Garcia would do whatever it took to protect his baby boy. This problem couldn't just be fixed with a phone call and a payoff, though. The father tried to stay focused.

"Who pays the rent on the place?"

"I do."

"Who signed the lease?"

"She did. I didn't want the liability."

Señor Garcia pondered his son's predicament. The liability on a lease was the least of his problems, but maybe it was a blessing in disguise. "That should give you some rights, but I'm no lawyer. I'll call Harrelson when we hang up. Go to a hotel. This call and its length will become an issue for the police. They'll want to know what we said. We'll need to get our stories straight as to what we discussed. It was about your loss of Robyn. You were inconsolable. Don't make any phone calls. I'll see you later today."

"I've got to call the Hewes County police when I check in. Detective Haber insists that I stay in Hewes County and that I let the police know where I'm staying."

"You'd better do as they ask. Let's assume they'll tap your hotel phone right away. After the call to the police, no more calls to anyone; don't even use your cell phone. They may get a tap on it as well."

Señor Garcia had dealt with the police in many jurisdictions. The laws of each country varied, but they rarely weighed heavily against the police. He had reason to be wary. He knew that in some of those countries the rights of the accused were not a concern. He also knew that the first day of any criminal investigation was critical to its outcome.

Charlie remembered he'd given Haber his cell phone number. Again his father interrupted his chain of thought. "I'm calling Harrelson right now. I'll hire a private jet, and we'll be in Nashville by nine. Can you pick us up at that private airport?"

"I don't have a car. My keys are in the apartment, and they won't let me back in it. Should I . . . ?"

"Don't do anything. You just sit there. Anything you do could be interpreted as incriminating. I'm calling Amy Pierce. I've got her home number. She'll pick us up at the airport, and we should be there before nine."

Charlie told his father he'd check into the Hewes Manor that was on the courthouse square. The cab arrived, and Garcia said good-bye to his father.

When he got to his room, Charlie called the Hewes City police and spoke to the desk sergeant.

"I've checked in. I've had a real bad day. I'm staying at the Hewes Manor. I'm in for the night. I'm not going anywhere. I don't have access to any of my clothing, and even my car keys are locked in that damn apartment. When can I get in?"

"You can call Detective Haber later today. She'll have a better idea when you'll get access to the apartment. Good night, Doctor, sleep well."

Charlie didn't like the way that son of a bitch said that. He thought about whether to call Robyn's mother but knew that Valerie had already done so. Mrs. Burton Eden didn't care for Charlie, never did. She was part of the Old South, and Charlie's foreign background was more than enough to cause her to dislike him. Now she'd hate him with every fiber of her being. Ultimately, Charlie chickened out. He'd make the call after meeting with his lawyers.

At ten fifteen, his father summoned Charlie to the lobby; he had no luggage, so he just walked out the door. His father gave him a big hug, which surprised Charlie. His father wasn't usually an emotional person. They got in the backseat of a waiting car. Harrelson and Pierce were in the front seat, with Pierce driving.

They went straight to Pierce's office. Pierce made Señor Garcia sit in reception while Harrelson and Pierce met with Charlie in the conference room. She insisted that only she and Harrelson meet with Charlie, something to do with attorney-client privilege and the fact that Señor Garcia could be subpoenaed. Pierce explained that because she and Harrelson were lawyers, they couldn't be subpoenaed.

Before she met with Charlie, Pierce met with Señor Garcia, who paid her a $50,000 retainer. Pierce emphasized that her fee would fit the crime, and these charges would be serious. She made it clear she would quickly exhaust the retainer.

Charlie provided his lawyers with as much detail as he could. Several times the two lawyers engaged in sidebar conversations about the law, which Charlie didn't understand. He did freeze when Pierce mentioned the word *murder!*

"Murder? What murder? She was a drug addict, and she died. That happens every day, doesn't it?"

Pierce decided she'd answer Charlie's question: "Drug addicts die every day, yes, but not with their doctor having sex with them on camera. Add to those unusual circumstances that the physician-boyfriend recently surrendered his Tennessee medical license and that he's on probation for a drug overdose involving the same victim, and it's not an everyday occurrence. Let's not forget who her sister is."

"Whose side are you on, Ms. Pierce?"

"I'm on your side. I'm your lawyer. But I'm not going to sugar-coat it for you, Charlie. You'll be charged with second-degree murder, and depending on what's on that tape and whether it's admissible, you may be convicted."

Harrelson took out his gold pocket watch and chain and nervously began twirling the watch. This kid needed to wake the hell up. Nobody told Dr. Charles Juan Batista Garcia the straight truth. It had always been sugarcoated. That was a big part of the problem.

"Well, Charlie hasn't even been charged yet."

"David, stop kidding yourself. We owe it to Dr. Garcia to shoot straight with him. The death of Robyn Eden is a serious problem that's not going away."

Harrelson wanted to say something encouraging. "Don't worry, kid. Your father and I still have a few tricks up our sleeves. One thing I can assure you of, this won't be a fair fight. Your dad and I will not pull any punches. This may get rough, but you'll survive. I promise . . ."

Pierce broke in and said, "I suggest that you call either the sister or the mother and offer your condolences. If you don't call this morning, it's a sign of guilt. I'll script what you should say, and we'll tape the conversation. If the conversation goes poorly, we can always erase the tape."

Pierce explained to Charlie and Harrelson that in Tennessee both parties to a telephone conversation do not need to know that the conversation is being recorded. Harrelson commented that New York required consent by both parties. Pierce resumed, "Did either the sister or the mother know about Robyn's drug problem?"

"Her sister, Valerie, certainly did," Charlie replied. "She and I spoke a few days ago, and we agreed that Robyn needed to go into rehab. Convincing Robyn to go into rehab was my primary purpose for visiting her. I doubt her mother knew."

Pierce ignored Charlie's attempt to rationalize his conduct. She thought, *This guy is unbelievable.* Pierce spent the next fifteen minutes scripting the phone call to the sister. She went over the script with Charlie and explained that whatever happened he was not to get angry or defensive. She explained that juries didn't like angry people. He needed to be the grieving boyfriend.

Charlie dialed Valerie Daniels's cell phone number, and he started crying before the conversation began.

"Senator Daniels here."

Between sobs, Charlie asked, "How are you doing, Valerie?"

"You've got a lot of nerve calling me, Charlie. She was already

258

dead when you called me last night. You're a real shit."

"That's unfair. I loved her, and I hoped to get her help. You know that I was trying to get her into rehab. I was trying to save my baby."

Both started crying.

So far, Charlie was giving an Academy Award performance. This tape would play well with a jury. He moved in for the kill. "We both know she was struggling."

"As a doctor, couldn't you tell this weekend that she was high?"

"Yes, but I couldn't be with her twenty-four hours a day. In retrospect, she must have taken the drugs when she went to the bathroom."

"You should have stopped her, Charlie. You're a doctor. You were in the best position to save her, and you didn't. You also claimed you loved her."

It was weird talking about Robyn in the past tense.

"If all it took were love, both of us would have been able to stop her. She was absolutely reckless. Despite her pregnancy, she continued to use. I was nine hundred miles away, but you had easy access. You lost a sister, and I lost someone I loved and my child."

Charlie hesitated and then burst out, "My child's dead, and Robyn killed him."

Pierce felt like Steven Spielberg, and Charlie was bringing home the Oscar. The strained conversation ended fairly abruptly. Charlie promised to call, which was a lie. He hoped he never spoke to Valerie again.

After the difficult conversation, both Pierce and Harrelson complimented Charlie on how well he'd handled the call. The tape would be helpful, although it was far from exonerating. It simply placed Charlie in a sympathetic light. However, once the police and eventually the jury saw the sex video, Charlie's credibility would be severely damaged, probably irreparably.

CHAPTER FORTY

YOU'RE UNDER ARREST
Thursday, July 13, 2000

O n July 13th, Charlie got the call he'd been dreading. It was from Pierce. He needed to surrender himself to the Hewes City police because he was under arrest.

His father and Harrelson, who had remained in Nashville, accompanied him to the police department. Pierce met them at the station house and expedited the booking. When Charlie was finally taken into custody, Harrelson thought he looked scared, and he hoped that he truly was. This was no joking matter.

Pierce instructed him, "Don't say anything. Not one word."

Two officers led Charlie and Pierce into an interrogation room, where they were left alone for what seemed like an hour but was only twenty minutes.

Detective Haber walked in and smiled. "Hello, Dr. Garcia, fancy meeting you here."

Charlie didn't respond. He had to use all of his restraint not to throw a punch.

"I feel like I know you pretty well. I've watched all of your videotapes. You're one sick person. You actually taught me a thing or two. I can't believe that poor young girl allowed you to sodomize her the way you did. It must have hurt like hell. I can't imagine she got any satisfaction at all." Haber was trying to goad him into a reaction.

Charlie wanted to tell Detective Haber what she could do with one of his toys, but he kept his cool. Pierce warned him that they would try to provoke him into talking, but he was not to take the bait.

"We found all the drugs and the syringe in the nightstand, and we know you were the source. You're looking at murder in the second degree. That's twenty-five years to life. This is Middle Tennessee. We're conservative here, not like your hometown of New York. A Tennessee jury isn't going to like what you did to that poor girl. This is a missionary position town. A guy might get a blow job on his birthday, but that's about it. There won't be one woman on the jury who's taken it up the ass and certainly none with a ten-inch dildo. You're a dead man."

Pierce had been patient. She couldn't see a camera, but if Haber were recording this, she would play badly before a jury. Pierce quickly concluded that Haber wasn't recording. She was simply trying to provoke her client. She figured it was a good test for Charlie; a lot worse was yet to come.

Pierce asked, "Are you finished with this interview? Do you have any questions? I haven't heard one. My client is heartbroken, and a police station is nowhere to grieve the death of a loved one."

Haber glared at Pierce. These two powerful, determined women were about to butt heads.

"We've got a search warrant for your New York apartment. I suspect the New York Police Department will find more tapes and more sex toys, won't they?"

Charlie tried not to change his expression, but it was hard because he knew she was right.

"I also bet they'll find a bunch of drugs. I bet there will be several drugs that are of the same type, dosage, and lot as were found in Robyn Eden's apartment. If they have the same manufacturer and batch number, then it's life, my friend."

Pierce looked hard at Haber. "I still haven't heard a question."

Charlie was sweating at this point. He wanted to scream at the top of his lungs for the detective to go to hell, but he didn't. Harrelson would be proud of him. He needed to get to either Harrelson or his father to tell them about the New York search warrant. His father had to get to the apartment before the police. It never dawned on him that a police department in Tennessee could initiate a search of his apartment in New York City.

Haber just sat there across from him. She'd given it her best shot, and he wasn't talking. As she left, her last comment was, "See you in court."

"What was that all about?" asked Charlie.

"She's just trying to intimidate you. Did it work?"

"A little."

"Look, you don't talk to anyone. The Hewes County jail is full of snitches. Guys are going to come up to you, and they either want to rat on you or do worse. Keep to yourself. That's my advice, not necessarily legal."

Charlie was taken to a cell, where he remained about two hours. Around four o'clock he was taken before a judge, whose nameplate read *Honorable Joe Tanner*. Harrelson, Pierce, and Señor Garcia were waiting in the courtroom. An assistant DA was at one table, and Detective Haber was sitting in the audience.

Judge Tanner took charge. "This is the bond hearing for Dr. Charles Juan Batista Garcia, who is charged with second-degree murder and reckless homicide in connection with the death of

Robyn Eden, a human being, a citizen and resident of Hewes County, Tennessee."

The court got each of the parties to acknowledge the jurisdiction of the court and that the court, in its discretion, could set bond in this case.

"General, what do you have to say as to the appropriate dollar amount of bond?"

The young DA, Jill Hoskins, began, "Dr. Garcia has dual citizenship in the United States and Majorca. I've not had time to study the extradition procedure from Majorca to Hewes County, but I'll bet at the very least it would be time consuming and expensive for our small county. For that reason I request a bond of $2 million. Your Honor, that's not the only reason for a high bond. I predict that Ms. Pierce is going to ask this court to allow Dr. Garcia to travel freely between New York and Nashville because of his employment. Dr. Garcia lost the privilege to practice medicine in Tennessee; he was forced to surrender his license."

"Objection, Your Honor. Dr. Garcia voluntarily surrendered his Tennessee license." Pierce started arguing that the DA was trying to poison the well.

Judge Tanner refused to let Pierce's remark go unchallenged. Tanner knew, and he wanted everybody else to know, that he was in charge of his courtroom and these proceedings. "Stop your bickering right now. I expect decorum in my court, and I will not tolerate unprofessional conduct. If you've got an objection, stand. I will recognize you, and you can make your objection. I will not have counsel talking over each other. It's disrespectful to this court, and the court reporter can't do her job. Anything else, General?"

The young DA shuffled her papers and started again. "This isn't

Dr. Garcia's first brush with the law. He was convicted of improperly prescribing drugs to Robyn Eden and recklessly endangering her life in Jefferson County, Kentucky, last year."

Pierce stood and was recognized by Judge Tanner. "Your Honor, the DA has just provided the court with inaccurate information. Dr. Garcia was not convicted nor did he plead guilty to anything in Kentucky. He entered into a pretrial diversion with the Jefferson County DA and is on an eighteen-month probation.

"But it involved the same victim."

Loudly the judge pointed out, "Did I recognize you, General?"

"No, sir."

Tanner directed the next question to Pierce. "Did the Kentucky charges involve Ms. Eden, Ms. Pierce?"

"Yes, sir."

"Anything else, General?"

By this time the young DA was a little gun-shy. She shook her head and sat down. She looked defeated to Harrelson.

Pierce went on attack. She was confident, eloquent, and yet humble. Charlie needed a little humility right now. She talked about Dr. Garcia's busy practice in New York and that his patients needed him. Pierce made Dr. Charles Garcia seem more like Mother Teresa than a man accused of second-degree murder.

Tanner sat there, taking it all in. When Pierce finished, the judge set bond at $500,000.

Señor Garcia had certified funds in that exact amount. He also had certified funds in larger amounts. Señor Garcia was taking no chances; his son would be out on bond.

As they were walking from the courtroom, Charlie whispered to his father, "They got a search warrant for my New York apartment."

"Don't worry, son. My men have gone through your place with a fine-toothed comb. They'll find nothing worthwhile, except what we want them to find."

Charlie decided that he'd let his father handle matters, as usual.

CHAPTER FORTY-ONE

A PAID FRIEND

Friday, July 14, 2000

D avid Harrelson didn't think Charlie was stupid, just arrogant. He didn't accept responsibility for his own actions. Harrelson believed that arrogance was the fault of his parents. They spoiled him and enabled him by solving all of his problems. In reality it was Harrelson who solved all his problems. Charlie never suffered any consequences.

Harrelson wasn't close to Charlie; he didn't even like the kid. But since his arrest, they'd been in constant contact, and that drew them closer—not necessarily a good thing. From their conversations Harrelson knew that the death of Robyn Eden forced Charlie to reexamine his life and the mistakes he'd made. These troubling thoughts made Charlie angry, not remorseful. In the past the consequences of his actions amounted to nothing more than a minor inconvenience. This was different. He was facing real jail time.

In response to Charlie's anger, Harrelson reminded him that at least he was out on bond and not in jail until trial. Harrelson knew that Charlie wouldn't survive in either jail or, heaven forbid, prison. The extremely handsome doctor would wind up some con's close personal friend. Harrelson smirked at the thought of someone sodomizing Charlie. He couldn't take what he dished out. The lawyer's job was to keep him from being incarcerated, by any means necessary. Harrelson played fast and loose. The key was not getting caught.

Under the law, Charlie was innocent until proven guilty beyond a reasonable doubt. Harrelson knew that was a heavy burden. Despite Charlie's conduct, that would be a difficult thing for the state to prove.

Charlie's parents assured him he wouldn't serve a day in jail. Harrelson never made such a promise. He explained that the legal system moved at a snail's pace and that even if he was found guilty, the appeals process lasted years.

Although he volunteered to do it, Harrelson dreaded his next phone call. He'd promised to call Alan Baxter, Charlie's Kentucky probation officer. As a condition of his probation, Charlie was required to inform the state of Kentucky about his arrest in the state of Tennessee. The arrest itself wouldn't revoke Charlie's probation, but a conviction would. Harrelson was disappointed but not surprised that Charlie couldn't stay out of trouble for eighteen months. He got close, fourteen months, but those four months would be a real problem.

Charlie was on good terms with Baxter. At Harrelson's insistence he followed the terms of his probation to the letter. He was required to call Baxter once a week and meet with him once a quarter.

Even prior to Robyn Eden's death, Harrelson had his firm's investigator check out Baxter. That report and information he gathered from Charlie created a detailed profile of Baxter.

Alan Baxter, a sixty-five-year-old black man, was over six feet tall, with snowy white short hair. He had a Morgan Freeman quality about him, including the actor's signature deep voice.

From his investigator Harrelson learned that Baxter was about to retire because he was mad at the system. He'd worked in the probation department for more than thirty years and hadn't accumulated anything. Harrelson knew exactly how much money Baxter had in his checking account and 401k. The meager amounts did not reflect a lifetime of work. Over the years, on behalf of his clients, Harrelson bribed many public officials. It was an art, and Harrelson had the talent. He could tell from his investigator's report that there was an opportunity to get to Baxter.

Dr. Charles Garcia wasn't Baxter's typical parolee. Baxter had dealt with the dregs of society, rapists and child molesters, as part of his job. It was obvious to Harrelson that even though Baxter didn't like his job, he didn't have much choice.

"Mr. Baxter, David Harrelson here, Charlie Garcia's attorney." Harrelson took his watch out of his vest pocket and nervously started twirling the chain.

"Yes, sir, I spoke to Charlie last week. He's due to call me today."

"Right. He asked that I call you first on his behalf. There's been a tragedy. Ms. Robyn Eden's dead. Drug overdose. The woman was on a self-destructive path. Unfortunately, Charlie was with her when it happened. He was there at the request of her sister to try to convince the girl to enter rehab. Hewes City police have charged him with her murder. His only crime was agreeing to try to get her into rehab and failing to convince her."

Baxter didn't say anything. Both men knew there was a purpose to this call. Harrelson took Baxter's silence as a green light to proceed.

"He's out on $500,000 bond."

"That sounds pretty serious. I guess murder is always pretty serious. Where'd he get the $500,000? I know he's a doctor, but that's a lot of money."

"His parents are rich. He was born into the golden sperm club. His parents will bail him out. You know how the system works." Harrelson let his words float there a minute.

Baxter spoke next. "Sounds like Charlie could use a friend."

Bingo, in every bribe there was the moment when the bribee made it clear that the bribe was possible. Now it was a matter of price. That didn't need to be determined in this conversation. The dollar amount was a moving target, calculated based on what needed to be done and how much help would be needed.

"I'm glad to hear you say that. Dr. Garcia at some point may need some help from you if his Kentucky probation becomes an issue. He may need a friend."

"Well, Dr. Garcia has been a model parolee. I could certainly testify to that."

Harrelson had hooked his fish.

"We'd appreciate that. You could be very helpful in the future."

"Just doing my job."

There was no point in pressing the point. Charlie Garcia's criminal case would proceed slowly, and they needed to figure out what type of help their new friend Alan Baxter might provide.

"We'll be in touch if we need anything. Can we just count my call as Charlie's scheduled call for the day?"

"No problem. You filled me in. Good luck with those charges. If I can be of any help, just let me know."

Harrelson hung up, turned, and opened his safe. He took out one hundred non-sequenced hundred-dollar bills and put them in an envelope. He printed Alan Baxter's home address on the outside, no return address, stamped it, and mailed it later in the day.

CHAPTER FORTY-TWO
AN UNUSUAL REQUEST
Friday, July 21, 2000

Davis decided he'd sleep in. It was out of character because he was usually the first in the office and the last one out.

He opened his eyes, glanced over, and saw to his surprise that Liza wasn't in bed. She was usually a late riser, and she was always asleep when he left the house.

When she entered the bedroom with two cups of coffee, he smiled. He liked being waited on. She handed him his mug, which read *World's Greatest Dad.* The mug was more than ten years old, one of a set made many years ago for him by his son, Jake. He kept the other ancient mug made by his son at the office and used it every morning there. It was his go-to cup.

Bella and Sammie argued that the chipped mug wasn't very professional looking, but Davis didn't care. Morty taught him to be his own man and not to care about what others thought, as long as he did the right thing. The mug felt right to Davis, so what others might have thought just didn't matter.

Liza walked to his side of the bed, looked down, and gave him a dumbfounded look.

"What are you still doing here? It's eight thirty. My lovers are due to arrive starting in forty-five minutes."

"Well, we've got forty-five minutes then."

Davis grabbed his wife's hand, pulling her toward him and down to the bed. It was an awkward move, causing her to spill her coffee on the floor.

"I can't believe what you made me do," she protested and started to rise from the bed to get something to clean up the mess.

"Forget about it!" Davis said in a stronger than usual Brooklyn accent, sounding like a Mafia don. "Your freakin' boyfriend can clean it up when he gets here."

Liza blushed, and Davis gave her a hard kiss while fondling her backside. From the back, he began kissing her neck. He bit her right earlobe a little too hard, and she yelled.

"Easy, fella, I don't want to be missing any parts after this is over."

"Your boyfriend told me you like it rough. I'm just following his instructions."

She giggled, and they made love. Fifteen minutes later, Davis was in the shower, and Liza was cleaning up the spilled coffee. The floor was hardwood, no damage done. He dressed quickly and kissed his wife good-bye.

"Do you think we can do this again later?"

"Once a day is my limit. You'll have to wait till tomorrow."

"I guess your boyfriend's just out of luck then?"

"That's once a day per customer."

"I'll see you tonight, and we'll renegotiate. Remember I know where you sleep, and I can wake you up at midnight, which would be technically the next day."

"You do, and you'll be singing soprano."

Davis waved and walked out of the bedroom and a minute later out the front door.

It was a beautiful summer morning, and he drove to the office with the top of his chocolate Bentley down. As usual Davis's longish hair would be disheveled by the time he arrived. It took less than twenty minutes to get to the office. When he walked into reception, trying to fix his hair, Bella and Sammie were at Bella's desk talking, and they abruptly stopped when he entered the room.

"What's up, ladies?"

There was no direct response, but finally Bella spoke, "You've got several messages."

Davis waited for Bella to continue, but she let the words hang in the air.

"I'll bite. Who called?"

"Bill Alexander from the *Tennessean*, Lester Kahn, and Senator Daniels."

He ignored the first two messages. "Did the senator say what she wanted?"

"An appointment with Morty and you, and she said it was important. I scheduled her for your first available at three o'clock today. Was that okay? I called Morty. He's upstairs and available."

"I guess she wants to talk about Robyn's trust. I didn't think there was anything left. Please pull that trust file."

At two forty-five, Morty, Sammie, and Davis were in the conference room waiting on their three o'clock. At five to three Bella walked in with Valerie Daniels behind her. Davis got up and gave her a hug, and the others exchanged hellos.

Morty, as the most senior person in the room, began, "How can we be of service, Senator?"

"My family needs your help."

They all sat there waiting for her to be more specific, but she seemed to be having difficulty finding her words, which was quite unusual for a politician. She finally said, "I want you and Ben to act as special prosecutors and bring Dr. Garcia to justice for the murder of my sister."

That wasn't what Davis or the other two expected to hear.

Morty responded, "That's the job of the Hewes County district attorney, not Ben or me. We're private citizens. That's the job of the state of Tennessee."

"Look, I know how poorly our legal system works. I'm part of the system. I know how talented the two of you are. I've seen you in court, and I've asked around. I can't let this bastard get off. I want him convicted of second-degree murder. I don't want some young DA, who's well intentioned but doesn't know what the hell he or she is doing. I also don't want some plea bargain and a slap on the hand.

"Morty, you've known my family for more than fifty years, and you and Ben are what my family and my sister need."

Morty looked at Davis, who was stunned by the request. Davis never tried a criminal case, and although over the years he represented many criminal defendants, Morty wasn't a prosecutor.

Continuing to speak for the lawyers, Morty replied, "What you're asking is not feasible for many reasons . . ."

Daniels interrupted, "With all due respect, Morty, I know it's feasible. What about the Nichols case in 1964?"

Davis knew exactly where this conversation was going. The senator was prepared and wasn't going to take no for an answer.

"That was personal. I knew the man. We grew up together. It was more than thirty-five years ago. That's an awfully long time ago. I was a hell of a lot younger."

"Are you saying you're not up to the challenge? You're Morty

Steine, for God's sake. You're not going to let this asshole get away with killing my little sister. You knew her also. This should be personal, just like the Nichols case."

Davis was concerned that the senator was getting the better of the old man. She was playing on his heartstrings, but it got worse.

Her next words played on the old man's ego, and she said them with complete authority and confidence: "Morty, in your career, besides the Nichols prosecution, you've defended and tried six manslaughter cases, and you've won them all. By my count, you've represented more than fifty criminal defendants, and only four of them went to jail. Those four must have been guilty, and you plea-bargained them a good deal. You've never lost a criminal trial. I suspect that many of your clients were guilty and that your ability made the difference . . ."

It was Morty's turn to interrupt: "You're confusing two roles in our legal system. A defense lawyer thinks and acts differently than a prosecutor."

"That's right. You know how the other side thinks. You also know Garcia's attorney, Amy Pierce. You and Ben beat her in the Plainview cases, and her license was suspended for three months. She'll be more concerned about you than some assistant DA."

"It's been fifteen years since my last murder trial, and the Nichols prosecution was more than thirty years ago, as I reminded you. I hate to admit it, but I've slowed down since then."

"That's why I want Ben to participate. You bring the brains, and he brings the stamina."

Davis had been silent until now. "I've got no criminal law experience, except holding his briefcase through some white-collar matters. A murder trial is a big deal. You need seasoned lawyers prosecuting and defending. I'm not right for that."

"I know, but you're a trial lawyer. Judges and juries like and respect you. More important, they believe you. If you say Charlie Garcia killed my sister, then there will be a conviction."

Davis turned to Morty, "When was the last time the state appointed a special prosecutor?"

Morty thought a moment. "It's most commonly evoked when a politician is charged with corruption. The courts and the state want someone independent to prosecute the case to avoid even the appearance of impropriety or party politics."

The senator came prepared. "The technical name for a special prosecutor is 'an attorney pro tempore.' Both the Tennessee Constitution and the Tennessee legislature have provided for such a special prosecutor."

Sammie got up, went to the bookcase, and pulled the first volume of the Tennessee Code Annotated, the T.C.A., all of the laws passed by the Tennessee legislature, starting with the Tennessee Constitution. She began reading out loud, "Article VI, Section 5, provides that an Attorney General for the State shall be appointed by the Judges of the State Supreme Court and shall hold this office for a term of eight years. In all cases where the Attorney General for any district or circuit fails or refuses to attend and prosecute according to the law, then the Court shall have the power to appoint an Attorney pro tempore."

Sammie went on to read that the order appointing the attorney pro tempore was not required to state a reason. The logic was that for whatever reason the state was not in a position to prosecute, the Tennessee Supreme Court had the power to find the right person for the job.

Sammie turned to Morty and Davis with half a smile on her face. She was enjoying watching the older man squirm. "What stronger authority do you need than the Tennessee Constitution?"

Daniels chimed in, "There's also a Tennessee statute, T.C.A. 8-7-106, passed in 1858, which follows the constitutional provision."

Sammie pulled that volume from the shelf and read it to herself before commenting, "The senator's right. There's ample authority for the Supreme Court to appoint you."

Davis didn't like being pushed, particularly outside his comfort zone. He said, "You've forgotten about one important condition that can't be satisfied. The district attorney general of Hewes County wants to prosecute this case. In fact, at the last motion hearing he handled it himself and refused to delegate the motion to an assistant DA. If his office wants to prosecute, there can't be an attorney pro tempore."

The senator sighed and then smiled. "I've spoken to the governor. He's the attorney general's boss, who's the boss of the district attorney of Hewes County. I think there just may be an opening to try this case."

Davis looked at Morty and Sammie and then turned to her, "How did you convince the governor to push so hard?"

"I made him an offer he couldn't refuse."

Everyone in the room knew the line came from the *Godfather*, but no one other than Daniels understood what she meant.

Morty let the drama linger and then responded, "I guess we've just left private practice to go work for the state of Tennessee."

Davis wouldn't argue with the old man. He'd done so much for him personally and professionally. "I hear the pay stinks, but the fringe benefits are worse."

It was a done deal. The senator shook everyone's hand and silently left the room.

CHAPTER FORTY-THREE

AN AWKWARD HANDOFF

Thursday, August 3, 2000

Morty, Sammie, and Davis entered the Hewes County DA's office, and all eyes fell upon them. The entire staff knew they were there to replace them. General Andrew Palmer felt compelled to warn his office that the Davis team would be taking over the Garcia prosecution. General Palmer did so with grace and class. He insisted that everyone give Mr. Steine and Mr. Davis their full cooperation and support. He told them, "We're all on the same side. We want a conviction."

Palmer led the Davis team into an office with two desks and a folding table. "This will be your office away from home. Anything you need, ask Jill Hoskins. She'll be your contact with this office because she has the greatest familiarity with the Garcia case. Jill will be valuable, but she's upset that you've stepped in. I suggest you keep that in mind and play nice. She's a good prosecutor, with great potential, but she's young and she's been hurt. If you have any problems that Jill can't handle or if you just want to talk and bounce an idea off me, my doors always open."

Morty grabbed General Palmer by both arms and squeezed tightly. "General, thank you for being so gracious."

"From what I understand none of us had much of a choice. I almost forgot. All of you raise your right hands."

Morty, Sammie, and Davis did as General Palmer instructed and repeated the oath taken by assistant district attorneys.

"All three of you are assistant DAs. Starting salary is $4,000 a month. Welcome aboard."

Morty laughed. "At least it's honest work."

The three sat down at the desk and opened the first file. It contained the three search warrants and a list of all the items seized from Robyn Eden's apartment.

The next file pulled was the indictment. Dr. Charles Juan Batista Garcia had been charged with two counts, second-degree murder and reckless homicide.

Davis asked Sammie, a recent law school graduate who also recently studied for the Bar, to identify what they'd have to prove to convict on each count.

Rather than wing it, Sammie pulled volume 7 of the Tennessee Code Annotated from her briefcase. "There are two subsections to second-degree murder. The first part is 'a knowing killing of another.' The other definition is 'a killing of another which results from the unlawful distribution of a Schedule I or Schedule II drug when such drug is the proximate cause of the death of the user.' It's a Class A felony."

Morty took over. "We can't prove the first definition, but hopefully we can prove the second. We need to determine if Garcia 'unlawfully distributed' the drug to Eden. Sammie, confirm what Robyn took was a Schedule I or II drug." He pointed out, "I'll bet there will be conflicting testimony as to the cause of death. Harrelson is smart. He'll find an expert who will testify that the proximate cause of death was something other than the drugs."

Davis said, "So we don't have to prove that Garcia killed her with deliberate purpose as long as the drugs are found to be the cause of death. What are the minimum and maximum sentences for second degree?"

Sammie answered, "Minimum, ten years. Maximum, life."

Morty was getting into his groove. "Tell me about reckless homicide."

Again Sammie knew the answer. "It's when a killing is caused by reckless conduct."

Morty connected the dots. "So Garcia can be convicted if he should have done something and also if his action was reckless. What class felony is it?"

"Class E, punishable by at least a year, but not more than five."

Morty looked serious and softly said, "I'm surprised. There are several crimes in between a Class A and Class E felony, such as manslaughter, that should have been charged. It's too late now. The die has been cast."

A young woman knocked on the door and, when acknowledged, walked in. She was petite and brunette, no more than twenty-six or seven.

"I'm Jill Hoskins, and I'm here to help. What have you looked at so far?"

"The indictment and the search warrants."

"Well, we just got two motions from Pierce. We were expecting the first but not the second."

Davis took the bait. "What's the first?"

"Motion to suppress the evidence discovered from the three search warrants."

"And the second?"

"A motion to recuse Judge Tanner."

Hoskins made copies for them, and they sat there and read.

Sammie spoke first, "I can't comment on the motion to suppress, but the motion to recuse is a suicide mission."

"I get it," Morty said out loud. "Pierce realizes that the jury, not the judge, will decide her client's guilt or innocence. Tanner is a hard-ass and will be angered by this motion. Pierce will push the judge, hoping to push him into reversible error, which would allow her client to remain on bond, out of jail, until the last appeal is exhausted. How much is Garcia's bond?"

Hoskins was the only one who knew the answer. "It's $500,000. His father put up cash."

Surprised, Morty looked at Hoskins and said, "That's much too low. We need a much higher bond for this rich kid. At least $2 million! Sammie and Jill, you work on that motion to increase bond."

"The judge won't increase bond," Hoskins said. "Did you know that Garcia was on probation under pretrial diversion? A New York lawyer named Harrelson negotiated the deal for Garcia in Kentucky. It was before Eden's death. They went to the Derby, and Eden od'd. The Jefferson County DA agreed to an eighteen-month probation rather than go to trial. Garcia had already surrendered his Tennessee license, so Tennessee didn't care."

Davis smiled and said, "We'd better check in with Dr. Garcia's Kentucky probation officer."

Morty commented, "We've got our work cut out for us. Pierce is one hell of a lawyer, and she's sneaky to boot."

CHAPTER FORTY-FOUR
A CHIP PLAYED
Wednesday, September 27, 2000

Harrelson felt better now that Alan Baxter was on the payroll. Through careful planning, Harrelson and Pierce determined Baxter's contribution to the defense. The time had come to communicate to Baxter his role and only his limited role.

Pierce made it clear to Harrelson that Judge Tanner was above reproach. He'd served ten years and didn't need or want money. He was smart, liked by the Bar, and would run with little opposition in six years. He'd be fair, but Harrelson wasn't interested in fair. He didn't want to leave anything to chance.

Harrelson didn't trust juries. They certainly weren't his peers. He'd discussed with Pierce the possibility of getting to a juror. That was dangerous; there were long sentences for a lawyer who got caught. It would be the ultimate hedge of one's bet, but if it backfired, someone would go to jail, probably Charlie, but possibly Harrelson or Pierce. Charlie Garcia wasn't worth that risk. Pierce was an excellent lawyer, smart and cunning, but she had to be cautious, having already had her license suspended for three months.

Through the investigator for Harrelson's firm, prior to her hire, a complete background check on Amy Pierce was provided. She was a single mother, with a son, Carter, age twelve. She graduated number two from the University of Virginia Law School, married number one, and both worked several years at big New York law firms. The marriage dissolved, she came home, and her ex-husband, Dan Smith, went to rehab, which didn't help. He was an addict with no self-control. As far as the investigator could tell, Dan had little or no contact with Pierce and their son. After five years at Dunn, Moore & Thomas she made partner.

The report described the Plainview cases and the disciplinary charges brought against Pierce and another lawyer named McCoy. Reporting another attorney to the IRS, solely for revenge, wasn't illegal, but Pierce breached a confidential clause and her conduct was in such bad faith, it was unethical. The board basically slapped her on the wrist with a three-month suspension.

The client, an issuance company, was impressed with her commitment, so when she left her law firm, DMT, two years later to form her own firm, she took the anchor client with her. She now had two former DMT associates working for her. She was tough, and Harrelson liked and respected her.

She'd been caught once, but Harrelson's big question was, how many times had she actually broken the rules? More important, how many times did she get away with breaking the rules? The report didn't say. Was she smart or just lucky? The consensus of Señor Garcia and Harrelson was that Pierce was dishonest and could be trusted by them in executing their plan. All co-conspirators were completely on board. Baxter was part of the plan but didn't know the plan.

Harrelson dialed Baxter's number. "Mr. Baxter, David Harrelson, how've you been, sir?"

"About to retire the end of next month. I'll let you know how I'm doing after that. It will be weird not to come to the office every day."

Harrelson already knew about Baxter's retirement. Charlie received notice from the state that he'd be reporting to a new probation officer beginning November 1st.

"Will money be a problem?"

"I've saved and I'll have my pension, but money will be a problem. I'm just a public servant."

"We may be able to help each other. Dr. Garcia could use your help."

"How so?"

"We need help finding a witness. I need a drug dealer to testify at Charlie's trial that he sold Robyn Eden oxycodone, the week of July 2nd. These sales took place in or around Hewes County, so the witness must have been able to be in Hewes County whatever date he claims he sold the drugs."

"That would be quite an admission. Why would somebody agree he sold drugs to Robyn Eden that caused her death? He'd be inviting a murder charge, wouldn't he?"

Harrelson had anticipated that problem. He knew what he needed and knew it wouldn't be easy. "People will do many things for the right amount of money. You'll need to find someone who's already in trouble facing serious jail time or worse and who desperately needs the money."

"He'd have to be pretty desperate!"

"Think outside the box, and it doesn't have to be a he. A she with kids, going to jail for a long time, is a real possibility." Harrelson made a good point.

"Let's stop bullshitting. Are you taping this conversation?"

"Why would I? I have a law license to protect. Why, are you?"

"That's the million-dollar question. It would be pretty stupid if you ask me. This conversation violates several state and federal laws. Dr. Charles Garcia won't be the only one going to prison if this all blows up. I did a little research. They'd probably put you and me in prison for a dozen years. Garcia has nothing to lose, but you and I do. I could kiss my pension good-bye, and your law license could be used as toilet paper. I'm not doing this for $10,000.

"Before I make one phone call or lift a finger, I'll need fake paperwork to get me out of the country in case our little scheme falls apart. After we've worked out the details, but before I take any action, I want $250,000 deposited in an offshore account of my choosing, where the banking laws protect the identity of their customers. This payment is my protection if everything just goes to shit, and despite my efforts, Charlie is convicted anyway. If that happens, our deal ends, I move on to Bora Bora, and Charlie spends the next twenty-five years to life in Brushy Mountain Prison in West Tennessee.

"Now, if there's a not guilty verdict or even if Charlie gets off on appeal, when he's a free man, I get another $250,000 for my help toward his victory. Charlie's happy, his parents are happy, and I'm happy.

"But, Mr. Harrelson, let me warn you. If you do try to double-cross me, I'll bring the house of cards down, and you'll go to jail and lose your law license. That's a promise."

Harrelson knew that Baxter was susceptible and basically dishonest, but how far the paper pusher thought through his options surprised him. Harrelson took his pocket watch out of his vest and started rubbing it between his thumb and middle finger. He preferred Baxter's greed as long as the man did his part and remained silent.

Taking charge, Harrelson said, "We need to create reasonable doubt. A jury shouldn't be able to convict if reasonable doubt exists. If the jury concludes that the drugs came from a source other than Charlie, the jury shouldn't be able to convict him of murder in the second degree. The jury for murder must find that he was the distributor or the source that proximately caused the victim's death."

Baxter immediately seized on the direction of Harrelson's defense strategy. "I'll need as much information about Robyn Eden as possible. I will need to know her drug background and, most important, her drug of choice. We need to determine Robyn's calendar the week of her death. It's critical that we discover when she may have been in the company of other people. I need to feed the right information to the drug dealer. Our witness isn't going to be the brightest person in the world, but he must be under my absolute control. I've got a few good candidates. They're more than willing to be a false witness; they've broken most of the Ten Commandments . . ."

Harrelson interrupted, "We'll have to figure out how to present this testimony. I'm not a trial lawyer, and I'm not licensed in Tennessee. We're going to have to find the witness, and then my co-counsel, Amy Pierce, will work with the person."

CHAPTER FORTY-FIVE
THE DEFENSE'S PLOY
Friday, November 10, 2000

At nine sharp, Judge Tanner took the bench with lightning speed, wasting no time. "There are three pending motions, two scheduled to be heard today. The third, the motion to suppress, is scheduled two weeks from today. I will first hear arguments as to why I should recuse myself in this case. After that, we'll address the bond issue. Ms. Pierce, how much time do you need to argue your motion to recuse?"

"I'd like unlimited time, Your Honor. I don't think such an important motion should be hamstrung by a time limit restriction."

Davis thought, *Pierce is just baiting Tanner.*

The judge's retort was an old Rolling Stones' song, which he practically sang, "Well, you can't always get what you want."

Davis recognized the lyrics. He sang them to his children on many occasions.

"I'll give you half an hour. That should be more than sufficient."

Pierce was just preserving the record for an appeal. She'd argued that Judge Tanner's failure to recuse himself was reversible error. "Please note my objection."

"Let's hear why I'm unqualified to sit on this case."

"This is a simple motion. Judge Tanner issued three search warrants for Robyn Eden's apartment, and they contained inaccurate information provided by the Hewes City Police Department. The affidavit of Detective Haber, upon which the search warrants were issued, was based on the assertion that Dr. Garcia had been convicted of possession of a controlled substance, possession of drug paraphernalia, and endangerment. These statements were not true. The only criminal record of Dr. Garcia was a pretrial diversion in Kentucky for dispensing and prescribing a controlled substance."

Pierce was correct. Haber's affidavit was inaccurate because the information provided by the Deputy Clerk of Jefferson County was incorrect. Judge Tanner issued the three search warrants on the bogus affidavit.

Pierce continued, "As the court stated at the beginning of this hearing, in two weeks the motion to suppress will be heard, and it is the defendant's position that Judge Joe Tanner shouldn't hear that motion because of his involvement in the issuance of the search warrants.

"Under Tennessee law and the Code of Judicial Conduct, the court must recuse itself. The question is not whether His Honor is biased, but rather to the ordinary citizen, is there the appearance of impropriety? The court's search warrants uncovered the evidence that the defendant is entitled to exclude. We submit that the average citizen on the street would be concerned that this court, because of its involvement in securing the search warrants, would conclude that Judge Tanner could be biased, therefore the appearance of impropriety."

"Mr. Davis, what do you have to say?"

"We've briefed this issue. We think the second and the third search were consensual. The apartment manager gave consent to the second. Senator Valerie Daniels, the victim's sister and guarantor of the lease, gave the Hewes City police permission for the third. We also contend that whether the search warrants were properly issued isn't relevant to this court's ability to hear this case. We also believe that the court is eminently qualified and that there isn't even the appearance of impropriety."

Judge Tanner was known for his bench rulings. Unlike most judges, he was prepared and didn't take many matters under advisement. "I've heard arguments, and I've read the briefs. I am prepared to rule."

The judge read from a piece of paper. He'd obviously handwritten what he was going to say before the hearing. "The defendant has moved to recuse the court because the court issued three search warrants, which the defendant asserts were based on an affidavit containing inaccurate information. The defendant asserts that the discovered evidence should be excluded. In 1979, the Tennessee Supreme Court in Hawkins v. State rejected such an argument as the basis for recusal. In conclusion, the court finds that no reasonable person would question the court's impartiality.

"The hearing on the motion to suppress shall proceed in two weeks."

He turned to Davis and said, "Mr. Davis, you have a motion to increase the existing bond. You've asked to submit evidence in support of this motion. What evidence?"

"That depends, Your Honor. I've asked Ms. Pierce to stipulate as to the conditions of her client's probation in the Jefferson County, Kentucky, Criminal Court. Ms. Pierce has not responded. The court could take judicial notice of those conditions."

"And what would you prove, Mr. Davis?"

"That Dr. Garcia knowingly and intentionally violated his conditions of probation by leaving the continental United States and going on vacation with Ms. Eden in Nassau, Bahamas. The court can also take judicial notice that Nassau is not part of the United States. I can present plane reservations for flights and receipts for purchases on the island."

"When did this trip occur?" Tanner asked impatiently.

"Ten weeks before Ms. Eden's death. That's when he impregnated the victim."

The judge hadn't yet read the autopsy report. He was shocked, which was the effect Davis wanted. The courtroom was silent about two minutes while the judge digested this latest information. He decided to just move on with the pending motion.

"What do you have to say, Ms. Pierce?"

Pierce stood and addressed the court, "I've been advised that Dr. Garcia's probation officer, Mr. Baxter, was aware of that trip and gave him permission to go."

Davis jumped to his feet. "I remind the court that Dr. Garcia was born in Majorca and holds dual citizenship. I've not been able to communicate with Mr. Baxter. He recently retired and hasn't returned my telephone calls or responded to my letters."

Pierce set Davis up beautifully. She produced the affidavit of Alan Baxter, retired probation officer, that confirmed he gave Garcia permission to leave the country for the vacation.

Pierce then added, "Dr. Garcia will also sign an agreement not to make application to the Majorcan government for a substitute passport, which can be provided to that government."

"Does that satisfy you, Mr. Davis?"

"No, sir. Dr. Garcia has access to money. Even without his passport he could disappear from the jurisdiction of this court. He's surrendered his Tennessee medical license, neither he nor his parents live in the state, and the Kentucky probation has not restricted his travel outside the country. I'd like to ask the court to deny bond and hold him till trial, but I know that would be overreaching."

Tanner stated, "You've asked to increase the bond to $2 million. I'll split the difference. The bond is increased to $1 million. Officer, please take Dr. Garcia into custody and process him in the Hewes County jail until he satisfies the additional $500,000 required for him to remain on bond."

A small victory, Davis thought. *Charlie Garcia will spend a short time in jail, and his parents will lay out more money.*

It was actually a better victory than Davis thought. Charlie spent two days in the Hewes County jail while Señor Garcia arranged the wire to the clerk's office. He had to move some funds around. In the meantime Charlie was intentionally placed in a cell with an inmate who might try to get to know Charlie better. Charlie remained awake more than forty hours to protect his honor.

CHAPTER FORTY-SIX
A CRITICAL HEARING
Friday, November 24, 2000

Charlie understood that today's hearing was critical to the defense of his case and his acquittal from all charges. If the three search warrants were held invalid, the sex video, sex toys, and drugs seized at the apartment would be excluded from evidence. If the jury never got to see the video, handle the sex toys, or learn about the drugs at the apartment, Pierce assured Charlie that the jury would have reasonable doubt as to murder.

The parties, through their briefs, had their opportunity to emphasize whatever legal points and precedents they felt were persuasive. The oral argument lasted all morning, first Pierce, next Steine, and then Pierce again.

Charlie begrudgingly had to admit that old man Steine had done a masterful job. He was also very satisfied with Pierce. She emphasized all of the reasons to exclude the evidence and hold the search warrants invalid, but something about Steine drew the listener, especially the judge, because Steine directed all of his attention at him. The old man was going to be a real problem at trial. Charlie needed to get his father to neutralize Steine.

Judge Tanner adjourned court until three and indicated at

that time he would rule on the defendant's motion to suppress the search warrants.

Pierce elected to have a working lunch, so Charlie, Harrelson, and his father lunched together. In a quiet voice at a restaurant in walking distance of the courthouse, Mother's, Charlie broached what was on his mind, "Steine's a real problem. He's too good. The judge respects him, and a jury will love the old bastard. Davis is good, but in a criminal trial, he's out of his element. How can we get Steine out of the picture?"

Harrelson, who had no problem bending the rules and often broke some, didn't like where this conversation was headed. "Charlie, you're already in a lot of trouble. We might not want to complicate things."

Charlie was prepared for this objection, "He's an old man with a heart condition. Why would an accident be suspicious? These proceedings must be stressful for him. I know they are for me, and I'm fifty years younger. We just need to figure a way to nudge him ever so slightly over the edge, and then he's gone."

Harrelson responded too loudly, "You're playing with fire."

Señor Garcia remained quiet throughout the conversation. Charlie could tell he was thinking and didn't want to commit one way or the other.

At three o'clock the parties returned to the courtroom. Judge Tanner took the bench, and after everyone was seated, he began, "This is the defendant's motion to suppress the July 5th, July 6th, and July 8th search warrants issued by this court."

Pierce stood and was acknowledged by Judge Tanner. "Your Honor, the defendant renews his motion for the court to recuse itself from ruling on this motion and to remove yourself from the case because the court erroneously issued the search warrants."

"I've ruled on that motion, Ms. Pierce. Don't push your luck."

Pierce was trying to goad the judge, hoping he might say something that would help on appeal. She wasn't afraid of him. Charlie didn't think she was afraid of anything.

"Judge, I just note for the record that it's the position of the defendant that the court is committing reversible error and that the trial of this cause will be null and void, a waste of taxpayer dollars."

"I'm sure that you and your client are worried about the taxpayers. I will not tolerate any further interruptions of my rulings. Sit down and shut up."

Charlie understood what Pierce was doing. She'd shared her strategy before they returned to court. If Judge Tanner was going to suppress the evidence, Pierce's exchange would make no difference in the outcome of the judge's decision. However, if Judge Tanner was going to hold that the search warrants were valid, then by her disrupting his ruling and angering him, Tanner was more likely to make a mistake and create appealable issues.

The judge got back on track. "The first question that must be considered is whether Dr. Garcia has standing to challenge the search warrants. The undisputed proof is that Dr. Garcia was a guest at Ms. Eden's apartment. Under the law an overnight guest does have an expectation of and is entitled to privacy. It is also an undisputed fact that Dr. Garcia over the last year gave money to Ms. Eden, which she used to pay her expenses, including her rent and other expenses associated with the apartment. However, the proof is also clear that Dr. Garcia was not a tenant on the lease. Ms. Eden and her sister, Valerie Daniels, were. Dr. Garcia did have his own key and did enter the apartment when he wanted, without the continuous permission of Ms. Eden."

Charlie whispered to Pierce. "Where's this going?"

"I don't know, but it seems to me like he's about to exclude the search warrants. Just listen."

"It is undisputed that twice on July 4th the Hewes City police at the apartment and then again at the Hewes County Hospital asked and were refused by Dr. Garcia to search. As an overnight guest, it was within his right of privacy to refuse the search."

Charlie smiled and squeezed Pierce's hand. She squeezed back. Charlie was confident for the first time that the search warrants would be thrown out. The system was about to work despite that convincing old man. Charlie refocused on the judge.

"Detective Haber on the morning of July 5th submitted to this court an affidavit, upon which this court issued the first of three search warrants. Detective Haber's affidavit contained inaccurate information. The affidavit asserted that Dr. Garcia had been convicted of improperly prescribing a Schedule III drug to the victim in Jefferson County, Kentucky, during the 1999 Kentucky Derby. This was not completely accurate. Dr. Garcia was not convicted. He pled 'no contest' and was placed on probation. There was no conviction or guilty plea. For this reason I must rule that the first search warrant is invalid and must be struck."

Charlie turned to Harrelson and his father. "One down and two to go."

"As to the second search on July 6th, which is based upon the consent of the manager of the apartment complex, I also hold that this search was invalid. The apartment manager testified that he was unaware that Dr. Garcia, who was at least a regular overnight guest, had refused to give permission to search. The manager also testified that on July 6th, he was told that there was a valid search warrant issued by this court the day before. For these reasons, I hold that the second search on July 6th was not consensual and was not valid."

Charlie got an encouraging look from both his father and Harrelson.

"The third search, on July 8th, based on the consent of Valerie Daniels, who was on the lease, is the most troubling. Did Ms. Daniels have greater property rights in the apartment than Dr. Garcia? She was a tenant, and he was an overnight guest. She did have a greater property right, even if Dr. Garcia gave Robyn Eden rent money. How she used the funds was in Robyn Eden's discretion. However, could Ms. Daniels, vested with her greater privacy rights, overturn Dr. Garcia's refusal to search? I hold that she did not, and therefore the third search was invalid."

Pierce grabbed Charlie by the arm. They were three for three. All three searches had been struck down. Charlie looked over at the Davis team. They didn't look despondent. In fact, Steine smiled at him.

"As discussed in Mr. Steine's brief, this court holds that despite the fact that the searches of July 5th, July 6th, and July 8th have been struck down, the court finds that the tapes, sex toys, and drugs found at the apartment are admissible into evidence under the Inevitable Discovery Doctrine, which is discussed in the last two pages of Mr. Steine's brief. According to the United States Supreme Court in the Nix case, if the evidence is in plain view and the police are on site for a legitimate law enforcement reason, a valid search warrant is not required for the police to take into evidence those items in plain view. It was Dr. Garcia who called 911. He had a reasonable expectation that the Hewes City police would come to the apartment and render assistance.

"On the floor of the bedroom was a dying Robyn Eden. In front of the bed was a camera on a tripod, and it was running. It was reasonable for Dr. Garcia to expect the police to want to view the tape, to determine what happened to Robyn Eden.

"At the time the police arrived, it was reasonable for the police to enter the bathroom of the apartment to see if anyone else was present or if there was anything in plain view that could assist them in the care of Robyn Eden or to determine what happened to Robyn Eden. In plain view were the drugs that proximately caused Robyn Eden's distressed medical condition and ultimate death. Also present at the bedside and in the bathroom in plain view were the sex toys depicted in the video used by Dr. Garcia with Ms. Eden. Whatever was found in the nightstand drawer was not in plain view and therefore inadmissible. All other evidence in plain view will be admissible at this trial. A written order will be filed tomorrow, consistent with my ruling.

"I'm also entering a gag order. We're not going to turn this case into a circus. As much as I don't want to, I've decided that the jury's going to be sequestered, so it makes sense to limit what the parties say to the press. Nothing will be said. Your only words will be, 'no comment.' Listen up, if anyone violates this gag order, especially the lawyers who are officers of this court, they will be my guest in the Hewes County jail. Don't test me, people."

With that Judge Tanner handed down a detailed pre-prepared gag order, which he was confident would be obeyed. The judge left the bench. Pierce and Charlie were stunned. They half expected at least one or more of the searches to be held valid, but Steine had placed so little emphasis on the Inevitable Discovery Doctrine that they were genuinely surprised by the fact that Judge Tanner had hung his ruling on that alone.

Charlie thought, *We've got to get rid of that old man.* He even growled at the old man as Steine and Davis left the courtroom.

CHAPTER FORTY-SEVEN
THE CONSPIRACY MOVES FORWARD
Thursday, December 21, 2000

Harrelson met Señor Garcia for an early lunch at the 21 Club on the Upper West Side.

"Hello, David, what do you hear from Ms. Pierce about Charlie's upcoming trial?"

It was a rhetorical question. Señor Garcia was in constant contact with both Harrelson and Pierce. He knew more about the defense than Pierce since he and Harrelson were orchestrating the defense and fabricating most of the evidence.

Harrelson and Señor Garcia were the only two who knew all of the details of the false testimony and contrived expert testimony. It was better that Charlie didn't know the details; Charlie actually liked it that way. Pierce would ultimately be fully informed because she would be the one introducing the evidence. They both knew Pierce had her price, and she'd do anything to win. She was ruthless. That's what they liked about her.

"Have you heard any more from Baxter?"

"He's got the witness lined up. She has agreed to twenty-five up front and another fifty after she testifies. He assures me that Nix will be convincing and that her testimony will be extremely damaging to the state's case. He has all the information he needs, so she'll testify with sufficient detail and she'll be believable. I'm still working on getting access to the evidence locker of the Hewes City Police Department. I've been looking through the personnel to find someone who has access and is desperate. I've got the DNA expert lined up if we can plant the evidence."

"How much will that cost?"

"The expert will be paid an hourly fee of $500, and who knows how much the cop will cost. I don't want to cut corners on that one. If that blows up and the cop turns, I go to jail. I need someone who needs the money, but it won't be cheap."

Despite his paternal instincts, Señor Garcia pointed out, "This trial is costing a fortune, and we need an acquittal. A hung jury just means more expense and more legal fees. My wife can't take much more of this. She loves Charlie, but he's been a big disappointment to her. We'll see it through, but he'd better get his act together after an acquittal. He's not a kid anymore. He needs to grow up."

Harrelson never heard his friend and client talk so realistically about Charlie. "What's up, Eddie?"

Señor Garcia handed Harrelson a certified letter from the New York State Medical Licensing Board. It read,

> Dear Dr. Garcia,
>
> It has come to the attention of the Medical Licensing Board that last year you pled no contest to a charge of improperly prescribing Schedule III narcotics and received an eighteen-month probation as a pretrial diversion.

It has also come to the board's attention that this year, you voluntarily surrendered your Tennessee medical license, under pending charges, and are currently under indictment for second-degree murder in Hewes County, Tennessee. For all of these reasons, please be advised that the State of New York Medical Licensing Board hereby summarily suspends your medical license pending a full hearing, in which you will be provided with due process.

This action is being taken to protect the general public, including your patients. Please cease and desist from the practice of medicine. Any further practice after receipt of this certified letter will constitute a Class C felony, subjecting you to up to ten years in prison and/or a $100,000 fine per occurrence.

We encourage you to seek legal counsel and suggest that your selected counsel contact Ralph Edwards of the New York State Attorney General's Office at 212-443-6434.

Robert O'Conner, MD, President of the New York State Medical Licensing Board

Harrelson just stared at the letter.

Señor Garcia opined, "I suspect calling the New York Licensing Board was Steine's idea. We've got to get rid of him before trial no matter what. Do it!"

CHAPTER FORTY-EIGHT

FINDING A LITTLE HELP FROM SOME FRIENDS
Sunday, December 31, 2000

The reality that the fruits of the searches—the sex video, sex toys, and drugs—would be admissible at his trial was too much for Charlie to bear. He was depressed. His parents canceled their New Year's Eve plans to be with him. Despite their sacrifice, Charlie wasn't talking. His father asked, "What's wrong, son?"

"How the fuck can you ask me what's wrong?"

As a rule, Charlie didn't curse around his father, He was civilized, and it offended him. His father gave his son a stern look, and with his eyes Charlie apologized.

"I won't minimize this setback, but that's all it is. Harrelson and I are mapping out your defense. You need a good psychiatrist."

"I am depressed."

Repeating what Harrelson scripted, Señor Garcia lectured his son, "Depressed. You may need a psychiatrist for that reason, but you'll need at least two psychiatrists who can testify that you're not a sociopath and also testify about your loving relationship with Robyn. They might be able to turn the failure of the relationship on the girl's drug use. The first one will be your treating physician, and the second should be an addiction expert. The second doctor can testify about your co-dependency toward Robyn. She was the addict, not you. You were a loving enabler."

"Why do we need two of each type of expert?"

"Corroboration. If one expert from a field says something, a jury might believe him or her, but if two eminent experts' testimonies support each other, the likelihood of their convincing a jury dramatically increases."

"That makes sense."

"What doesn't make sense is you and how you conduct your life. You're a huge disappointment to your mother and me, and we've come to the end of our rope."

Charlie looked into his father's eyes and recognized the intense disappointment. He needed to say something profound in order to avoid his wrath and disdain.

"Father, I've disgraced the family name, but even worse I've disappointed you. In the past my poor judgment created manageable problems, and you've always shielded me from the consequences of my mistakes, for which I've been grateful. This time David Harrelson and your money can't secure a quick fix. It's up to me. I've got to convince the jury that although I did use poor judgment, I shouldn't go to prison for my mistakes. I'll have to testify and persuade them."

"You're a Garcia. You'll rise to the occasion, and we'll rise above all this. Harrelson and I are working on your defense. By the time we're through, any Hewes County jury will acquit."

Charlie actually felt better after talking to his father. Señor Garcia was so confident; it came from a lifetime of being able to buy whatever he wanted, when he wanted.

Over the next week Harrelson spent his days looking at experts' resumes. He'd agreed to find the necessary experts, and Pierce, despite the fact that she was lead counsel, allowed him to conduct the search and perform the initial interviews. She insisted that the second non-treating physician had to be licensed in Tennessee but conceded that Charlie's treating psychiatrist had to be from New York because of treatment logistics.

Dr. Robert Townsend was a board-certified psychiatrist with more than thirty-five years of hands-on experience. He'd been treating the rich and famous of New York City for years. Despite the success of his practice, Townsend was broke, a habitual gambler. He owed $200,000 to high-end loan sharks, who he was barely paying his weekly vig. He was getting desperate.

Harrelson accompanied Charlie to his first appointment. After cordial introductions, Harrelson told Charlie to excuse himself. Harrelson got down to business and explained the nature of their problem and how Dr. Townsend could help.

"I can't promise what my opinions will be, but . . ."

Harrelson pushed six photocopied papers across Townsend's desk. They were his markers for $200,000.

"I've bought these. I own you. Your opinions will be what I tell you those opinions are. What's your normal hourly rate?"

"Five hundred a session, but . . ."

"You'll be paid that as we go. You'll be paid $10,000 to give a deposition and another $10,000 to testify at trial. Upon Charlie's acquittal, I'll tear up these markers. If he's found guilty, these markers will be the last things you have to worry about. I'll ask Charlie to come back in and leave the two of you to your first session."

With that Harrelson left the office, Charlie came in, and Townsend turned to him.

"Let's find out a little about you and this Robyn Eden."

CHAPTER FORTY-NINE

AN INTERESTING FLIGHT
Monday, January 1, 2001

He must have been out of his mind. He'd promised Liza he wouldn't fly with the old man anymore.

Her argument was simple: "He's almost eighty years old. He can hardly see, and he's got a chronic heart condition. What happens if he passes out or dies? Then you're the only stupid shmuck in the plane. It's common sense. I hope you have some and just let him fly solo."

Davis protested, "He needs the company. It's an important part of his life. He's got a valid license." As soon as the words came out of his mouth, he regretted them.

"You must think I'm stupid, Ben. I know he bribes an FAA friend to keep passing him despite his age and disability. Your children and niece are forbidden from flying with him. I'll not risk their lives. Yours is well insured, isn't it?"

"The policy is for $2 million with New York Life. I hope you and the second Mr. Davis have a good time with the proceeds."

Davis tried to kiss Liza, but she pulled away. When he walked out the door, he finally realized how angry she really was.

Davis picked Morty up at Squeeze Bottom, his longtime family farm. His driving was questionable. Davis thought, *If I won't drive with him, why do I fly with him?* The reason wasn't complicated. He loved the old man, and the old man loved to fly. He'd been flying and owned a plane since he was in his teens.

"How about we go fishing?"

Morty was far from stupid. He knew what Davis was trying to do, and he wasn't playing along.

"We're going flying. That was my New Year's wish. You gave your word, and as I've told you, your word is your bond, and always do the right thing. I don't care what Liza's orders are. You gave me your word. Just close your eyes, and it will be over soon enough."

"I only have to work with you. I have to live with her."

"I outrank her. You're following my orders."

"Yes, sir, General."

Davis drove the fifteen miles to John Tune Airport in silence. He was trying to think of a graceful way to get out of going on the flight. Five minutes later he was climbing into the cockpit behind Morty.

Davis had flown in Morty's Cessna 401 at least forty times. In earlier years, so had his children. He'd been flying less and less. Getting back in the air was a big deal.

They took off without incident. About twenty minutes into the flight, Davis looked over at the pilot, who had a contorted face.

"What's wrong? Are you ill?"

"No, but I don't feel good."

"In what way?"

"Our oil pressure dropped drastically, and I can't figure out why."

"What does that mean?"

"The engines are going to seize up."

Davis was now much more concerned than his old friend. "What the hell does that mean to us?"

"We'll have to make an emergency landing in some field if you can find one."

For the next ten minutes they looked for that field but had no luck.

Davis started getting very agitated and said, "Find a field. This is getting serious!"

With those prophetic words engine #1 cut off. Morty struggled a moment with the plane but regained control.

"Safest two-engine plane ever made. Lucky for you I know what the hell I'm doing. We'll be fine."

Davis thought, *Stop bragging and land this plane.*

On that thought engine #2 conked out.

They were gliding now. Morty still had the plane under control.

"If I don't find a field soon, I'm going to have to land on the highway."

"What?"

"Make sure your seat belt is as tight as possible, and when we hit, make sure your head is in your lap."

Davis didn't argue, but that was a physical impossibility. His belly was in the way.

Davis actually started praying. He figured it couldn't hurt: "Shema Yisrael, Adonai Eloheinu, Adonai Echad! Hear O Israel, the Lord is Our God, the Lord is One. . . ."

Morty repeated Davis's prayer. Just then he spotted a county high school, and one side of the football field was open-ended. He focused; he was unafraid, except for the life of his cargo. He hit ground at the fifteen-yard line and slid across the field. The plane stopped outside the other end zone. By now the engines were smoking.

When the plane came to a complete stop, Morty yelled, "Get the hell out of here as soon as you can. It could blow."

Davis was in shock but came to his senses. Davis released his seat belt and, for a man his size and weight, moved quickly. Morty moved a lot slower. Davis, who'd started running, went back to help his friend, and they fell about the five-yard line.

Morty was gripping his chest. Davis could tell immediately he was in severe pain. Morty pointed to his pocket, and Davis found his nitroglycerin pills. He opened the bottle and placed one under Morty's tongue.

Davis sat down and put his head between his knees and threw up. He heard sounds coming from his friend. He moved closer. The son of a bitch wasn't in pain. The sick bastard was laughing.

"What the hell are you laughing about? We almost died."

"I've still got it. We walked away from our landing. During the war, that was an acceptable landing. We'd live to fight another day. The pilots were even more valuable than the planes. We saved the world."

The old man was in sort of a trance back in time. Despite his laughter, he was still very shaken up. Davis helped him to his feet.

"No one would ever accuse you of thinking your glass is half empty. I've got to say, it's an easy call, and you're a half-glass-full kind of guy."

No broken bones or permanent damage, other than to the plane. Davis agreed the glass was half full, except he'd have to explain this to Liza. The water level of the glass just dropped a little.

"I love you like a father, but your flying days are over," Davis stated firmly.

With that remark Morty's mood changed, as angry as Davis ever heard. He said, "This is bullshit! Something was not right with my plane. My maintenance on that plane is impeccable! There's a reason both engines lost oil pressure. One would be unlikely, but losing both just doesn't happen. You can check the logs. Those engines were properly maintained. Something's not right! Listen to what I'm saying! I'm telling you this is bullshit! This wasn't my fault."

With that Morty's beloved Cessna burst into flames, and the old man started crying.

"There goes my proof!"

Davis could feel the heat of the explosion. It woke him up. They needed a plan.

Both men's cell phones were lost in the plane. It took Davis a moment to figure that out. They moved to the opposing thirty-yard line and rested. Still feeling nauseous, Davis concluded that they should stay put because someone would see the smoke.

Fifteen minutes later a Hewes County Fire Department truck was on the scene. Two minutes later two other trucks and an ambulance were on the scene. A paramedic with the nameplate *Mackey* approached them and asked them how they were. Davis told him about Morty's heart condition, and Mackey went to work. He gave Morty oxygen and checked his vitals.

When the news truck showed up, Davis knew he was in real trouble. Liza would see the local news report, which would include the name of the owner and his passenger. Davis borrowed a phone from a police officer nearby.

"Hi, honey, I promise this will be my last flight with Morty Steine."

Liza was a very direct person. In a firm, stern voice she asked, "What happened?"

He sheepishly told his wife about their flight and its abrupt end. He promised that not even Morty's friend at the FAA could save Morty's pilot license after this fiasco.

When she slammed down the receiver, Davis knew he was in for his own fiasco, which included hearing, "I told you so!" again and again.

What Davis didn't know was that he was being watched through high-powered binoculars as Mackey tended to Morty. The observer's arms were raised, forcing his sleeves to pull up and reveal a T-rex tattoo with fiery yellow eyes.

CHAPTER FIFTY
MOTIONS IN LIMINE
(Preliminary Motions)
Tuesday, February 6, 2001

Davis spent eighteen hours a day for the last three weeks getting their case ready for trial. Morty worked a third as much and was still exhausted at the end of each day. Sammie got the education of a lifetime. With the help of Bella she ran the office and tended to the needs of the firm's other clients. It was like being thrown into a swimming pool to learn how to swim. She did a great job; the clients loved her. Bella was the key. She'd been abandoned for a trial many times. She helped Sammie through this stressful time. When the trial started, with Sammie gone, it would be Bella who ran the office and handled the clients as best she could. Most were understanding, but not all. That was the nature of a small law office, with limited resources and personnel.

The Garcia case placed a terrible financial burden on the firm of Davis & Davis. On January 2, the day after the plane crash, Davis unveiled the new brass placard that he had commissioned. There was a little ceremony that Liza attended. Everyone was so proud of Sammie, especially the old man. He thought of her as his creation, like Professor Henry Higgins had done with Eliza Doolittle. He suspected she'd be a better lawyer than her uncle someday, and possibly as good as him—but not better.

Davis was spending much too much time at the DA's office. He'd go home to change, continuously eat, and sleep. He was tired and feeling the loss of income and accounts receivable. Morty, as Davis's landlord, agreed to waive Davis's rent, and Morty was paying Bella's salary. Morty had done the same thing during the Plainview cases. He had the money, and Davis was his primary beneficiary under his will anyway.

It was hard on Davis and Sammie, but it was too much for the old man. At eighty, he was physically exhausted, but his mind just kept on working.

Today would be a long one. Seventeen preliminary motions had to be argued. Morty, Sammie, and Davis were in their small DA office an hour from argument of those motions. Morty cleared his throat. There was an odd feeling in the air.

"Ben, since your display of grit in the Plainview cases, you've been the lawyer I'd hoped you would be. I'm so proud of you I could bust. This is a new chapter in your career, and you're prepared. You've read the Rules of Criminal Procedure and Evidence several times. It's just like a civil trial. You've got this. Just remember there are other lawyers, a judge, and a jury. You know how to deal with the lawyers, and you know how to work with a judge and charm a jury. This is your baby; I'm just here for support."

Davis felt his eyes welling up. He was struggling to keep from crying. Sammie was.

Morty broke the tension, "Just think, in twenty years you'll be having this conversation with Sammie, maybe sooner."

Davis would argue the preliminary motions. There were several motions filed by both parties. For the most part, they addressed pretrial evidentiary rulings. These motions were important for several reasons. First, each side needed to know what evidence would be admitted, so they could be prepared at trial. Second, these pretrial decisions allowed the trial to move quicker. A jury didn't tolerate delay, and whoever they believed was unreasonably delaying the trial would pay for it. Last, motions in limine preserved issues for appeal. They forced the judge to articulate his rulings, so they could be considered and ruled upon by the Court of Appeals.

In the courtroom Davis turned to Sammie and asked her to identify the defendant's pending motions.

Sammie spoke directly to Judge Tanner, "Well, there are a total of seventeen motions, thirteen by the defendant and four by the state. I don't know in what order the court intends to address them."

Tanner briskly said, "Just tell me what they are, Ms. Davis."

"Starting with the defendant's motions, (1) To exclude from evidence Dr. Garcia's probation for improperly dispensing drugs to Robyn Eden in Kentucky; (2) To exclude from evidence the fact that Dr. Garcia surrendered his Tennessee medical license; (3) To exclude from evidence the fact that the state of New York had suspended Dr. Garcia's New York medical license; (4) To exclude from evidence the sex video of Robyn Eden and Dr. Garcia made July 4th; (5) To exclude from evidence acts of violence by Dr. Garcia against Robyn Eden throughout their relationship; (6) To exclude the testimony of the state's expert witnesses because of a break in the chain of evidence; (7) To exclude from evidence statements made by Dr. Garcia to Detective Haber at Hewes County Hospital because he didn't receive his Miranda warning; (8) To require the state to explain what happened to certain cell phone photos taken by Dr. Garcia of Robyn Eden on July 4th; (9) For the court to sequester the jury, to live in a motel, after their selection; (10) To reconsider the court's ruling on the validity of the search warrants and the Inevitable Discovery Doctrine; (11) To exclude any reference to the two civil lawsuits filed in Davidson County, in which the Davis law firm represented Dr. Nichols; (12) To exclude any reference to the Princeton police report of Charles Garcia; and (13) To exclude any reference to Dr. Garcia's juvenile pretrial diversion for drug possession."

Sammie took a breath. She didn't envy Judge Tanner for his responsibility to decide each of those motions. "The state has four motions: (1) To exclude the testimony of the defendant's expert witnesses for opinions that are not based on good science; (2) To refer to the defendant as Mr. Garcia, rather than Dr. Garcia, because he no longer has a valid medical license; (3) To exclude the nude photographs of Robyn Eden and her old boyfriend Ron Harris taken in 1994; and (4) To exclude evidence of Ms. Eden's pregnancy."

Davis could tell that the judge was unhappy about the number of pretrial motions.

"I've got a headache just listening to you list them," Judge Tanner said, and he wasn't joking.

Louder than he intended, Davis whispered to Sammie, "I can't believe I've got to argue all of them."

"Just take them one at a time," Sammie responded.

Tanner as usual took control. "We have a lot of work in front of us before we begin this trial and select our jury. I've read all of the briefs, and it will not be necessary for us to have oral argument on all of the pending motions. Let the record reflect that neither party has waived oral argument on any of their motions, but several of these motions are in my sole discretion as a matter of law. Therefore, I have the right to refuse oral argument and rule on those motions."

Davis was surprised that Judge Tanner would refuse oral argument on any of the motions. It was common courtesy for the court to at least allow some argument if a party took the effort to file the motion. Often a court would limit the time of argument, but it was rare, particularly in a murder trial, to refuse oral argument. Davis just held his breath and waited for the court's rulings.

"First, I will sequester the jury. Despite the gag order, I expect this case to be heavily reported, locally and possibly nationally. I don't want our jury poisoned by publicity. It will be hard enough to find an acceptable jury without exposing them to the opinions of the media, which are often ill informed and wrong. This jury is going to base its decision on the evidence, the testimony from the witness box, and the documents and information that I deem admissible. I am also putting the parties on notice that I intend to liberally allow challenges for cause. I want a fair and impartial jury."

Davis didn't like the way that this hearing was starting. It sounded like Judge Tanner was going to bend over backward in an effort to have a clean but defendant-friendly trial. The state, unlike the defendant, certainly didn't want the judge to commit reversible error. A retrial, after an appeal, would be a financial nightmare for the state and for Davis personally and professionally.

"The defendant will be referred to as Mr. Garcia. He no longer holds a valid medical license."

Davis sighed with a little relief. At least this clown wouldn't be disrespecting the entire medical profession by being called "Doctor."

"On the motions to exclude the experts, well, I'm going to let the jury listen to their testimony, weigh the science supporting those opinions, and decide whose testimony they're going to rely upon. I will give each side great latitude in the effort to impeach that testimony, but bottom line, that's the job of the jury."

Tanner paused and took a sip of water. "We've all got our witness lists and three boxes of exhibits. We're going to use the exhibit

numbers from the exhibit list instead of introducing them in se-
quential order. Exhibit 133 will be introduced as Exhibit 133. You
know the drill."

Pierce and Harrelson risked failing to disclose Danny Nix on
their witness list. She would be an impeachment witness, who
would contradict evidence introduced by the state, but only if Tanner permitted her to testify.

Davis hoped the motion to exclude the defendant's experts
would be granted. The defendant's experts had impressive resumes,
and their testimony tried to establish that Mr. Garcia did not have
the requisite intent to kill Robyn Eden.

"Mr. Davis, that only leaves two of your motions for argument,
but before we begin, I must ask you a question. Is it the state's position that Mr. Garcia corrupted Ms. Eden and that he was the cause
of her unorthodox sexual behavior?"

"It's the state's position that Mr. Garcia did assert control over Ms.
Eden, in part through their doctor-patient relationship and in part
through their sexual role-playing and untraditional sexual behavior."

"In that case, I am going to allow the pictures of Ms. Eden and
Mr. Harris into evidence. A jury could find that Ms. Eden, based on
those photos prior to meeting Mr. Garcia, was willing to be photo-
graphed nude and had a long history of sexual deviance."

Those photos showed just that. Which was why Davis filed the
motion to exclude them.

"Now I want to discuss the state's motion to exclude the pregnancy. It's right there on the autopsy report. That's an important
piece of evidence. Why would the court agree to exclude proof of
the pregnancy, Mr. Davis?"

Davis knew the motion was a long shot. The pregnancy made
the drug-using victim look like a horrible person. The average

Hewes County citizen couldn't fathom why a pregnant woman would take drugs. The pregnancy also helped Garcia. Again the average Hewes County citizen would find it hard to believe a father would be complicit in giving drugs to the mother of his child. Davis needed to convince the judge to exclude this damaging evidence and preserve the issue for appeal.

"Your Honor, when the state received the autopsy report, the state was faced with the decision whether to charge the defendant with a double homicide for Ms. Eden and the child. The state chose to indict as to Ms. Eden's death only. The death of the child is not relevant to the murder of Ms. Eden and should be excluded."

The judge said, "That's a pretty creative argument, Mr. Davis, but motion denied. The fact that Robyn Eden was pregnant is a fact that both sides are going to have to live with. Quite frankly I don't know what a jury will do with this information, but I suspect that they will consider it important. They have a right to know."

Truthfully, no one knew how a jury would take it.

"Ms. Pierce, I'm not going to let in the juvenile drug possession or the Princeton police report. They are remote as to time, and therefore the prejudicial effect outweighs their probative value under Rule 403 of the Rules of Evidence. Even though the two civil lawsuits are close in time, they were mere allegations, and the cases were settled. It is my understanding there is a confidentiality clause in each of those settlement agreements, which I intend to honor. It's ironic, Mr. Davis, that your clients were also parties to those same settlement agreements, so through your clients, you and Mr. Steine, as Dr. Nichols's attorneys, are also bound."

At the time the confidentiality clause in the civil lawsuits made good sense. Davis thought he was through with Mr. Garcia, but he was wrong.

"It's fair to say that the relationship between Ms. Eden and Mr. Garcia was a complex and tumultuous one. I think the jury needs to sort through the facts and decide what that relationship was and what part each of them played. I'm letting in what happened in Kentucky and any other bad acts committed by either Mr. Garcia or Ms. Eden that explain their relationship. Let the chips fall where they may, and let the jurors come to their own conclusions. The probation, physical abuse by Mr. Garcia, sex tapes, still photos, and sex toys all come in."

It was clear to Davis that Judge Tanner had decided to let State v. Garcia be a knockdown, drag-out fight. That would be fine in a civil case, the kind Davis had always tried. The burden of proof was a mere preponderance of the evidence, a slight tipping of the scale. But in a criminal trial, the state's burden was beyond a reasonable doubt, and that was a much higher burden for Davis to meet.

"That leaves only two motions. I would like oral argument on the missing July 4th cell phone pictures and exclusion from the testimony of Detective Haber as to what Mr. Garcia said to her at the hospital. Mr. Davis, what's the state's explanation for these missing photos?"

Davis stood and replied to the judge, "Your Honor, neither my associates nor I were involved at the early stages of the investigation, and the first time we were made aware of this alleged problem."

"Mr. Davis, you're standing before this court as the state of Tennessee, not Benjamin Davis. You're responsible for the actions of all of the agents of the state, including the Hewes City Police Department, which controlled the crime scene and the evidence taken into its possession. Have you inquired about these photos?"

"There are two hundred seventy-two still photos. I'm not sure what I'm looking for."

"Which ones are missing, Ms. Pierce?"

"Your Honor, Dr. Garcia distinctly remembers that Ms. Eden on July 4th inserted a large black sex toy, first in her mouth, and Dr. Garcia took two pictures with his cell phone. Those photos were not produced by the state."

Judge Tanner corrected Pierce, "Your client, the defendant, is Mr. Garcia, not Dr. Garcia."

Davis waited a few moments to let Judge Tanner's rebuke of Pierce sink in.

"Your Honor, we question the veracity of Mr. Garcia."

"Well, we're going to let the jury hear the testimony and decide if the state destroyed these photos. I'm going to ask the jurors a preliminary question, and if they conclude the state did destroy evidence, then I will charge them accordingly."

The last thing Judge Tanner did was to hear testimony from Detective Haber about her conversation at the hospital with Mr. Garcia to determine whether such testimony should be heard and considered by the jury.

"Based upon what the detective has said, despite Mr. Garcia's affidavit, Mr. Garcia at the time of the conversation did not require a Miranda warning. At that time the apartment had not been searched, and Mr. Garcia was viewed as a grieving boyfriend and was not under investigation. Mr. Garcia can explain to the jury that when he spoke with Detective Haber, he felt threatened and under suspicion. The jury will determine who's telling the truth."

Judge Tanner looked at his watch and smiled. "Seventeen motions in less than three hours. That's got to be a world record. Let's hope the trial goes as smoothly. I'll see you all in court tomorrow to begin picking the jury. Hopefully we'll have another productive day." Then Judge Tanner walked from the courtroom, leaving the parties stunned that the motions had been decided.

CHAPTER FIFTY-ONE

PICKING A JURY AND JURY INSTRUCTIONS

Wednesday, February 7, 2001

I t was a big day for both the defense and the prosecution. That was true for the first day of any trial. Morty, Sammie, and Davis were prepared. They'd divided the responsibilities of the trial fairly equally among them, but Davis took the lead. Davis and Sammie were concerned that the old man might run out of steam. If so, they'd outlined contingency plans to take up the slack.

Bella was back at the office, like always, holding down the fort. There would be no Davis & Davis without her perseverance. Sammie would report to her at lunch.

Amy Pierce was equally prepared. Her two associates helped her get the case ready for trial, but they were back at the office. Pierce wanted all the credit. She also believed that if she sat alone at the defense table, while the state had three lawyers, it might appear to the jury that the defense was an underdog.

David Harrelson wasn't a trial lawyer, nor was he licensed in the state of Tennessee, so he was relegated with Señor and Mrs. Garcia to the audience. Charlie's parents were there for the duration, throwing their economic and emotional support behind their son.

Hewes County was an affluent community, clearly divided between Hewes City and the rest of the county. The total county population was just under forty thousand with almost twenty thousand living in Hewes City. There were two high schools, one inner city and the other rural. This lent itself to competition between the two schools. In general the population was educated, fifty-eight percent with college degrees and eighty percent with a high school diploma. Not everyone agreed whether this was a good or bad factor for Charlie Garcia. Davis felt it worked against him.

The newshounds were out in force. All of the local press and also *USA Today*, the *New York Times*, the *Washington Post*, and a few regional papers. This case had literally good sex appeal, and the media loved good sex appeal. Because cameras weren't allowed in the courtroom, the playing field was evened out between TV and print news media. The national news coverage of the trial would make picking a jury much more difficult. Judge Tanner made the right decision to sequester the jury.

All of the parties were subject to a gag order, so the lawyers avoided the reporters like the plague. Judge Tanner promised if they gave anything to the press, they'd be his guests in the Hewes County jail.

In many ways, even though his future was uncertain, Charlie was relieved that this day finally arrived. His arrest six months earlier had shaken his world, and he'd lived in fear of incarceration ever since. It was no way to live. Charlie was convinced that the trial was a necessary evil for him to move on with his life.

Judge Tanner took the bench precisely at nine. "Good morning, everyone. Let's pick a jury. Any preliminary matters before we get started?"

Neither side offered anything to the court, so the selection process began. All of the potential jurors had completed juror questionnaires. They started with a jury pool of one hundred eighty, and that number was reduced to one hundred thirty-nine based on their responses to questionnaires. For example, six jurors were excluded because they knew one of the lawyers, and two were excluded because they knew one of the potential witnesses. Judge Tanner excused thirty-three jurors because of either business or family commitments.

The selection process began with Judge Tanner spending the first fifteen minutes explaining what being sequestered meant: "This case is expected to last at least two weeks, and the jury will be sequestered at the end of each day of trial in an undisclosed hotel. You'll be away from your families and work for at least two weeks. Does this create an unbearable conflict for any of you?"

Surprisingly only seven hands went up. Davis expected more, even though several others had already been excluded. These seven did have commitments so the judge released them. The rest of the ninety-three jurors wanted to serve. The response was unprecedented. Any other panel would have dozens of persons seeking to be excused. The Garcia case, which was highly publicized, had titillated the community. Everyone wanted to hear the evidence and decide the case.

The judge continued to ask questions, and four other jurors were excused.

Davis stood and began the inquiry for the prosecution, "Ladies and gentlemen, Mr. Garcia has been charged with second-degree murder. The state alleges that he supplied the drugs, which proximately caused Robyn Eden's death. If the state proves that essential element of its case, would any of you be unwilling on moral grounds to find him guilty of murder, where Judge Tanner might sentence him to life in prison?"

No one raised his or her hand. Davis continued, "Without trying to be sensational, the state intends to introduce into evidence a videotape of Mr. Garcia and the victim engaged in various sex acts, which will leave   nothing to the imagination. This is not soft-core pornography . . ."

Pierce jumped up and objected, "Mr. Davis is characterizing the evidence, Your Honor. I object to him referring to the video as pornography, soft, hard, or otherwise."

The judge turned to Davis for his response. "The United States Supreme Court, through Justice Potter Stewart, proclaimed that it knew what was pornographic when it saw it. I'm confident that this jury will know what this video is when it sees it."

"I withdraw my question."

Without missing a beat, Davis asked another hour of questions, including ones about sex toys and drugs. Several of the older women looked uncomfortable when he referred to various sex toys. The men just looked horny, and some of the younger men couldn't take their eyes off Sammie. Davis suspected that several of them had erections from the combination of hearing his questions and looking at his niece.

After Davis sat down, it was Pierce's turn. She wanted to shame every woman over forty off the panel. She was convinced, and the prosecution agreed, that older women would blame the victim for her drug use and sexual promiscuity. Pierce wanted young men on the jury, the younger, the better. They were most likely to identify with Garcia and his lust and fetishes.

She asked, "How many jury members have used a vibrator in their lovemaking?"

It was Davis's turn to object, "Your Honor, that's a pretty personal question to ask these jurors. I don't think they should have to identify themselves and be embarrassed in this courtroom."

Pierce was ready for the objection. "Your Honor, a man's freedom for the remainder of his life is at stake. I need to find out which of these jurors are predetermined to guilt simply because my client and Ms. Eden used sex toys in their lovemaking."

Tanner pondered the issue a long minute and then ruled, "I'll allow it."

Sixty-one women were left on the panel. After a good two minutes, in staggered succession nearly half of the women raised their hands, and so did ten males.

Davis suspected that several others were too embarrassed to acknowledge the use of the marital aids.

Pierce finished her questions after eliminating four women, all over the age of sixty-five.

Judge Tanner broke for lunch. The court reduced the panel to ninety-three potential jurors, excusing the rest for cause.

After lunch, the remaining potential jurors filled the jury box by lottery, fifteen jurors in the box, and the lawyers had to use their preemptory challenges to exclude jurors for perceived bias or any legitimate subjective reason. It was illegal to exclude potential jurors on the basis of race, sex, or age, but it was done all the time. The judge had given each side six preemptory challenges. Race wasn't an issue in this case since both the defendant and the victim were white. Age and the sex of the jurors were issues. As one side or the other threw off a juror, a replacement candidate took the seat.

By four thirty, a jury of seven men and eight women had been selected. The average age was forty-six. The men ranged in age from thirty to fifty-five; the women were more diverse. Two women were in their late twenties and two in their seventies. Pierce ran out of challenges, and the last two seated were the old ladies.

Juror 1, Frank Bean, age fifty-one, was a car salesman in a blue blazer. Juror 2, Sandra Horton, age twenty-nine, was a dental assistant. David Thomas, juror 3, had shoulder-length hair and worked at a car wash. Also there were a college professor, an accountant, an assistant manager of Kroger, a few housewives, two state employees, and others from all walks of life.

The three alternates from the fifteen-member panel would be selected by lottery at the end of the trial. That way all fifteen paid close attention, and no one knew who the actual twelve jurors were until right before deliberation.

Davis was satisfied with the composition of the jury. He particularly liked the two older women. He hoped that the jury would be outraged by Charlie Garcia's conduct and pity the loss of Robyn Eden.

The judge finished the day by reciting from memory the preliminary jury instructions. He warned the jury, "Don't engage any of the attorneys. They know not to talk to you and will appear rude by ignoring you."

Judge Tanner also admonished the jury not to discuss the evidence among them until after he had given the final jury instructions and directed them to deliberate. "The guilt or innocence of the defendant will be decided by you based on the evidence. The evidence is the testimony of the witnesses and the documents that are introduced. You are the judge of the credibility of the witnesses. If you disbelieve any part of a witness's testimony, you have the right to discount or disbelieve all of that witness's testimony."

Davis understood that even the slightest inconsistency in testimony could destroy a witness's credibility. He'd learned that skill from his mentor and co-counsel Morty.

"What the lawyers assert in the opening and closing statements is not evidence. You are the judge of the facts. I, as the judge, instruct you on the law. The prosecutors are here to present the state's case against Mr. Garcia. In order for you to find him guilty, the state must prove each element of the charges beyond a reasonable doubt."

Judge Tanner explained to the jury each element of second-degree murder and reckless homicide. The instructions lasted more than an hour but provided them with necessary information. The verdict of this case was based upon the evidence but had to be decided within the confines of the law.

Judge Tanner banged his gavel and bid the jury good night. He told them that the Hewes County court system owned an excellent library of DVDs because the jury for the next two weeks couldn't watch TV, listen to radio, or read a newspaper or magazine.

CHAPTER FIFTY-TWO

OPENING STATEMENTS AND THE FIRST DAY OF PROOF

Thursday, February 8, 2001

A my Pierce was prepared to give her opening statement. She'd practiced it in front of her associates and in front of the mirror several times. Soon she'd stand before the jury and without notes open for the defense.

The state went first and last because the state had the burden of proof. She figured that was to her advantage. She got to hear the state's arguments and then could dismantle them one at a time.

Steine gave the state's first opening statement. It was short and to the point. Mr. Garcia was guilty of second-degree murder because he supplied the drugs that killed Robyn Eden. He distributed or gave her the drugs that proximately caused her death. He was her doctor and her lover, who knew she was an addict. He spent the last days of her life exploiting her addictions for sex and drugs.

"You'll notice that the parties throughout this trial will refer to the defendant as Mr. Garcia, not Dr. Garcia. At one time the defendant held two medical licenses: one from the great state of Tennessee and one from the state of New York. He surrendered his Tennessee license, and New York suspended the other."

Steine pointed out several inconsistencies in Mr. Garcia's statements given to the paramedics, the treating physician, and the police the night of the victim's death as well as his behavior that night. Steine argued that under the law, a person could be dishonest through his acts but also through his omissions. The failure to disclose a material fact was a lie because it misled the EMTs and the emergency room doctor.

Steine was very dramatic and expressive as he walked slowly around the courtroom. He reminded Pierce of an old lion, proud and dignified.

He posed some questions to the jury: "The defendant was a medical doctor. Unlike you and me, he was used to dealing with medical emergencies. Because of his training and experience, the law imposes even greater obligations on him. He needs to explain to you why he failed to disclose what he knew to the professionals who were trying to save Robyn Eden's life.

"The defendant was with Ms. Eden for several days. The proof will show they didn't leave the apartment. How did he not know what drugs she was taking? The drugs were left right out in the open, right next to the defendant's shaving kit.

"There is a graphic videotape that is the best evidence of what happened at the apartment. It's important not only that you pay close attention to what you might see in the video, but also please pay close attention to what you hear. The strongest evidence is what the defendant in his own words says. His own words prove his guilt."

Steine had the jury's attention. It wasn't difficult to keep their focus as he paraded around the courtroom talking about drugs and sex videos. He went on to describe the lesser offense of reckless homicide. Pierce thought the state overreached with its charge of second-degree murder. A jury verdict of reckless homicide was far more likely.

He argued that if the jury, in its wisdom, failed to find second-degree murder, it was a no-brainer to convict the defendant for reckless homicide. He pointed out that Mr. Garcia failed to disclose to the paramedics at the apartment and then later to the hospital staff that Robyn Eden was an IV drug user. He argued, "Mr. Garcia lied by omission. He possessed critical information that would have helped with the care of Robyn Eden, yet he withheld that information. He was a doctor. He knew just how critical that information was. He acted recklessly, and it caused Ms. Eden's death."

Steine thanked them for their service and their sacrifice of sequester. The opening lasted less than thirty minutes.

Pierce was up next. She reminded the jury that the defendant was innocent until proven guilty beyond a reasonable doubt. "My client doesn't have to prove anything. The burden is all on the state, and it won't meet its obligation. You're going to find Charles Garcia not guilty."

Next she explained the state's burden of proof beyond a reasonable doubt. She compared that heavy burden to that of a civil case, which was by a preponderance of the evidence.

The jury listened intently. Greg Jones, juror 8, the life insurance agent, kept his arms crossed during Pierce's opening statement.

Pierce thought, *Did juror 8, Mr. Jones, have his arms crossed during Steine's opening?* She couldn't remember. Danny Appleton, juror 6, the waiter at Outback, smiled, a good sign. Andrew Bremen, juror 13, the golf superintendent at the local country club, had kind of a frown on his face. Pierce understood just how important the jury's body language was in her effort to read where the jury's heads might be.

"I promise you this will be an interesting case. It's about sex, drugs, and country music. As you all know, sex is not illegal. It can be a beautiful thing between two loving adults. It can also be raunchy and beyond the pale. How it's performed is up to the imagination of the two consenting adults. It can be very different from what you and your spouse or loved one may engage in. If it is, it's still legal.

"Drugs are another story. Robyn Eden was a drug addict of the worst kind. Her worst crime was what she did to herself and her unborn child."

Pierce stopped and watched the jury carefully. She wanted to assess their reaction to the pregnancy. There definitely were different degrees of surprise. Pierce concluded that the greater reaction came from the women. The trial changed. It now involved the death of an unborn child, and Pierce claimed that Robyn Eden was the murderer.

"She killed herself and her baby slowly through her drug use. July 4th was the culmination of years of abuse. She was the proximate cause of her own death. The baby from inception didn't have a chance. That was my client's child. I want you to ask yourself what kind of person uses IV drugs when she knows she's with child? The answer is someone without hope who cares nothing about herself or her unborn child. Robyn Eden's death was inevitable and unpreventable.

"I can't argue that my client was just a bystander like you and me. He played a part in their relationship. Mr. Garcia and Robyn Eden used each other. There may have been feelings of love and talk of marriage, but bottom line, as consenting adults they had an arrangement. She was a beautiful woman who thought surgery would make her more beautiful. The defendant provided her with those surgeries that she desperately wanted. They both wanted unorthodox sex. It's clear from the video that they got what they desired. You can't hold those unorthodox sex acts against my client. Robyn

Eden demanded them from my client. If he didn't accommodate her, she would have gotten her sex elsewhere. The proof will show she got her drugs elsewhere.

"The state is calling my client a murderer. It must prove that Mr. Garcia gave her the drugs that killed her. There will be no proof that he provided those drugs. The state has no proof on this critical point. Its plan is to prejudice you against Mr. Garcia because of his unusual sexual preferences. That's a diversion. Don't fall for it.

"You're probably going to hear the testimony of Senator Valerie Daniels, Robyn Eden's sister. She's a powerful woman in Washington, DC. Remember she'll be sitting in the witness box as a sister, not a senator. I'm sure she loved her sister, but she knew Ms. Eden was an IV drug user, an addict. In fact it's her fault that Charles Garcia is here on trial today. Senator Daniels begged him to fly down to Hewes City and try to convince Ms. Eden to enter rehab. He'd separated himself from Ms. Eden because she was an addict and self-destructive. His head told him that leaving her was the right thing to do and in his best interest. He should have listened to his head, but instead he listened to his heart and admittedly another part of his anatomy. He may overcome those urges, but during their conversation, the senator played her trump card, his unborn child. How could he refuse? But for the call from Senator Daniels, her plea for help and his desire to save Ms. Eden and their child, he wouldn't be here.

"We're here today because a powerful politician brought pressure on the state to charge Charles Garcia with murder. The senator is trying to pass her guilt to my client, and that's not right.

"Thank you for your attention. The state gets to put its proof on first. It's important that you withhold judgment until you hear all of the proof by both parties. I'm confident after you hear all the proof, you'll bring back a verdict of not guilty."

Steine stood and looked squarely at the jurors. "I'm a man of few words. The defendant murdered Robyn Eden, and his lawyer just had the nerve to assert that her sister killed her. I'm outraged. You will be too. The state will prove that Charles Garcia is not only a liar but also a murderer, and you will convict him for his crime. Thank you."

Davis thought, *Morty's second opening was short, but he delivered it with such power that it jarred the jury. They're ready to go.*

Judge Tanner called a recess. All of the lawyers decided they needed a comfort break.

Pierce and Sammie availed themselves of the third-floor ladies' room at the same time. Pierce didn't care for her. She was smart and beautiful, but she was her competition, and Pierce didn't like any competition.

Sammie called as the state's first witness the 911 dispatcher. She established her identity and then played the 911 call.

"Did Mr. Garcia provide the correct address?"

"No, there was about a four-minute delay while we found the correct building number."

"How do you know it was a four-minute delay?"

"I was monitoring the call. I know the time they arrived and the time they entered the right unit."

The younger Davis handed the dispatcher over to Pierce.

"How many 911 calls have you taken?"

"I've been on the job twelve years. I work forty to fifty hours a week, and I take an average of two calls an hour."

Pierce picked up a calculator from the defense table and started doing some math. "That's about at least eighty calls a week. Fifty weeks a year, that's four thousand a year for twelve years. That's forty-eight thousand calls, right?"

"That's a good guesstimate."

"In all those years and all those calls you've observed how people act under pressure and in an emergency situation. You'd consider yourself an expert in emergency situations. Right?"

"It's my job, and I'm good at it. Over the years I've saved lives."

"In your opinion, did Mr. Garcia seem upset and emotional?"

"Yes."

"In your opinion, was he trying to get Ms. Eden help?"

"Yes."

"Do you think he gave the wrong address because of the stress of the emergency?"

"Yes."

Sammie stood and redirected. "In those forty-eight thousand calls, how many were from doctors?"

"Less than fifty."

"How many of those doctors were as hysterical as Mr. Garcia?"

Pierce objected, "There's no testimony that Mr. Garcia was hysterical."

Sammie didn't wait for Judge Tanner. "In your opinion, was he hysterical?"

Pierce protested, "That calls for a medical conclusion."

The judge overruled.

"I think so."

Sammie continued, "How many of the forty-eight thousand callers gave the wrong address?"

"I've had only six or seven, maybe as high as ten wrong addresses."

The day ended on that note. The judge wished the jury a pleasant evening at the hotel and thanked them for their service. He warned them not to discuss the case among themselves or with anyone else for that matter.

CHAPTER FIFTY-THREE

AN HONORABLE DOCTOR
Friday, February 9, 2001

Judge Tanner started court an hour late because he had to deal with another matter that couldn't wait till lunch or the end of the day. At ten, the jury entered the jury box, ready to resume the trial.

Davis could see the anticipation on the jurors' faces; they wanted to hear the juicy stuff. The first witness was Willie Whatley, the younger of the two paramedics who responded to the 911 call at the Eden apartment. He seemed a little nervous to Davis as he took the oath from the judge's court officer. His right hand was shaking.

"Mr. Whatley, I'm Benjamin Davis. I represent the state of Tennessee. Have you ever testified before?"

"No, this is my first time."

"Are you nervous?"

"Very."

Davis told him not to be nervous. He was providing a very valuable service by telling the jury what happened on July 4th. That seemed to calm him down a little, but his voice still squeaked when he spoke.

The proof established that Whatley, by July 4th, 2000, had been on the job only three weeks. Using a diagram of the apartment,

Whatley showed the jury where Robyn Eden was found naked on the bedroom floor. He also indicated on the diagram where the camera and tripod were set up.

The diagram and the camera and tripod were introduced into evidence. The parties to expedite the trial had pre-numbered the exhibits and stipulated to their admissibility with a few exceptions. This was done so the trial would move smoothly and quickly. Neither side wanted the case to get bogged down in front of the jury. Before the trial began, the judge and the lawyers knew where the evidentiary fights were. The judge ruled on some before the commencement of the trial and preserved them for appeal, while Judge Tanner reserved ruling on others, so he could decide the dispute in context.

The EMT testified that Ms. Eden was completely naked. The naked pictures of Robyn Eden taken by Whatley were admitted and passed to the jury. Davis and Steine decided they needed to expose the jury to the themes of the case early in the trial. They'd be seeing a lot of strange sexual proof during this trial. The thinking was that they might as well let them know that from the start.

The pictures showed Robyn Eden lying next to the bed, her large breasts and clean-shaven pubic area for everyone to see. It was interesting to watch each juror's reaction to the photos. Gretchen Bieber, juror 11, who sang in her church choir, looked particularly uncomfortable. Some jurors passed the exhibits quickly while others, three men in the back row, lingered over them.

Davis knew that the jury would have some reaction to this evidence because he did when he first saw the photos. He was only human. He'd been both aroused and saddened by them. These photos motivated Davis to take on the special prosecution. Robyn looked so vulnerable. From the photos, he couldn't see her dark side, her addiction. Admittedly the senator pressured him into the case, but after he examined the evidence, he was glad she forced him into the prosecution. He was convinced that Charlie Garcia was responsible for the death of Robyn Eden. Now all he had to do was prove it.

EMT Whatley described for the jury the treatment he provided Ms. Eden and the information provided by Dr. Garcia. Davis had to keep correcting him with Mr. Garcia.

"Did you ask Mr. Garcia if she'd taken any drugs?"

"My partner did. I was working on Ms. Eden, and he was questioning Dr. Garcia. I mean Mr. Garcia."

"Did you hear their conversation?"

"Yes, I was only a few steps away. I could tell she was on something, but all Mr. Garcia would acknowledge was that she'd drunk a significant amount of vodka, and she'd smoked some joints. He also stated she was an addict, but he didn't know what she'd taken."

"Did that make sense to you as a paramedic?"

"No, she was definitely on something other than pot or alcohol."

"Did you go in any other room after entering the bedroom?"

"I walked through the living room to the bedroom when we arrived and back out the same way to leave."

"You didn't go into the master bathroom?"

"No, my partner asked Mr. Garcia if he could, and Mr. Garcia told him to take care of his patient and get her to the hospital."

"So he refused access to the bathroom?"

"I guess you could say that."

Whatley described in detail what happened in the apartment and then how they met two Hewes City police officers at the elevator.

Davis sat down, and Pierce jumped up.

Whatley admitted that he was a rookie and that he was busy tending to the patient and not listening carefully to his partner's conversation with Mr. Garcia. He also admitted that Mr. Garcia was most concerned about getting Ms. Eden to the hospital, not wasting time searching the apartment. He agreed that by the time they were at the elevator, Mr. Garcia was anxious to get Ms. Eden to the hospital.

Under the law, Pierce was allowed to ask leading questions, and she did that very effectively. She made some good points with the younger EMT, who was afraid to disagree. It was a tactic any good lawyer used with a malleable and scared witness. The key was not to go too far to the point that the jury understood what was happening. Pierce stopped just when she should have.

The next witness called by the state was EMT Louis Mackey. Under Sammie's questioning, she established that he was a twenty-four-year veteran of the Hewes City Fire Department and that he responded to the July 4th 911 call of Charles Garcia. Using the diagram, he located the patient and the camera. He was not shown the photo. The Davis team agreed to save it for later so as not to anesthetize the jury to its impact.

Mackey was asked to describe the condition of the apartment.

"It was a mess. Not to speak ill of the dead, Ms. Eden was no housekeeper. Styrofoam food containers were everywhere. I saw at least two empty vodka bottles, several empty soda bottles, and other garbage all around the bedroom. There was a video camera on a tripod and sex toys and pill bottles on each of the nightstands."

He was shown pictures of five different sex toys and confirmed that they were on the nightstand next to the bed. When those pictures were passed to the jury, several male jurors looked at Sammie with either embarrassment or lust in their eyes. This jury was paying close attention.

No risk of anyone falling asleep, thought Davis. That wasn't unheard of; it kinda depended on how boring the nature of the subject matter of the case.

Mackey described Ms. Eden's condition and the treatment EMT Whatley provided. When asked about his conversation with Mr. Garcia, he replied, "He told me they were having sex, and she went into cardiac arrest. He claimed to have performed CPR. He explained they'd just finished a sex marathon. I asked about what drugs she'd taken. He was vague. He reported that she drank at least two liters of vodka and smoked several joints. I pressed him and he confirmed she was a drug addict, but he didn't know what her current drug of choice was. He walked over to the nightstand and handed me with a tissue three of the four bottles."

"What were the drugs he gave you?"

"Xanax, Prozac, and hydrocodone."

"What was his response?"

"He indicated that she did take Xanax and Prozac for her anxiety. That she took hydrocodone for headaches."

"What was the fourth bottle?"

"He told me that the Viagra was his and he'd taken several doses over the course of the weekend."

Viagra was only recently available on the market, and the manufacturer had conducted an extensive advertising campaign. Davis wondered how many jurors pictured Charles Garcia with a four-hour erection.

Sammie next questioned Mackey about his request to search the bathroom for medications and why that might be important. He explained that since Mr. Garcia was uncertain about what she'd taken, he put the three bottles in a plastic bag and got back to the patient.

"He refused to allow me into the bathroom. He told me to tend to my patient and get her to the hospital. I was surprised by his refusal, but I wasn't going to argue with him. He was her fiancé and her doctor."

"Who told you that Mr. Garcia was Ms. Eden's fiancé?"

"Mr. Garcia told me. I now know that wasn't true."

Sammie let that lie just sit there. "If you knew what Ms. Eden had taken, how would that have affected your treatment of her at the scene?"

Pierce objected as leading, and it was sustained.

Mackey testified that knowing what she overdosed from was critical because depending on what it was, there might be a counteragent.

Mackey confirmed that Mr. Garcia also refused the Hewes City police access to the apartment when they got to the elevator.

"What happened when you got to the hospital?"

"We transferred the patient to the emergency room staff at the door. I spoke briefly with Dr. Mann and provided him with the evidence bag containing three bottles that were on the nightstand. I did tell him that the patient's doctor accompanied us in the ambulance and that he might want to ask him what she'd taken."

"Why did you tell him that?"

"I guess I wasn't satisfied with Mr. Garcia's explanation of what happened and his vague answer concerning what she'd taken. I thought maybe doctor-to-doctor, Mann might get more information than I did."

Pierce on cross went back to the fact that Mr. Garcia saved the patient's life by doing CPR. Mackey was asked about the three pill bottles, and the witness confirmed he'd placed them in a plastic bag and given them to Dr. Mann.

"That was the last time I saw them."

"You are aware that those pill bottles have been conveniently lost by the Hewes City police?"

Mackey didn't respond, and Pierce ended on that question. Davis thought Pierce was skittish with Mackey, unlike with Whatley. When Pierce ended, they broke for lunch.

Before court, Tanner met with the lawyers in his chambers. He wanted to know whom the state planned to call in the afternoon.

Davis informed him they would be Hewes City Police Officer Donald Dawson, who'd be a ten-minute witness, and then Dr. Mann, the emergency room physician.

Davis was true to his word. Officer Dawson took a total of ten minutes. He testified he and another officer met the gurney at the elevator, and he requested access to the apartment, which Mr. Garcia refused.

Asked what he did next, he testified, "I called the station and spoke with Detective Haber, who instructed me that the apartment was a potential crime scene. I was to deny anyone access, return to my patrol car in the apartment complex parking lot, and await further orders."

On cross Pierce asked, "So Detective Haber, at the time of your call-in, thought a crime had been committed?"

"She told me to treat the apartment as a potential crime scene."

"And she thought that Mr. Garcia was a suspect."

Before Davis could object, Officer Dawson answered, "You'll have to ask her."

Pierce sat down.

Dr. Randolph Mann took the stand. He was a tall black man with a deep, smooth, polished voice. Under Steine's questioning, it was established that he was born and grew up in North Carolina, attended the University of North Carolina, and went to Meharry Medical School in Nashville. He was board certified in emergency medicine.

He described Ms. Eden's condition upon arrival in the emergency room. "I could go into a long medical explanation, but she was barely alive. She already had a line in, and I administered epinephrine.

"I'd spoken to EMT Mackey, who'd told me that her doctor was transported with the patient. I stepped out of the treatment room and met Dr. Garcia."

"That's Mr. Garcia, not doctor."

"What do you mean? He represented himself as a doctor."

Steine stopped and looked at the judge for guidance. When he got none, he offered, "Well, he was a doctor at that time, but he no longer holds a medical license. Tell us about your conversation with Mr. Garcia."

"He asked me about her condition. I provided him with her vitals and told him I'd given her epinephrine. I asked him what drugs she'd taken. He told me that over the long weekend she drank at least two liters of vodka and smoked several joints. I asked him what other drugs she'd taken. He admitted that she was a drug addict and that she'd abused a number of drugs, but he wasn't certain what she'd taken over the weekend. He claimed that she'd disappeared into the bathroom several times and must have used there.

"I asked him about the pill bottles provided to me by EMT Mackey, and he begrudgingly admitted that she'd probably taken the Xanax, Prozac, and hydrocodone over the weekend and that he'd taken the Viagra. He volunteered that they'd engaged in a sex marathon, which at the time I thought was a very odd thing to say. It wasn't in the context of our conversation. I took his remarks as almost bragging."

Steine paused, letting Mann's testimony and observation linger.

"Why do you say it was odd?"

"I was fighting to save Ms. Eden's life. Trying to get critical information about her drug use to determine what protocol to follow to save her life, and this clown is talking about a sex marathon!"

Mann actually got mad. Steine paused for effect.

Pierce objected to the use of "clown." Davis smiled to himself.

He was sure that several of the jurors agreed with the description. Steine knew exactly what he was doing. He was the master.

"What happened next?"

"I went back into the treatment room to try to save the patient. At that time I made two important discoveries. The first was that the patient was pregnant. The fetus never had a chance. It expired before the patient reached the hospital. It was a blessing. There was no way the fetus would have survived to birth because of the drug use."

Davis and Morty decided that in light of the fact that the state lost its motion to exclude pregnancy, they'd better bring it out at the earliest possible opportunity.

"What was the second important discovery?"

"The patient had a linear set of puncture wounds in the femoral or groin area."

"What's the importance of that discovery?"

"Before I'd spoken to Mr. Garcia, I'd checked the patient's arms for track marks and found none. That is the most common place for IV drug use. Those small puncture marks at her groin were evidence of IV drug use through the femoral artery, which is a highly unusual site. I'd actually never seen it used by a drug addict before. In fact it's a very dangerous site to inject."

"Why is that?"

"A punctured or torn femoral artery can be fatal. It's an area that is not as accessible or visible. Someone had to have injected her. I'd say it was someone with medical training."

"Is that speculation or with a reasonable degree of medical certainty?"

"I'm not speculating. The linear nature of the injection sites indicates that whoever helped her was very precise, almost surgical."

"Like a trained surgeon?"

Pierce objected, and Judge Tanner turned to Dr. Mann.

"Dr. Mann, I'm going to let you answer the question, but don't speculate. Any opinion you testify to must be with a reasonable degree of medical certainty."

"Your Honor, I can state with a reasonable degree of medical certainty that whoever injected Ms. Eden had medical training. I can't testify that the person was a surgeon."

Davis thought that was a good place to stop. So did Steine because that's just what he did.

Pierce moved slowly. She didn't like that last answer. It satisfied by circumstantial evidence a critical element of the state's case.

"You didn't mention the injection sites near the femoral artery to Mr. Garcia, did you?"

"I discovered them after our conversation."

"But it was you who notified Mr. Garcia that Ms. Eden had died?"

"Yes."

"So after you'd seen the sites, you still didn't mention them?"

"What would have been the point? She was dead. I needed that information when she was alive."

"How many IV drug users have you treated?"

"Not many. Most of the addicts I've dealt with were pill abusers. IV drug use isn't that common in Hewes County, thank goodness."

"Do you understand how IV drug users inject oxycodone?"

"Yes. They crush the pills into a powder, then mix it with a liquid, usually water, and inject the mixture by syringe."

"Do you understand why they elect to inject the drug rather than ingest it?"

Davis thought that Pierce was being a little condescending with the doctor.

"Drugs administered intravenously render the user a high more quickly and more intensely. If you ingest the pill, it must first go through digestion before the brunt of its effect can be achieved."

"Do you know what's in oxycodone?"

"The active ingredient is the same as hydrocodone, and there are some fillers. But I don't know what they specifically are."

"So there are things you don't know about the drugs and addiction?"

Steine objected, and the judge sustained on the grounds that the question was argumentative.

"So you're not an expert in addiction, are you?"

"No, but I'm a medical doctor, and I'm board certified in emergency medicine. Addiction is part of the study of medicine."

"There's not a course in addiction?"

"There are courses that touch upon it."

"But there are experts in addiction. You're just not one of them."
"Yes."

Pierce defiantly asked, "Have you ever heard of Dr. Lawrence Porter?"

"He's a professor at Vanderbilt who is an addiction expert," Mann responded.

Davis objected, but he knew the damage had been done. Mann's testimony bolstered Pierce's own expert's testimony. Davis admitted, *Smart move, bitch.*

Steine looked at Davis, without using words, asking him if he should keep going. Davis thought about whether he wanted to end the day's proof on that note. Unless Steine or he could think of a great comeback, they needed to quit while the quitting was good.

Steine stood, whispered to Davis, "Here goes," and slowly walked past the jury. As he did, he gazed at each juror, trying to gauge where they were in formulating their verdict.

He smiled at Dr. Mann and asked, "Did you work last night?"

"Yes, sir, twenty-four hours."

"When did you go to bed?"

"I got home at 8:00 a.m. and spent two hours with my family unwinding. I slept three hours and then came here."

"Save any lives yesterday?"

"I brought two people back. An eighty-year-old man and an eleven-year-old boy."

Pierce objected as to relevance and outside the cross. Tanner sustained the objection.

Davis smiled. The old man was about to make a great point. The two men thought alike. Steine was a very good teacher.

"You don't deal with addiction every day?"

"No."

"But you do work daily with persons who were in an emergency situation, like Robyn Eden on July 4th?"

Mann looked straight at the jury and in a strong and convincing voice guaranteed, "That's exactly what I do every day. I'm board certified in emergency medicine. Those are the types of people I treat and save every day."

That's the note I wanted to end on, thought Davis.

CHAPTER FIFTY-FOUR

A TOUGH COP
BUT A BAD WITNESS

Monday, February 12, 2001

Amy Pierce got up early. She needed to spend some time with her son, Carter, an eighth grader at Montgomery Bell Academy. He was an honor student, and Pierce was driven to provide him with the best. In her mind, that did not include his father, Dan Smith. He'd struggled with addiction for about fifteen years. He'd sold drugs and been arrested. He'd been calling because he wanted to reestablish a relationship with Carter. He was a thorn in Pierce's side who was interfering with her desire to protect Carter and her deep need to be in control of her life. Dan Smith was simply not part of her plan. He was more than a bump in the road; he was an obstruction.

Despite her commitment to the Garcia case, her office was functioning fine, and her two associates were serving clients and managing the office. They'd helped her get prepared for the Garcia trial, but now it was her show. She wanted the glory. This morning she could afford to spend time with Carter. Court wasn't scheduled till ten. Tanner was delaying court for another matter.

As they ate breakfast together, Pierce asked, "How's school, darling?"

"It's fine. I aced my math test, and we won our debate."

"Sorry I missed that. I couldn't help it; I was in court."

Carter just shrugged his shoulders, which made Pierce feel guilty. She'd realized spending her time away from home was the price of a successful practice.

Court opened with an insincere apology from Judge Tanner. Pierce knew the judge looked at his courtroom as his kingdom, and there was no question who was king.

Davis called Chief Detective Haber to the stand. Both sides knew she was going to be a dangerous witness.

Pierce composed herself and got in the zone as the oath was given. She needed to listen carefully so she could twist Haber's testimony on cross in the afternoon. She'd take detailed notes during Davis's examination and prepare her cross at lunch.

She was tired of this case and Charlie Garcia. Harrelson was no longer any help. He relegated himself to the audience, whispering into the father's left ear.

Davis spent a good twenty minutes having Haber recount her background. She'd been to the Body Farm adjacent to the University of Tennessee campus in Knoxville twice for seminars organized by the TBI, the Tennessee Bureau of Investigation. The Body Farm was a world-renowned homicide and pathology facility that trained law enforcement officers. It was an honor to attend and was a reflection of the officer's abilities. She'd been on the force sixteen years and rose through the ranks to chief detective. Her job was to assign a detective to appropriate cases.

Under Davis's questioning, she explained that she first heard about the Eden case when the 911 calls came in. Looking at her report, she testified that at ten twenty-six Officer Dawson called in and confirmed the transport of a white female to the county hospital. He also informed her it was probably a drug overdose.

"Following protocol, I told him to seal the apartment from the public and to wait in the apartment parking lot for further orders. I assigned myself the investigation and drove to the hospital."

"Is it unusual for you to take the lead in an investigation?"

"No, I do that from time to time. I like to get in the field so I don't get rusty."

Pierce watched the jury as they watched Haber. She spoke with both authority and brashness. Pierce was biding her time. She'd get a bite out of Haber after lunch.

Haber described what happened when she arrived in the hospital. She first met with Dr. Mann, who confirmed the overdose, provided the three pill bottles, and told her that the patient's doctor was in the waiting room and was with her when she collapsed. Haber took a picture of the bottles and put them in an evidence bag to be sent to the TBI lab.

Pierce knew what Davis was doing. He was about to expose the weakest part of his case. That was the right thing for a good lawyer to do, bring up your case's worst problems first and diminish the hurt.

"Where are those bottles now?"

"Gone. We discovered they were gone during a periodic audit of the evidence locker."

"You lost them?"

"Not me personally. They were signed in, but they're not in the locker any longer."

"You never checked the bottles for fingerprints?"

"We couldn't. They were gone."

Pierce thought Davis's effort was a good one. He'd minimized the sting.

"Dr. Mann was pretty busy, so I first sat and watched Mr. Garcia. After observing him, I went up and spoke to him. He was sitting in the waiting room with his face in his hands. I walked up and introduced myself."

"We've all seen it on television. Before you spoke to Mr. Garcia, did you read him his Miranda rights, a right to an attorney, etc.?"

"That wasn't necessary. He wasn't a suspect at that time. I treated him as if he'd just lost a loved one."

Davis, despite the fact that Judge Tanner denied the defendant's motion on this issue, knew that Pierce would bring it up on cross, and it was much better if the state brought it out first.

She testified that she learned in that conversation that he was more than her doctor. He was also her fiancé. She discussed the specifics of what Mr. Garcia told her about the long weekend. He described it as a sex marathon. He mentioned that Robyn had been sick the whole time, suffering from nausea and headaches.

"Despite those problems, he told me that she kept having sex."

Haber testified that he admitted taking several doses of Viagra to keep up with her. He admitted she disappeared into the bathroom and was high on something but wasn't sure what. He'd seen her consume two liters of vodka and smoked several joints.

"When I pressed him on what she might be on, he turned doctor on me. He gave a very technical answer about her being an addict and not having any specific drug of choice. He said he didn't want to guess."

Haber explained that while they were talking, Dr. Mann walked up and informed them that Robyn Eden was dead. After a few minutes Mr. Garcia asked to be excused to call the Eden family. Haber testified that Mr. Garcia was visibly shaken and walked away without a good-bye.

"You mentioned that Mr. Garcia told you he was Ms. Eden's fiancé."

"I later determined that he wasn't."

There was that unnecessary lie again. Charlie Garcia was his own worst enemy. Pierce knew it, Harrelson knew it, Señor Garcia knew it, and even Charlie knew it.

Pierce looked into the faces of the jurors, trying to read into their minds. What was their disposition at this moment? Did they like Haber? More important, what did they think about Charlie Garcia? She didn't care if they didn't like him or thought that he was a disgusting pig. The critical question was, did they think he was a murderer?

Most of them had good poker faces. If she had to guess, jurors 3, 7, 8, 12, 13, and 15 were leaning against her. Jurors 1 and 2 had smiled at her several times. They at least liked her. The rest looked undecided. Pierce reminded herself that all she needed was one juror, and it was a hung jury. Tennessee law required a unanimous guilty verdict, and proving guilt beyond a reasonable doubt was a tough burden.

Haber testified about the three search warrants and that the court found they were invalid because of inaccuracies in her affidavit. She swore she wrote down exactly what the Jefferson County Clerk told her.

Davis asked to approach the bench. He asked Judge Tanner if he could read the court's order concerning the motion to suppress. Instead the judge announced he'd explain his ruling to the jury from the bench.

"The state on July 5th, 6th, and 8th searched Ms. Eden's apartment. I've held that those searches were invalid because the affidavit of Detective Haber was not technically accurate. She mischaracterized Mr. Garcia's criminal record. I also held that, under Tennessee criminal law, what was in plain view in an apartment where there was a suspicious death was admissible in this case. I'm marking and entering into evidence as the next exhibit my writ-ten order so that you can read my order when you deliberate and understand what transpired. The important thing is that you as the jury get to weigh the value of this evidence, which is only a piece of the puzzle we're asking you to consider."

Pierce again thought Davis did a good job minimizing a bad problem. He next admitted the evidence list created by the Hewes City Police Department, and Haber testified how the document was generated. There were three hundred sixty-two items.

"There were one videotape in the camera and thirty-two videos in plain view on a shelf; two hundred seventy-two still photos from two cell phones that were in plain view; and five sex toys."

Using the evidence list, Davis spent the next hour and a half parading items from the evidence list before the jury. He would from time to time ask the court's clerk to pass an exhibit to the jury. Pierce watched the jurors' faces as they handled naked photo-graphs of Robyn Eden. Several depicted her inserting a sexual de-vice in all available orifices. The men looked at the sex toys in plas-tic evidence bags, and a few of the women seemed to brighten up.

Pierce figured the photos hurt Eden as much as Garcia or more. Davis didn't mention that three of the photos were of Eden and another man. She wondered whether that was intentional or an oversight.

Davis turned his attention to the video. He was brief. Judge Tanner ruled that the video could not be characterized. It was to be played, and the judge wanted the jurors to draw their own conclusions.

Tanner ruled the video was just another piece of the puzzle in the jury's ultimate decision, murder or not. The courtroom was darkened, and the video started. Every eye in the courtroom was glued to the monitor.

It was raw and graphic. It wasn't what the jury considered lovemaking. It was much better than amateur quality. They used good equipment and from practice knew how to stay in frame. The audio was excellent. No one looked away; no one took a breath. The sessions lasted a total of two hours. A Friday night episode and a Saturday episode together lasted forty-one minutes. Each time Charlie turned off the camera within a minute or two of completing sex.

The last session, when Robyn overdosed, started with her entering the frame and bleeding from her crotch, and Charlie commenting that she was bleeding like a stuck pig and then yelling at her to put pressure on it. Then there were ten minutes of sex, and Robyn's cardiac arrest was captured on audio with Charlie and Robyn just off camera. The jurors heard the 911 call and then Charlie talking to Robyn as he gave CPR. Charlie did give the wrong address. They could hear the arrival of the paramedics. They could hear some but not all of the conversation between Charlie and paramedic Mackey. When Charlie got the three pill bottles, he came into frame, and off camera he described what they were. The jurors could hear his description of the drugs and why Robyn took them.

The jury heard him talk about the Viagra and boast about the sex marathon. It was very damaging evidence, yet the jurors also heard the stress in Charlie's voice. Eventually after Robyn was taken from the apartment, the camera ran out of tape.

The most damaging evidence was when the tape showed Robyn returning from the bathroom. In his own words, Charlie proved that he knew that Robyn Eden was injecting something IV into her femoral artery.

It was the biggest problem with Haber's testimony, and Pierce still hadn't figured out how to counter this proof.

Davis continued with the witness through lunch and into the early afternoon. Haber did well; she recovered from her slow start.

Davis then brought up the final weakness of Haber's testimony, the erased last four photos on Robyn Eden's cell phone. Pierce knew Davis must have had more questions for this witness because he wouldn't end on this proof.

"I don't know what the erased pictures were. I was trying to e-mail them to my phone, and they accidentally got erased," Haber said.

Davis ended with proof that Mr. Garcia's shaving kit was found in the master bathroom where needles and crushed pills were in plain view. Another very damaging puzzle piece. He couldn't bring up the white powder and syringe in the nightstand because they weren't in plain view and therefore weren't admissible under Judge Tanner's ruling.

Pierce needed to attack Haber's credibility, so she stated accusingly, "You gave a false affidavit upon which this court issued an invalid search warrant."

Davis objected, and Tanner agreed. He reminded the jury the affidavit was inaccurate.

"You lost the pill bottles, didn't you?"

"They're gone. I didn't lose them. I turned them over to the evidence locker, and then they went missing."

"If you hadn't lost them, we'd know that Mr. Garcia's fingerprints weren't on them." That was a big jump, but Pierce was willing to take it.

Haber didn't know what to say.

Davis objected, and the court instructed Pierce to move on.

"You erased the last four cell phone pictures of Robyn Eden."

"It was an accident. I was trying to e-mail them to myself."

Pierce asked the court to instruct the jury about lost evidence. He explained that since the evidence was in the state's control, it is to be presumed that the lost evidence was relevant to the defendant's innocence and supported that innocence.

Haber confirmed that Ms. Eden's computer was on the evidence list. Pierce handed to Haber the history of the sites visited by Ms. Eden. There were 304 sites, and more than 25 were about oxycodone. Another 65 related to securing pharmaceuticals online, on such sites as drug dealer.com and homedelivery.com. Then there was the pornographic stuff. Pierce introduced some of the drug-related sites and pornographic ones as separate exhibits individually and then made the hard drive an exhibit.

"Ms. Eden made these site visits independent of Mr. Garcia?"

"Yes."

"She was the drug addict, not him."

"Yes."

"She visited these pornographic sites without Mr. Garcia?"

"How would I know that?"

"Didn't Mr. Garcia live in New York, and weren't these downloads done over a period of several months?"

"Yes."

"So she was engaged in perverted sex without Mr. Garcia?"

"Yes."

She answered too fast before Davis could object, but in fairness it was pretty perverted.

"It was Robyn Eden's idea to make these videotapes and to take these photographs?"

"I don't know. You'll have to ask Mr. Garcia."

"Well, before she met Mr. Garcia, she'd made lewd and pornographic photos with other men."

"Yes."

Pierce introduced the two photos of Robyn Eden and Ron Harris, which Davis tried to exclude. They left nothing to the imagination involving oral sex and intercourse.

Davis watched the jury carefully. The two older women made faces of disgust. Those jurors felt no sympathy for Robyn Eden.

"Did Mr. Garcia tell you why he'd come to Tennessee?"

"He said he'd had a sex marathon. I figured he came in for that."

"We now know he was invited to Hewes City by her sister to convince Ms. Eden to go to rehab."

"Right."

"He came down to help, and now he's charged with her murder."

"Yes."

It was four fifty-three, a good time to end the day and the witness.

CHAPTER FIFTY-FIVE
A FOOLED PHYSICIAN
Tuesday, February 13, 2001

The TBI lab administrator was the first witness of the morning under Steine's examination. He testified as to the chain of evidence and that all of the samples tested based on photographs of the bedroom and master bathroom were in plain view. He introduced the forensic chemistry report into evidence. Steine had the TBI agent summarize the report and dumb it down for the jury. There were three syringes: two used and one still in its wrapper. The two used syringes had residue of oxycodone and acetaminophen. He explained that both drugs were painkillers. There was a too lengthy discussion of the difference between a Schedule II drug compared to a Schedule III drug. The lower the schedule, the more serious the drug. Heroin was a Schedule I. What Eden took was a Schedule II. *Not the most exciting witness,* Davis thought, *but the proof went in and later witnesses can rely on that evidence.*

The next witness was a young woman technician from the TBI lab. Sammie questioned her. The testimony was concise. The sex toys in plain view were tested for DNA evidence, and the only DNA found was that of Robyn Eden. Neither Mr. Garcia's nor anyone else's DNA was found. The sex toys were deposited in the evidence locker.

They were removed once, and the chain of evidence was preserved. The witness handed the items directly to an independent DNA testing facility at the instruction of a court order. After the tests, the items were handed directly back to the Sheriff's deputy and deposited in the evidence room. Pierce had no questions for the witness.

Davis next called Dr. Thomas Barnard, Ms. Eden's internist. Davis moved into evidence Barnard's office record of Ms. Eden. The doctor had seen her twice and prescribed Xanax, Lexapro, Ambien, Norco, and hydrocodone twice.

"Why did you prescribe each of those medications?"

"Xanax and Lexapro are for depression. Ambien is for sleep. Norco and hydrocodone are for headaches."

Davis reviewed with Barnard his two physical examinations of Robyn Eden. He knew she was a former IV drug user. He checked her arms but not her groin area. It would not have been pertinent to his exam. Davis asked if that was a common site to inject recreational drugs.

"The arms and the legs are where most users go. I wouldn't check the groin unless I was doing a gynecological examination."

"Is it an easy site to get to?"

"You can't see, and the femoral artery is real fragile. It would be very difficult to inject oneself. If the femoral artery were to tear or be punctured, that could be fatal. It really takes a skilled user or a second person who is trained to give injections."

Davis wanted to keep this witness short and limit the subject matters addressed. He established that Dr. Barnard would not have renewed the prescription of hydrocodone if he'd known Robyn was a drug seeker.

He discussed her symptoms, especially her headaches. He was convinced they were real. Davis had no choice. He had to put the doctor on the stand, and he expected Pierce to make points on cross.

Pierce started slowly and established that as her doctor, he wanted what was best for his patient.

She then asked, "A patient has responsibility in her own care and treatment, right?"

"Absolutely."

"As a doctor, you rely on what a patient tells you to help diagnose and treat her?"

"Absolutely."

"You knew from her history that she was a former IV drug user, right?"

"Yes."

"She was an addict?"

"Yes."

"Addicts are liars?"

"Yes."

"They engage in deceptive behavior?"

"Yes."

"Robyn Eden lied to you and deceived you?"

"Yes."

"It was her deceptive and self-destructive behavior that caused her death?"

Davis objected, asserting that such an opinion usurped the duty of the jury. Tanner held that the jury could hear his opinion and place whatever weight it deemed appropriate.

Dr. Barnard opined that Robyn Eden's conduct contributed to her death. Davis could tell Pierce was proud of that one. It would play well in her closing argument.

Davis thought Pierce's timing was excellent since at that moment Tanner announced it was time for lunch and they'd resume court at two o'clock sharp.

The state called as its next witness Dr. John Davenport, the county medical examiner. Davenport served in his position twenty years. He knew his stuff, but he couldn't communicate with the average person. Unfortunately juries are made up of average persons. Davis and Morty learned about this problem from talking to the man during the months before the trial. He just didn't know how to communicate. The jurors needed to understand the cause of death to find a guilty verdict. They had to tie Charlie Garcia's conduct to her death. If they didn't, he'd be acquitted on the murder charge. Davenport's explanation of his autopsy report and what happened to Robyn Eden got bogged down in medical jargon.

Davis and Morty decided that Davis would conduct the direct and, as the questioner, make contact with the jury.

Davenport took his seat after taking the oath. He looked and was pretty pompous in the thick golden oak witness box. The American and Tennessee flags were draped from poles on either side of the witness box.

Davis stood, opened the courtroom closet, and removed a six-foot skeleton complete with multicolored rubber organs. The heart was red, the lungs were blue, and the kidneys were yellow. He placed the prop between Davenport and the jurors but didn't block their view of each other. Davis was armed with a laser pointer. There'd been an argument about whether to use the laser or a wooden pointer, and Davis won out. Sometimes Morty was too old school.

By alternating leading questions, Davis got Dr. Davenport's background presented. Watching the jurors, Davis concluded that they accepted his expertise, so they'd rely on his testimony in reaching their verdict.

"Doctor, would you introduce our friend here to the jury and explain why he's here today?"

"This is my friend Irving, and I've asked him here to help me explain what happened to and caused the death of Robyn Eden on July 4th of last year."

Davis and Dr. Davenport reviewed with the jurors the different organs and their functions. They spent ten minutes reviewing the heart and lungs and how the heart pumps the oxygenated blood to the rest of the body. It was like a good version of freshman biology. In order to accurately point the laser Davis was standing right next to the jury. Davis believed that his close proximity to the jury created a bond between them. He smiled at them, and they smiled right back.

He reviewed with the witness the diagram of Ms. Eden's body, which noted all the surgical scars from the operations performed by Mr. Garcia or other doctors at his request. That bite of information didn't seem important, but it would be used in closing argument. Morty and Davis always thought ahead. In order to argue a point in closing, there had to be a factual basis introduced into evidence through either testimony or a document.

They introduced the autopsy report and reviewed portions of the document. Davis briefly discussed the dead child. Davenport kept referring to it as a fetus. Davis preferred child. He decided he'd better move on with this bad witness. He asked Davenport about the cause of death.

"Acute combined multiple drug overdoses."

"Explain to the jury what that is, please."

Davis looked at the old man, and in response with his eyes, Morty said, *That's too open-ended a question for this egghead. Go back to using Irving.*

Davis caught himself and decided to break down the question. "Let me ask that a different way. What were the multiple drugs that killed Ms. Eden?"

"Oxycodone, hydrocodone, and Alprazolam."

Keep his answers short and sweet, Davis thought.

"What are those drugs, and how are they different?"

"Before I explain how they're different, let me tell the jury how they are all the same. Oxycodone and hydrocodone are opiates, narcotics. They're painkillers. Oxycodone is the more serious of the drugs and is designated in Schedule II while the hydrocodone is Schedule III. They're all highly addictive when taken orally. However when crushed and mixed with a liquid, such as water, their potency increases exponentially. Xanax is a benzodiazepine. It's for anxiety, like Valium. It's designated as a Schedule III."

Using the autopsy report, Davenport discussed the levels of each drug in Ms. Eden. They were incredibly high, indicating chronic use. He also testified that Robyn Eden on July 4th required a greater amount of these drugs to become high because of her built-up tolerance.

"Each time she had to do a little more to achieve her desired high."

"Which drug actually killed her?"

"Based upon the toxicology on July 5th, I am of the professional opinion with a reasonable degree of medical certainty that the oxycodone killed her. It was the cause of her death. She was injected with the oxycodone mixture in her femoral region, and it caused respiratory depression and her death."

Davis was glad to hear that important answer. He had drilled into Davenport that he had to testify that it was the oxycodone because it was a Schedule II, not a Schedule III drug. Davenport also had to hold his opinion as to cause of death with a reasonable degree of medical certainty. Those were two key elements to the state proving murder.

The state wanted the jury to find that Robyn Eden died from

oxycodone, not the other drugs. Robyn had three prescriptions for the hydrocodone and another three for the Xanax. Those six prescriptions were dispensed by different pharmacies and prescribed by Dr. Barnard and another doctor. Garcia didn't prescribe either hydrocodone or Xanax! The state needed to prove beyond a reasonable doubt that she died from the oxycodone and that Mr. Garcia dispensed it.

Dr. Davenport, again relying on his autopsy report, discussed the size of Ms. Eden's lungs and the fact that at the time of the autopsy, he discovered pulmonary edemas. When he lost the jury in his explanation, Davis pulled him back on track.

Using Irving as a guide, he explained why Ms. Eden's excessive drug use resulted in hypertension, which also contributed to her death. Davis and Morty knew Pierce would bring that out on cross, so they decided to steal her thunder. They debated whether to bring up the filler and decided they'd better or Pierce could cause greater damage.

Davis said, "Ms. Eden also abused pills, which contained both hydrocodone and Xanax. The police found three pill bottles at her apartment."

Pierce objected as leading, and Tanner sustained the objection.

Pierce was going to make Davis work to damage her cross of this witness.

Dr. Davenport with difficulty explained why the hydrocodone and Xanax weren't the causes of death. He touched on the fact that the pills contained filler but denied that an accumulation of the filler in small vessels was the cause of death.

Through that testimony, Davis attacked Pierce's best argument as to what caused Robyn Eden's death. Davis knew that Pierce would be fierce on cross. He sat down.

Pierce got up, put her arm around Irving, and made a sexy gesture as she told him she was single. The jury loved it. Davis had to admit it was a brilliant move. It made her vulnerable and funny at the same time. He had to admit despite his ill feelings toward her, she was a beautiful woman, and the jury knew that. She was also smart as hell, and he hated to admit that.

"Ms. Eden was a drug addict?"

"Yes."

"Drug addicts are liars. They lie to doctors to get prescriptions, don't they?"

Without answering her question, Davenport answered it.

"Ms. Eden had prescriptions for hydrocodone and Xanax from Dr. Barnard, her treating physician, and Dr. Connor within two days of each other."

Pierce showed Davenport a picture of Robyn Eden's medicine cabinet, which had three shelves with dozens of prescriptions. She handed Davenport a typed list of medications in the medicine cabinet.

"The parties have stipulated that this list identifies the number of prescriptions Ms. Eden filled and were still at her apartment.

"How many opiates are listed?"

Davenport started counting out loud, "One, two, three . . . eleven."

"Do you see the column marked number of pills?"

"Yes."

Pierce handed him a calculator.

"How many pills?"

Davenport started punching buttons. He stopped and obviously had to start again.

"456."

"That's a lot of opiates?"

"Absolutely."

"Would you agree that if someone took that many opiates, she would inevitably die of a drug overdose?"

Davis actually jumped to his feet and loudly stated, "Objection, speculation."

Tanner sustained, but it was too late. The jury had just been told by the state's medical examiner that it was inevitable that Robyn Eden would die of a drug overdose. Davis and Morty knew he was a bad witness, They just didn't know how bad.

Pierce got Davenport to admit Robyn was using an IV, and that intensified the drugs.

"She used an awful lot of hydrocodone. Based on that list, it was her drug of choice?"

"Absolutely."

Davis cringed.

"Hydrocodone pills are two-thirds filler and one-third active ingredient?"

"Yes."

"That's a tremendous amount of filler in a short period of time?"

"Correct."

Using Irving, Pierce explained to the jury how the filler blocked the smaller vessels. "It's like a cork blocking the blood from flowing, right?"

Davenport explained how the pressure builds up, and the result is high blood pressure, which can under extreme circumstances cause death.

Pierce asked if she could pass to the witness Exhibit 131, a cell phone picture of Ms. Eden. Davis didn't have a clue where Pierce was going. It was a picture of Robyn inserting a very large vibrator into her vagina. It had been passed to the jury. Davenport looked very uncomfortable.

"What is the time on that cell phone picture?"

"Ten o one."

"The parties have stipulated that Mr. Garcia called 911 at ten ten and that after that call, he performed CPR and revived Ms. Eden. Those are stipulated facts.

"Would you say that Ms. Eden is posing in that picture and that it took some dexterity for her to insert that sex toy into her vagina the way she did?"

"Correct."

"Does she look like she's in respiratory distress?"

"She seems active and not in distress."

"I want you to assume that there are four cell phone photos after ten o one that reflect similar activity by Ms. Eden.

"Does this photo impact your testimony that the mechanism of death was respiratory depression?"

Davenport sat there for what seemed like a very long time. The jury noticed the delay in his response. He was obviously thinking.

"This photo proves she didn't die of respiratory depression. She was much too active right before her death. My autopsy report is wrong as to the mechanism of death."

"You've never seen this cell phone photo before?"

"No."

"Do you know why Mr. Davis or the police didn't show it to you?"

"No."

"You were never told there were four missing photos taken later in time than this one, were you?"

"No."

Pierce stopped on that damaging point.

Davis got Davenport to restate that the cause of death was the oxycodone, but it wasn't clear that the jury heard or understood the difference between cause of death and mechanism of death or the importance of that anymore.

Davis thought by using Irving, he could make Davenport's testimony more interesting to the jury. He couldn't help that Dr. Davenport was hopeless as a witness. Sometimes a lawyer has no choice but to try to put on the proof and weather the cross.

It was past six, and Tanner recessed for the day.

CHAPTER FIFTY-SIX

ABOVE REPROACH

Wednesday, February 14, 2001

Harrelson was tired of sitting on his backside on the hard oak pews of the Hewes County Courthouse. He wanted to sit with Pierce at the defense table, but he didn't have the experience. He excused himself from the Garcias and walked out the courthouse front door into the cold February morning. He sat at a bench that faced a Civil War cannon, pulled his cell phone out, and faked making a call.

He didn't have to wait long. Alan Baxter sat down on a bench right behind Harrelson's and mimicked making a call. The two men's heads were inches apart facing in opposite directions. There was nothing suspicious about two men on two separate benches making two separate phone calls.

Speaking into his phone, Baxter said, "It's no dice. I can't get to him. He's above reproach."

Cold and tired of sleeping in a hotel bed, Harrelson snapped back, "Everybody's got a price or a weakness we can exploit. You've disappointed me, Baxter, you know that. You just needed to dig deeper, but it's too late now. He's their next witness."

"I'm telling you I've tried. He's the DA. You just can't walk up to him and offer him a bribe. He's a man of principles."

"I'm very disappointed in you, Baxter. We needed your help, and you didn't deliver."

Harrelson rubbed in Baxter's failure. He got up and walked back into the courthouse. He sat down and reported to Señor Garcia, "We've got a small problem. We couldn't get to the DA."

"He's going to try to crucify Charlie. We'll put Baxter on as part of our case to try to nullify the DA's testimony."

Judge Tanner took the bench and called his court to order.

Davis called his first witness, District Attorney Peter Taylor of Jefferson County, Kentucky. The completely bald DA was immaculately dressed in a blue three-piece suit.

Davis took him through his background and the fact he was an elected official. He was responsible for all criminal prosecutions in his county. Davis asked him whether he'd ever met Mr. Garcia.

Taylor testified that the defendant in 1999 was indicted for "count one, unlawful prescribing and administering a narcotic; count two, wanton endangerment; and count three, unlawful possession of drug paraphernalia."

"What was the drug Mr. Garcia unlawfully prescribed?"

"Hydrocodone."

"And who did he prescribe it for?"

"Robyn Eden, the victim in this case."

"At the time Mr. Garcia was a doctor, wasn't he?"

"Yes, but Kentucky doesn't let out-of-state physicians prescribe Schedule III narcotics."

Davis stopped to let the importance of that testimony sink in.

Neither party disclosed the Derby incident in opening statements. The jury was about to learn that July 4th was not the only time Charlie Garcia was around when Robyn Eden overdosed.

"Can you tell the jury what transpired to cause the indictment of Mr. Garcia?"

Taylor was an experienced litigator. He went to court for a living and was very comfortable providing the narration of the 1999 Derby weekend.

"Ms. Eden overdosed from a combination of injecting a hydrocodone mixture into her groin area and consuming the remainder of the bottle. She had to be hospitalized. I interviewed her in the hospital. She got in an argument with Mr. Garcia after she injected herself and then took the remainder of the bottle orally. She had to have her stomach pumped. He caused her overdose in May 1999."

Davis let that testimony just sit there. It was a gotcha moment.

He waited so long, Judge Tanner asked, "Anything else, Mr. Davis?"

"Yes, sir, Your Honor."

He asked the DA, "What happened to the charges against Mr. Garcia?"

"I'm sorry to say I cut a deal. I accepted a plea bargain. Mr. Garcia accepted pretrial diversion and probation for eighteen months. We placed the charges in abeyance, and if he stayed clean, the charges got dismissed."

"Why did you do that?"

"Two reasons. First, I believed Mr. Garcia when he said that he didn't realize he couldn't write a prescription for a Schedule III narcotic in Kentucky. Second, Robyn Eden became uncooperative."

"What do you mean?"

"She recanted her testimony and refused to cooperate. He had absolute control over her."

"Mr. Garcia got eighteen months. He didn't quite make it, did he?"

"He was arrested for murder after fourteen months."

"You're here voluntarily. You're not under subpoena?"

"You couldn't subpoena me. I live outside the state of Tennessee. I'm here because I feel guilty. If I'd prosecuted this man, he would have been convicted, and that young woman would be alive today."

Pierce objected on the grounds of speculation, "He has no idea what outcome would have occurred if he tried Mr. Garcia. He obviously had very serious concerns, or he wouldn't have suggested pretrial diversion."

Tanner sustained the objection, and Davis sat down.

Pierce opted to ask no questions. Taylor was a dangerous witness, and he'd done his damage. No sense in giving him more of an opportunity to do more harm to her case.

Lunch was called.

CHAPTER FIFTY-SEVEN

WINDING DOWN THE STATE'S PROOF

Thursday, February 15, 2001

In the afternoon Davis started by calling Jasper Wright, a musician and friend of Robyn. He played in several bands with Robyn and spent years on the road with her. He testified about Robyn's addiction and her fear of needles. The purpose of his testimony was to humanize Robyn.

On cross-examination Pierce ripped him up. He admitted he was an addict, only clean sixteen months. He admitted that addicts lied to get what they wanted, whether it was drugs or something else.

"You want my client punished?"

"I think he murdered my friend."

"You want revenge?"

"Yes. He killed her."

"You're an addict. You'd say anything to get what you want, right?"

No response from Wright.

"You want revenge, right?"

"Yes."

Pierce next showed him pictures of the needle marks in Robyn's groin. In response he testified he'd never been intimate with Robyn, and Pierce snidely inferred he was the only one.

Davis next called Melissa Lemon, senior pharmacy tech at the Hewes County Super AAA Pharmacy off Highway 96. Davis used her because she was a familiar face in the community. Some people knew her by name, but most just knew her face. Her testimony boiled down to one point: you couldn't just walk into a drugstore and purchase the syringes used by Robyn Eden. Eighteen-gauge syringes were special order, and ten millimeter required either a prescription or evidence of insulin dependence, such as producing a vial of insulin. Ms. Lemon testified that was her company's policy and, to the best of her knowledge, every other chain pharmacy in the state.

On cross, Pierce got Ms. Lemon to acknowledge she didn't know the policies of independent drugstores selling syringes. The inference that Garcia provided Robyn Eden with the syringes was destroyed.

Judge Tanner addressed Davis, "It's four thirty. Who is your next witness?"

"I've got two more witnesses to present. Neither of them will be short. I would prefer to complete these witnesses at one time rather than break them up."

He explained to the court that one of them was his expert, and his last witness was Senator Daniels.

Judge Tanner explained the situation to the jury. He suggested a fifteen-minute comfort break, and they'd either go late tonight or they'd call it a day. The foreman of the jury, Randy Mayer, informed the court the jury was ready to plow on.

Davis called Dr. Brian Limbaugh.

Dr. Limbaugh strode to the witness box with absolute determination and confidence. He was a professional witness first and a psychiatrist second. His credentials were impeccable. Harvard undergrad, Johns Hopkins medical school, and he did his residency and fellowship in psychiatry at Bellevue Hospital in New York. He taught at Columbia and lectured worldwide. He came at the request of Morty Steine, who'd represented and saved from ruin a life-long friend of the doctor.

The moment he started to speak, Dr. Limbaugh commanded respect. His voice was warm but authoritative. The jury seemed to hang on every word.

Davis asked why the doctor was testifying.

"I'm here at the request of the state, so I'm here on behalf of citizens of this state, Tennessee. People like these jurors."

The line was actually Morty's, and it worked.

Davis turned to Limbaugh's compensation. Dr. Limbaugh explained that he'd spent three hours interviewing Charles Garcia, read depositions that Mr. Garcia had given in other legal matters, and read the pleadings filed by both sides of the case. He'd spent a total of twenty hours of his time forming his medical opinions, to which he intended to testify.

"I've agreed to a fee of fifty dollars an hour for my time. Mr. Davis refused to let me testify for free."

It was like playing softball. Davis lobbed the questions in, and Limbaugh hit them out of the park. Davis asked only about five questions, and Limbaugh spoke for thirty-five minutes. He used technical terms but explained them in the course of his testimony. He was not complimentary of Charles Garcia.

"In layman's terms, plain English, he's a schemer and as egomaniacal and self-centered as a person can be. He sees the world as a place for only his purposes and everyone as his pawn to control and manipulate.

"He spent his days making women who were his patients into his image. That confirmed he had absolute control over them. But after surgery, they went home to their husbands and families, and he lost that control. That's why he needed Robyn Eden. She was his own private canvas. Even if they were a thousand miles away, he still controlled her.

"They both at times believed that they were deeply in love and that their relationship was beautiful and meaningful. But then reality set in, and after rational review, they saw it for what it was: perverted and self-destructive."

After Davis asked Dr. Limbaugh whether Mr. Garcia felt any remorse for Ms. Eden's death, Pierce objected.

Tanner ruled, "I'm going to let the jury hear his testimony, but remember these are Dr. Limbaugh's opinions. You give them whatever weight that you deem appropriate."

Dr. Limbaugh looked straight at the jury. There was no question he was focused just on them and no one else in the courtroom.

"Dr. and now Mr. Garcia feels deep remorse but not for Robyn Eden. His remorse is for himself. He's lost everything, and he's lost control. The loss of control and the fact that he must be here in this courtroom to answer for what he's done are the worst things that have ever happened to him. To him, control of his life and others meant everything. I'm sure he's in a deep depression."

He deliberately turned and looked into the soul of Charlie Garcia.

"You were her doctor. Ethically you never should have been her lover. If you wanted to be with her, ethically you were required to stop treating her. She died on your watch, and as her doctor, you knew the highest principle is first do no harm."

Davis sat down.

Pierce rose and announced, "It's six thirty-eight. Why don't we call it a night? I'll reserve my cross for tomorrow morning." She was shaken by Dr. Limbaugh's testimony and wanted the night to plan her cross. She outsmarted Davis. His expert's testimony was broken up after all.

Tanner agreed, and the jurors were taken by bus to dinner at a local steakhouse and then on to the hotel. Although Dr. Limbaugh entertained them, Davis knew it was time to wrap up the state's case.

CHAPTER FIFTY-EIGHT

A RESTLESS NIGHT
AND A BROKEN WOMAN

Thursday-Friday, February 15–16, 2001

Amy Pierce tossed and turned all night debating her cross-examination of Dr. Limbaugh. He'd be a tough witness, and then Davis would get to go all over again on redirect. Pierce was ready for Senator Valerie Daniels. Why not let the show begin rather than spend any more time with Limbaugh?

Her evening was also marred by a phone call from her ex-husband, Dan. He wanted to resume visitation with their son, Carter. Pierce didn't want her son hurt again by a father who'd abandoned him and was unstable. He was a drunk and a drug addict. He'd been a lawyer, so he at least understood that she was in the middle of a trial. She was able to convince him to postpone their discussion until after the trial.

In that frame of mind Pierce announced the next morning, "No questions. Let's get to Mr. Davis's final witness so the defense can put on its case."

She watched Davis's face. She'd caught him a little flat-footed. He wasn't prepared to start with Daniels first thing this morning.

Daniels was eating breakfast at Mother's on the square, waiting on his call for a progress report. Judge Tanner ordered a comfort break while Daniels walked to the courthouse.

Valerie Daniels knew how to speak to a jury. They were voters, right? Davis spent only a few minutes on her background. She came from privilege, and because of that she had very little in common with the jury.

Pierce knew Daniels was a two-edged sword, and in the end Pierce would find the sharper side.

She was her sister's conservator and was legally responsible for her. "She was family. I loved my sister despite all of her faults. She was an addict. If you spent fifteen minutes with her, you'd know that. Mr. Garcia certainly knew it. He took advantage of my sister because she was an addict. She . . ."

Pierce objected, and Tanner sustained.

"Mr. Davis, ask a question, and I direct the witness to answer only that question."

Pierce thought that Daniels on direct did a good job but was not very exciting. Limbaugh would have been a better choice as the last state's witness. *I do believe that Davis goofed.*

Pierce questioned Daniels in detail about her childhood and her relationship with her sister. Those subjects were fair game. "You and your sister lived a privileged childhood."

Davis objected, and Tanner told Pierce to move on. The jurors could form their opinion without her characterization.

After that, Pierce got rough. She got Daniels to admit that she knew about Robyn's addiction and that her use began long before she met Charlie Garcia.

"She'd used IV drugs before she met him?"

"Yes."

"She made pornographic photos before she met him?"

"Yes."

"Everything you did failed to save her?"

"Yes."

"Your sister was pregnant with your niece or nephew, and she still couldn't stop using IV drugs?"

"Yes."

"That child didn't have a chance, did it?"

"I don't know."

Daniels was about to lose it. She was a hardened politician, but this was a personal attack, not a political one.

"Why did you think that Charles Garcia would have better luck than you had?"

"I thought as the father, he might be able to convince her."

"In fact he's in this mess because you dragged him into it. He wasn't a drug addict, but he was addicted to her?"

"Yes."

Pierce then played the telephone call between Daniels and Garcia the day after Robyn's death. He came off very sympathetic, the grieving boyfriend. She came off angry at the world. It was powerful proof, and the state just had to sit there and take it.

After that, Daniels was like a punching bag. Davis objected a few times, trying to help Daniels catch her wind, but it didn't work.

"You even had an intervention after she was terminated from Nichols & Garcia for stealing drugs out of the medicine closet?"

"Yes."

"Mr. Steine and Ms. Davis participated in her intervention, didn't they?"

"Yes."

"Mr. Davis refused to participate, didn't he?"

"He didn't refuse. He thought because he was the one who'd fired her, his involvement would be counterproductive."

"The intervention worked. She went into rehab, but she relapsed, didn't she?"

Davis always felt bad that he didn't participate in that intervention. At this moment he felt even worse.

Daniels was a powerful woman and tried her best, but Pierce overpowered her. She pounded Daniels for more than two hours.

Davis tried to rehabilitate Daniels on redirect, but it was evident that Daniels's heart wasn't in it.

Pierce did a short recross, and Davis closed his proof.

Judge Tanner addressed the jury, "Ladies and gentlemen, the state has closed its proof. I'm letting you go to the hotel early today. I've got to hear some motions, and we'll reconvene at nine on Monday. Have a good weekend, and remember: don't talk about the case. I promise you'll get an opportunity to deliberate when all of the proof has been presented."

The jury filed out.

Tanner asked Pierce, "You have a motion to make, Ms. Pierce?"

"Yes, sir. The defendant moves for a directed verdict."

In layman's terms she was asking the judge to dismiss all charges without the need to put on any proof.

"I can save us some time, Ms. Pierce."

"It's your courtroom, Your Honor."

"I've read the briefs, and I've heard the proof. There's a jury question here. I'm letting both counts go to the jury. Anything else?"

She hated that the jury would decide the case, but Tanner wasn't going to get reversed on this call. Almost everyone had left the courtroom to either enjoy the afternoon or get to work on other matters. Pierce planned to go home and spend some time with Carter.

CHAPTER FIFTY-NINE

A CONVINCING LIAR

Monday, February 19, 2001

Monday morning, the defendant's proof began with Baxter first up. Pierce suggested him because he'd be an easy witness. She was right. He described Charles Garcia as the model parolee.

"You get to know your parolees. They open up to you. Mr. Garcia was highly intelligent, and he was dedicated to being a doctor."

He went on, he knew the man; they'd spoken weekly. They actually talked about Robyn Eden and his relationship with her. Her addiction dragged him down. He wanted to save her, but she was too self-destructive. Baxter said, "Dr. Garcia's crime is, he failed to convince her to go into rehab."

Davis, by objection, got the last answer thrown out, but a jury never really forgets an answer, no matter what the judge instructs.

Pierce next called Dr. Gene Albertson from Bio-Tech Labs.

Davis jumped to his feet and asked if the jury could be excused rather than addressing his objection in open court or by a sidebar. The court recognized that this dispute was considered by Davis important and granted Davis's request. When the jury was gone, Davis moved to the podium.

"Dr. Albertson is not on the defendant's witness list, and I assume that because he's a doctor, he's also an expert witness."

Judge Tanner turned to Pierce. "What do you have to say, Ms. Pierce?"

"Dr. Albertson is an impeachment witness, Your Honor. The state put on proof through the TBI lab technician that the only DNA found on the sex toys was that of Robyn Eden. That's not true. This court by its order allowed the defendant to conduct independent DNA testing, and Dr. Albertson is here to tell the jury his contradictory findings. That makes him an impeachment witness, and therefore his name didn't need to be on our list."

Tanner now turned to Davis. "Well, Mr. Davis?"

Davis turned to Sammie, who addressed the court. "Your Honor, in early September 2000, after the independent DNA testing, I spoke with Ms. Pierce, and she told me that the report would not be on her exhibit list. She implied that its findings were consistent with those of the state and therefore not necessary."

Pierce spoke up, "Ms. Davis is partially correct. I did say the independent report would not be on my exhibit list, and it wasn't. I never stated or implied that it was or wasn't consistent. She must have assumed that conclusion, and she was wrong. I assure the court this is critical evidence, and to exclude it would be reversible error."

"Ms. Davis, other than my order are there any written communications with Ms. Pierce on this subject?"

"No, Your Honor."

"I can't rely on the conflicting memories of two lawyers. Dr. Albertson is a conflicting witness, an impeachment witness. He will testify, and his report will come into evidence despite the fact he wasn't on the witness list."

Sammie sat down at the prosecution table. Morty leaned over

and said softly, "Lesson learned. Always send a confirming letter. You can't trust your opposing counsel, especially Amy Pierce."

Dr. Albertson testified that he tested five sex toys and that Robyn Eden's DNA was on each of them. He also testified, "I did find another person's DNA on Exhibit 146, a double dildo. Ms. Eden's was on one side, and the DNA of Danny Nix was on the other."

He explained that Ms. Pierce introduced him to Danny Nix at his lab; that he sampled her DNA and determined it was on one side of Exhibit 146. His report was made an exhibit.

Davis asked for a fifteen-minute comfort break, not to relieve himself but to talk to his team. He knew what was coming next, Danny Nix. The consensus was, if you don't know the answer to a question, then you shouldn't ask the question. There were no further questions for Dr. Albertson.

Danny Nix, a forty-year-old self-proclaimed lesbian, was up next. Davis renewed his objection for the record, but Tanner directed Pierce to begin her questioning.

She'd known Robyn Eden for four or five years. With one look at her, anyone could tell Nix had once been a beautiful woman, but she'd hit hard times. Two nasty divorces and alcohol abuse aged her. She sold drugs but knew not to use them. She had a special relationship with Robyn Eden. Pierce got right to the point.

"I traded drugs for sex at least fifteen times. I supplied her with hydrocodone and oxycodone, and she did whatever I asked."

"What do you mean?"

"I enjoy strapping on a dildo and going at it. Robyn for a few pills would accommodate my desires. She was very accommodating."

Harrelson thought her testimony was credible. He knew the jurors wouldn't like her. That wasn't what was important, though. They needed to believe her.

She looked at several pictures of the sex toys found in Robyn Eden's apartment in plain view as a result of the three search warrants. She pointed out four she claimed she actually used with Eden.

When she got to Exhibit 146, she said, "This one was our favorite. I'd insert one side inside me, she'd insert the other side in her, and we'd meet in the middle."

Then Pierce asked the key question of the examination, "When did you last have sex with Robyn Eden?"

"It was right before the July 4th holiday, on June 30th."

"Are you sure of that date?"

"Absolutely. It was our last time. I'll never forget it. Sex with Robyn isn't something you'd forget."

"What, if anything, did you give Robyn in return for sex on June 30th, 2000?"

"I gave her eight oxycodone pills. She loved those babies. She'd crush them up and inject them. She got a quicker and better rush. The mixture went right into her bloodstream."

"Did you ever see her inject herself?"

"Many times."

"Where did she inject herself?"

"She'd shoot up between her toes and in her groin."

Harrelson sighed with relief. The critical testimony was in evidence. In his mind reasonable doubt existed. Who supplied the oxycodone and who injected Robyn Eden were now disputed facts. The jury should acquit on the murder charge.

Pierce finished up quickly. The critical points had been made. The waters had been muddied.

Steine got up and tried to cross Nix. Yes, she was a drug dealer. Yes, she traded sex for drugs. Jill Hoskins, the young DA, left the gallery to get Nix's computerized rap sheet. Before Steine's cross ended, she'd handed it to him.

"You've been arrested, correct?"

"Yes, several times."

"You were arrested on October 4th for distribution of narcotics?"

"Yes."

"And you faced serious jail time, fifteen years?"

"Yes."

Harrelson didn't like this line of questioning. All he could do was sit there.

You received immunity in that case, right? You turned on the drug dealer that sold to you?"

"Yes."

"So you're a snitch?"

"Yes."

On redirect Pierce pointed out that when Nix acted as a snitch, she did it for the state of Tennessee. "You snitched for Mr. Steine and Mr. Davis's client?"

"That's right."

Tanner called it quits for the day. He wished the jury a good evening and warned them not to discuss the case. He promised that their service would end soon. Court would resume two days hence because of another pressing matter for him. It had been a good first day for the defense. The liar was convincing.

CHAPTER SIXTY
A BIG DECISION
Tuesday, February 20, 2001

It was a beautiful morning for court to be recessed in Middle Tennessee when Charlie, his father, and Harrelson met with Pierce in her office. Everyone was in good spirits, especially Charlie. Judge Tanner had another criminal matter to attend to, so everybody got the day off. Pierce looked at the day off two ways. Either they were losing momentum, or the jury had an opportunity to chew on yesterday's testimony. She rationalized that the delay was a positive development.

Charlie thought the first day of the defendant's proof went exceptionally well, and everyone praised Pierce for the job she'd done so far.

The purpose of the meeting was simple. They were to answer the question, should Charlie testify?

It was Pierce's office, and she was the trial lawyer, so she went first. "As I see it, you've beaten the murder charge. There is reasonable doubt as to who supplied the oxycodone. If the jurors find that's what killed her, then they should acquit. We still intend to present contradictory medical evidence that it was the accumulation of hydrocodone and filler that caused her death. That should create even greater reasonable doubt. My best argument comes from the state's own medical examiner, Davenport. According to him, she was going to die anyway, and she took the child with her. No one on that jury feels any remorse for her. I'm of the opinion that to secure a not guilty plea on the murder charge, we don't need Charlie's testimony. Reckless homicide is a different story. I think the jury right now will convict on that count. Sorry, but I do."

Charlie didn't like that opinion one bit. He didn't mean to, but he yelled at Pierce, "That's not fair! I loved her and tried to save her. Daniels played on my heartstrings. She said, 'If not for Robyn, then the child.' My only crime was that I didn't get her into rehab."

The sad thing was, Charlie really believed that. He'd convinced himself of that lie. Everyone else in the room, even his own father, knew Charlie was guilty of something.

"I want to testify. I can convince them to let me go free. I've suffered enough."

Instead of responding to Charlie, Harrelson asked the right question: "If convicted of the second count, what could Charlie expect as a sentence?"

"It's hard to say. Maybe two or three years and he'd serve about two-thirds of his sentence. It would be at a minimum-security facility, so it wouldn't be too bad."

Charlie lost it again, "I'm not going to jail for two years! Father, do something."

Señor Garcia looked straight into Charlie's face and, with harshness in his voice, chastised his son, "I've shielded you from all your mistakes. You've used really bad judgment. Ms. Pierce has done an exceptional job defending you. She even got some outside help from Harrelson and my wallet, but you're not innocent. You need to make the smart decision and listen to Ms. Pierce. She knows what she's talking about."

Harrelson had been following the exchanges and added, "Charlie, if you'd been represented by a public defender and didn't get that outside help, you'd be going to jail for at least twenty-five years. Quit while you're way ahead. Finish the trial, don't testify, and take your medicine like a man. If you testify, you could potentially screw this up. Davis or, even worse, Steine will destroy you on the stand. Pierce will be picking up the pieces on redirect. Don't do it, boy. Don't waste all this hard work and money. Who knows? You could get as little as a year and serve only nine months."

Pierce agreed that such a sentence was a possibility.

Charlie sat there thinking. All three of his advisors were adamant against his testifying. Each of them had the reasons, and the arguments were pretty consistent. He was ahead in the game, his testimony wasn't necessary, and it could be disastrous.

Charlie announced he wanted to think about it.

Pierce acknowledged that if he elected to testify, she was prepared to go forward. The last thing she said to him was, "It's your call, Charlie. I've given you my best advice and my honest opinion, but it's your life, not mine or Harrelson's. You think about it and let me know before tomorrow morning, so I can prepare to put you on the stand."

After the meeting, Pierce got a phone call from Dan asking to see Carter for the upcoming weekend. She explained that she was still in trial and he'd have to wait until it was over. He wasn't happy with that answer. He started whining loudly about his rights as Carter's father. She couldn't stop him from seeing her son. He'd drag her into court. She'd be a defendant, not a lawyer. She didn't give a damn about his threat. As he spoke she became more determined to keep him from seeing Carter. Dan seemed equally determined to spend time with his son and enter Pierce's life again.

From her perspective the day went from bad to worse. After she spoke to Dan, Charlie Garcia called to say that he wanted to testify.

CHAPTER SIXTY-ONE
HIS OWN WORST ENEMY
Wednesday, February 21, 2001

Before going to the courthouse, Pierce tried to persuade Charlie that his testimony interfered with her strategy. It was just plain stupid. Why take the risk? Even if there was a guilty verdict as to reckless homicide, there'd still be a two-year appeal.

Pierce speculated with more authority than she should have, "I can get Tanner to continue your bond and home detention. He'll probably increase the bond a million or two, but what do you care? Your father is willing to invest a couple more million for your freedom. You know you're costing a fortune. I'm not cheap, Harrelson certainly isn't cheap, and your father's paying all the expenses, including renting your house. It all adds up. Please don't screw this up."

Charlie looked thoughtful and shook his head no.

Pierce changed gears mid-thought. She had to. She walked over to the courthouse. Charlie was escorted each morning by a deputy sheriff.

Judge Tanner began the morning with a pep talk. The jury needed encouragement. Pierce took that time to analyze where she was with the jury. It was all on her. Her associates were at the office making her money. She didn't want to share the recognition with anyone. Like Charlie Garcia, she required absolute control. They were too much alike.

The judge finished his talk, and despite her anxiety, Pierce dug deep and mustered absolute determination. She rose and said, "The defendant will testify."

The importance of the moment was not lost on the jury. They'd seen enough TV to realize that a defendant didn't usually testify; it had something to do with an amendment or something. No one in the courtroom knew whether Garcia would testify. Judge Tanner started thinking of what issues the testimony of this witness might give rise to. Davis thought about his cross-examination, and so did Steine.

Pierce watched Davis and Steine huddle in the corner. She'd given them something to think about.

Morty squeezed Davis's right arm. It was a loving gesture. "Look, Ben, this is your moment. To get our murder charge to stick, you need to knock this guy out. You can do it; he's so arrogant. Just keep the pace fast and his ego will get ahead of his brain and he'll slip up. If I haven't told you lately, I'm very proud of you. Now murder this arrogant son of a bitch."

Pierce intentionally started slowly with Charlie. She knew he'd be on the stand all day and probably several hours tomorrow. She downplayed his background, just as Davis did with Daniels. His education and training were above reproach.

He described in some detail how he got to Nashville. He didn't mention the breach of contract, and Pierce hoped that Davis wouldn't. He did admit to two sexual harassment suits that were settled without admission of any guilt. He admitted that he surrendered his Tennessee medical license, but there was no finding against him, only the claims of the two women. He said, "I elected not to get in a long, drawn-out fight. I had my New York medical license, and I wasn't remaining in Tennessee anyway. At the time it seemed like the right thing to do. I didn't know I'd be defending myself against a murder charge."

He also bitterly testified how the New York licensing board suspended his New York medical license without any hearing or opportunity to defend.

His life was ruined. "I've lost everything, including Robyn. I know the jury's heard some strange things about our relationship, but I did love her. She was an addict long before she met me. She was in love with herself, and I like to think with me also. She went through all of the surgeries voluntarily, and I accommodated her. It was good for business since she sat out in reception."

Pierce spent the next thirty minutes discussing Charlie's relationship with Robyn, through his eyes.

"After I left Nashville, Robyn joined me in New York. She was a great singer. I loved to listen to her. She occasionally got a gig at a club and played three or four nights. Then the headaches started, cluster headaches right above her eyes. She wasn't faking. They were very real. I prescribed hydrocodone twice until I realized she was abusing it. The last time was the 1999 Derby weekend."

Pierce stole Davis's thunder on several damaging points. She hoped he'd skip some of them now. Charlie testified why they separated but explained that he couldn't live without her. She felt the same way, and they'd get back together and then she'd use.

He told what happened at the 1999 Derby. That weekend he was trying to get her into rehab, but he failed. She wound up in the hospital instead. He took pretrial diversion rather than go to trial. He didn't admit he'd done anything wrong.

Pierce had Garcia describe what their relationship was like during their separation. She moved into evidence eighty-six e-mails from 1997 through June 2000 in support of their loving relationship. Pierce had Garcia read seven and then stated that the rest would be available for the jury to read during deliberation.

"Look, she was ordering pills online. I'd didn't sell her or give her any drugs other than the ones I testified to earlier. She played doctors and could get drugs on the street. She also had real medical problems. Her headaches were real, and so were her anxiety attacks."

He testified that he pleaded with her. He warned her she was going to kill herself.

Under Pierce's questioning, he described the long July 4th weekend. He explained that during that time, he didn't go into the master bathroom. Robyn must have taken his shaving kit in there. All they did was have sex, eat takeout, and watch movies. They also videotaped or took cell phone pictures of themselves.

He admitted he wasn't an angel. He'd smoked pot before and abused alcohol. He abused sex. He was addicted to her. He was addicted to Viagra. He had to take it to keep up with Robyn. He didn't corrupt her; she used drugs and engaged in weird sex before they ever met.

Pierce showed him two photos of Robyn and a man. Both were naked, and the man was bent over Robyn.

"Do you know the two persons in these photos?"

"Robyn and Bobby Bowers. He's a friend of Robyn, a real good friend."

Using the date stamp on the photos, Pierce established that the Bowers pictures were taken during one of Robyn's separations from Charlie.

She showed him the two pictures of Ron Harris and Robyn, taken before she ever met Garcia, that had already been introduced into evidence. Pierce asked that the four photos be passed to the jury. She then asked Charlie about the video. It wasn't Robyn's first. She'd made videos with him and with others. She lived for the camera.

"You saw the tape. She was sick and had a headache. Can you imagine what she was like on a good day?"

"Why did you make the video?"

"It was her idea. She liked to watch them while we made love. As I said, we'd done it several times before. But that July 4th holiday was a sex marathon."

Pierce brought up that the video showed Robyn holding gauze by her groin. He admitted he suspected she was injecting some kind of crushed pill.

Pierce didn't like that last answer, but to fail to address that proof would have been a tactical mistake. She forged ahead. She asked what brought him to Hewes City for that July 4th holiday.

"Senator Daniels asked me to come down to get her into rehab. She told me that Robyn was about ten weeks pregnant and that Robyn was killing herself and my child. I was shocked to hear that I was going to be a father. She admitted that she'd tried everything. I loved Robyn, so I agreed. It was the biggest mistake of my life. I tried my best to get her into rehab, but I was weak. It turned into a sex marathon, and she went into the bathroom to do drugs. I didn't know what drugs she was doing, and I didn't want to guess. I tried to save her. I performed CPR and brought her back, but it was too late. She died at the hospital."

Pierce took Charlie through the scene at the hospital. He described a hostile Detective Haber. It was now clear to him that he was a suspect. "No, she didn't read me my Miranda rights."

Charlie ended his direct testimony with a condemnation of Dr. Peter Nichols and Davis, 'I'm being prosecuted by the state, but I'm being persecuted by Mr. Davis! This is personal."

Pierce stopped for the day. Davis's cross would be tomorrow. Direct went well, but Pierce knew that cross would be brutal.

CHAPTER SIXTY-TWO

A CROSS-EXAMINATION OF A LIFETIME

Thursday, February 22, 2001

The day started with Charlie Garcia back on the witness stand. Davis wanted to draw blood quickly. "Mr. Garcia, you've testified that you wrote only two prescriptions of hydrocodone for Ms. Eden, correct?"

"Yes, sir."

"In fact, over the years, you've prescribed several different types of drugs for her?"

"Absolutely not."

"That's false testimony."

"Absolutely not!"

"Well, isn't it true in 1995 and early 1996 you performed several surgeries on Ms. Eden? After those surgeries, on almost a weekly basis you prescribed and she used various drugs?"

"Yes, she was in pain after those surgeries."

Using Robyn's chart from Nichols & Garcia, Davis established that Garcia injected her with Demerol eleven times.

"You introduced Robyn to an IV needle?"

"I don't know."

"Ms. Pierce has stipulated that according to Robyn's medical records, her first IV use was in 1995 with a surgery you performed."

"Then I guess I did."

"According to her medical records in 1995–96, a four-month period, you prescribed hydrocodone five times for a total of one hundred fifty pills. That's more than one a day?"

"Your math's right."

"You got her addicted to hydrocodone?"

"That's not fair. I prescribed that pain medication because she was in pain and suffering from severe headaches."

"At the 1999 Derby you went too far, and she wound up in the hospital and you wound up facing criminal charges?"

"Again you're not being fair. In a locked bathroom she injected one dose and then took the rest of the bottle. That's what put her in the hospital."

"But you did know that she was an IV drug user more than a year before her death?"

"Yes."

"And you were the one to introduce her to hydrocodone and IV use?"

"Yes, but Robyn was a drug addict long before we met. Her sister had been dealing with her drug abuse at least five years before I met her."

Using several still photos, Davis got Garcia to admit that Robyn and he engaged in some very different sex games. He made Garcia handle the sex toys. They were his, and Davis wanted the jury to see him with them.

He asked Garcia about how they made the videos and then watched them while they had sex. He played the first part of the July weekend videotape. The night of July 4th, that portion of the video was more than fifty minutes long. That Viagra really worked.

It was pretty rough stuff. Even if some members of the jury had used sex toys before, they'd never used them the way Robyn Eden had.

Next, Davis played the video of Robyn's last day alive in her apartment. First, Robyn started the camera and jumped into bed. She complained about her headache. With Garcia next to her in bed she picked up one of the bottles on the nightstand and took a pill. The two went at it for a good ten minutes. Several women on the jury gave Charlie Garcia hard stares. It was clear to Davis they didn't like the man or care for his taste in sex.

When both grunted in climax, Robyn jumped from the bed and disappeared, presumably into the bathroom. The camera stayed on Garcia alone in the bed, and he yelled, "What the hell are you doing?"

She yelled back, "Masturbating. I'll be right out!"

She flew out of the bathroom. It was clear she'd taken something while in the bathroom by how animated she became when she returned on camera. When she got on her back and invited Garcia to get on board, viewers could actually see she was bleeding around her shaved pubic area. Clear as a bell they could hear Charlie Garcia say, "You're bleeding like a stuck pig. Get some gauze." Everyone in the courtroom heard the defendant's voice: "And put pressure on it."

Davis stopped the video there.

"Don't insult this jury. You knew she was shooting up a crushed pill in her groin."

"I didn't know. I suspected."

"That's your answer to this jury."

"That's my answer," Charlie responded.

"Did you think she just spontaneously started bleeding down there? You're a medical doctor."

No response from Garcia. There wasn't a good answer.

"She'd just come from the bathroom where next to your shaving kit was the crushed oxycodone that she used, which caused her femoral bleeding?"

"I don't know that. I never went into the master bathroom."

"How did your open shaving kit get in there? Walk in by itself?"

"She must have taken it out of my bag and put it there."

"She took it in the bathroom, opened it, took out the oxycodone you'd brought with you, crushed it, and used it?"

"Absolutely not. I didn't bring any drugs other than the Viagra."

That was a lie, but Davis couldn't prove it.

"So you say. She must have taken your shaving kit into the bathroom because she needed a shave?"

"I don't know."

"And we can't ask her?"

"No."

"You held absolute control of Robyn Eden?"

"No. If I controlled her, I could have stopped her from doing drugs. I could have talked her into rehab."

"You liked her on drugs? Drugs made her weak and easier to control? You took advantage of this impressionable young woman?"

Pierce yelled her objections.

Judge Tanner sustained, but Davis knew more than half the jury agreed with his little speech.

"You lied to the paramedics?"

"I didn't make full disclosure."

"They could have better helped Robyn if they knew she'd injected a narcotic?"

"Yes."

"You could have walked into the bathroom and brought them the syringes and determined she'd crushed oxycodone, right?"

"I didn't think of that. I was panicked. I'd just performed CPR and saved her life. I wanted her to live."

"You had a second chance at the hospital to disclose what she'd taken when Dr. Mann questioned you?"

"I again didn't tell him the whole truth."

"Are you familiar with the Hippocratic Oath?"

Pierce objected on the grounds of relevance.

Judge Tanner overruled and added, "I want to hear the answer to this question."

Garcia stumbled over his answer. He testified that it could be traced to the Greeks, that it required that physicians provide care, and that they first do no harm.

With the court's permission Davis read the oath and then asked Garcia, "You were Robyn Eden's doctor?"

"I was one of them."

"Did you violate your oath as her doctor?"

"I guess I did."

"When you called Valerie Daniels on the evening of July 4th, you didn't inform her that her sister had died, did you?"

"No."

"That was another example of you not telling the whole truth?"

"Yes. I wasn't thinking right. I was nervous and upset."

"You're nervous and upset right now, aren't you?"

"Yes."

"You're not telling this jury the whole truth, are you?"

"I've tried to."

"Well, you've done a pretty miserable job."

Pierce objected, and before Judge Tanner could rule, Davis sat down and announced no further questions.

CHAPTER SIXTY-THREE

THE DEFENDANT'S EXPERT PROOF

Friday, February 23, 2001

Harrelson's private eye earned his fee when he turned up the medical records proving Robyn Eden had two abortions. Using those documents, Pierce forced Davis into a stipulation, which Judge Tanner read to the jury. "The parties have entered into the following stipulation based upon authenticated medical records. The parties stipulate that Robyn Eden had an abortion on June 15, 1990, and December 29, 1993. The defendant was not the father in either of these pregnancies."

Pierce figured that Davis believed the stipulation was better than allowing Pierce to prove the abortions. In the end the abortions would be proven. Pierce actually liked how concisely these important facts entered into evidence.

She next called the first of her experts, Dr. Lawrence Porter, a toxicologist at Vanderbilt. He gave an impressive PowerPoint. His presentation was very factual, and he spoke in a very commanding voice.

Porter testified that oxycodone belonged to a class of drugs called narcotic analgesics; it is a painkiller. "Its active ingredient is oxycodone, and it comes in five doses: 10, 20, 40, 80, and 160 milligrams. It goes by the street names 'term,' 'kicker,' 'oxy,' 'Oxycotton,' 'pill ladies,' and 'pharming.' Robyn Eden used the two stronger doses of 80 and 160 milligrams.

"According to a recent National Survey on Drug Use and Health, approximately 2.8 million use oxycodone at least once recreationally. In 1999, sales of oxycodone exceeded $1 billion. That dollar amount has dramatically increased over the last two years. This opiate is highly addictive. It stimulates the brain to produce an artificial feeling of pleasure."

Professor Porter testified that oxycodone placed a strain on the cardiovascular system and that an overdose caused slow breathing, seizures, loss of consciousness, coma, vomiting, and severe diminished mental functions. Porter explained that IV use of the drug intensified the symptoms of the drug. He also stated that oxycodone withdrawal was truly horrific.

He testified that less than ten percent of oxycodone users achieve remission after one year on the drug. He testified that only four percent of IV users of oxycodone ever kick their habit. He testified, "Only twenty-four percent survive more than ten years of using the drug."

His testimony painted a dismal life expectancy for Robyn Eden. He further testified that seventy-four percent of the time the addict destroys the life of a loved one, who is unable to deal with the addict's use. He added, "Charles Garcia didn't have a chance. His relationship with Robyn Eden was statistically destined to fail."

Pierce kept it short and sweet. Davis asked five questions on cross but couldn't attack the statistics.

The judge called a comfort break, and when they returned, Pierce called Dr. Robert Townsend. Harrelson brought his IOUs to the courtroom; they were safe in his inside jacket pocket.

Dr. Townsend took the oath and, under Pierce's direct examination, laid out his education and professional background. He admitted he was being paid his normal hourly rate of $500 an hour. He failed to mention that his $200,000 IOUs would be ripped up if Charlie were acquitted. He lied and claimed he'd been treating Charles Garcia since 1998. He'd falsified his office records to support the lie.

When Pierce felt the jury was comfortable with Townsend, she started asking open-ended questions.

"Explain how you diagnosed Charles Garcia."

"I've spent one hundred forty hours interviewing Charles Garcia. One day I spent ten hours in therapy with him. It's a proven method. If I talk to patients long enough in a session, they reveal things about themselves they didn't intend to. I learned a lot about Charles that day. I've also interviewed his parents and his lawyers. I've read pleadings from various matters, Charles's depositions, and more than a hundred e-mails between Charles and Ms. Eden. I understand and I know Charles Garcia better than anyone, including the state's expert Dr. Limbaugh. He spent a few hours with Mr. Garcia. I read the testimony he gave last week, and I strongly disagree with him."

Townsend testified that Charles Garcia was the worst case of any enabler he'd ever seen. Charles Garcia wasn't an egotist and someone who sought to control, but a person who takes on hopeless causes, anticipating that he'd fail. "Enabling is a term often used in the context of a relationship with an addict. Usually the enabler suffers the effects of the addict's behavior, rather than the addict doing the suffering. Enabling removes consequences from behavior of the addict. Co-dependents often feel compelled to solve other people's problems. Enablers start off wanting to help but then get caught up in desperate situations.

"His last desperate act was to try to save his child. The child was doomed from inception. Charles Garcia sought to save lost souls.

"Why else would he get involved with Robyn Eden? Yes, she was beautiful, but Charles could have dated and pursued most women. Why pick an addict, and why stay with an addict? To pick the addict would be bad judgment. To stay with an addict and to keep coming back for more are the bases for his self-destructive syndrome.

"He testified to this earlier. Coming back at Senator Daniels's request was the biggest mistake of his life. He's lost everything that was important to him: his medical license, his freedom, and most of all, Robyn. I'm absolutely sure he loved her, as he understood love. He engaged in some outrageous behavior, but that was for Robyn, to serve her desires. He knew she'd have gone elsewhere, which was unacceptable to him."

Pierce had Townsend explain how Robyn and Charles fed off one another.

"She was an addict. It's what drove the relationship, and it's what drove him to try to save her. He failed, but that's not a crime. He shouldn't be punished any more than he has already. To do so wouldn't bring Robyn back. To do so would be to punish someone for an illness. It wouldn't be justice."

Pierce turned Dr. Townsend over to Davis for his cross-examination. Davis began slowly, but he was determined to crack the doctor's testimony.

"What is the term for the medical condition that Mr. Garcia is suffering from?"

"He has enabler syndrome. He can't help himself from trying to take on lost causes."

"And it's Mr. Garcia's behavior that supports your diagnosis?"

"Yes."

Davis pointed out that under the Tennessee Rules of Criminal Evidence, he was permitted to ask expert witnesses hypothetical questions.

"Hypothetically, if Mr. Garcia had sex with a woman going through a divorce, whose world had been turned upside down, would that be consistent with Mr. Garcia's syndrome?"

"That would be consistent with the syndrome."

"Hypothetically, if a woman had survived several failed relationships and had two abortions, would having sex with such a desperate woman be consistent with his syndrome?"

"Yes."

"So Mr. Garcia's syndrome is a license to abuse the weak and unprotected?"

"No. You're looking at the syndrome from the wrong side. Yes, the people he associates with have problems, but it is his behavior that is defined by the syndrome. He can't help himself. He's drawn to these losers."

Davis figured the collective jury would see Townsend's answer for what it was. He spent the next hour sparring with Dr. Townsend without a great deal of luck.

Davis sat down, and Pierce announced that the defendant was closing his proof.

Davis put Dr. Limbaugh on the stand as his rebuttal proof. Dr. Limbaugh pulled no punches. He'd been sitting in the audience during Dr. Townsend's testimony. Limbaugh called Dr. Townsend's professional opinions rubbish, paid-for mumbo jumbo.

Pierce objected several times. Judge Tanner ruled that each expert was entitled to his or her own professional opinions and that it was the job of the jury to sort them out.

It was close to the end of the day, so Judge Tanner called it quits. He promised the jury that they were getting close to the end of their journey. Then he posed a question to them: Did they want to work and deliberate over the weekend? He insisted that it was their choice and that they could announce their decision after they'd had an opportunity to discuss the issue.

The jurors adjourned to talk it over. Within a few minutes they returned, and the furniture store owner foreman reported, "The jury unanimously voted to deliberate both days and bring this process to a close, Your Honor."

CHAPTER SIXTY-FOUR

THE STATE'S FIRST CLOSING ARGUMENT

Saturday, February 24, 2001

The Davis team knew this was going to be an important day. Bella sat in the front row with Liza next to her.

Today explained why Judge Tanner had sequestered the jury. Local print, radio, and TV media were everywhere. Courtesy of Judge Tanner the *Hewes City Gazette* had a reserved place in the first row. The coverage had been very slanted against Charlie Garcia and his lifestyle.

The big boys were out and about too. The *New York Times, Washington Post, USA Today*, and AP had their knives sharpened. It was a good thing that the jury was allowed to only listen to music and watch movies on DVD. Open access to the media would have required a reversal of trial. Tanner would have no problem defending that ruling in front of the Court of Appeals.

Sammie and Morty were giving Davis a pep talk in the hallway. It was mere formality. He didn't need one.

The clerk came into the hallway to retrieve them; court was about to start. Judge Tanner and the jury walked in as they got to their table.

Judge Tanner wished everyone a good morning, then he turned to the jury foreman and stated, "A trial is supposed to be an orderly process. I want to commend the lawyers for their part of moving this case along. I'd also like to thank the jurors for their attentiveness and service.

"We're getting near the end of the process so I want to plan the rest of it out. Today we'll have three closing arguments, the first by the state. See, the state goes first and last because it's got the burden of proof. I remind you that the defendant doesn't have to prove anything. This is a serious case, and there are three hundred forty-six trial exhibits, most of which were exhibits from the Hewes City Police Department's investigation. I'm sure they will not review all of them with you, but they are going to cover the highlights.

"I suspect we will be hearing from the lawyers for several hours, well into the afternoon. I propose that we break for the day whenever the lawyers are finished. The next step in the process is the jury charge. That will take about an hour, and then we begin deliberations. I suspect that will begin about ten thirty on Sunday. I'm not here to tell you how to deliberate, but it would be reasonable to go through the exhibits and talk about each witness's testimony. Then you'll debate guilt or innocence on each count."

The judge completed his remarks, and he motioned for the state to give its closing argument.

Davis got up slowly. He was in the zone, focused only on that jury.

"Ladies and gentlemen of the jury, before I begin my remarks, on behalf of the state of Tennessee and Hewes County, I want to thank you for your service. Did you know it's a constitutional right to have a jury trial for any crime? You've been an instrument of the Constitution. You have a right to be proud."

Davis knew how to butter up a jury. He'd learned from the master.

"Ladies and gentlemen, I hope I'm not distracting you, but I've got to move around during this closing, so I can keep the blood in my legs flowing. Judge, I hope you won't tether me to this podium."

Judge Tanner respectfully responded, "I know you'll conduct yourself appropriately, Mr. Davis."

Davis thought that was a little help from the judge. He was telling the jury to listen to this guy; he's been around the block a time or two.

His plan was to get physically close to the jury. How an attorney conducted himself in a courtroom was part of being a great lawyer. Yes, you had to ask the right questions, clearly and authoritatively, but presence in the courtroom could be the swaying factor. It was a skill that could be taught. Morty learned it on his own and taught Davis and Sammie. Pierce had the skill too.

Davis moved closer and resumed, "I'm not going to handle many exhibits during this first closing. I certainly am never going to handle Mr. Garcia's sex toys. You've seen what he did with them. All of the exhibits will be available during your deliberations.

"Over the next hour or so, I want to prove to you that Mr. Garcia is a liar. The state has to prove the elements of each charge: second-degree murder and/or reckless homicide. I'll focus on those issues in my second argument.

"You may be wondering why I'm spending this valuable time to prove Mr. Garcia a liar. Ms. Pierce will argue so what if he's a liar? That doesn't prove he's a murderer. Well, that's true, but if you conclude that he's a liar, then as Judge Tanner will instruct you, his whole testimony can be thrown out, and you can base your verdict on circumstantial evidence. As the finder of the facts, you may make reasonable inferences from the evidence.

"My point is, if you disregard Mr. Garcia's testimony, then all of the circumstantial evidence that supports the charge of murder has greater weight and supports a conviction. I'll explain this point later in my closing."

Davis had the jurors' attention; they were hanging on his every word. He'd become each juror's professor in a school room, wise by years of experience.

"How plausible is this part of the defendant's testimony? Mr. Garcia claims that he didn't know that Robyn Eden was injecting narcotics by IV. That's an outright lie. His testimony is insulting to your intelligence. Don't forget Dr. Limbaugh's testimony. You're all pawns to be deceived and manipulated for Mr. Garcia's own purposes. At the time he was a medical doctor. He had lived with her and had the most intimate contact with Ms. Eden. You saw how close he got to her femoral area. He saw those linear injection sites. You're reasonable people. He suspected her use. Another insult to your intelligence!

"What about his shaving kit found in the master bathroom, where the crushed oxycodone and syringes were in plain view? He never explained why the kit was there. He claimed that he never went into the bathroom. He lied about not being in that bathroom.

"Ms. Pierce will argue that all the state has is circumstantial evidence as to the murder charge. That's not true. We have Mr. Garcia in his own voice and words proving his perjury. Remember this part of the video."

He played the snippet of video where Mr. Garcia stated clearly, "Put pressure on it."

"He didn't tell the paramedics that Ms. Eden had taken narcotics through an IV at her groin. No question from the video he knew she'd injected herself; she was bleeding. You heard the testimony of the paramedic, which was admitted by the defendant; he failed to disclose the IV drug use. That lie killed her. That information could have made a difference in her treatment and the outcome. He could have walked into the bathroom, collected the crushed oxycodone and the syringes, and given them to the paramedics. His testimony claims he didn't think of it. Another lie. He was a doctor. He knew better than you and I what was going on in that bathroom. You saw the video. She flew out of that bathroom like a top.

"He had one last chance when Dr. Mann questioned him at the hospital. He lied again. He fails to tell Dr. Mann about the IV drug use. This isn't a mistake. This is intentional. He made a mistake when he gave 911 the wrong address. That cost Ms. Eden four minutes and brought her that much closer to her death.

"And what about Dr. Mann's testimony? He was the only physician who actually examined Ms. Eden. Dr. Mann testified that the injection sites were linear. Both he and Dr. Davenport testified that only someone with medical training could have made such a pattern. Mann testified that whoever injected Robyn had medical training. Mr. Garcia was a licensed surgeon. She was a songwriter/receptionist."

Davis was under no time constraint. He talked straight through to lunch, and he did an articulate and convincing job.

Judge Tanner made a joke that maybe he should have put a time limit on the lawyers, but it was too late now.

CHAPTER SIXTY-FIVE

THE DEFENDANT'S CLOSING ARGUMENT

Saturday, February 24, 2001

Davis had put Pierce in a difficult position. There would be four hours of court time this afternoon, and if Pierce took as long as Davis, he might give his second closing argument the next day. That wasn't acceptable to Pierce. She called for a bench conference and forced Tanner out of fairness to require Davis to tell them how long his second close would take. His response was less than two hours, and she got Judge Tanner's commitment to finish closings today or, if necessary, tonight.

Pierce had to focus on the murder charge. Charlie Garcia was without question reckless. She'd argue to the contrary, but acquittal on count two was a long shot.

Pierce began, "We're almost at the end of our journey together. We've all invested a lot of time and energy, and after you're instructed by the judge, you'll deliberate and render a verdict. That's the whole purpose of this process. It's important that you get it right. A man's freedom for a very long time is at stake.

"As you have been told a number of times and will be told again in the jury charge by Judge Tanner, the burden of proof is on the state. In order to convict, it must prove beyond a reasonable doubt each element of each crime charged. It is critical that when you deliberate, you remember the definition of *beyond a reasonable doubt*, which is 'the standard that must be met by the prosecution's evidence in a criminal prosecution: that no other logical explanation can be derived from the facts except that the defendant committed the crime, thereby overcoming the presumption that a person is innocent until proven guilty. If the jurors or judge have no doubt as to the defendant's guilt, or if their only doubts are unreasonable doubts, then the prosecutor has proven the defendant's guilt beyond a reasonable doubt and the defendant should be pronounced guilty. The term connotes that evidence establishes a particular point to a moral certainty and that it is beyond dispute that any reasonable alternative is possible. It does not mean that no doubt exists as to the accused's guilt, but only that no reasonable doubt is possible from the evidence presented.'"

Pierce paused for effect. She wanted that definition to sink deeply into the minds of the jurors. She pointed out that Mr. Garcia claimed he didn't prescribe or give Robyn Eden the oxycodone. The state failed to prove that was a lie. The state would have introduced evidence of the prescription if there was one.

"Mr. Davis made certain predictions as to what I might say. He did that because he's a very smart man, and he knows the law. He was right that I'd argue that proving my client a liar does not prove he's a murderer."

Pierce figured she might as well give some fake deference to Davis; it brought her closer to the jury. "I'm sure you don't like Charlie Garcia. In your eyes he was born with a silver spoon in his mouth, had an incredible education, earned a profession, and then blew it. Dr. Townsend testified that he had no control of his own downfall.

Mr. Davis would say that's a lot of rubbish. You heard the testimony. You decide."

She was certain that the women on the jury despised Charlie Garcia. She was equally confident that the men didn't like him either, but a few envied him. He satisfied the fantasies of each man on the jury and then some.

Pierce walked back to the podium and got a drink of water. She didn't want to break up her next thought. She took three deep breaths and moved very close to the jury.

"Yeah, Mr. Davis is a very smart man and a good attorney, but he still can't answer these next few questions. Why doesn't Danny Nix's testimony create reasonable doubt as to who distributed or provided Robyn Eden with the oxycodone?

"Ms. Nix testified that she gave Ms. Eden eight pills for sex on June 30th. Her DNA was on Exhibit 146, so we know she was telling the truth about knowing Robyn Eden in the biblical sense. That proof alone creates reasonable doubt as to one of the critical elements of second-degree murder."

Again Pierce stopped for effect. This part of her argument would save Charlie Garcia from serving twenty-five years in jail.

"Mr. Davis could call Ms. Nix a liar, like he did Mr. Garcia, but why would she lie? Arguably the defendant has at least a motive to lie: avoid prison. What's her motive? I submit that by admitting that she traded the drugs that caused the death of Robyn Eden for sex only puts her in harm's way. The state might try to arrest her and prosecute her. She has no motive to lie. Let Mr. Davis explain that one.

"We know that Ms. Nix testified that she was intimate with Robyn Eden. We've got the best evidence to corroborate that testimony, her DNA on one side of Exhibit 146. It was drugs for sex, oxycodone."

Pierce was feeling pretty good. A murder conviction wasn't likely to happen.

"Danny Nix's testimony is fatal as to the murder charge. There's no proof the oxycodone came from the defendant. Maybe Mr. Davis can explain. Listen carefully when he stands up and summarizes the proof.

"Oh, yeah, let's not forget Robyn Eden's searches on the Internet for all different types of drugs including oxycodone. She got the drug through Nix, the Internet, or somewhere else on the street. There's more than reasonable doubt on this point."

Pierce spent the next twenty minutes arguing that there was reasonable doubt through expert testimony if the oxycodone actually was the cause of the overdose. Robyn Eden had taken hydrocodone for years, both orally and by IV. It was possible, with a reasonable degree of medical certainty, that the filler over time clogged her small arteries, causing death. She reminded the jury that if the proximate cause of death wasn't the oxycodone, a Schedule II drug, then there was no possibility of a murder conviction.

She said, "If the cause was anything else, then you can't find beyond a reasonable doubt that Charles Garcia murdered Robyn Eden. If you find that the oxycodone killed Ms. Eden, then you must find beyond reasonable doubt that the source was the defendant. In light of Ms. Nix's testimony, you must acquit on the murder charge."

Over the next thirty minutes Pierce discussed reckless homicide and why the jury shouldn't convict. She could tell from the jurors' faces that Charlie was in trouble. It was difficult to argue convincingly that Charlie Garcia didn't act recklessly.

She finished by reminding them, "Charles Garcia doesn't have to prove anything. That's the state's burden. The judge will charge what all of the elements of that crime are, and the state must prove them beyond a reasonable doubt."

Pierce thanked the jury and sat down. It was four forty-five.

Judge Tanner gave the jurors a comfort break, and when they returned, he told them that Mr. Davis was up last and they'd finish tonight. The jury chose to take an early dinner and come back at six to hear Mr. Davis after they'd eaten.

CHAPTER SIXTY-SIX

THE LAST WORD

Saturday, February 24, 2001

The Davis team elected to skip dinner and talk about Pierce's closing and how Davis should respond to the questions she posed. They went back to their small office in the DA's offices. Davis found some peanut butter and crackers and shared them with his co-counsel. He ate twice as many as either Morty or Sammie. He was famished. He'd eaten nothing since lunch and was feeling a little anxious.

They sat around the small conference table and asked the same question they'd asked before. Somehow it seemed very relevant again. How the hell did Pierce find Nix? She testified that she'd never met Charlie Garcia. That was probably a lie, but the state never proved that lie. Who else, other than Garcia, could have found this witness?

Davis was the one under fire, so he broke the ice. "I've got to call Nix a liar, and I'm confident she is, but what's her motive? Did she hate Robyn, or is this self-proclaimed lesbian in love with Charlie Garcia? If we had video of any combination of a threesome, I could explain their testimony and even Nix's DNA and the lie. I bet there is a video of a threesome; it just wasn't in plain view. Even if we could find those videos today, it's too late. They're not in evidence."

411

Davis announced that the tail he put on Nix after she testified confirmed she'd left not only Hewes County but also the state of Tennessee. That information was provided to Davis courtesy of the TBI. Davis was a state prosecutor, so he called in a favor with the TBI. Nix got on a plane to Atlanta and then had reservations to go to Rio. She was gone and with her a motive.

"What about the old faithful motive of monetary gain?" suggested Sammie.

Morty was quick to respond, "We didn't prove it."

Davis stayed quiet a few minutes. Morty and Sammie were watching him carefully, waiting for him to share his thoughts.

Finally he spoke, "We ask the jury to infer it from her character. Is Nix the type of person who would engage in a threesome? Is Nix the type of person who would take money for false testimony? Pierce will object and Tanner might sustain, but the seed will be planted. I've got nothing better. That's what I'm going with."

No one had a better suggestion so that became the response to Pierce as to Nix's motive.

They entered the courtroom, and Davis marched straight to the podium. It was six on the dot. Davis knew he had to be mindful of the time. Pierce had successfully limited his argument to less than two hours, and it would have been a mistake to keep the jury the full two hours until eight o'clock.

For forty-five minutes Davis methodically went over the important exhibits and testimony with the jury. It wasn't as theatrical as his first closing, but it was informative and refreshed the jury's recollection of the proof. He then turned to Pierce's questions. He answered the easier ones first.

"As to the motive behind Ms. Nix's testimony, I want you to know I've given this a lot of thought. Danny Nix admitted she exchanged

412

drugs for sex. You got to watch her testify and are the sole judges of her credibility. Did you think she was a truthful witness? She testified that sex with Robyn Eden was the best she ever had. Maybe she engaged in a threesome with Robyn and Charlie Garcia?"

Pierce jumped up and yelled, "Objection, there's no proof of that in evidence."

Judge Tanner didn't rule right away. Davis suspected he was contemplating the impact on appeal if he overruled Pierce's objection.

He cleared his throat and said, "The jury is the judge of the credibility of the witness. If this jury believes Ms. Nix lied and gave false testimony, then the jury can infer whatever motive the jury deems plausible. Mr. Davis is suggesting a possible motive. The jury must determine whether that motive is valid. Overruled, Ms. Pierce."

With a green light from Tanner, Davis floated the idea that Nix accepted monetary compensation for her testimony. There really wasn't a factual basis, except that the allegation was true.

Davis finished up by thanking the jurors for their service and wished them good luck in their deliberations. It was seven thirty-eight, and Judge Tanner let the jurors go to their hotel.

CHAPTER SIXTY-SEVEN
JURY CHARGE
AND THE VERDICT
Sunday, February 25, 2001

Judge Tanner welcomed the jury and explained how the day would proceed, "I'm about to read to you the jury charge. A copy of this document will be available in the jury room, just like each of the exhibits. Listen carefully, but remember if you need to refresh your recollection, it will be in the room for your review.

"After I instruct you, I will randomly draw three names, and those jurors will be excused. The remaining twelve will begin deliberations."

Judge Tanner gave the preliminary charge, the portion of the charge that applied in every criminal case and every jury trial. He explained that as a jury, they were a collective body, and it was each member's obligation to listen to each other. They were to weigh the evidence, the documents made exhibits, and the testimony from the witness stand. They were the judges of the facts. They had to sort through the conflicting testimony and find the truth.

The judge explained that the judge charged the defendant with two counts: second-degree murder and reckless homicide. "Each of these crimes has separate elements that must be proven to convict. You can prove second-degree murder two ways. These are two distinct subsections. If you prove either of them beyond a reasonable doubt, then you must convict for second-degree murder. The first is the knowing killing of another that results from the unlawful distribution of a Schedule II or I when such drug is the proximate cause of the death of the user.

"The question you must answer under the first definition is whether the state proved beyond a reasonable doubt that Charles Garcia knowingly killed Robyn Eden.

"Under the second subsection, you must ask yourself the question, did the state prove beyond a reasonable doubt that Charles Garcia distributed, either sold or gave Robyn Eden oxycodone, a Schedule II drug, and that such drug was the proximate cause of her death. If you find those elements beyond a reasonable doubt, then you must convict for second-degree murder. If you find that the hydrocodone was the cause of Robyn Eden's death, then you must acquit on the second-degree murder charge because hydrocodone is a Schedule III drug, not I or II.

"Second-degree murder is a Class A felony punishable by a minimum prison term of ten years to a maximum of life imprisonment."

Judge Tanner next discussed the elements of count two, reckless homicide: "A reckless homicide is a killing by reckless conduct. A defendant acts recklessly when the state proves beyond a reasonable doubt that he or she is aware of, but consciously disregards a substantial and unjustifiable risk of such a nature that its disregard constitutes a gross deviation from the standard of care that an ordinary person would exercise under all of the circumstances.

"Reckless homicide is a Class E felony. It is punishable by an imprisonment of a minimum of one year to a maximum of five years."

The judge spent twenty minutes discussing the law and the jury process, "I want each of you to take pride in what you're about to do.

You're part of a very important process. I have absolute confidence you'll sort through all the evidence and find justice for the defendant, the victim, the victim's family, and our community. Go and deliberate."

The jurors filed out to do their job.

Davis, Sammie, and Morty went back to the DA's offices and found some cards and started playing gin. Davis sucked one Tootsie Pop after another. His favorite flavor was raspberry; he avoided the chocolate ones. Morty and Sammie played the first hand, and then the winner played Davis. Morty was the better player, and he quickly started racking up the points. Davis got tired of cards and suggested that they walk over to Mother's and get some lunch.

They told the judge's clerk where they were going in case the judge needed them. They didn't even get a chance to order. The judge's clerk showed up and informed them that the jury had three questions. Everybody rushed back to the courtroom.

Pierce and Garcia were waiting.

Judge Tanner took the bench and announced, "We've got three questions. The first is, can they see the videotape? Any objection? It's an exhibit."

No one objected, and arrangements were made to deliver the necessary equipment to the jury room.

The second question required more debate. The jury wanted a layman's definition of the elements of second-degree murder and reckless homicide.

In the hope the jury would understand the crimes, Davis argued for the court to simplify the terms, but Pierce objected, "The law is the law." She suggested that the judge simply direct them to the pages of the charge that defined the terms. She argued that the jury was obligated to apply that law even if it was difficult to understand.

Tanner agreed and sent a note directing the jurors to pages 11, 15, and 16.

The third question was very telling. The jury asked if the fact that the defendant was a doctor was to be considered in whether he acted recklessly. There was some debate, and Tanner ruled that the fact that he was a doctor was one of the circumstances of the case. They should consider his conduct as an ordinary person with medical training.

Davis, Sammie, and Morty returned to Mother's, where Davis ordered steak and biscuits, French fries, and a chocolate milkshake. Sammie and Morty split a turkey club. After they ordered, there was a long silence.

Sammie broke the ice: "I can't believe they wanted to watch that video for a third time. Do you think it was for the audio portion where he directs her to put pressure on the bleeding wound or for the sexual escapades?"

"The sex. It's both horrifying and titillating."

"Morty Steine, that's disgusting!"

"Sammie, you might be right, but that doesn't make it any less true."

Davis agreed, and they ate lunch with no more conversation. He ate when he was nervous, and his full plate gave an indication of how he was feeling. The other two were nervous also. The afternoon dragged out; more cards and Morty kept winning. Davis drank one Fresca after another. Waiting on a jury was the hardest part of practicing law.

At three o'clock the phone rang, and Sammie picked it up. The jury had reached a verdict.

The Davis team scampered over to the courthouse. Judge Tanner was already on the bench when Pierce walked in. Escorted by a sheriff's deputy, Garcia took his place next to Pierce.

Judge Tanner addressed the parties, "Before we hear from the jury and know the outcome of this trial, I want to commend the lawyers for the fine job they did. This was a complicated case, and they conducted themselves in an ethical and professional manner. Sure, we had our disputes and heated moments, but that's just part of the process. We each play our parts trying to move it forward. It was an honor to preside over this case."

The jury was brought in. Tanner wasted no time with pleasantries. He wanted to get to the verdict. "Have you reached a unanimous verdict?"

Randy Mayer, the foreman, responded, "Yes, sir."

"As to count one, second-degree murder, how does the jury find?"

"Not guilty."

Charlie Garcia squeezed Pierce's hand. Harrelson, in an unusual exhibition of emotion, hugged Eddie Garcia. Charlie's mother, Kiki, was in tears. The Davis team was visibly shaken.

"Reckless homicide, how does the jury find?"

"Guilty as charged."

Tanner asked both sides if they wanted to poll the jurors and have them announce their verdict individually. Both sides declined.

Judge Tanner told the courtroom that if a juror wanted, and only if a juror wanted, he or she could share with the lawyers the deliberations and reasons behind the verdict. Some jurors wanted to leave the courthouse, but most were willing to talk to the lawyers.

Judge Tanner announced that Mr. Garcia would remain in the custody of the Hewes County sheriff pending sentencing, which he scheduled for Wednesday, February 28th.

Tanner adjourned court, and Pierce and the Davis team ran to engage the jury. As planned, they separated, covering three times the ground that Pierce could. They formed little pockets of one or two jurors with each lawyer.

Sammie sat with the assistant manager of Kroger and two of the housewives. Davis spoke with the foreman, Mayer, and the car salesman. Morty held court with four or five jurors. Pierce sat with the two older women. She was interested in their view of the sexual evidence. It all didn't matter; she'd gotten Charlie off on the murder charge. She earned her fee. It was a madhouse but informative.

The jury had little debate about whether the defendant's conduct was reckless. He was found unanimously guilty on that count on the first vote after they reviewed the exhibits and the testimony. Based upon the interviews, the Davis team learned that the jury despised Charlie Garcia. They also didn't think much of Robyn Eden. Most jurors had no sympathy for her.

No one bought Dr. Townsend's diagnosis or testimony. The jury thought that Dr. Limbaugh got it right, yet the jury did not convict for murder. Davis learned at one point it was eight to four to convict for murder, but the minority successfully argued that Danny Nix's testimony created reasonable doubt as to who gave or sold her the oxycodone.

As a basis for the finding of not guilty, each juror cited Ms. Pierce's unanswered challenge: Why would Nix lie? Davis's explanation did not answer the question beyond a reasonable doubt.

The jury also found there was reasonable doubt about what killed her. The oxycodone or the filler combined with the hydrocodone over time?

In a way a guilty verdict only on reckless homicide would be much easier to defend on appeal than a murder conviction. All of the lawyers in the courtroom and Judge Tanner knew that unless Garcia was sentenced to probation, there would be an appeal.

Morty, Sammie, and Davis left the courthouse licking their wounds.

CHAPTER SIXTY-EIGHT

SENTENCING

Wednesday, February 28, 2001

Although the verdict disappointed the Davis team, Charlie Garcia's sentencing would be a joyous event. His recent conviction wasn't Charlie Garcia's only problem.

Charlie's first problem was his conviction violated his probation in Kentucky. He no longer had protection from the retired Baxter, and DA Peter Taylor hated him. The day of the verdict Davis called DA Taylor and notified him of Garcia's parole violation. He was a convicted felon. Taylor assured Davis that Garcia would soon be arrested, be ushered in front of a judge, and be serving his three-year sentence by April 1st.

Convicted of a Class E felony, Garcia faced a minimum sentence of one year to a maximum sentence of five years. Under Tennessee law, Judge Tanner had absolute discretion as to the term of the sentence. He heard the proof. The Court of Appeals would just affirm the length of the sentence as long as the evidence supported the jury verdict.

Under Tennessee law, there were thirteen enhancement factors that the state could argue suggested the maximum sentence should be imposed, and there were thirteen mitigating factors that indicated the minimum was appropriate. Not every factor was applicable to each case.

In the Garcia case the state had filed a brief, which argued that three of the thirteen enhancing factors applied. The state asserted that Mr. Garcia had a previous relevant criminal history, he was on probation, and his conduct violated that probation.

The defendant in briefs argued several mitigating factors were applicable. He asserted that his conduct was excused or justified; that he had no intent to violate the law; that he'd been under intense psychiatric counseling; and that jail wouldn't rehabilitate this defendant.

The state went first and last. Davis called Valerie Daniels to the stand. She was dressed immaculately and didn't appear nervous. She took the oath, and Davis asked if she had a prepared statement.

She responded affirmatively and began to read, "I want to thank the jury and the court for all their effort in the prosecution of Mr. Garcia for the murder of my sister Robyn. I know we fell short on the murder charge. That was because the jury was compelled to find murder beyond a reasonable doubt. It's a tough standard to prove. You heard the proof, and in sentencing you're not bound by that high standard. For example you can, based upon Dr. Mann's testimony concerning the linear pattern of the injection sites, find that Mr. Garcia injected Robyn in the groin during the long holiday. He was the instrument of her death. I understand you'll be hearing Dr. Limbaugh's testimony again. He was the most credible expert witness, I heard. The testimony of Dr. Townsend was insulting to our intelligence.

"The death of my sister cannot be reimbursed. There is no amount of jail time that would satisfy me, but that's not the purpose of this hearing. Justice is what needs to be satisfied, not me.

Justice dictates the maximum sentence of five years. Thank you for listening to my thoughts on this matter."

Davis thought Daniels did a much better job this time in court than under Pierce's cross-examination. The statement allowed her to speak her mind without Pierce's interference. In fact Davis knew the words weren't those of Daniels but of her speechwriter in Washington.

Davis called Dr. Limbaugh and conducted an abbreviated examination. Judge Tanner heard his testimony recently so Davis hit only the highlights. Dr. Limbaugh's opinion of Charles Garcia hadn't improved. He testified that based on the pleading filed by Ms. Pierce, it was clear that through the mitigating factors relied upon, Garcia was trying to manipulate the court. He testified that when Charles Garcia took the stand, every other word would be a lie spoken for the sole purpose of reducing his sentence. Davis thought that was probably true of every convicted defendant who testified at his or her sentencing hearing.

Davis gave a short summation, since he knew he'd have the last word. He hoped that Pierce would make the mistake of putting Dr. Townsend on the stand.

In conclusion Davis argued, "The court knows that I am not an experienced prosecutor. I promised the citizens of Tennessee to do my best. I did secure a conviction for reckless homicide. I submit the proof on that count was overwhelming. I've looked at the enhancement and mitigating factors that are applicable to this case, and one factor overshadows them all.

"In 1999 this man was given probation, not only for the same conduct, but also in regard to the same victim. He learned nothing from his narrow escape and just repeated his reckless conduct. This man needs to serve the maximum sentence. Thank you."

It was the defense's turn. As anticipated, Pierce had Charles

Garcia read a statement. Like Davis, Pierce didn't want her client cross-examined. The statement was a lot cleaner and safer. Charlie talked about how much he'd learned about himself from this tragedy. He attested his love for Robyn and the sorrow he felt without her. The loss of his child only added to his pain. He read with tremendous emotion, but his words fell on deaf ears. Dr. Limbaugh had convinced everyone in the courtroom, including the judge, that his attempt at remorse was simply self-serving lies.

Even Charlie realized his statement was falling short so he skipped the last four paragraphs and went to the conclusion: "A longer prison sentence isn't going to rehabilitate me. Jail isn't going to rehabilitate me. I've lost everything, including Robyn, who I loved with all my heart. If placed on probation, I would dedicate myself to helping others. I do have skills, even if I can't be called Dr. Garcia."

In summation, Pierce had a few choice words. She criticized the state for charging her client with murder. She argued that the decision to appoint Mr. Davis as a special prosecutor was politically driven and that Mr. Davis and Mr. Steine had their own agenda. She made several of the same arguments that she made in closing to the jury. After fifteen minutes she sat down, figuring she did her job when the jury acquitted Charlie on the murder charge. Charlie Garcia was about to be sentenced to whatever amount of time Judge Tanner deemed appropriate. She'd make money on the appeal.

Judge Tanner went over the elements of the crime and the enhancing and mitigating factors applicable to the case: "This defendant started life with everything. God gave him the intelligence to go to the best schools, which he was lucky his parents could afford. He was given the best training and had a good profession. He was not a kid from the streets who was born with two strikes against him.

"A young woman died as a direct and proximate result of his

reckless conduct. I think he lied several times during his testimony, which clouded the murder charge. I can't prove it, but I think he suborned perjury. I seriously question the testimony of Ms. Nix, but the state failed to sufficiently challenge that testimony. I agree with the jurors that her testimony did create reasonable doubt as to the murder count and so that count should have been dismissed.

"I agree with Mr. Davis that all of the enhancing and mitigating factors pale in comparison to the fact that the defendant was on probation for almost identical conduct involving the same victim. I use that term loosely. Ms. Eden, despite the testimony of the experts from both sides, was a willing participant in her own destruction, but there's no question in my mind that the defendant pushed her along.

"I remind the defendant of a portion of the Hippocratic Oath, 'Into whatever patient setting I enter, I will go for the benefit of the sick and will abstain from every voluntary act of mischief or corruption and further from seduction of any patient.' I've viewed that videotape too many times, but there's no question the defendant violated that part of his oath.

"For the reasons stated I hereby sentence the defendant to the maximum time prescribed by the statute, five years."

He asked, "Ms. Pierce, do you have a motion?"

Pierce made a motion for a new trial, which was denied before Mr. Davis could stand up. The motion was a mere formality for the appeal.

Judge Tanner inquired about whether Ms. Pierce intended to file a notice of appeal.

"Yes, sir. I'll file the necessary documents tomorrow. The defendant moves for the defendant to remain on bond during the pendency of the appeal."

Before Davis could stand, Judge Tanner ruled, "Ms. Pierce, I'm going to grant that motion for fifteen days, to be reviewed after the expiration of that time period. I will also add a few additional conditions. The bond is increased from $1 to $4 million. As further security, Sheriff Buford Dudley will assign a deputy to the defendant's leased residence, 24/7, to further guarantee that he remains there under house detention with the ankle bracelet. The defendant shall reimburse the sheriff's office the cost of these assigned deputies. Are those conditions agreeable, Ms. Pierce?"

"Absolutely, Your Honor."

Judge Tanner smiled and signed the prepared order relating to the continuation of the bond. Davis noticed a devilish smile on Tanner's face. He didn't have to wait long.

"I'd like to share a phone call I received this morning from DA Peter Taylor. He assured me that within the next two weeks he'd be extraditing Mr. Garcia to Kentucky to begin serving his three-year sentence. After that and the exhaustion of your appeal, Mr. Garcia can be a guest of the state of Tennessee."

Without another word, Tanner left the bench.

CHAPTER SIXTY-NINE

CONFRONTATION WITH AN EX
Monday, March 12, 2001

Until recently, Dan hadn't asked to see Carter. He wasn't much of a father, even though Carter wanted to know him. Pierce wanted to prevent it and protect her son. She was contemplating what to do.

Other than the reappearance of Dan in Carter's life, Pierce's life was going pretty good. Her firm was prospering. The Garcia appeal was progressing. It would take years and would mean hundreds of thousands in fees. She deserved it; Charlie was acquitted for the murder of Robyn Eden; reckless homicide was manageable. Charlie was out on appeal under house arrest, but unfortunately he'd simultaneously be serving twenty months or so of the three-year 1999 Derby sentence.

That was Charlie Garcia's problem, not hers. She'd done a great job, and as a reward for herself and for Carter, she'd decided to put in a swimming pool and was looking forward to summer. The swimming pool company had dug the hole, and the plan was to install the rebar and pour the concrete tomorrow.

Carter was spending the night with Pierce's great-aunt, the one who was the librarian at Pierce's alma mater, Harpeth Hall, and who'd raised her.

Pierce answered the knock on the door. Dan, her ex, was standing there and gave her a hug. It was one of those awkward hugs where both parties stick their backsides out, avoiding any genital contact.

She explained that Carter was spending the night elsewhere, so they could discuss Dan's visitation of their son openly and candidly. Pierce insisted that if he were going to begin seeing Carter on any regular basis, there had to be ground rules, and those rules would be reduced to writing. She took his jacket and hung it in the hall closet.

"You've got to be kidding. After everything I've done for you, you're going to make me jump through hoops to see my son? You're making a big mistake if you think you can treat me like that."

Their discussion was going south quickly. Pierce needed to take charge of the situation. That wasn't hard when her ex-husband was a drunk, an addict, and still madly in love with her.

Dan wanted to reenter Pierce's life, and the first step was to negotiate visitation of Carter. He believed if he could get a foothold, he could wiggle his way back into Pierce's life. Pierce had no such plans. Her plan was to get the drunk permanently out of their lives.

"Let's have a shot of tequila and bury the hatchet."

They did four, and the mood mellowed. Pierce served crab cakes and little eggrolls as appetizers to start. The conversation was pretty normal, except Dan began to slur his words after the sixth shot. He said, "I'd like to see Carter every Saturday if that's all right with him."

"I'll agree, but only if you agree to random drug tests."

Dan exploded, "Go to hell, you crooked bitch. Don't get high and mighty with me. I know you for what you are. You're no better than me. You'd do anything to win: lie, steal, and falsify evidence. I've got the power over you. If I wanted, you'd be disbarred, and you'd go to jail."

Pierce bit her tongue and excused herself to get the main course.

When she came back, Dan was still fuming. "And another thing, I want some respect around here. You can't treat me like dirt. If you're not careful, I'll spill the beans and destroy you."

She set the plates down. She had prepared a stir-fry with chicken, shrimp, pineapple, and a ton of fresh vegetables.

"Let's eat, and we'll argue some more after dinner. We might as well eat while it's hot."

She started eating with chopsticks, and he followed. She didn't cook much, but this was one of their favorite homemade dishes when they were a couple living in New York City.

Dan started coughing, which got progressively worse. Pierce suggested that they have dessert out on the patio, and she showed him the hole for the new pool. Even though it was March the weather was warm enough to construct the pool and pour the concrete. After a few minutes, Dan started clearing his throat, a noise their son made when he was having an allergic reaction.

"You shouldn't threaten me, Dan. It's a big mistake. I'm smarter than you, and it's just plain dangerous."

He cleared his throat again, louder this time. His color changed. His normally pale complexion went bright red. He was having some problems breathing.

Pierce smiled and looked hard at her ex. He'd underestimated her. What a fool!

He tried to talk to her, but a strange noise, not words, came out. His throat was tightening. He and Carter had the same allergy to nuts.

Maybe she shouldn't have cooked the stir-fry in peanut oil. It wasn't an honest mistake. Dan was suffocating in front of her, and she intended to do nothing, even though there was an EpiPen in the refrigerator for Carter, and Dan brought one in his inside coat pocket. Either of those pens could have reversed his distress.

Dan tried to stand up, presumably to get to his jacket, but he fell down hard on the patio. Pierce just watched, offering no assistance. His breathing got very shallow, and within fifteen minutes he was dead. Pierce checked his pulse to confirm the threat was terminated.

Dan was a disease that Pierce wouldn't let back into her life or Carter's. He'd served his purpose. All he was now was an unnecessary liability.

No one knew about this dinner. Carter wasn't expected home until the next afternoon. Pierce took a few minutes just staring at Dan's lifeless body. He'd hurt her, but even worse he'd hurt Carter. She smiled. *Dan Smith got what he deserved.*

Pierce took another shot of tequila. She dragged his body to the edge of the pool hole and rolled Dan into it. She took off all her clothing, except her bra and panties, and grabbed a shovel that she had strategically placed earlier.

She jumped into the pool bottom. The ground was soft as part of the pool prep. She looked down at Dan, who had a twisted smile on his face, and started digging. After about an hour she had dug a four-foot-deep hole. She pushed the body in the hole and placed the bottle of peanut oil in Dan's right hand. Pierce had a strange sense of humor. When she was finished, Dan's body just became part of the landscape. The next day it would be covered by concrete.

The threat was gone. He'd never threaten her again. He'd never bother Carter again. Pierce cleared the dishes and any evidence that Dan Smith had reentered her life. He was a part of her past and represented the sleazy side of her. Carter represented the best part. She planned on focusing on him and her law practice.

She looked in the mirror and thought, *I've made it. All my hard work and determination has paid off. The end justifies the means.*

CHAPTER SEVENTY

JUSTICE IS KINDA SERVED

Thursday, March 15, 2001

After sentencing, DA Taylor ran into obstacles in extraditing Charlie Garcia. Several days passed, and Garcia was still in his rental house under guard by the Hewes County Sheriff's Office. The notice of appeal for the reckless homicide conviction had been filed. It would be years before the Tennessee Court of Appeals would either reverse or affirm the conviction. If not for the Kentucky parole violation, Garcia would remain under house arrest for the next few years.

In a meeting in Judge Tanner's chambers, the judge continued the conditions of bond, except he increased the bond by another million, to $5 million. Visitation was limited to his parents, his lawyers, and his treating psychiatrist, Dr. Townsend. Judge Tanner drafted an order with these conditions of house detention. The order set a term of three months, and then the conditions would be reviewed. Tanner expected Kentucky to take possession of Charlie Garcia long before the order expired.

Charlie Garcia remained in the Hewes County jail for two days while his father raised the additional funds. Davis felt a little satisfaction that Garcia spent two days behind bars.

Davis monitored Charlie Garcia's home detention through his old friend Hewes County Sheriff Buford Dudley. Davis got informal weekly reports. According to Dudley, Charlie Garcia was despondent and under intense psychiatric care. The logs showed that the doctor came three times a week and stayed at least an hour. The log also showed visits from Pierce, Harrelson, and Señor Garcia.

Davis thought that Garcia got off easy, and he felt no sympathy for him. He still got to read, watch TV, and Davis was sure, look at Internet porn. Davis didn't forgive and forget. Robyn Eden couldn't do any of those things.

Since the trial, Davis reflected on what went wrong and what went right. He wanted to learn from the Garcia trial, not simply lick his wounds and move on. The first big mistake was the state trying to satisfy the demands of Valerie Daniels. Because of her power and influence, she forced the state to overreach in its charge of second-degree murder. That wasn't his team's fault; they inherited the indictment.

Second, the Hewes City police screwed up the investigation in many ways. Haber gave a false affidavit to obtain the first search warrant. She didn't do it intentionally, but in the rush of the early morning of July 5th, serious mistakes were made. Haber also lost the three pill bottles, or they magically disappeared from the evidence locker. Then she erased the cell phone pictures.

Haber was lucky the jury didn't convict her of a crime instead of Garcia. It was just like the OJ trial. Pierce put the police on trial. Again, the police investigation and the faulty search warrants were before Davis's appointment as special prosecutor. That was baggage he was stuck with.

Third, Robyn Eden was not a sympathetic victim. She was young and beautiful, so women jurors resented her from the start. She wasn't satisfied with what God gave her, and in return for sex she received free surgical services. She also used powerful drugs when she knew she was pregnant. A jury might excuse an occasional glass of white wine, but IV drug use was criminal. That didn't play well with any of the jurors. She was a sexual deviant and a drug addict. The jury didn't identify with her, and she became less than human, something dirty. Davis reminded himself that you don't get to pick the victim; the murderer does that.

Fourth, the testimony of Nix muddied the water as to the source of the drugs. Davis knew from interviewing jurors after the verdict that they begrudgingly accepted the testimony of the drug dealer because Nix's DNA placed her with Eden. The consensus, after much debate, was that Charlie Garcia knew what drugs she was using and knew that she was injecting the drug in her groin. The audio of the videotape proved that.

The fifth and final factor was the burden of proof. Davis as a civil trial lawyer operated under the restriction of having to prove his case by a preponderance of the evidence. All he had to do was tip those scales of justice ever so slightly in his client's favor. He'd been taught well and knew how to do that. In that setting the lawyer's skills and effectiveness often made the difference in the outcome of the case. In a criminal trial the state was required to prove its case beyond a reasonable doubt. That was an incredibly difficult threshold to meet.

Davis wondered whether in the Garcia case justice would be served. Garcia lost two medical licenses and a bright future, and he was facing jail time. The trial was complex, so the appeal had meat to it, and a reversal and a new trial were always possibilities. Davis dreaded the possibility of a retrial. If asked, he would do it because it would be the right thing to do, but he wouldn't like it. That made accepting the responsibility even more important.

Things were getting back to normal at the office, and Bella's life improved. She finally had other bodies in the office. She'd been running it almost exclusively by herself, with a little help from Sammie. After taking a few days off, Davis was back in the swing of things. He and Sammie were solving other people's problems. Morty spent most of his day napping in the ninth-floor loft but joined the team for lunch and some of his storytelling.

Davis was enjoying his second cup of coffee and leftover apple strudel brought in by Bella. His piece was twice the size of one a normal person would choose. Everyone had an addiction. At least his was legal.

Bella buzzed in. "I've got Sheriff Buford Dudley on the phone."

"Put him through." Davis figured his weekly report was a day early.

"Morning, Ben. I'm going to get right to the point. Charles Garcia is dead. Looks like a drug overdose. Looks like he took several pills orally. We'll know more when we get his complete blood work back. His heart just gave way. Isn't that the same cause of death as Robyn Eden? Do you find that ironic? We've declared it a suspicious death, and there will be an autopsy. I never liked Garcia, so I'm not going to shed any tears. I figure he got what he deserved."

Stunned, Davis said nothing.

Dudley continued, "I can't figure out how he got the drugs. He never left the house, and the visitor log over the last two weeks identifies his psychiatrist, Dr. Townsend; his lawyer, David Harrelson; his father; and Amy Pierce. It had to be one of them who supplied the drugs, but which one?"

Davis finally gained focus and answered Dudley, "Buford, who had the most to gain from Charlie Garcia's death?"

"I think that's the right question, Ben. I'm glad that someone else will have to figure out the answer. The Tennessee Bureau of Investigation has jurisdiction. I've turned the matter over to the TBI; let them figure out this mess."

Davis thought a minute, "If I were a guessing man, I'd speculate that the psychiatrist was prescribing medications for Garcia's depression and anxiety and, based on his history, a medication for sleep. If you save up enough Prozac, Xanax, and Ambien, you can overdose pretty easily."

Davis continued, "I don't think Pierce had anything to do with it. Garcia was her meal ticket. She stood to make close to half a million dollars on the appeal, and who knows what she'd make on a retrial?

"Same argument goes for Harrelson. He made a lot of money off Charlie Garcia over the years. I know for a fact he charged $800 an hour.

"And then there's Señor Garcia. Charlie had to be a big disappointment for him and his wife."

He'd dishonored the family name, which Davis knew was important to that aristocratic fool.

"Besides with Garcia's death, the $5 million bond is returned to the father. Disgrace and money are pretty good motives. But as you say, it's not our problem."

Dudley was digesting Davis's reasoning. He asked, "What will happen to Garcia's appeal in light of his death?"

"I guess it will be dismissed."

Two days later, Davis got the answer to the question.

Pierce didn't file a motion to dismiss the appeal. Instead she filed a motion to dismiss the charges against Garcia, arguing that a dead person couldn't be convicted of a crime. Therefore all charges should be dropped. The Court of Appeals agreed and directed Judge Tanner to enter an order dismissing all charges against Mr. Charles Juan Batista Garcia, deceased. Judge Tanner reluctantly did so.

Davis, Sammie, Morty, and Valerie Daniels were furious. Justice had not been served.

A week later Davis was sitting at his desk, reading a deposition in a medical malpractice case, when Bella interrupted him.

"I've got a messenger here, and he has a large envelope for you. He insists that it must be hand delivered to you and only you. He's got a release for your signature."

Annoyed but intrigued, Davis went to reception to sign and accept delivery of the envelope. He scribbled his name, the young man left, and Davis went back to his office.

Davis looked at the return address: Lee, Foster & Dee, a law firm in Salt Lake City. The law firm's envelope was taped to the outside of the manila one. In big red bold print it said, *INSTRUCTIONS; PLEASE READ BEFORE OPENING.*

Davis opened the instructions, which read,

> Dear Mr. Davis,
>
> We were instructed by our client Dan Smith to deliver this envelope to you if he did not call this office by the 10th of each month. Mr. Smith did not contact our office this March 10th so our delivery has been made. If you have any questions, please do not hesitate to contact me.
>
> Yours very truly,
>
> Marc Foster

He tore open the manila envelope, and an audiotape, a sheet of paper, and an eight-by-ten glossy fell onto his desk face up. Davis stared at the photo. It was of Amy Pierce, younger but very recognizable at the beach in an electric blue bikini. He first noticed her figure, but after that startling image, his eyes moved to the man standing next to her. He was in swim trunks, shirtless and athletic. On his right forearm was a tattoo. It was a T-rex with fiery yellow eyes. A shiver went down Davis's back.

He picked up the sheet of paper, which read,

> I am Dan Smith. I was married to Amy Pierce. In 1993 at her direction, I, together with two others, beat you up at your downtown office. You might recall, I told you "life's a very fragile thing."
>
> This New Year's Day, at the direction of Amy Pierce, I sabotaged Mr. Steine's plane, causing him to make an emergency landing.
>
> These admissions and accusations are proven by the enclosed audiotape. I figure you'll take it to the DA, and you'll get my ex disbarred and prosecuted.
>
> If you've received this envelope, then I'm dead. I loved her, and that was my weakness and downfall. She's devious and capable of anything. I learned that the hard way.
>
> I direct your attention to the fact that this handwritten affidavit is notarized and should be considered a dying declaration since it was transmitted only if I believed I was dead.
>
> I'll meet Amy in hell and deal with her then.
>
> Dan Smith

Davis leaned back in his chair and put his hands behind his head. He thought about the Plainview beating and his near death experience in Morty's Cessna earlier in the year. He no longer had to wonder who was at the bottom of those life-changing events. He now knew that it was Pierce who tried to scare him into submission in both the Plainview and Eden cases. If he'd been a scared man, who didn't have Morty Steine in his life to set his moral compass, he might have backed down. But Davis knew that the most important principle a man could strive to achieve was to always try to do the right thing.

Davis sat there deep in thought. He was thinking about the future. He often did that, trying to think five or six steps ahead of his adversaries. He concluded that despite the reliance on false evidence, it was too late to retry Charlie Garcia for the murder of Robyn Eden. Amy Pierce was another story. She was at risk of going to jail for a very long time. Justice might be served.

EPILOGUE
Wednesday, July 4, 2001

The Davises were preparing for their annual July 4th barbeque. They expected more than two hundred guests. It was a hot, humid day in Middle Tennessee, and the crowd would be hungry and thirsty. Davis was prepared.

It had been almost four months since the suicide of Charlie Garcia. That was the finding of the TBI. According to the report, Garcia accumulated pills provided by his treating psychiatrist, Dr. Townsend, and overdosed. Davis read the actual report and thought the TBI took the easy way out. Davis knew Pierce was capable of murder, and he suspected both Harrelson and Señor Garcia had their motives. The TBI ignored them and simply closed its investigation.

Despite the death of Charlie Garcia, his path of destruction continued. In early June, his mother, Kiki, died of a heart attack. Some say it was from a broken heart. According to sources, Señor Garcia was inconsolable for the loss of his wife and fled to the seclusion of his home in Majorca.

Liza stuck her head in Davis's home office and announced that Buford Dudley was in the foyer. He would like to have a few minutes. Davis walked to the front door and once inside his office offered Dudley a soft drink and a seat.

"I'll get right to the point. The TBI called me this morning and informed me that Danny Nix was found stabbed to death in an alley in Rio. They suspect it was a drug deal gone badly. She was one hell of a liar."

The death of a drug dealer wasn't that surprising. But what Davis and Dudley didn't know was that drugs had nothing to do with Nix's death. Greed killed Nix. About ten days after Charlie's conviction, Nix called Harrelson and demanded the balance of her money. Harrelson correctly pointed out that the second payment was due only if his client was acquitted, and he was convicted of reckless homicide. She was only entitled to a second payment if the appeal succeeded and the charges were dismissed. After Charlie's death and the dismissal of the conviction, Harrelson knew he was going to have to deal with Nix, one way or another. He decided that the better use of the $50,000 was to end the threat rather than feed it. Harrelson knew people, and Nix was history.

Davis turned to Dudley and asked, "What's the status of Pierce's indictment?"

Dudley turned a little red, and his voice squeaked, "The DA's office is getting cold feet. No body, no murder. Pierce is screaming harassment because she beat the Garcia murder charge. She claims her ex wanted visitation with their son, and when she refused he fabricated his own death. Her claims that he was a worthless addict and drunk have been confirmed. He was off the grid for years, and the DA's office thinks he faked his death and went off again."

"What about the letter? Smith went to a lot of trouble to set this up. Do they really think that letter is some elaborate hoax to create problems for Pierce?"

"I can't tell you what they're thinking, but she won't be indicted."

Dudley stood, shook Davis's hand, and left on that disappointing note.

Davis sat there fuming to himself, "That bitch is going to get away with murder. It was bad enough when she bent the rules to get Garcia off his murder charge. Then Garcia, by his own hand, escaped serving a day in either a Kentucky or a Tennessee prison. Is the system just falling apart? Is justice truly blind?"

Feelings of discouragement started to weigh Davis down, threatening to overwhelm his holiday spirit. Then he remembered all of the clients he'd helped. Some were all about the money, but others were life-changing events. He'd made a difference in the lives of his clients time and again. He was a great lawyer, who'd been taught to operate in a broken and flawed system. His job was to fight for his clients within the bounds of the law and ethics and to always try to do the right thing.

GLOSSARY
OF LEGAL TERMS

Answer—the responsive document filed by a defendant to a complaint.

Attorney pro tempore—appointment of private citizen as a special prosecutor.

Bad faith—when an insurance company has an opportunity to settle within its insured's policy limits and fails to do so.

Beneficiaries—the parties who receive money or property under a will.

Beyond a reasonable doubt—the burden of proof in a criminal case. The highest possible burden of proof, no other logical alternative.

Breach of contract—when a party to a contract materially fails to perform.

Co-executors—two parties who jointly administer an estate.

Complaint—the document that starts a lawsuit and spells out what the defendant did wrong.

Counterclaim—when the defendant turns around and sues the plaintiff who brought the lawsuit.

Cross-examination—when the opposing attorney asks a witness questions.

Defendant—the party who is sued.

Direct examination—when an attorney puts a witness on the stand and asks questions.

Fiduciary duty—the highest duty that can be owed by one person to another, such as attorney and client.

Guarantee—when one party stands for the debt of another.

Impeachment evidence—when evidence is presented that contradicts evidence already introduced.

Impeachment witness—when a witness contradicts the testimony of a previous witness.

Malpractice—when a professional provides services that are below the standard of care expected of a reasonable professional.

Motion for a directed verdict—when a defendant asks the court to dismiss the charges after the state has closed its proof.

Motion for summary judgment—when a party claims that there are no material facts in dispute, and the case as a matter of law should be decided by the judge, not the jury.

Motion in limine—preliminary motion filed by a party to resolve evidentiary issues prior to trial.

Negligence—an act or omission that falls below the standard of care expected of a reasonable person.

Non-compete clause—a contractual provision that prohibits an employee from working in competition with a former employer within a certain geographic area for a specific amount of time.

Non-solicitation clause—a contractual provision that prevents an employee from hiring an employee or customer of a former employer for a specific amount of time.

Overruled—the judge disagrees with the objection made by an attorney.

P.C.—a professional corporation, where only licensed professionals can be shareholders.

Plaintiff—the party that brings the lawsuit.

Preemptory challenges—each party is given a predetermined number of elections to release a juror for an unexplained reason, just because that side wants to.

Preponderance of the evidence—the burden of proof in a civil case. The successful party must tip the scales of justice just over 50%.

Probate of estate—the filing of a will so the assets can be distributed to the beneficiaries.

Recklessness—conscious disregard for the safety of others.

Recross examination—when an opposing counsel gets to question witnesses.

Redirect examination—when an attorney gets a second chance to ask his witness questions.

Respondent superior—an employer is liable for the acts of employees within the scope of their employment.

Sequester—when a judge in his or her discretion limits a jury's access to information and publicity about the case. The jury, when not in the courtroom or jury room, is excluded from others, usually in a hotel or motel.

Sustained—the judge agrees with the objection raised.

Ultra vires acts—an employer is not liable for the acts of employees outside the scope of employment.

ABOUT THE AUTHOR

A. Turk was born in 1954, in Brooklyn, New York, and he grew up on Long Island. He earned a BA from George Washington University, an MBA from the Vanderbilt Owen Graduate School of Business, and a JD from Vanderbilt School of Law. He was licensed to practice law in Tennessee in 1980. In 1983 he also was licensed, but never practiced, in New York because of a promise he made to his mother.

A. Turk for more than thirty years was a prominent Nashville attorney and a veteran of fighting courtoom battles. He garnered national media attention in 1994 when he won a unanimous US Supreme Court decision, which held that 2 Live Crew's parody of Roy Orbison's song "Pretty Woman" did not require a copyright license. With the support of NBC, HBO, Time Warner, *Mad Magazine*, and others, A. Turk won this landmark case preserving the right of commercial parody under the Fair Use Doctrine.

A. Turk in 2010 retired to begin his second career as an author of courtroom dramas based upon his personal experience. *First Do No Harm* was A. Turk's debut novel, where he introduced his fictitious alter ego, Benjamin Davis. *Second Degree* is the second installment of the Benjamin Davis Series, which will explore and address the same legal issues and moral dilemmas that A. Turk faced during his legal career.

A. Turk has been married to his wife, Lisa, for thirty-four years, and they have two adult children, Jessica and Ben, as well as two pugs, Neuman and Cosmo. A. Turk currently splits his time between Nashville, Aspen, and Highland Beach. Mr. Turk has already begun working on the next installment of the Benjamin Davis Series, which he hopes to release in 2015.

ACKNOWLEDGMENTS

The release of *Second Degree* validates there is a Benjamin Davis Series; two books are a series.

In writing *Second Degree*, I followed the same process used when I wrote *First Do No Harm*, my debut novel. I finished the first draft of *Second Degree* while living in Highland Beach, Florida. Every day I sat on a deck and wrote while staring at the Atlantic Ocean.

I then submitted my manuscript to thirty-one friends and friends of friends. These Focus Group members were divided into three groups, who met independently in Nashville, Memorial Day week 2014.

The three Focus Groups provided consistent criticism, which I accepted, and those changes impacted the final product. There were also significant differences of opinions and heated discussion from which I gained insight. Several members raised unique points that were made and incorporated in the final manuscript.

Detailed notes were taken at each Focus Group meeting by my daughter, Jessica, my editor, Dimples, and me. I took those notes with me to Aspen and rewrote my manuscript several times. From pool side looking at the Snowmass Mountain, I completed *Second Degree*.

I would like to thank my Focus Group participants: Denise Alper, Amy Anderson, Robert Anderson, Gayle Brinkley, Brandon Bubis, Martin Bubis, Anita Dowdle, Doug Dowdle, Amy Flynn,

Charles Patrick Flynn, Mary Forsythe, Tom Forsythe, Bob Garrett, Harriett Garrett, Karen Goldsmith, Steve Goldsmith, Elliot Greenberg, Jay Lefkovitz, Steve Lefkovitz, Adam Little, Laura Little, Dee Ann Melton, Paula Milam, Tom Milam, Terry Murray, Ben Rosario, Kristin Rosario, Tommy Thompson, David Tiner, Janina Tiner, Kate Vorys, and Becky Waldrop.

As a practicing attorney, I've come to appreciate the importance of relying on experts to polish and present your case. I'd like to thank my editor Dimples Kellogg for her contribution to my finished work. I'd also like to thank Dan Swanson for the cover and Darlene Swanson for formatting the book.

My daughter, Jessica, was my collaborator throughout my process and my strongest critic. I love her and thank her for her contribution.

I'm proud of *Second Degree* and the Benjamin Davis Series. I've begun the third installment in the series, titled *Third Coast.* Thank you for reading and for giving your continued support.

A. Turk

CPSIA information can be obtained at www.ICGtesting.com
Printed in the USA
LVOW12s0557011014

406715LV00003B/4/P

9 780989 266633